Praise for the incomparable

ROSEMARY ROGERS

"Sizzling sensuality, seduction and danger, along with a fine overview of Russia and the political intrigues of the Romanov court, come together with a powerful, skillfully told love story that's not only very satisfying but also vintage Rosemary Rogers."
—*Romantic Times BOOKreviews* on *Scandalous Deception* (4½ stars)

"The grand, sweeping romance filled with passion and adventure rides again as one of love's leading ladies, Rosemary Rogers, whisks us into a tale of daring passion."
—*Romantic Times BOOKreviews* on *A Daring Passion*

"Rogers' legion of readers will be delighted to find that her latest historical romance features the same brand of arrogant, bold, and sexy hero; stubborn, beautiful, and unconventional heroine; and passionate plot that first made this genre wildly popular in the early 1980s."
—*Booklist* on *Sapphire*

"Her novels are filled with adventure, excitement, and always, wildly tempestuous romance."
—*Fort Worth Star-Telegram*

"Ms. Rogers writes exciting, romantic stories... with strong-willed characters, explosive sexual situations, tenderness and love."
—*Dayton News*

"Her name brings smiles to all who love love."
—*Ocala Sta*

Also by

ROSEMARY ROGERS

Scandalous Deception
A Daring Passion
Sapphire
Jewel of My Heart
Return to Me
Surrender to Love
An Honorable Man
Wicked Loving Lies
A Reckless Encounter
Sweet Savage Love
Savage Desire

ROSEMARY ROGERS

BOUND BY LOVE

HQN™

ISBN-13: 978-0-373-77396-1

BOUND BY LOVE

This edition published by arrangement with Harlequin Books S.A.

www.HQNBooks.com

Printed in U.S.A.

Readers and book lovers the world over, I salute you!

CHAPTER ONE

1821
St. Petersburg, Russia

COUNTESS NADIA KARKOFF'S house just off the Nevsky Prospect was not the largest mansion in the neighborhood, but it was by far the most luxurious.

In the finest tradition, the facade was designed along sleek, classical lines with a great number of windows and a wide, columned terrace. From the roof, Greek statues overlooked the upper balustrade with cold expressions of superiority. Or perhaps they were revealing their disapproval of the large gardens that surrounded the house. There was nothing classical about the brilliant profusion of flowers and ornamental shrubs and marble fountains that the Russian aristocracy adored.

The interior was equally elegant, with large rooms and soaring ceilings that were decorated in rich golds and crimsons and sapphires. Lush colors that created a sense of warmth during the long, dreary months of winter.

The furnishings were a mixture of satinwood and cherry, the style more French than Russian as suited the Countess's current fancy and contrasted nicely with the dark, brooding paintings by Flemish masters. Only the jewel-encrusted ornaments and jade figurines scattered through the rooms were entirely native.

It was the view, however, that was the crowning glory of the house.

From the upper windows it was possible to admire the churches and lavish palaces, with their glittering spires and golden domes, that adorned St. Petersburg. The stunning panorama allowed one to appreciate the beauty of the city without sensing the brittle tensions that ran rampant through the busy streets.

Having lived her entire two and twenty years in the house, Miss Leonida Karkoff offered only a brief admiring glance out the window of her bedchamber, more pleased with the late-spring sunlight than the familiar landscape.

Moving to seat herself before the mirrored dresser, she allowed her maid, Sophy, to smooth her long, golden tresses into a complicated knot atop her head, leaving a few curls to brush her temple. The severe style complemented the perfect oval of her alabaster skin, emphasizing her delicate bone structure and the startling blue of her heavily lashed eyes.

She would never possess her mother's dark, smoldering beauty, but she had always been considered quite pretty, and perhaps more importantly, her golden hair and clear blue eyes so closely resembled her father that there could be no mistaking her parentage.

Rather an odd circumstance considering that for all practical purposes she was a bastard.

Oh, Count Karkoff willingly claimed her as his child. And he was indeed married to her mother when she was born, which made Leonida entirely legitimate in the eyes of society. But there were few in all of Russia, and perhaps beyond, who did not know that her mother had been involved in a torrid affair with Alexander Pavlovich, the Emperor, when she had been hurriedly wed to the Count. Or that the Count had suddenly come into enough rubles to restore his crumbling estate outside of Moscow, an estate he rarely left, while the Countess was gifted with this lovely house and a large enough allowance to keep her in elegant style.

It was one of those secrets that was known by all, but

spoken by no one, and while Alexander Pavlovich did occasionally send an invitation to Leonida to visit him when he was in St. Petersburg, he was more a vague, benevolent figure that drifted in and out of her life than a parental figure.

Not that she desired any additional parental figures, she ruefully acknowledged as her mother swept into the room, her lush form swathed in cherry gauze over a slip of silver satin with matching silver ribbons in her dark, glossy curls.

Her beauty was as dramatic as her entrance, although it was rather ruined by her grimace as her dark eyes glanced about the blue and ivory damask that Leonida had insisted be used for her private chambers.

Nadia Karkoff would never comprehend Leonida's preference for simplicity.

"Mother." Leonida turned on her seat to regard the Countess in wary surprise. There was never a doubt that the two loved one another deeply, but Nadia possessed a ruthless will and a habit of squashing anything that might stand in her path. Including Leonida. "Whatever are you doing here?"

"Sophy, I will speak with my daughter alone," Nadia announced.

The plump maid, who was the daughter of Leonida's English nurse, bobbed a curtsy, sending Leonida a covert wink. She was all too accustomed to Nadia's love of melodrama to take offense.

"Of course."

Waiting until the maid had left the room and closed the door behind her, Leonida rose from her chair and squared her shoulders.

It was always better to face the Countess on her feet.

Not that she was any less likely to be bowled over.

"Has something occurred?" she demanded bluntly.

Now that she had her daughter alone, Nadia appeared oddly reluctant to come to the point. Instead she drifted toward the wide bed canopied with ivory silk.

"Can I not simply desire a private conversation with my daughter?"

"You rarely do," Leonida murmured. "And never at this hour of the morning."

Nadia chuckled. "Tell me, *ma petite,* am I being chided for my indolent habits or for being a less than devoted mother?"

"Neither. I am merely seeking an explanation for this unexpected visit."

"Mon Dieu." Nadia plucked the delicate fawn-colored muslin gown from the bed, studying the double row of garnets stitched along the demure neckline. "I wish you would allow my *modiste* to make your gowns. One could easily be forgiven for mistaking you for a member of the tedious bourgeois rather than a young and beautiful member of Russian nobility. You must think of your position, Leonida."

It was a familiar argument, and hardly one to lure her mother from her bed at such an early hour.

"As if I am ever allowed to forget," Leonida muttered.

Nadia turned her dark gaze in Leonida's direction. "What did you say?"

"I prefer my dressmaker, Mother," Leonida said, her voice firm. On this subject she would not budge. "She comprehends that my tastes are more modest than other females'."

"Modest." Nadia heaved an impatient sigh, her gaze flicking over Leonida's slender form, which would never possess the seductive softness that most men preferred. "How many occasions must I remind you that a woman in society has no power unless she is wise enough to use what few weapons God has given her?"

"My gown is a weapon?"

"When designed to tantalize a man's hunger."

"I prefer warmth to tantalizing," Leonida retorted with unapologetic honesty. Despite the spring weather that had grudgingly arrived, there was a blazing fire in the white, gold-veined fireplace. She was always cold.

Nadia tossed the dress aside with a shake of her head. "Foolish child. I have done everything possible to ensure your future. You could have your pick of the most influential gentlemen in the empire. You could become a princess if only you would follow my lead."

"I have told you I have no desire to become a princess. That is your ambition, not mine."

Without warning, Nadia crossed to stand directly before Leonida, her expression hard.

"That is because you have never known what it is to be without wealth or an established position among society, Leonida. You may sneer at my ambition, but I assure you that your precious pride will swiftly be forgotten if you are impetuous enough to believe you can survive on love. There is nothing charming in being cold during the winter or darning your gowns to hide frayed hems." Her eyes darkened with remembered pain. "Or being excluded from society."

"Forgive me, Mother," she said softly. "It is not that I do not appreciate the sacrifices you have made for me, but…"

"Do you?"

Leonida blinked in confusion at the abrupt interruption. "I beg your pardon?"

"Do you appreciate all I have done?"

"Of course."

Nadia reached to take her hands in a tight grip. "Then you will agree to do what I must ask of you."

Leonida hastily tugged her hands free. "I love you, Mother, but my appreciation is not without boundaries. I have told you that I will not accept Prince Orvoleski's proposal. Not only is he old enough to be my father, but he reeks of onions."

"This has nothing to do with the Prince."

Leonida's wariness deepened to outright anxiety. There was something in her mother's expression that warned her that this was more than just another of the theatrical scenes Nadia adored.

"Something has happened."

Nadia twisted her hands together, jeweled rings glinting in the morning light.

"Yes."

"Tell me."

Instead of answering, Nadia drifted toward the window, the scent of expensive perfume drifting behind her.

"You know a small part of my childhood."

Confused, Leonida turned to study her mother's stiff back. Countess Karkoff never discussed her humble beginnings. Never.

"You have told me that you were raised in Yaroslavl' before coming to St. Petersburg," she answered, her words tentative.

"My father possessed distant ties to the Romanovs, but after he argued with Emperor Paul he was too filled with stubborn pride to apologize and he was forever banished from court." Nadia's scornful laugh echoed through the room. "Stupid man. We lived in a frozen monstrosity of a house, miles from the nearest village, with only a handful of peasants to keep it from utter ruin. I was buried in the midst of savages with only my nurse to bear me company."

Leonida's heart softened with sympathy. This vivacious, extroverted, highly fashionable woman stuck alone in a gloomy old house? It must have seemed like hell to her.

"I cannot imagine you in such a setting," she breathed.

Nadia shuddered, one hand lifting to stroke the diamond necklace around her neck, as if to reassure herself that her grim memories had not stolen it away.

"It was a misery, but it did teach me that I would do anything to escape," she rasped harshly. "When my aunt decided it was her duty to invite me to her home, I ignored my father's threat to disown me. What did he have to offer me beyond years of lonely isolation? Instead I sold my few pieces of jewelry and made my way to St. Petersburg alone."

Leonida chuckled in admiration. Of course she had.

Nothing would be allowed to stand between Nadia and her dreams.

"You are truly amazing, Mother," she said. "There are few women who would have possessed such courage."

Nadia slowly turned, a rueful smile touching her lips. "It was more desperation than courage and, had I known I was expected to be more a servant than a guest beneath my aunt's roof, I am not entirely certain I would have been so eager to endure the grueling journey."

"I am certain. You have never allowed anything to stand in the path of what you desire."

Her mother shrugged. "True, but not even my considerable determination would have given me the opportunity to enter society without the assistance of Mira Toryski."

It took a moment for Leonida to place the name. "The Duchess of Huntley?"

"Her family were neighbors of my aunt," Nadia explained. "She was already a favorite among society, of course. How could she not be? She was beautiful, wealthy and yet astonishingly kind. I shall never understand why she took pity on me and convinced my aunt to allow me to attend a few of the smaller gatherings, but I shall forever be grateful."

The Countess's deep affection for her girlhood friend could not be mistaken. Strange, considering Nadia preferred to surround herself with handsome young officers rather than the ladies of society.

"That is when you met Alexander Pavlovich?"

"Yes." The dark eyes softened as they always did at the mention of the Emperor. "He was so handsome and charming. I had only to glance at him to know he was a man destined for greatness."

Leonida resisted the urge to prod for more details of her mother's relationship with Alexander Pavlovich. There were some questions better not asked.

"This is all very fascinating, Mother, but I do not entirely comprehend what is troubling you."

Nadia's hands shook as she smoothed them over the gauze skirt. "I need you to understand my deep affection for Mira."

"Why?"

"Not long after I came to St. Petersburg Mira was introduced to the Duke of Huntley. She, along with most of the women in society, lost her heart to the handsome Englishman and returned with him to London to be wed." Nadia grimaced. "I was devastated by the loss of my dearest friend. She was…well, let us just say that my only comfort was exchanging letters so we could continue to be involved in one another's lives."

"Perfectly understandable," Leonida said gently.

"Perhaps, but I was still foolishly young and when Alexander Pavlovich began to make his interest in me known, I was eager to share every detail with Mira."

If anything, Leonida was only more confused. "From all I have heard, your affair with Czar Alexander was not precisely a closely guarded secret."

"No." Nadia shrugged, as always unrepentant at her intimate connection to the Emperor. "Our…relationship was a source of endless gossip, but our private conversations were never intended to be shared. Not even with a dear friend whose loyalty to the Romanovs could never be questioned."

Leonida stiffened. "You revealed Alexander Pavlovich's private conversations to the Duchess of Huntley?"

Nadia's expression became defensive. "I knew she could be trusted and it was not as if I could share my most intimate thoughts with anyone else. There was not a woman in society who was not consumed with jealousy by my relationship with Czar Alexander."

"As they still are." Leonida hastily soothed the older woman. She would get nothing out of Nadia if she were pouting. And Leonida had a terrible foreboding she needed to know precisely what was happening. "But you are rarely so indiscreet."

Nadia was far from appeased. "How could I possibly suspect that anyone beyond the Duchess would ever see them?"

Leonida's heart stuttered. "Someone else has seen them?"

"I do not need you to point out that I was a reckless idiot. I am painfully aware of my mistakes."

"Very well." Leonida sucked in a calming breath. "I presume that these letters hold information that might prove uncomfortable for the Czar?"

"It is much worse than that. In the hands of his enemies they might very well destroy him."

"Destroy him?" Leonida blinked in shock. "Surely you must be exaggerating?"

"I only wish I were."

"Mother?"

With a graceful motion, Nadia sat on the brocade window seat, the morning sunlight revealing the shadows beneath her eyes and lines that bracketed her full lips.

It was the first occasion that Leonida could recall her mother actually appearing her age.

That was more frightening than all the melodramatic insinuations of imminent danger.

"Being the leader of the Russian empire is never a simple task," she said in low tones. "Unrest is always brewing among the citizens, while treachery is a mandatory game for the nobility, but matters have become even more perilous over the past few years. Alexander spends too much time away from his throne as he travels about the world. It gives his enemies encouragement to plot against him."

"They hardly need encouragement."

"Perhaps not, but they grow more bold with every passing day."

Leonida licked her dry lips. "And there is something in the letters that would offer Alexander Pavlovich's enemies the means to harm him?"

"Yes."

"What..."

Her mother held up an imperious hand. "Do not ask me, Leonida."

Leonida's first instinct was to demand an answer. If she were to be involved in whatever mess her mother had created, she deserved the truth.

Then she wisely swallowed the words hovering on her lips. She held a great love and respect for Alexander Pavlovich, but she of all people understood he was just a man, with all the failings and frailties of any other. And, in truth, there had always been a melancholy air that shrouded the Emperor, as if he carried with him a deep and painful secret.

Did she truly wish to know what caused him such sorrow?

"Then you must write to the Emperor and warn him of the dangers," she said briskly. "He will surely wish to return to St. Petersburg."

"No," her mother denied sharply.

"You cannot hide the truth, Mother."

"That is exactly what I must do."

Leonida frowned, unable to believe her mother could be so selfish.

"You will put Alexander Pavlovich at risk because you do not wish to confess your indiscretion?"

The dark eyes flashed with annoyance. "*Mon Dieu.* Have you not been paying attention over the past months?"

"You mean the uprising?"

"Alexander is devastated." Nadia paced across the polished wood floor, her expression tight with unmistakable concern. "He considered the Semyonoffski Regiment the most faithful of all his soldiers and their betrayal has been like a knife in his heart. I fear for him, Leonida. He is so fragile. I am not certain he could bear what he is certain to believe is yet another betrayal."

"We are all concerned for his welfare, but he is the Emperor," Leonida pointed out softly. "He must know of any threat to his throne."

Coming to a halt, Nadia turned to meet Leonida's gaze with a tilt of her chin.

"I intend to ensure that any threat is brought to an end before Alexander returns."

"How? If someone has managed to get their hands on the letters you wrote..."

"I am not convinced that anyone has actually seen the letters."

Leonida lifted her hands to rub her throbbing temples. "You are giving me a headache, Mother. Perhaps you should start at the beginning."

Drawing in a deep breath, Nadia pressed her hands to her stomach as she sought to gain command of her composure.

"Last week a masked man calling himself the Voice of Truth approached me at Count Bernaski's masquerade. The ridiculous man claimed that he possessed the letters I had written to Mira and that he would make them public unless I agreed to pay him one hundred thousand rubles."

"One hundred thousand," Leonida whispered in shock. It was worse, much worse, than she had dreamed possible. "Good lord. We could not possibly pay such a sum."

"I have no intention of paying so much as a ruble," Nadia snapped. "Not until I am convinced the bastard truly possesses the letters, which I assure you I am not."

"Why not?"

"Because as soon as the man turned to leave I motioned for Herrick Gerhardt to have him followed."

Leonida grimaced. Herrick Gerhardt was Alexander Pavlovich's closest advisor and the most alarming man she had ever encountered. Nothing escaped his dark, penetrating gaze. And his fierce devotion to the Emperor meant he would willingly destroy any threat without a hint of remorse.

It was impossible to be in his company without fearing you might be hauled to the nearest dungeon.

"Of course," she muttered.

Nadia shrugged, not nearly so frightened of Gerhardt as she should be.

"This is not the first threat I have endured. My position often attracts those who would hope to use me to influence Alexander Pavlovich."

Well, her mother was not alone. Leonida was shocked at the many occasions the members of society would approach her in hopes she could sway the Emperor.

As if she had any power. It was ludicrous.

"I assume Herrick managed to follow the man?"

"Yes. His name is Nikolas Babevich. His father is a Russian officer and his mother is—" Nadia gave a delicate shudder "—French. Disgusting people. They are never to be trusted."

Leonida ignored her mother's prejudice. Nadia possessed a vivid memory of Napoleon's invasion and the costly war.

"Was he captured?"

"Herrick decided it would be better not to allow the fiend to realize we had discovered his identity."

Leonida shook her head. Had her mother taken leave of her senses?

"I will be the first to admit that I know very little of government affairs, but if you know who and where this villain is to be discovered then why on earth would you not have him arrested?" Leonida demanded in confusion.

"Because we cannot be certain he is acting alone."

"Did Herrick at least retrieve your letters?"

"He searched the man's house, but could find no letters."

Leonida made a sound of frustration. "They could be anywhere."

"He is being constantly watched so if he does have them hidden he will eventually lead the guards to the location."

Leonida realized there was no use in pressing to have the horrid blackmailer arrested. If Herrick had decided to allow the man to remain free, then nothing she said would alter the situation.

Instead she concentrated on her more pressing questions. "Why do you suspect he is lying about having the letters?"

Nadia returned to her pacing, her fingers toying with the large drop diamonds of her necklace. A sure sign she was not nearly so composed as she would have Leonida believe.

"When he first approached me, I demanded that he show them to me. He claimed that he did not have them on his person, so I requested that he reveal precisely what they said. Again he refused, saying that he would offer no proof until I had paid his outrageous sum."

"That does seem odd. Surely he must realize that anyone with the least amount of sense would demand evidence before paying?"

"Most gentlemen underestimate women. No doubt he assumed I would be so panicked that I would give in to his demands without thinking." Nadia's voice revealed her contempt for such stupidity. "And there is something else."

"What?"

"Mira and I quite often traded secrets, so we devised our own code when we wrote to one another in the event our letters fell into the wrong hands. It was silly and no doubt childishly easy to decipher, but the man said nothing of having managed to translate the words."

Leonida had to agree that it did sound suspicious. Even assuming the man thought a woman could be so easily culled out of such a large sum of money, he surely would have felt compelled to brag at his cleverness of deciphering the code.

In her experience, gentlemen never lost the opportunity to reveal their utter superiority to women.

"So, if he does not have the letters, how did he discover they exist? And how did he know they might be damaging to Alexander Pavlovich?"

"That is why Herrick allowed him to remain unaware we know his identity," Nadia explained. "He believes that Nikolas Babevich is merely a pawn being used by others."

Leonida shuddered, knowing it was more from apprehension rather than the chill of standing in the middle of the room wearing nothing more than her shift and corset.

The thought that there were more enemies seeking to harm her mother was not precisely reassuring.

"Then it seems there is nothing to do but wait until the man leads you to his associates."

There was a tense silence before her mother halted to stab her with a narrowed gaze.

"Actually, there is a very important task that must be done."

Leonida took an instinctive step backward. She knew that tone of voice. And it never boded well.

At least not for her.

"I am not certain I wish to know."

"Someone must travel to England and search the Duke of Huntley's estate for the letters," Nadia said, ignoring Leonida's words of reluctance. Typical. "If they are still there then we can be certain Nikolas Babevich is nothing more than a fraud."

The shimmering unease in the pit of her stomach became outright panic.

Good lord. She had not seen this coming. Stupid, really. Nadia thought nothing of making the most outrageous demands of her only child.

"But…" She struggled to capture her elusive breath. "If the letters are still hidden in England, how could anyone know of them?"

Nadia shrugged. "Perhaps the current Duke or his brother, Lord Summerville, mentioned seeing them to someone. Edmond was here in St. Petersburg, after all, only a few months ago."

Leonida seized on the words as if they were her salvation. "Then why not simply write to them and demand the letters back? The Duchess has been dead for years—they could have no interest in your correspondence."

Nadia gave an impatient wave of her hand. "Because

they are first and foremost Englishmen with loyalty to the Prince Regent.... Oh, I suppose the hideous man has now become King." She grimaced. "In any event, it is well known that the portly monarch was not at all pleased by Alexander Pavlovich's last visit to celebrate the end of the war. If the King knew that those letters contained information that could harm the Emperor, I do not doubt he would demand they be given to him."

Leonida wanted to argue, but she had heard the rumors of King George's lingering resentment toward Alexander Pavlovich's distant manner during his brief visit. Hardly surprising. The two rulers could not be more different.

The Emperor detested gaudy displays and false bravado.

She swiftly sought another excuse to avoid the appalling mission to England.

"One can hardly search the Huntley estate without permission. An English duke must possess an entire battalion of servants. I would not get past the door without being caught."

Nadia smiled. "You could if you were a welcomed guest."

"Mother..."

"The arrangements for your journey are being made as we speak," Nadia interrupted, her tone resolute. "You will leave by the end of the week."

It was Leonida's turn to pace the floor, the rising panic making it difficult to think clearly.

"Even if I were willing to agree to this absurd scheme, which I assure you I am not, I could not possibly intrude upon the Duke of Huntley. Not only would it be extremely rude, but he is a bachelor."

"I have already written to Lord Summerville and his new bride to inform them that Alexander Pavlovich has decided you are in need of a proper introduction to English society. They could not possibly turn you away."

Dear heavens, this just became worse and worse.

"Does Lord Summerville live with his brother?"

"No, but the King has given the couple Lady Summerville's previous home, which is less than a mile from Meadowland. No doubt you will often be calling on the Duke."

Leonida shook her head in disbelief. "So you simply foisted a complete stranger on the newlyweds without regard to how awkward it will be for all of us?"

Nadia's expression hardened. She had made her decision and nothing Leonida might say would sway her.

"Leonida, not only would I be ruined if those letters are indeed in the hands of my enemies, but Alexander would never be able to withstand the scandal," she said, her voice harsh with warning. "Not again."

Not again?

What the devil did that mean?

Leonida's temper stirred. This was hardly the first occasion her mother had devised some outlandish scheme, but this…

"So you wish me to travel to England, intrude on a newlywed couple who have never met me, sneak into a duke's well-guarded home and retrieve letters that might or might not be hidden there?"

Her mother did not so much as blink. "Yes."

Leonida snorted. "Then, supposing I am to accomplish this unlikely feat, what am I to do? Burn the evidence?"

Nadia widened her eyes in shock at the mere notion. "No. I want you to return the letters to me."

"For God's sake, Mother. Have they not already caused enough trouble? They have to be destroyed."

With a flurry of gauze and silk, Nadia crossed to stand directly in front of Leonida.

"Do not be a fool, Leonida. I need them."

Caught off guard by her mother's sharp insistence, Leonida frowned. "Why?"

Nadia paused, clearly choosing her words with care. "Alexander Pavlovich has always adored me, and over the years he has been quite…generous to us. But we both know that the Emperor's brothers have never approved of me or Alexander's continued support of our small household. If something were to happen, God forbid, I fear we might find ourselves cut out of any inheritance that rightfully should be ours."

"I do not..." Leonida gasped in shock as realization hit. "Oh, no. You mean to use the letters to extort money from the next czar? Have you gone completely mad?"

Nadia's lips thinned in annoyance. "One of us must think of the future, Leonida."

"I am thinking of the future, Mother." Whirling on her heel, Leonida marched to stare blindly out the window. "I just hope you enjoy the damp prison cell that is no doubt awaiting us."

CHAPTER TWO

Surrey, England

AT A GLANCE, THE TWIN gentlemen who were currently strolling through the traditional English garden appeared startlingly similar.

Both possessed raven-dark hair that fell onto their wide foreheads in charming disarray. Both possessed the angular, Slavic features of their Russian-born mother. Both were blessed with dark blue eyes that had been sending women into a swoon since they left the cradle. And both had the sort of leanly muscled bodies that were shown to perfection beneath their tailored jackets and buckskins.

A closer study, however, would reveal that the elder twin, Stefan, the current Duke of Huntley, had skin a few shades darker than his brother, Edmond, Lord Summerville. And his shoulders were just a tad broader. A result of the hours spent overseeing his vast farms. Stefan's features were also a trace more delicate than Edmond's. Elegant rather than powerful.

The physical differences, however, were nothing in comparison to the differences in personalities.

Edmond had always been a restless soul, or at least he had been until he had wed Brianna Quinn several weeks before, while Stefan was deeply devoted to his estate and the vast number of people who depended upon him. Edmond was charming, swift to anger and frighteningly courageous. He had willingly risked his neck on several occasions during his time as advisor to Alexander Pavlovich.

Stefan, on the other hand, was far more reticent, preferring to remain in the background rather than calling attention to himself. He was also prone to speak the truth rather than offer flattery, which perhaps explained why he was more comfortable in the company of his tenants rather than the aristocrats scattered about the neighborhood.

They both, however, shared a shrewd intelligence and fierce loyalty to each other, as well as those who depended upon them.

It was that loyalty that had brought Edmond to Hillside on this late spring morning.

Strolling through the gardens of Hillside that were being ruthlessly manicured after fifteen years of neglect, he slid a covert glance toward his brother, who was walking silently at his side.

"So, your guest has arrived?" he murmured.

Edmond's lips twitched; no doubt he easily sensed Stefan's looming lecture.

"She has."

Stefan tossed aside any notion of subtlety. It had never been his talent.

"I cannot comprehend why you allow yourself to be taken advantage of by Alexander Pavlovich," he growled, stepping around a pile of branches that had been cut from the now tidy hedge. "You are not one of his advisors."

"I have never been an advisor to King George either, but that does not halt him from taking advantage," Edmond pointed out. "Of either of us."

Stefan ignored the reminder of King George's incessant demands. Instead he concentrated on the two women currently entering the garden from the rambling Palladian-style home.

Brianna was easily recognizable by her vibrant red hair

and her swift, rather unladylike stride. In many ways she was as impulsive and reckless as Edmond.

A familiar, fond warmth filled his heart before Stefan was turning his attention to the tiny woman struggling to keep pace with Lady Summerville.

"Is that her?" he demanded.

"Yes. Miss Leonida Karkoff."

In that moment the woman turned her head and Stefan stumbled to a startled halt.

It was not the female's beauty.

Well, at least not entirely.

She *was* lovely. Hair as golden as a morning sunrise, alabaster skin, and a slender form that was currently shown to advantage by her moss-green walking dress that was modestly scooped at the bodice with tiny puff sleeves.

No, it was the unmistakable line of her profile and the potently sweet curve of her lips.

He would bet his last quid her eyes were the color of a summer sky.

"Good God."

Edmond chuckled. "Lovely, is she not?"

"Lovely, and remarkably familiar."

"Yes. There is no mistaking her father," Edmond agreed. "A pity he was already wed to Elizabeth before meeting Leonida's mother. Nadia would have made a formidable czarina who might have given Alexander Pavlovich the courage he needed to defy the nobles and insist upon the reforms he desired when he was still young."

"His grandmother would never have allowed him to wed a provincial chit with nothing but beauty and sheer cunning to recommend her."

Edmond flashed him a wry glance. "Never underestimate a determined woman."

"Which is why I prefer a more timid female," Stefan smoothly countered. "Life is much more peaceful."

Edmond grimaced. "Tedious."

Stefan returned his attention to the approaching women. "How long does Miss Karkoff intend to linger?"

"She has not revealed her plans."

No, he did not imagine she had. Or was likely to.

"It hardly makes sense for the Emperor to send her to this remote part of Surrey if he desired her to mix among English society."

"The London season is at an end." Edmond's expression was suddenly sly. "Besides, why toss the lovely Leonida among a crowd of other lovely ladies when she could be the only eligible female within miles of an unwed duke?"

"You think…" Stefan shook his head, not about to fall for such an obvious ploy. "No. Not even Alexander Pavlovich is so lacking in finesse as to blatantly dangle his daughter beneath my nose."

"Perhaps not, but her mother would."

"No."

Edmond arched a raven brow. "Why are you so certain?"

"I am not so isolated that I haven't heard the usual gossip that trickles from London. From all accounts, the Countess Karkoff has her heart set on nothing less than a prince for her daughter."

Edmond shrugged. "A wealthy English duke would surely trump a destitute prince from a principality that is little more than a spot on the map."

"Not if that principality possessed soldiers that Alexander Pavlovich could count loyal to his throne," Stefan retorted. "I have many things, but no army to lend aid."

"No, but you do have the ear of the English king. A most powerful ally."

"A king that has peevishly proclaimed his disapproval toward the Czar."

Edmond chuckled, clearly enjoying himself. He, better than anyone, understood Stefan's abhorrence at the thought of being wed for his title.

"Maybe this is Alexander Pavlovich's attempt to make peace."

"Then the wench should be in London," Stefan growled. "I do not doubt she could easily wrap the King about her finger."

Edmond narrowed his gaze. "Why are you so suspicious of the poor chit?"

"I have not forgotten the last occasion you became involved in Russian affairs." Stefan frowned. "Both you and Brianna were nearly killed."

"Hardly Alexander Pavlovich's fault."

Stefan could not argue. It had been yet another plot to overthrow the Czar, but of course, it had been Edmond who was tossed directly in the middle of danger.

"Perhaps not, but he is never hesitant to put you at risk for his own cause. I do not wish to see you once again entangled."

Edmond tossed an arm around his shoulders. "Do not worry, Stefan. Much to my surprise, Leonida is not only charming, but utterly lacking her mother's ambition and her father's Machiavellian plotting."

"Hmm." Stefan was not so easily convinced, but it was obvious Edmond was not prepared to heed his warnings. It would have to be Stefan's duty to keep a careful watch on the unwelcomed guest. "Does she at least realize that she is intruding into the privacy of newlyweds?"

A wicked humor twinkled in Edmond's eyes. "You are surely familiar enough with me, Stefan, to know that when I desire to spend time alone with my exquisite wife I allow nothing and no one to stand in my way."

"True enough," Stefan was forced to concede. "I cannot recall how many dinners I have attended at Hillside only to find myself shown to the door before I could even finish my port."

"Someday, my dear brother, you will understand."

"I believe one Huntley blinded by the agonizing throes of love is quite enough." His tone was flippant, disguising the dull ache of loneliness that had plagued him over the past year. That was a secret he intended to keep to himself. "Think of our reputation."

"Should I think of my reputation as a frivolous rake or your reputation as a dull farmer who pays more heed to his cows than to society?" Edmond teased.

"Surely not dull?" Stefan protested. "I have always thought I possessed a small measure of wit."

"A very large measure of wit. Unfortunately it is rarely on display outside Meadowland. I fear you may become as moldy as your books."

Stefan pulled away from his brother's arm, discomfited by the turn of the conversation. He would stab a dagger in his heart before he would allow Edmond to realize just how jealous he was of the happiness he had discovered.

No one deserved it more than Edmond.

"My books arc not moldy, and neither am I."

Edmond's gaze was searching, perhaps sensing his brother's unease. "It would not hurt you to practice your social skills."

"Ah, I begin to understand your devious plot." Stefan deliberately turned the conversation from himself. "You wish me to keep Miss Karkoff distracted so you can spend more time alone with your bride."

"My only thought is for you, dearest Stefan."

Laughing at his brother's pious tone, Stefan abruptly realized they were no longer alone. A curious tingle inched down his spine as he turned to smile into Brianna's astonishing green eyes, only grudgingly turning his attention to the woman at her side.

Without warning his breath was wrenched from his lungs as he encountered the clear blue gaze that shimmered with a guileless innocence.

Christ. It was no wonder Alexander Pavlovich had sent this female to do his bidding. Leonida Karkoff was every man's fantasy. Sweet, untouched purity combined with a golden beauty that stirred a primitive need to sweep her off her feet. Who would not be dazzled by such a vision?

Even Stefan.

It was the sound of Brianna delicately clearing her throat that made Stefan realize he was staring like a damned fool, and with a silent curse at allowing himself to be distracted for even a moment by the dangerous siren, he determinedly returned his gaze to Lady Summerville.

"Good day, Stefan," she murmured, her smile impish.

"Lovely Brianna." With a deliberate motion, he grasped her hand and raised it to his lips. He enjoyed provoking his twin. "As always you brighten my day."

On cue, Edmond shifted to place a possessive arm around his wife. They both knew that Stefan regarded Brianna as a beloved sister, but some reactions were too instinctive to be denied.

Perhaps that explained why he was so vividly aware of the innocent blue gaze still fixed to his profile, and the enticing scent of jasmine that filled the air.

Instinct.

Thankfully obtuse to Stefan's uncharacteristic distraction, Edmond waved a slender hand toward his guest.

"Stefan, may I introduce you to Miss Karkoff? Leonida, my brother, the Duke of Huntley."

With no choice, Stefan grimly ignored the peculiar race of his heart, and turned to watch Miss Karkoff perform an elegant curtsy.

"Your Grace." Her voice was low, with only a trace of accent to mar her perfect English.

The dip of his head was just short of rude. He would not forget his suspicions.

Not even if Leonida Karkoff did possess the face of an angel.

"I hope you are enjoying your visit to Surrey?"

Her smile was dazzling. Of course. Everything about her was dazzling.

"Very much, thank you. Lord and Lady Summerville have been most welcoming and I have discovered a great deal of beauty in the English countryside."

"It must be a bit tedious in comparison to St. Petersburg. As I recall there is a constant variety of entertainments offered to young and beautiful women."

She shrugged, drawing attention to the delicate line of her shoulders and the slender neck that was circled by a perfect strand of pearls.

"I prefer the peace," she countered, a hint of curiosity in her eyes, as if able to sense his distrust. "And to be honest, I am pleased to be in the country where I can truly bask in your summer warmth."

He curved his lips into a smile, taking her arm to firmly lead her down the paved pathway. Obviously he would have to take greater care if he were not to put her on guard.

"Like a cat?"

She stiffened, as if caught off guard by his touch, then with a smile that was as false as his own, she fell into step beside him.

"Yes, I suppose I do feel rather like a cat," she said, lifting her face as if enthralled by the warm sunlight. "At home I rarely leave the house without being wrapped in at least a shawl."

"What a pity to conceal such skin." Against his will, Stefan's gaze skimmed over her delicate features. God, but she was beautiful. "It shimmers with the beauty of alabaster in the sun."

"I am confused, your Grace."

"And why is that?"

She turned her head to stab him with a penetrating stare. "I understood that your brother was the practiced flirt while you preferred substance to charm."

"I seem to be referred to as a stodgy bore with depressing frequency of late. I never realized I was so dull."

"Substance is not dull."

His brow lifted at her vehement tone. "No?"

"Quite the opposite." She pinned the stiff smile back on her lips. "Lady Summerville mentioned that you possess the finest library in Surrey."

"You are interested in books?"

"Far more than my mother approves of, I fear. If I were allowed to have my way, I would spend my evenings curled before a warm fire with a good book rather than attending the seemingly endless gatherings Russian society adores."

His heart missed a beat. She preferred books to society? No. It had to be a lie. Just a part of the act she performed so well.

"An unusual preference for a young lady."

"I disagree."

"Do you?"

"It is more that young ladies are rarely asked what their preference might be."

His eyes narrowed. Beautiful and clever. Dangerous.

"Touché," he murmured.

"Forgive me." She coyly lowered her head. "I am inclined to speak my mind too frankly."

"There is nothing to forgive. I prefer *honesty.*" He deliberately emphasized the word. "And to prove my own sincerity I offer you an open invitation to make use of my library during your stay."

She stumbled, a faint blush touching her cheeks. "That is very kind, your Grace, thank you."

A rather odd reaction to his offhand invitation. "Not kind, merely sympathetic. For all your claims to enjoy the quiet it cannot be particularly inspiring to have only my brother and Brianna as company. I have spent enough time with the newlyweds to know they have a tendency to forget there is anyone else in the room when they are together. You at least should have some means of wiling away the hours."

"They are very devoted to one another."

"Besotted."

Coming to a halt, Stefan turned to discover that Edmond and Brianna were standing near a crumbling fountain. They made a perfect vision of marital bliss, with Brianna's head nestled against Edmond's shoulder while his hand stroked tenderly down her back. Stefan, however, did not miss the concerned expression on his brother's face.

"I find myself quite envious," Miss Karkoff murmured. "It is not often a woman is allowed to wed for love."

"And even less often for a gentleman."

"Truly?"

His shifted his attention to catch her disbelieving expression. "Why are you surprised?"

"I would think that a gentleman with your wealth and position could wed any woman of his choosing."

"You have lived among the most powerful families in St. Petersburg, Miss Karkoff, you comprehend how treacherous a courtship can be."

"Treacherous?"

He shrugged. "Accept one invitation to a ball while declining another and you offend half the members of the House of Lords. Speak with one maiden for a moment longer than another and the room buzzes with rumors. And God forbid I request a few friends to Meadowland without including every unwed sister, cousin or passing acquaintance they might possess. To actually propose marriage..."

"Yes, it would no doubt cause another War of the Roses," she said, her voice so smooth it would be easy to miss the mockery. "Very wise to remain unwed and allow each ambitious papa and title-hungry mama to continue dreaming they might capture you for their daughter."

His smile became genuine. Despite his suspicions, he appreciated quick wits and a refusal to bore him with insincere flattery.

"My thought precisely."

"No doubt that is why you prefer to avoid society?"

Ah, obviously Brianna had been sharing her annoyance

with his refusal to accept the endless invitations that arrived each morning.

"One of many reasons." He paused. "Ah, but perhaps I should keep my less than favorable opinion of society to myself."

"Why?"

"That is why you have come to England, is it not? To be introduced into English society?"

"I…my mother thought it might be beneficial."

"But not you?"

"I am here, am I not?" she said, her light tone belied by the stoic set of her expression.

Odd. Had she been compelled to England against her will? Not that it truly mattered. If she intended to involve Edmond in one of the Emperor's schemes then Stefan intended to have her run out of Surrey.

"So you are. Rather surprising."

"What is surprising?"

"There are numerous Russian diplomats in London. I would think your mother would prefer for you to be launched into society by a more formal introduction."

This time she was prepared. Her smile never faltered as she met his gaze squarely.

"My mother is stubborn, but she is no fool. I, alas, did not inherit her ability to be at ease among strangers. She no doubt hopes that by sending me to Lord and Lady Summerville I can make a few acquaintances without causing too much embarrassment."

"Hmm."

She arched a golden brow. "Yes?"

"I was just thinking it was rather a stroke of fortune that Edmond decided to wed at such an opportune moment. Otherwise your visit might never have occurred."

Her magnificent eyes flashed with annoyance at his pointed words. Ridiculously, Stefan found himself pleased to have provoked her first genuine emotion.

"There is no need for you to point out that my visit is…awkward considering that Lord and Lady Summerville have only been wed a few weeks," she said tartly.

"I am certain you are quite welcome, Miss Karkoff."

"Are you?"

"Of course."

Her lips thinned. "I did attempt to convince Mother that it was not entirely appropriate to thrust myself upon his lordship, but she was insistent."

"And do you always do what your mother commands?"

She turned to regard a nearby rosebush, the sunlight outlining the pure lines of her profile.

"Not always, but family loyalty is a strange and powerful thing, your Grace. Even for a woman who considers herself a sane, rational being."

He frowned, struck by her low words. Was she confessing that she had been sent by the Emperor?

"Family loyalty?"

"Ah, there you are," Edmond intruded, stepping next to Stefan with a mysterious smile. "I have convinced Brianna to return to the house, and I am certain she would appreciate your company, Leonida."

"Of course." There was no mistaking Miss Karkoff's relief to be away from Stefan as she offered a hasty dip. "Your Grace."

"Miss Karkoff."

Barely waiting for his nod, she spun on her heel and hurried toward the house.

Stefan watched her progress in silence, still churning with a strange mixture of emotions.

Anger, suspicion and, over all, a potent fascination.

Who the devil was Miss Leonida Karkoff?

And why was he suddenly missing the sweet scent of jasmine?

"Could you not even make an effort to charm the poor female?" Edmond drawled.

"I do not trust her," he retorted, not adding he was also unwillingly captivated by the clever minx. "I think she was deliberately sent here by the Emperor for his own devious purpose."

"Even if she was, I am quite capable of protecting what is mine." Edmond's voice held a hard edge of warning. "For all of Alexander Pavlovich's faults, he is wise enough to realize what would happen if Brianna was harmed."

"But do you have the sense to protect yourself?"

Edmond shrugged. "I am learning."

Stefan smiled, folding his arms across his chest. "So, do you intend to share your announcement?"

"What announcement?"

"I may be dull and unsociable, but I am capable of noticing that you are even more overprotective of your bride than usual."

Edmond's eyes widened in surprise. "*Mon Dieu.* I forget that behind your pretense of being a staid farmer you are far more perceptive than any person I have ever known. Nothing gets past your notice, does it?"

"Very little."

Edmond snorted, shaking his head. "You are fortunate that neither the King nor Alexander Pavlovich know of your talent. They would never allow you to leave their side."

"And you are very accomplished at evading an answer," Stefan retorted.

Edmond grimaced, allowing his deep concern to shimmer in his eyes. "We suspect that Brianna might be increasing but it is very early days yet. We cannot be certain."

Stefan understood his brother's unease. Brianna had thought she was increasing once before only to lose the child. It would be hellish to endure yet another loss.

Still, she was young and healthy. It seemed reasonable she would be able to bear her child.

He reached out to clap his brother on the shoulder. "You have my deepest congratulations, brother."

Edmond nodded, but his gaze was searching. "Do I?"

It took a moment for Stefan to realize his brother was referring to Stefan's proposal to Brianna months ago.

At the time he had been moved by the knowledge he had failed his childhood friend and that he could make amends by protecting her future. There had also been the comfort of familiarity.

Now he could only be relieved that she had possessed the sense to choose Edmond.

"Never think otherwise," he assured his brother. "You and Brianna were destined for one another. Besides, I can now hope that any need to wed and produce the proper heir has been removed. Just ensure Brianna has a boy."

"Matters are out of my hands, I fear." Edmond's concern eased and he smiled with wicked amusement. "And besides, you would be a fool to become overly comfortable in your role as bachelor."

Stefan arched a brow. "And why is that?"

Edmond laughed. "I highly doubt that I am the only one destined to tumble into the clutches of a woman. It is only a matter of time, dear brother."

CHAPTER THREE

IT TOOK THREE DAYS FOR LEONIDA to acquire the nerve necessary to walk the mile from Hillside to Meadowland.

Stupid, really. She had discovered from Brianna the first day she arrived in Surrey that the Duke of Huntley made a habit of spending his afternoons assisting his tenants and inspecting his vast lands. There had truly been no reason to hesitate so long.

After all, the quicker she found the damnable letters, the quicker she could return to Russia.

She told herself that her reluctance was nothing more than revulsion. She was no prude (how could she be with Nadia as her mother?), but she did draw the line at behaving like a common thief.

Deep inside, however, she knew it was not just her moral outrage that kept her from the inevitable.

No, it had far more to do with her reaction to the Duke of Huntley.

Odd how her entire body had seemed to tingle with excitement the moment he had glanced in her direction. He was stunningly beautiful, of course. But so was his brother and she had felt nothing but gratitude toward Lord Summerville. Well, gratitude and a horrid guilt.

Certainly her heart did not race and her knees feel weak whenever he happened to be near. Nor did she have the unpleasant sensation that his penetrating gaze could see through her flimsy excuses to lay bare her true reason for being in Surrey.

At last she could delay her duty no longer.

Waiting until Brianna had excused herself to rest after luncheon, Leonida quietly slipped through a side door and meandered aimlessly through the gardens. Only when she was certain she could no longer be seen from the house did she slip through the nearest gate and head across the open meadows.

Away from the house she allowed her steps to slow, enjoying the warmth of the sunlight that had made an appearance after the damp morning. Her nurse had told her fascinating stories of England, speaking of her own childhood in a small village in Derbyshire and the lovely countryside. But it was even more charming than Leonida had expected.

It was all so very…green.

Avoiding the various cottages, Leonida entered the thick woods rather than crossing the open fields. Although she did not intend to sneak into Meadowland, she preferred not to have word of her arrival spread throughout the neighborhood. The last thing she needed was the Duke of Huntley rushing home early.

Careful to follow the path, it was not long before she stepped from the trees, her eyes widening as she caught her first sight of Meadowland.

It was not nearly so vast or grand as the palaces in Russia, and even from a distance there was a hint of scruffiness, like a well-worn slipper, but Leonida discovered herself drawn to the rambling mansion.

There was a comforting timelessness to the sturdy stone structure, she decided. With its massive bays, sash windows and carved stone balustrade, it appeared as if it had sprung naturally from the surrounding parklands rather than having been thrust there by man.

She allowed herself a brief moment of silent appreciation before forcing her reluctant feet back into motion. It would be far too easy to give in to the panic fluttering in the back of her mind and flee back to Hillside.

You will not be a coward, Leonida Karkoff.

Pretending a confidence she was far from feeling, she followed the winding, tree-lined path that led past the ivy-covered tower gate and, at last, climbed the shallow steps. Not surprisingly one of the double oak doors was pulled open as she crossed the wide terrace. The Duke of Huntley struck her as a gentleman who would inspire complete loyalty among his staff.

Her courage briefly wavered beneath the formidable glare of the thin butler attired in a black-and-gold uniform. The elderly servant made no effort to disguise his dislike at her intrusion, but obviously having been warned by his employer that Leonida had been issued an invitation, he grudgingly led her through the marble foyer that offered a view of the impressive staircase and down a wainscot-paneled hallway to the library.

Opening the door with a bow, the butler disappeared into the bowels of the house, leaving Leonida alone to enter the vast room.

She breathed a sigh of pleasure at the towering shelves soaring two floors toward a ceiling painted with a stunning panorama of the local landscape. Along one wall was a bank of towering windows that overlooked a pretty deer park filled with trees and wildflowers. And at the end was a massive marble fireplace with two wing chairs and a narrow pier table situated before it.

Eventually, her gaze shifted to the heavy walnut desk and matching chair near the windows.

She briefly wavered. Did she dare try to sneak up and search for the Duchess's private rooms, or did she begin here?

In the end cowardice won the day. The mere thought of trying to slip past an army of servants to intrude into a dead woman's privacy made her stomach twist with dread.

Besides, it was entirely possible that the Duchess of Huntley used this beautiful room to write her correspondence.

Her decision made, she crossed to the desk and, bending down, she jerked open one of the upper drawers. She grimaced at the sight of the deep pile of papers, realizing this might take more time than she had first assumed.

Dividing her attention between the papers and the door leading to the hallway, she reached the last drawer when the unmistakable sound of footsteps had her slamming it shut and racing toward the nearest shelf, her heart in her throat.

She was blindly studying the leather-bound books when someone entered the room. With a pretense of indifference, she glanced to the side, fully expecting the grim butler to request she take her leave. Instead it was the Duke who stepped over the threshold, his expression hard as he studied her with an unnerving intensity.

Leonida froze. Good lord, he was beautiful. Disturbingly beautiful with his dark, perfectly chiseled features and his muscular body shown to advantage in his blue coat and buckskins.

At the moment his raven curls were tumbled from the wind and his cravat loosened to reveal the strong column of his throat, a testament to his hours in the fields, but his casual appearance only added to his potent attraction.

But it was the relentless intelligence in his dark blue eyes that sent a chill down her spine.

This man was no fool and she sensed he already had suspicions of her arrival in Surrey.

Dangerous.

The silence lasted for several painful heartbeats, then with a smile that did not meet his eyes, he was smoothly moving forward to take her hand and lift it to his lips.

"Miss Karkoff," he murmured. "My butler informed me I would find you here."

She tugged her hand from his grasp, unsettled by the tingles of pleasure that raced up her arm.

"I..." She halted to clear the husky fear from her voice. "I did not expect you."

He arched a brow. "No?"

"Lady Summerville mentioned you spent most afternoons in your fields."

Something flashed through his eyes. Curiosity? Suspicion? "As a rule, although I do occasionally spend time with my accounts."

So much for trusting in luck. She would not make that mistake again.

"I hope you do not mind my intrusion, your Grace?"

"Of course not." He casually leaned a shoulder against the sturdy shelf, his powerful presence filling the room as his gaze slid blatantly over her sprigged muslin gown with tiny satin roses sewn along the scooped bodice. At last he returned his attention to the blush staining her cheeks. "I did invite you to make use of the library. Have you not discovered anything of interest?"

She managed a meaningless smile. She had not spent years among the treacherous Russian society without developing some skill in dissembling.

"I was indulging in my love for browsing. Your collection is quite magnificent."

"In all fairness I must confess that I inherited a large portion of the collection from my various ancestors, although I do occasionally add a few books."

She glanced to the wrapped packages sitting on the scrolled satinwood table near the door. She would bet her favorite pearl necklace they held newly arrived books.

"How occasionally?"

"Perhaps *occasionally* is not quite the proper word," he conceded, a heart-melting twinkle entering his eyes.

Her stomach quivered. She was too aware of his potent appeal.

"I did not mean to disturb you. I will return…"

Without warning, he reached out to grasp her arm and steered her toward the wing chairs.

"Please have a seat, Miss Karkoff. I have requested that

Mrs. Slater bring us tea. I believe you will find her seed-cake to be the finest in England."

She briefly debated the odds of making it to the door before he could catch her, only to swiftly dismiss the ludicrous thought.

She had been well and truly cornered, and there was nothing to do but brave it out.

She sank gracefully into one of the chairs and folded her hands in her lap, hoping the penetrating blue eyes did not notice they were shaking.

"Thank you."

Taking his own seat, the Duke stretched out his legs, crossing them at the ankle and putting at risk the fine gloss on his Hessians.

"Tell me what you have seen of the house."

She stiffened. Seen of the house? *Mon Dieu.* Did he suspect she had come to search Meadowland?

"I beg your pardon?"

"I thought perhaps Goodson had given you a tour. He is inordinately proud of the rambling old place and inclined to haul unsuspecting guests from room to room regardless of their boredom."

"No." She breathed a silent sigh of relief. "Of course, I did have the opportunity to admire the front foyer and your very fine marble staircase. I can readily understand your butler's pride."

"Edmond claims that it shall soon be a shabby ruin if I do not devote myself to renovations."

"It is hardly a ruin," she protested, faintly smiling at the lift of his brows. "Although it might be a tiny bit frayed," she conceded. "Still, it is perfectly understandable you would be reluctant to have the house altered in any way."

"And why do you believe me to be reluctant?"

"As I recall, you lost your parents at a very young age. It is only to be expected you would cherish their memory, especially within your home."

He sucked in a sharp breath, as if startled by her words. Strange. From all her discreet inquiries regarding the Duke of Huntley it seemed perfectly obvious to her that he still mourned his parents. Did he believe he kept his pain hidden?

Whatever he might say, however, was halted as the door was opened and a young maid entered carrying a large tray.

"Ah, tea," he murmured, waving the maid to place the tray on the table set beside Leonida's chair.

Completing her task, the pretty maid with a mass of brown curls and big brown eyes dipped a curtsy.

"Is there anything else you need, your Grace?"

The Duke's gaze never wavered from Leonida. "That will be all, Maggie. Thank you."

The maid left and closed the door behind her.

"If you will pour, Miss Karkoff?" he requested as the maid scurried from the room.

"Certainly." She reached to arrange the fine Wedgewood china. "Sugar?"

"Just milk."

Happy to have something to distract herself from his unwavering gaze, Leonida poured the tea and filled two plates with the tiny sandwiches and seedcake.

Unfortunately, he merely set aside the refreshments, continuing to study her as if she were a weed that had dared to stray into his well-tended field.

Sipping her tea, Leonida attempted to appear impervious to his rude stare, allowing her own gaze to travel over the nearby fireplace to the large portrait hung over the mantle.

"Is that a portrait of your parents?"

"Yes, it was done shortly after their marriage."

She studied the couple, not surprised that the previous Duke was a tall gentleman with dark hair and an air of power visible in the strokes of his handsome face, while the Duchess was a small, slender beauty with the brilliant blue eyes she had blessed on her two sons.

"The Duchess is just as lovely as my mother said she was," she murmured. "They were dearest friends, you know."

"So I have heard."

She sipped her tea, quashing her fierce desire to flee and instead stiffened her backbone. For goodness' sakes. This was the perfect opportunity to discover the information she needed. Why was she hesitating?

"I am not certain that my mother ever forgave the Duke for stealing away her beloved Mira," she said, forcing herself to meet that shrewd blue gaze. "Indeed, she confessed her only comfort was writing endless correspondence to the Duchess."

"She was not alone. As I recall my mother devoted several hours each morning to answering the letters she received."

"Well, this is a beautiful room for such a task."

His eyes narrowed. "Actually my mother preferred the private parlor that connected to her bedchamber. It is situated to catch the morning sunlight and she had a perfect view of the lake, which she always loved."

She silently tucked the information away. She at least now knew she needed to discover a means of searching the Duchess's private parlor and that it was on the east side of the house.

Enough for now.

"I cannot imagine a room that does not have a lovely view," she said lightly. "Your parkland is quite magnificent."

"Somewhat less formal than your Russian gardens, although my mother did insist her rose garden be designed with the memory of the Summer Palace in mind. There are a great number of statues and marble fountains."

She glanced toward the windows with their view of the deer park. "While you prefer a less tamed landscape?"

He steepled his fingers beneath his chin. "Nature is a fine enough artist for me."

"And yet you spend hours taming your fields."

She turned back in time to catch the hint of genuine amusement that softened his features.

"So I do, but not, I must point out, for artistic purposes."

"No, your work is far more important."

His gaze lowered to linger on her lips. "Take care, Miss Karkoff, or you will quite turn my head."

Her heart missed a beat and she hastily set aside her cup and shoved a piece of seedcake into her mouth. Anything to distract herself from the heat that suddenly swirled through her body.

"Somehow I doubt that anything or anyone easily turns your head, your Grace," she at last muttered. "You are very…"

"What?"

"Shrewd."

"Thus far I am substantive and shrewd." He smiled, but Leonida detected a faint hint of pique in his voice. "More traits that one desires in a man of business than a gentleman. Perhaps I will not have my head turned after all."

She lifted her brows in surprise. "You would prefer I think of you as shallow and stupid?"

He caught and held her gaze. "I would prefer handsome and charming."

For a startling moment, Leonida found herself lost in his stunning eyes, momentarily forgetting her mother's pleas, the damnable letters and even the suspicion that this man was toying with her much like a cat with a cornered mouse.

Her only thought was that this gentleman stirred sensations in her body that were as shocking as they were delicious. And if they had encountered one another in a Russian drawing room, she would have done everything in her power to try and captivate him.

Abruptly realizing that his expression had become speculative as she gawked at him in silence, Leonida set aside her plate.

"You were correct, your Grace."

"I was?"

"These are the tastiest seedcakes I have ever eaten."

"Ah." His lips twitched. "Tell me, Miss Karkoff, how do matters stand in Russia?"

She blinked at the unexpected question. "I am not certain what you mean."

"When my brother left St. Petersburg he had just assisted in halting a near rebellion."

Her lips thinned at the unwelcome reminder of the uprising among the Emperor's guards. As her mother had so recently pointed out, the politics in Russia were always a murky affair, with a dozen secret societies and foreign powers plotting to overthrow the Czar at any given time, but the betrayal by his own army had been designed to strike Alexander Pavlovich directly in his heart.

"Yes, it was an unfortunate incident."

"Rather more than unfortunate," he drawled.

Her chin tilted with offended loyalty. "England is not without a few revolts by the people."

His smile widened at her sharp tone. "True. I was merely curious about the mood in St. Petersburg."

"Much as it always is, I suppose."

"Has the Czar returned from his travels?"

She considered her words, wondering if his interest was merely passing curiosity or something more.

"He had not when I left, although I believe he was expected shortly. The Emperor does not keep me informed of his movements."

"According to my brother, the Emperor rarely keeps *anyone* informed of his movements."

Well, that was true enough. Unfortunately.

"Do you have a specific interest in Czar Alexander?"

The handsome features hardened with an unmistakable warning. "I am very fond of Alexander Pavlovich, but he does possess a habit of putting my brother at risk when it suits his purpose."

She blinked in confusion. "I understood that Lord Summerville had resigned his position with the Emperor?"

"Yes, he has."

Was that his suspicion? That she had come to Surrey to lure Lord Summerville back to Russia?

Hastily she was on her feet, hoping to disguise the flood of relief that raced through her.

"I should return to Hillside before Lady Summerville begins to worry."

"But you have not yet chosen a book," he protested, rising from the chair to stand at her side.

"Perhaps another day. A woman in Lady Summerville's condition must not be made anxious."

"Condition?" His brows lifted. "Did Brianna tell you she is increasing?"

"Not precisely, but it was not difficult to surmise considering..." She broke off her words, suddenly realizing it was not her place to reveal that poor Brianna spent most mornings battling her nausea.

"So, I am not the only who is shrewd."

"Hardly shrewd," she denied. If she had a bit of sense she would never have agreed to her mother's insane plot. "Goodbye, your Grace."

With a hasty curtsy, she was heading for the door, not at all surprised that before she could yank the thing open, the Duke's voice was halting her escape.

Nothing was easy when this man was near.

"I shall see you at dinner, of course."

Reluctantly she turned, rather disconcerted to discover that he had moved to stand behind his desk.

"Dinner?"

"My brother has very kindly invited me to dine at Hillside."

Her heart jerked at his words, but she knew it was not from fear. "I see. Then until later, your Grace."

"A moment, Miss Karkoff," he murmured, once again

halting her escape, bending down to pluck something from the floor.

"Yes?"

Straightening, he held out his hand. "Your hairpin, I believe."

This time it was fear that made her heart leap and her blood run cold. Damn. How could she have been so careless?

Frozen in place, she frantically searched her mind as he smoothly crossed the room.

"I…it must have fallen out while I was admiring the view," she managed to croak, her throat dry as she met his brooding gaze.

"No doubt."

Praying her hand did not tremble, she reached to pluck the diamond hairpin from his outstretched palm.

"Thank you."

"Did you enjoy it?"

She jumped at the abrupt question. "What?"

"The view. Did you enjoy it?"

"Yes, I…very much." Oh lord, she had to get away from that all too knowing gaze. She felt as if he could see into her very soul. "Goodbye, your Grace."

With that unnerving swiftness he had grasped her hand, lifting it to his lips to caress her knuckles with a slow, intimate kiss.

"*À bientôt,* my angel."

LEANING AGAINST THE DOORJAM, Stefan listened to the swish of muslin as Miss Karkoff rushed down the hallway. Just for a moment, he allowed himself to savor the lingering scent of jasmine and the memory of her warm flesh beneath his lips.

Christ. He had never been so aware of a woman. The delicate line of her profile. The lush curve of her mouth. The gentle mounds of her breasts that begged for a man's touch.

His body didn't give a damn why she was in Surrey. Only how swiftly he could get her into his bed.

Thrusting aside the dangerous thoughts, Stefan waited for the inevitable arrival of his butler. Goodson had not been pleased by Stefan's invitation to allow Miss Karkoff to make use of the library. The servant had devoted his life to ensuring that Stefan was protected from even the least disruption.

While he appreciated Goodson's dedication, Stefan intended to ensure the poor servant put aside his protective nature. At least until he discovered what the blazes Miss Karkoff was plotting.

When Stefan had casually suggested to Miss Karkoff that shc visit his library, it had been with a vague hope of earning her gratitude, and perhaps luring her into revealing some hint of her true purpose in Surrey. He had not truly expected her to accept the offer. Not if she were here to sway Edmond into some foolish scheme for the Emperor.

Now he had to wonder if he was mistaken.

Oh, he was still suspicious of the beautiful woman. She was hiding something. He was as certain of that as he was certain that she had been searching his desk before he had so unexpectedly returned home.

But what?

He was brooding on the puzzle when the thin, silver-haired butler silently slid down the hall to stand before him.

"Ah, Goodson."

The servant offered a bow. "Your Grace?"

"When did Miss Karkoff arrive?"

A sour expression settled on the dignified face. "Precisely at a quarter past one."

Stefan gave a slow nod. He had arrived back at the house at exactly two o'clock.

"So, she was here some time before I returned."

"You did say that you had invited her to make use of the library. I hope I did not do wrong to allow her to stay?"

"Not at all." Stefan absently toyed with the gold signet ring that every Duke of Huntley had worn since the time of Henry the Eighth. "I must say I extended the invitation in the hopes of learning more about the chit, but I did not truly expect her to make an appearance. Now I must reconsider my entire theory."

Goodson frowned. "I beg pardon, sir?"

"I assumed she had come to Surrey with some ploy to lure my brother into Alexander Pavlovich's schemes. Now I must wonder…" Stefan shook his head in aggravation. He was not accustomed to anyone being capable of playing him for a fool.

Miss Leonida Karkoff would pay.

And he could think of the sweetest of punishments.

"I shall make certain she is not allowed to cross the threshold again," Goodson swore, thankfully unaware of Stefan's erotic thoughts.

"No, Goodson. I wish you to make her feel a welcomed guest whenever she arrives."

The butler scowled. "Are you certain, your Grace?"

"Quite certain."

"If you do not trust her, then surely she should not be given the opportunity to cause mischief?"

Stefan's lips twisted. "I have no genuine reason not to trust her, to be honest. She is most likely precisely what she seems to be. A young Russian noblewoman who is anxious to become acquainted with English society."

"But?"

"But, in the event she is not, then I desire to know precisely what she is doing here. And the only means to do that is to keep a close eye upon her."

Goodson clicked his tongue. "So I am to allow her to freely roam about your house?"

"Allow her to roam, but I want a close eye kept upon her," Stefan corrected. "Just ensure she is not aware that she is being watched."

"As you wish."

The servant heaved a heavy sigh, but Stefan was confident that the efficient butler would fulfill the command with his usual efficiency.

Of course, efficiency was not all that the delicate situation demanded.

"Goodson."

"Yes, your Grace?"

He straightened from the doorjamb, his expression one of warning.

"Be sure that Miss Karkoff has no reason to suspect she is anything but an appreciated guest."

Goodson dipped his head in ready understanding. "Very well."

CHAPTER FOUR

LEONIDA TOSSED ASIDE PRIDE and even dignity as she scurried from Meadowland and headed back to Hillside at a pace hardly suitable for a proper lady.

She only wished that she could return to St. Petersburg at an equally swift pace.

What a fool she had been to come to England. It was not, after all, as if she had actually believed her mother's blithe assurances that it would be a simple matter to slip into a duke's grand manor house filled with a few dozen servants and waltz out with a packet of letters that had been hidden for the past twenty or thirty years. And that was before she had met the Duke of Huntley.

Why did the man have to be so annoyingly perceptive?

From the moment they had been introduced he had regarded her with a brooding suspicion that he barely bothered to conceal beneath his smooth charm. And after today…

She halted just outside the gate leading to Lady Summerville's private garden, glancing down at the diamond hairpin clutched in her hand. Well, needless to say, she had done nothing to ease his distrust of her presence in Surrey.

And worse, that maddening fascination she felt whenever he was near refused to be squashed, no matter how desperately she warned herself that it threatened to ruin everything.

For the moment, the Duke of Huntley stood between her and those letters she so desperately needed. She had to think of him as the enemy. Not as a gentleman who made her heart race and her stomach churn with a painful excitement.

Giving an angry shake of her head, Leonida reached to open the gate, pausing as she heard the unmistakable sound of footsteps from behind her. Turning about, she expected to discover one of the innumerable servants or tenants. Unlike Russia's vast expanses, the English countryside seemed to be crowded with people.

Strangely, however, there was no one to be seen. It was as if whoever was there had hastily ducked behind one of the numerous trees.

"Hello," she called, decidedly unnerved by the sensation of being watched by unseen eyes. "Is anyone there? Hello."

"Miss Leonida, whatever are you doing?"

With a squeak of alarm, Leonida whirled back to the gate, discovering her maid standing there with a frown on her round face.

Pressing a hand to her pounding heart, Leonida sucked in a steadying breath. "I was certain I heard someone following me."

"The Duke?"

"I..." She shook her head, reaching to pull open the gate. She did not believe that Stefan would lower himself to sneaking behind her, but she did blame him for putting her so on edge that she was jumping at shadows. "It was probably just my imagination. My nerves are rather unsettled."

"And no wonder." Wrapping a protective arm around Leonida's shoulders, Sophy led her toward the nearby house. "Your mother has no right to involve you in such foolishness."

Leonida hastily glanced around the empty garden. "Shh, Sophy, you must take care."

Sophy snorted. Leonida had been forced to reveal that her mother had sent her to England to discover a hidden object, but nothing more. It was not that she did not trust her maid, but the fewer who knew the better.

"Did you find what you were searching for?"

"No." Leonida reached to pluck a pink rose from a nearby bush. "I shall have to return."

"Not today, you will not," Sophy muttered. "You look in need of a long nap."

"I hoped you packed my headache powders."

A sly smile curved Sophy's lips. "No, but I did manage to get my hands on a bottle of vodka. The finest in your mother's cellars."

AS USUAL, STEFAN CHOSE TO WALK the short distance to Hillside rather than calling for his carriage. Not that he was foolish enough to wander around on his own. His position as Duke offered some protection, but a desperate thief could put a hole through his heart as easily as if he were any other man.

Besides, his servants would be horrified if he walked through the dark alone. They expected him to behave in a manner befitting a duke, even when he felt as if he were being slowly strangled by the rigid custom.

Reaching the gardens of Hillside, Stefan commanded the two grooms to go to the kitchen to enjoy dinner and stepped through the gate. Once alone, he followed the torchlit path until a faint sound had him reaching into his pocket to grasp the pistol that was loaded and primed to fire.

A shadow loomed from behind a fountain, then Stefan's tension relaxed as the flickering firelight revealed his brother's familiar features.

Pulling his hand from his pocket, Stefan gave a lift of his brows. "Edmond. Were you laying in wait?"

Edmond shrugged, his gaze narrowing as it skimmed over Stefan's tailored jacket in a dove gray that he had matched with a black waistcoat stitched with a gold thread. Stefan shifted, uncomfortable. He had no desire to explain why he had felt a sudden need to call for the local tailor.

"I did wish to speak with you before you entered," Edmond admitted, a mysterious smile playing about his lips.

"Has something occurred?" Stefan's brows snapped together. "Is it Brianna?"

Edmond held up a reassuring hand. "Everything is well, Stefan."

"Then why did you wish to speak with me?"

"The King sent a messenger earlier to demand my appearance at Court."

"Damn." Stefan grimaced. George had been more demanding than ever of his loyal subjects since the death of his father. "What does he want on this occasion?"

His brother shrugged. "He claims that he desires to discuss the details of his approaching coronation."

"And what is his true purpose?"

"I suspect he desires me to ensure that Queen Caroline comprehends that her presence at the ceremony is distinctly unwelcome."

Predictable. After the farcical trial where the King failed to dissolve his marriage to the Queen, he had done everything in his power to humiliate her.

"Does he not have a dozen fawning sycophants to negotiate the royal domestic squabbles?"

Edmond shoved his fingers through his dark curls. A sure indication he was not as calm as he appeared.

"None with the least amount of diplomatic skills."

"As if diplomacy has ever swayed the Queen from her outrageous behavior."

"Yes, it is rather a pity she did not remain abroad," Edmond muttered. "Still, I am not without pity for her. The marriage might have been less a tragedy if she had not been treated with such open contempt by her husband and those who surrounded him."

That was true enough. The King had not only flaunted his mistress with utter disregard, but he had made no effort to disguise his disgust for his new bride.

"I agree, but there is no healing the wounds after all these years. She will go to any lengths to have her revenge.

And what could be more tempting than embarrassing the King during such a public spectacle?"

Edmond heaved a sigh. "I must at least make the attempt."

"When do you leave?"

"Tomorrow morning."

Stefan blinked in surprise. "I have always known Brianna to be efficient, but surely not even she can prepare to undertake a journey so swiftly?"

Edmond's features hardened. "Brianna will be remaining in Surrey."

"Good lord. Have you told her?"

Edmond's short laugh echoed through the shadowed garden. "She was not pleased to say the least, but she eventually had to concede that traveling any distance in a carriage is beyond her at the moment."

Stefan's concern was not eased. "I am happy to know she is being sensible, but do you truly think that she should be left alone here with Miss Karkoff?"

"*Mon Dieu*, Stefan, you do not believe the woman is here to harm my bride?" Edmond demanded in exasperated tones.

Stefan recalled his violent confusion of emotion when he had stepped into his library to discover Leonida. Suspicion, anger and a raw, relentless desire at the sight of her simple beauty that seemed to glow in the slanting sunlight.

"I have no notion why she is here, and that is what troubles me," he muttered.

There was a pause before Edmond folded his arms across his chest.

"Then you will be pleased to discover that Leonida is as concerned for Brianna's welfare as you are."

"What do you mean?"

"She seems to believe you would make a suitable chaperone."

"Me?"

"The implication was that Brianna, and Miss Karkoff of course, would stay at Meadowland until my return."

Stefan stilled. "Miss Karkoff suggested that they stay at Meadowland?"

"Yes."

"Now that is intriguing."

"And not entirely unpalatable, eh, Stefan?"

Unpalatable? Stefan's lips twisted. A wicked heat speared through his body at the mere thought of having Leonida so close at hand.

"It will be much easier to keep an eye upon her if she is under my roof."

"And is your eye the only thing you desire to keep upon her?" Edmond drawled.

Stefan regarded his brother with a bland smile. "I cannot imagine what you are implying."

"I have seen the manner in which you stare at Leonida."

"And how is that?"

"Like I stare at Brianna."

Stefan shook his head. No. Edmond was captivated with his bride beyond all reason. What Stefan felt for Leonida was an explosive combination of suspicion and smoldering lust.

"I will not deny she is a beautiful woman."

"And you want her in your bed?"

He sucked in a sharp breath, easily imagining Leonida spread across his sheets, her alabaster skin drenched in moonlight and jasmine.

"My bed and the women who might warm it are not a subject I discuss with anyone," he warned. "Including you, Edmond."

Edmond chuckled. "I am just pleased to know that you are not entirely determined to live as a monk."

Stefan arched a brow. There were several lovely widows in Surrey who would be shocked by the mere suggestion.

"Hardly a monk."

"Why, you cunning fox. Who is she?"

"Shall I come in the morning to collect Brianna and Miss Karkoff?" Stefan firmly put an end to the conversation.

Edmond's smile was taunting, but he willingly allowed himself to be diverted. "If you do not mind the intrusion?"

"On the contrary." Stefan glanced toward the brightly lit Hillside where he could see the silhouette of a slender woman standing near the window. Leonida. "I have rarely looked forward to something with such anticipation."

THE PRIVATE QUARTERS of Meadowland proved to be as exquisite as the rest of the estate, if a bit shabby.

Left alone in her chambers, Leonida wandered through the small parlor decorated in soothing shades of ivory and gold, her hand lightly stroking over the back of a satinwood sofa before she headed into the matching bedroom. A canopied bed draped in cream satin was set in the center of a Persian rug and above the ceiling was painted a blue sky with tiny cherubs. Across the room, a large armoire was situated next to a bay window that overlooked the ornamental lake.

A lake.

So…her rooms must be set near the Duchess's, she realized, unconsciously licking her dry lips. Yet another stroke of fortune.

Oddly, Leonida did not feel particularly fortunate.

She had spent last night tossing and turning after her impetuous suggestion that she and Brianna come to stay at Meadowland. This might be the perfect opportunity to discover the letters, but she was wise enough to sense that she was walking directly into a trap.

Unlike most aristocrats, the Duke of Huntley was no fool. If he allowed a woman he did not trust into his home, then it was only because he had his own devious plot in mind.

Leonida could only hope that she was clever enough to outwit him.

She shivered despite the heat in the room, then with a

tilt of her chin, she forced herself to thrust aside her cowardly thoughts and begin a thorough search of the armoire. It hardly seemed likely the letters would be hidden in a guest chamber, but she would leave no stone unturned.

Besides, she dare not seek the Duchess's room until she could be certain she would not be seen.

Finding nothing in the armoire but the clothing that Sophy had unpacked just moments before, Leonida turned her attention to the mirrored dressing table, pulling the drawers open to discover a silver-backed mirror and matching brush as well as several expensive bottles of perfume. She had just tugged open the bottom drawer when a familiar tingle raced over her skin, warning her that she was no longer alone.

Slamming the drawer shut, she rose jerkily to her feet and turned to discover Stefan leaning against the doorjamb, his arms folded across her chest.

Despite the fact she had seen him less than an hour before, her heart gave its familiar jerk as she met his dazzling blue gaze.

He was so damnably gorgeous. Even attired in a plain green jacket and buckskins, his dark beauty was enough to steal the breath of any woman.

"Your Grace," she murmured, refusing to glance down and ensure her white muslin gown with a black ribbon threaded through the bodice and seed pearls stitched along the hem was not wrinkled from her short journey. It was bad enough her hand had already lifted to touch her curls that had been twisted into a complicated knot on top her head.

"I wished to assure myself that you were settled. I hope the chambers suit you?"

"Very much, thank you."

His gaze shifted over her shoulder, lingering on the dresser. "You appeared to be searching for something. If there is anything you need…"

"No, I was simply assuring myself that Sophy had packed all that I requested," she interrupted, her voice rushed.

"Ah." His expression was impossible to read. "And did she?"

"Yes, I believe so."

"If not, you need only let me know and I shall send one of my servants to collect it for you."

"That is very kind of you."

A slow, tantalizing smile curved his lips. "I desire you to feel welcome at Meadowland."

Her mouth went dry, reminding her that there was more than one danger in residing beneath the same roof as the Duke of Huntley.

"Where is Brianna?"

"Saying farewell to my brother."

"I see. Perhaps I should say goodbye, as well."

His wicked laugh brushed over her skin like a caress. "I doubt they would welcome the interruption at this precise moment."

She bit her bottom lip. "Oh."

"Hmm." Without warning he reached to brush a finger down her cheek. "I wonder if that blush is real. Are you as innocent as you appear to be?"

She hastily backed away, not halting until her back was pressed against the carved post of the bed. A mere touch should not make her stomach clench with excitement.

"Your Grace."

Prowling forward, the Duke did not halt until he was close enough for her to feel the heat of his body through her gown.

"My name is Stefan." He reached to grasp the post just above her head, his brooding gaze trained on her lips. "Say it."

A voice whispered in the back of her mind to slap his handsome face. It would be a disaster to allow this man to realize just how susceptible she was to his potent masculinity.

That voice, however, went unheeded as her body softened and her pulsed raced. How was she supposed to think when his spicy male scent was clouding her senses?

"Stefan," she breathed.

His head dipped down to stroke his lips over the pulse fluttering at the base of her throat.

"Again."

She trembled. "Stefan."

"Beautiful." He gently nipped her skin, his hand skimming up the curve of her waist. "You are so beautiful."

Her knees went weak and Leonida was forced to grasp the lapels of his jacket to keep upright.

"Why are you doing this?" she asked huskily.

His fingers shifted to trace the edge of her bodice, the light touch making her stomach clench again with a thrilling sense of exhilaration.

"Because I must know."

"Know what?"

His mouth traced a path of kisses up the line of her throat. "If your skin is as smooth as I have fantasized it to be." He nuzzled the hollow beneath her ear. "If your hair smells of jasmine." He explored the heated skin of her cheek before hovering just above her mouth. "If your lips taste as sweet as they appear."

"You must not…"

Her words were halted as he covered her mouth in a fierce, shockingly brazen kiss.

Leonida's breath tangled in her throat and her heart forgot to beat as her lips parted beneath his insistent demand. Over the years she had occasionally been kissed by hopeful gentlemen. A few had even been quite skilled. But never had such a simple caress seared through her, melting her resistance with a terrifying ease.

His lips tasted of brandy, as if he had sipped the spirit before entering her room, and his tongue teased hers in an oddly erotic dance. She felt dizzy, his male scent stirring her senses as surely as the clever fingers that cupped her breast in a possessive gesture.

She shivered, her lips moving beneath his with a ready response she could not hide. This was precisely what she had desired from the moment she had laid eyes on the magnificent Duke of Huntley.

It was, at last, the achingly sweet excitement blooming in the pit of her stomach that sent up a shrill of alarm through her mind.

Mon Dieu.

She had devoted the entire morning to preparing herself to ignore Stefan's intoxicating presence. Had she not paced her room at Hillside, listing all the reasons her attraction for the Duke was such a ghastly notion? Not the least of which was the risk of being distracted from her true reason for being in Meadowland.

And here she was, melting in his arms, just minutes after her bags had been unpacked.

Pressing her hands against his chest, Leonida turned her face from his devastating kiss.

"No…this is…"

"What?" he rasped, stroking his lips over the line of her jaw.

"Dangerous."

He pulled back to regard her with smoldering eyes. "Are you afraid?"

Afraid? Her heart was pounding and her knees weak, but she knew that it was not from fear.

"I would be if I had any sense," she muttered.

He searched her wide eyes, a stain of color splayed along his high cheekbones.

"Do you have a lover waiting for you in Russia?"

She stiffened at the harsh question. "Of course not."

"It would not be so shocking, little dove. You are an exquisite temptation that few men could resist."

"Just because my mother…"

He frowned as she allowed her defensive words to trail away. "This has nothing to do with your mother."

With a wiggle, she slipped from his arms, her hand pressed to her churning stomach as she regarded him with a wary gaze.

"Please, your Grace, Sophy might return at any moment."

His expression hardened. "My name is Stefan."

"Fine." She blew out an exasperated sigh. "Stefan."

"Until later."

With a stiff bow, the Duke turned to make his way toward the door. Abruptly, Leonida realized she was about to allow a perfect opportunity to slip through her grasp.

"Your…" She swiftly corrected herself as Stefan turned to stab her with a warning frown. "Stefan."

"Yes?"

"I hope you do not mind if I explore your beautiful home while I am here?"

Despite her determinedly casual tone he stilled at her request. He looked like…what? A predator that had spotted his prey?

"I will be pleased to take you on a tour before dinner."

"No, I…" She halted to clear her throat. "I would not want to take you from your duties. I am quite capable of wandering around on my own."

He offered a slow dip of his head. "As you wish."

Waiting until he had left her chambers, Leonida moved to sink onto the edge of the bed, burying her face in her hands as her body trembled with frustrated need.

"Mother, what have you gotten me into?" she muttered.

LEAVING THE IVORY CHAMBERS, Stefan was forced to halt and battle the desire that raged through him like wildfire.

Damn.

He had deliberately gone into Leonida's room to catch her off guard. Not a particularly admirable ploy, but it had succeeded. A mere glance at her rummaging through the drawers of the dresser had proven she had been searching for something. Something she obviously thought was hidden at Meadowland.

Not that he could imagine what it might be.

And within a few moments in her company, he no longer gave a bloody hell.

At the mere sight of her standing next to the bed, her jasmine scent filling his senses, he had been lost.

If she had not pushed him away, he would have taken her then and there.

Christ, he wished that he had taken her. At least then his body would not be aroused to the point of pain.

"Sir."

The familiar voice of his butler was nearly as good as being tossed in the middle of a freezing lake.

The savage need faded—although he suspected it would never be truly gone, at least not until he had Leonida spread beneath him—and he was able to turn to face his servant with a measure of composure.

"Yes, Goodson?"

"It may be nothing, but I thought you should know."

"What is it?"

"Benjamin caught two ruffians in the copse of woods just south of the house."

Stefan frowned. "Poachers?"

Goodson gave a lift of his hands. "They claimed they were staying in the local village and were merely admiring the grounds."

"Were they armed?"

"Yes, and Benjamin claimed they spoke with a strange accent." There was a deliberate pause. "He was certain it wasn't French."

Stefan clenched his hands. Foreigners. Were they connected to Leonida?

There was only one means to discover the truth.

"Have Benjamin travel to the village and see if he can

catch sight of the trespassers. I would be very interested to know where they are staying."

Goodson nodded, his gaze shifting to the door that Stefan had so recently closed.

"What of Miss Karkoff?"

"You may leave Miss Karkoff to me."

The butler sniffed his disapproval. "As you wish."

CHAPTER FIVE

TWO DAYS LATER, LEONIDA joined Brianna in a slow stroll through the Duchess's formal garden.

It was a beautiful creation.

The main avenue was paved with a pale pink stone and lined by fountains topped with sirens on each side. At the end of the avenue a refectory pool was surrounded by marble benches and in the center of the pool was a large golden sculpture of Apollo surrounded by lions spewing water from their mouths.

Several smaller paths led to the flower beds that were framed by precisely cut hedges, and set just beyond the pool was a pretty domed grotto that offered a magnificent view of the surrounding countryside.

Soaking in the welcome warmth of the afternoon sun, Leonida slowly felt her tense muscles relax.

The past few days had been stressful, to say the least.

Lord, she had known that Stefan must employ a small battalion of servants, but she had not realized that it was impossible to step from her rooms without tripping over a half dozen of them. Chambermaids, under maids, footmen, pages, a housekeeper, a butler…

Even the one occasion she had attempted to slip toward the Duchess's chamber in the middle of the night, she had nearly been caught by a uniformed servant who seemed to have no other task than keeping an eye on the candles burning along the corridor.

She might as well have been attempting to steal the Crown Jewels.

To make matters worse, there was no escaping the time she was forced to spend in Stefan's company.

Oh, he was unfailingly polite, even charming. What else could he be when Brianna was always near? But Leonida was acutely aware of his brooding gaze that held a terrifying mixture of distrust and blatant sexual need.

Unaware that her feet had faltered to a halt, Leonida gave a sudden jerk as Brianna touched her arm.

"Well?"

Turning her head, Leonida regarded her companion's expectant expression, belatedly realizing that Brianna assumed her bemused manner was due to their beautiful surroundings.

"It is as stunning as you promised," Leonida said, happy to be distracted from her worrisome thoughts. "It reminds me of home."

Brianna smiled, her hair shimmering like fire in the sunlight. If Leonida had been an envious sort of person, she would have hated the slender woman with her tilted green eyes and perfect features. Even simply attired in a morning gown of twilled French silk, she seemed to glow with feminine beauty. Leonida, on the other hand, knew she was pretty enough in her rose-and-ivory striped walking dress with satin flowers along the hem, but she would never possess Brianna's dramatic appeal.

Thankfully, Leonida had never been petty and she found herself enchanted with Brianna's artless charm.

"Yes, the Duchess was most insistent that it resemble the garden she had known when she was a girl in St. Petersburg," Brianna explained. "She loved Meadowland, but she never forgot her devotion to Russia. No doubt that is why Edmond felt compelled to offer his services to the Emperor when he came of age."

"The current Duke does not seem to possess his brother's sense of dedication to Russia."

"No, Stefan is very much an Englishman, as he should be," Brianna readily agreed. "His duty is to his estates and to the British Crown. He has a great number of people who depend upon him."

"So I have noticed," Leonida said dryly, recalling the unwelcome servants who filled the house.

"He is a very fine duke. Just like his father."

Leonida pretended an interest in a nearby rose bloom. She suspected that Brianna was aware of far more than she allowed others to believe.

"Did you know the previous Duke well?"

"Yes." With a faint sigh, Brianna moved to settle on a nearby bench. "I was in London when he and the Duchess died, but I spent a great deal of my childhood here. My own parents…well, let us just say they were unsuited to wed and even more unsuited to have a child. My only solace was coming to Meadowland where I was welcomed as one of the family." She glanced toward the sprawling mansion. "This was a place of great joy and great love."

Leonida nodded. She had easily been able to sense the happiness that seemed to have seeped into the very stone of Meadowland, as if just waiting for an opportunity to fill the air once again.

"Did you know then that you would wed Edmond?"

"Good heavens, no." Brianna's chuckle filled the rose-scented air. "He terrified me. I was much closer to Stefan."

Leonida felt a ridiculous pang. Not that she believed that Brianna was anything but devoted to Lord Summerville, but there was no denying that she held a special place in Stefan's heart.

"I see."

"He was like a brother to me," Brianna said, an odd hint of amusement in her voice. "Now he is truly my brother. I could not be more delighted."

Leonida stroked the velvet petal, considering Stefan and Edmond.

"I cannot claim your acquaintance with the brothers but I must admit that I find the Duke far more…" She searched for the proper word. "Intimidating than your husband."

"You are very perceptive."

Leonida turned to meet Brianna's startled gaze. "Why do you say that?"

"Most people are fooled by Stefan's quiet manner and dislike for the foolishness of society, but beneath his calm composure is a formidable intelligence and a ruthless will." She deliberately paused. "I would not desire to cross him."

Leonida could not halt her shiver. "No."

"On the other hand, he is intensely loyal and would do anything in his power to protect those he loves."

Leonida returned her attention to the roses, unable to dismiss her insatiable fascination with the Duke of Huntley.

"It is odd that he has not yet wed."

"You must recall that Stefan and Edmond were raised by parents who were utterly devoted to one another. Neither could be satisfied with anything less in their marriage."

Leonida's heart sank at Brianna's words. Stupid. Of course, a gentleman such as Stefan would choose a woman he could love without reservation. A woman of beauty and grace and charm. A woman of unshakable morals whom he could always trust.

She hastily quashed the dangerous thoughts. The next Duchess of Huntley was none of her concern.

None.

"Edmond certainly found such devotion," she murmured.

"Yes, well, it might not be so simple for Stefan." Brianna laughed wryly. "Not that Edmond's and my courtship was without its difficulties, but Stefan is consumed with his duties as Duke. I think he always fears that he will somehow fail his father. A ludicrous notion, but…"

"But he feels the weight of his responsibilities?" Leonida finished for her companion.

"Too much. He never gives himself the opportunity to meet a woman who can win his heart. I worry for him."

Leonida shrugged. "He is still young."

"And extraordinarily attractive," Brianna pointed out, as if Leonida was not already painfully aware of Stefan's lethal allure. "It is grossly unfair that two men should possess such beauty. I always feel remarkably dowdy in their presence."

Leonida snorted. "I know precisely how you feel."

"Yes, perhaps you do."

Leonida stiffened at Brianna's soft words, sensing that the woman was far too aware of her potent awareness of Stefan.

Squaring her shoulders, she sternly reminded herself that she had a purpose in coming to Meadowland, and it was not to fantasize about the Duke of Huntley.

"Were you close to the Duchess?" she asked with artful innocence.

"She was always very kind to me."

"As she was to my mother. They were great friends. In fact, she told me that she was so lonely that she wrote endless letters to the Duchess after she left Russia to travel to England." She covertly glanced toward Brianna, watching her expression. "Did you ever happen across any of them?"

"Not that I can recall." Brianna frowned. "Wait, it does seem… Oh, of course."

"Yes?"

"I remember asking Edmond why he and Stefan held their cousin Howard Summerville in such contempt." She grimaced. "He lived not far from here and I occasionally crossed his path, so I knew he was a petulant little snitch who delighted in spoiling the fun of others, but their violent hatred seemed a bit extreme."

Leonida managed a smile, although she couldn't imagine what Howard Summerville had to do with her mother's letters.

"What did he say?"

"He said that Howard was always dunning them for money, and worse, they caught him more than once stealing objects from Meadowland that he could sell in London."

Leonida blinked in shock. *"Mon Dieu."*

"Edmond said they were usually small things, snuff boxes or statuettes, but once Stefan caught Howard in the Duchess's rooms trying to stuff packets of old letters into his pockets."

"Letters?" Leonida's fingers tightened on the rose, sending a shower of crimson petals across the path. Had Howard Summerville managed to read the letters? Was he the one behind her mother's blackmail? "You are certain?"

"I believe that is what Edmond said. Why?"

"It seems an odd thing to steal."

"A dangerous thing to try and steal as it turns out." Brianna laughed. "Stefan had bloodied Howard's nose and cracked three of his ribs before Edmond could pull him off."

Leonida froze. "I...see."

"I do not mean to imply that Stefan is a violent man, but he is intensely protective of his parents' memories."

The dread that had been growing with every passing day coiled through the pit of her stomach.

She did not believe Stefan would physically harm her if he learned the truth of her quest. He had been raised a gentleman. But he might very well hate her.

And she could not blame him for a moment.

"Quite understandable," she muttered.

"Stefan never forgave his cousin," Brianna continued, unaware of Leonida's shiver of regret.

Struggling to concentrate on the realization that there had been letters in the Duchess's rooms, even if she could not know for certain they were the ones she sought, Leonida blinked in astonishment as a large dog bounded through the nearby hedge, dancing around her with his tongue hanging out and his ears flopping.

"Oh."

Brianna laughed. “Do not fear, Puck would not harm you, would you, old boy?”

“Puck?”

“Puck the second, actually,” a dark voice drawled, making Leonida jerk her head up to watch Stefan step from behind the fountain.

“Stefan, you are home early.” With a smile of welcome, Brianna rose to her feet. “We did not expect you until dinner.”

Stefan’s gaze never wavered from Leonida’s guarded expression. “I discovered I could not concentrate on drainage ditches when I had two such lovely guests staying beneath my roof.”

Brianna chuckled. “It must be your loveliness that has lured him from his beloved fields, Leonida, since he has on more than one occasion forgotten that he was to join me for tea at Hillside.”

Stefan’s lips twitched. “Only because I knew your annoying husband would be hovering about to ruin my appetite for sponge cake.”

“You are a terrible liar and it is time I lay down for a rest,” Brianna said, glancing from Stefan to Leonida with a hint of satisfaction. “It is excessively inconvenient to always feel so weary.”

Recalling his manners, Stefan moved to take Brianna’s hand and lift it to his lips.

“Inconvenient, but wondrous.”

“Yes.”

“If you have need do not hesitate to call for me.”

“All I need is rest. I shall see you both at dinner.”

Leonida watched Brianna follow the path back toward the house, only belatedly realizing she was being left alone with Stefan. Her heart fluttered in alarm. She had gone to great efforts to avoid this precise situation.

“Perhaps…”

Without warning, Stefan had moved to grasp her arms. “No.”

STEFAN GAZED DOWN AT THE FACE that had haunted his nights. The clear, innocent blue eyes. The delicate features. The stubborn line of her jaw.

The lush lips that begged for his kiss.

Christ. He was tired of waiting for her to reveal her nefarious reasons for being at Meadowland, and even more tired of playing the role of proper host.

He wanted her in his bed. To hell with anything else.

As if sensing his smoldering tension, Leonida licked her lips, her eyes darkening with a need she could not entirely disguise.

"No?"

"You were about to suggest that you follow Brianna to ensure she is well or perhaps you have discovered a sudden need to change your gown or any of the other excuses you have used over the past two days to avoid being alone with me."

Her lips thinned at his mocking tone. "If you are so confident I am attempting to avoid you then it would seem odd you would insist that I remain."

Skimming his hands down her bare arms, he took her hand and firmly tugged her down the path.

"Since I have done everything in my power to make you feel welcome at Meadowland, I think it only fair to have an explanation as to why you would take such a dislike to my companionship."

She ducked her head, hiding her expressive features. "I do not dislike your companionship."

"Then why do you avoid me?" he demanded. "Is it because I kissed you?"

"You should not have."

Stefan's short laugh was without humor. Did she believe that he had a choice in the matter?

"Perhaps not, but that will not halt me from doing so again."

He felt her shiver and, quickening his pace, he led her around the small pool to climb the steps of the private grotto. Bloody hell, he had to kiss this woman before he went stark raving mad.

She gasped as he yanked her into the shadows of the grotto that was painted with lovely Grecian frescoes, his arms wrapping around her to haul her firmly against his chest.

"Is this why you returned early?" she demanded, her glare at odds with the rapid pulse beating at the base of her throat.

Miss Karkoff might pretend indifference, but she desired him. Her words could lie, but not her body.

"I returned because I could not stay away." Dipping his head, Stefan buried his face in the curve of her neck. "Jasmine."

"What?"

"You smell of jasmine."

She shuddered, her hands lifting to clutch at his shoulders.

"Stefan, what do you want of me?"

"I should think that obvious." He pulled back to regard her with a grim determination, his fingers easily dealing with the ribbons that held her chip bonnet tied beneath her chin. "But if you wish, I shall reveal precisely what I want of you."

She made a sound of annoyance as he casually tossed the hat onto the flagstone floor.

"That is my favorite bonnet."

Heat spread through his lower body, stirring his muscles in sharp anticipation.

"A charming concoction, but as you know I prefer a more natural beauty." With a few practiced motions he had the pearl studded pins plucked from her hair, allowing the golden curls to tumble over her shoulders. With a low groan, he thrust his fingers through the thick curls. "Silken sunshine."

Her fingers tightened on his shoulders. "You are trying to distract me."

He brushed his lips over her brow, pausing to nuzzle the pulse hammering at her temple.

"Am I succeeding?"

"Damn you," she said huskily.

"Such language, little dove. Those lips were meant for a far sweeter purpose." Framing her face in his hands, Stefan angled it upward, seeking her lips in a kiss of sheer possession. *Mine,* a voice whispered in the back of his mind. Parting her mouth with his tongue, Stefan tasted deeply of her sweet innocence, a savage hunger humming through his body. For a moment she went rigid, as if startled by his invasion, then with a sigh, she arched closer to his body and tangled her fingers in his hair. "Yes," he muttered against her lips, his hands smoothing up her back as he skillfully unhooked the pearl buttons.

He swept his lips over her eyes, the perfect line of her nose, before returning to her pleading lips. At the same moment, he was shifting her arms so he could tug her gown down until it pooled at her feet.

Leonida groaned, pulling back to regard him with dazed eyes. "The servants…"

"Will not trouble us here," he promised, nuzzling that tender spot at the base of her throat that always made her shiver.

"Do they know this is where you lure hapless women?" she rasped, even as her head tilted back to allow him greater access.

"Hapless?" He laughed as he shifted to press her against the wall, his fingers tracing the scooped bodice of her shift. Her skin was as soft as the finest silk. "You are the most dangerous woman I have ever encountered, Miss Karkoff. The Emperor is wiser than I ever suspected."

Her breath caught at his accusation. "What do you mean?"

"You are the one with the answers, not I," he muttered, far more interested in removing her lacy corset than in discovering the truth. The undergarment dropped to the ground, swiftly followed by her thin shift. She shivered. Stefan wrapped her tightly in his arms. "And until I have the truth from you I intend to enjoy what has been offered me."

"Stefan..." She gave a startled squeak as he bent his head to take a puckered nipple between his lips. "Oh."

"Shh, my dove," he murmured, savoring the sweet taste of Leonida's skin as he explored the curve of her breast, his fingers stroking down her lower back and over the flare of her hips.

She was tiny, but perfectly shaped, and so exquisitely soft. Flawless. With a muttered curse, Stefan ripped off his cravat and jacket, his waistcoat swiftly following. Then, jerking his linen shirt over his head, he reached to grasp her hands and pressed them to his chest.

"Touch me," he commanded roughly.

With a tiny groan she arched back to regard him with a troubled gaze.

"I have warned you that I am not my mother."

He frowned, gripping her hips to press her firmly against his aching erection. This was hardly the moment to chat about her mother.

"So you have said, although I haven't the least notion what this has to do with the Countess," he growled.

Her hands trembled, but she did not pull them away from his chest. "You are not the first gentleman to presume I am eager for an affair just because my mother enjoyed such a blatant liaison with the Emperor."

Just for a moment Stefan's heart twisted at the sight of the vulnerability that shimmered in her wide eyes. She appeared so damned innocent with her flushed cheeks and her bright curls tumbled about her face. It stirred a protective instinct that sent a chill of alarm down his spine.

He narrowed his gaze as he studied the angelic face that might very well disguise the heart of a viper. He would be a fool to forget that for a moment.

"And you would not be the first woman to return my

kisses with the hope of trapping a duke into marriage," he smoothly countered.

She blinked, as if shocked by his words. "I would never—"

"And neither would I," he interrupted, kissing her with a fierce demand. "I desire you," he rasped, his lips moving down the line of her collarbone. "I ache for you. It is that simple."

"Dear lord," she moaned, her fingers skating over his chest as he once again found the tip of her breast to suckle her with a growing insistence. "There is nothing simple about this."

She was right.

Lust was simple, but this…

Grimly thrusting aside the voice of warning in the back of his head, Stefan nudged her legs apart with his knee, his hand moving over her hip until he could tease the inner skin of her thigh.

She gave a small cry of pleasure and Stefan hastily covered her lips in a smothering kiss. It was not fear of discovery that troubled him; it was fear he might very well shoot anyone stupid enough to walk through the door and interrupt him.

Returning his kiss with an untutored enthusiasm, Leonida dug her nails into his back. Stefan growled his pleasure, his hand seeking the intimate cleft between her legs. She was already damp and his finger slid through the slick folds, a sweet temptation that made his erection pulse with an angry demand for release.

Guided by her soft pants and moans, Stefan caressed her with a growing urgency, goading her to even greater pleasure. She began to stir restlessly in his arms, seeking a relief to the tension he could feel clenching her muscles.

"Easy," he murmured, grasping one of her wandering hands to press it against his arousal.

He groaned at the raw pleasure. Even through his buckskins he could feel the heat of her fingers as they curved tentatively around his shaft.

Using one hand to guide her fingers over his arousal, he used the other to continue pleasuring her, their rasping breaths the only sound to break the silence of the grotto.

"Stefan…I need…"

"I know, my dove, trust me," he muttered, barely recognizing the irony of his words.

In this moment he could think of nothing beyond the sight of Leonida's beautiful face as her eyes widened and her mouth parted in a silent scream of pleasure.

Her first taste of passion, but not her last, he silently swore.

Struck by her beauty, Stefan was caught off guard when her fingers tightened around him. With a strangled moan, he thrust his hips forward and his powerful release exploded. Gasping for air, he leaned heavily against her, struggling to remain upright as the shattering climax pulsed through his body.

Christ, what had the woman done to him?

CHAPTER SIX

WAITING UNTIL THE DINNER GONG had echoed through the vast house, Leonida glided through the thankfully empty corridor to slip into the Duchess's room.

She knew she was taking a risk. Although a large number of the servants would be busy in the kitchens, either assisting with the meal or enjoying their own, there were always a few drifting about the house, their sharp gazes missing nothing.

But what choice did she have? She might try and convince herself that giving in to Stefan's skillful seduction was the perfect means of keeping him distracted from her true purpose for being in Surrey, but she was not stupid.

Her violent explosion of pleasure had nothing to do with plots or schemes or her loyalty to Russia. She was quite simply incapable of resisting the handsome Duke of Huntley. And every moment that she spent in his company only deepened her fascination.

She had to find those letters and flee before her revulsion for deceiving Stefan overcame her devotion to her mother.

Her decision made, Leonida had sent word to the kitchen that she preferred a tray in her room and, waiting until she was certain that both Stefan and Brianna had gone down to dinner, she had posted Sophy near the stairs and darted through the shadows to the state rooms.

Grasping a candle in her hand, she entered the Duchess's bedchamber, casting a quick glance around the vast room.

Unlike most of the estate, the Duchess had chosen to

remove the aging wainscoting and replaced it with crimson damask wall panels. The ceiling was molded and trimmed with gilt, and in the center a cut glass chandelier reflected the candlelight with a shimmering beauty. Set near the white marble fireplace, the four-poster bed was draped in emerald-green velvet that matched the cushions on the gilt gesso chairs.

Despite the air of emptiness, the chamber was kept ruthlessly clean, reminding Leonida that a servant might enter at any moment. The quicker she finished her search, the better.

The question was…where to begin?

Beyond the fabulous gilt-framed pictures by Gainsborough and Reynolds that could all possibly cover a hidden safe, there was a pair of mahogany cabinets, a rosewood writing table and a French marquetry pedestal bureau.

And she had not yet entered the private parlor that was just beyond the connecting door.

With a sigh, she moved toward the writing table. Surely it was the most obvious place to begin her search?

Obvious, but fruitless, she soon discovered, finding nothing more than the usual items. Parchment, quills, ink, wax and the Duchess's formal seal.

"*Mon Dieu.* Where can they be?" she muttered.

She was just moving to the pedestal bureau when the door to the room was pressed open and Sophy was waving a frantic hand.

"The Duke is coming up the stairs," she hissed. "You must hurry."

Muttering a curse, Leonida raced across the room, shutting the door behind her. Then, grasping Sophy's arm, she hurried them both toward her chambers.

"Why does the aggravating man not leave me in peace?" she hissed, as aggravated by the joyful leap of her heart as by his untimely approach.

Sophy snorted, casting Leonida a knowing glance. "Aye, I wonder."

Leonida blushed. "He is suspicious of my presence in Surrey."

"Why would he be suspicious?"

"He seems to believe I am here to lure his brother into some plot devised by the Emperor."

"Ah." Sophy nodded. "Well, the rumors were that Lord Summerville did put himself at risk on a number of occasions for the Czar Alexander. Perhaps the Duke has cause to worry."

Leonida's lips twisted. "If Alexander Pavlovich desires Lord Summerville's assistance I would be the last person he would send. He rarely even recalls that I exist."

"Such a man has much on his mind," Sophy murmured.

Of course he did. Alexander Pavlovich carried the weight of a vast empire upon his shoulders. But that did not lessen Leonida's sense of abandonment when months, even years passed without a word from the Emperor.

Perhaps it would not have been so noticeable if her mother had been a more…affectionate parent.

Oh, Nadia loved Leonida, but she had no interest in raising a child. Not when she could be devoting her attention to ensuring her place as a leader among society or dabbling in the dangerous games of politics as she sought to protect Alexander Pavlovich's throne by whatever means necessary.

As a result, Leonida had been raised by her English nurse and a series of governesses who rarely remained more than a few months.

Was it any wonder that she had never truly felt important to anyone?

"Yes, well, we all have a great deal on our minds," she muttered, pulling Sophy into her parlor and closing the door.

Then, as if she could truly avoid the impending encounter, she continued on to her bedchamber, crossing the floor to stare out the window.

"Do you want me to inform the Duke you're not receiving?" Sophy asked softly.

Leonida wrapped her arms around her waist. "You are welcome to make the attempt."

She kept her gaze trained on the distant lake that reflected the fading sunset in muted hues of pink and violet. The beauty spread before her, however, went unnoted as the sound of Sophy's raised voice echoed through the air, followed by Stefan's low, composed response.

A grim smile touched her lips as Sophy continued to squabble. The maid was a ferocious protector of Leonida, but she was no match for the Duke of Huntley. He might hide his ruthlessness behind a quiet charm, but it made him no less perilous.

Indeed, he was by far the most dangerous gentleman she had ever encountered.

At last, Sophy fell silent, her anger turned aside by Stefan's calm, unyielding determination. There was the sound of shuffling feet, then a door closing. Leonida remained poised at the window, a tingle of excitement inching down her spine as Stefan's spicy male scent filled the room.

"I thought we had put an end to your little games, my dove," he drawled, his footsteps coming ever closer.

"Games?"

His slender fingers closed around her upper arms, forcing her around to meet his smoldering gaze.

"You cannot avoid me."

"Obviously not," she snapped, refusing to acknowledge the thrill of pleasure that darted through her body. "What have you done with Sophy?"

His gaze seared over her stubborn expression. "I requested that she join the other servants so she could enjoy her dinner. It hardly seems fair that she should suffer because her mistress is a coward."

"I am not a coward, I am simply tired. And since you are so concerned for my maid's welfare I assure you that I requested that two trays be sent up, so there was no fear she would be sent to bed hungry."

His lips curled into a humorless smile. "Ah yes, the trays."

"Is there a problem?"

"Not now. I informed Cook that she need not bother since you would be joining Lady Summerville and myself in the dining room."

"Are you so high-handed with all your guests?"

His fingers skimmed over her lips, which had thinned in annoyance. "Only those who insist on being unreasonable."

She struggled to breathe. His dark, compelling beauty was overwhelming. Irresistible.

"It is hardly unreasonable to desire a quiet evening."

"It is when I want your companionship," he countered, his fingers stroking the line of her jaw.

"And because you are a duke you always get what you want?"

His smile widened with genuine humor. "I always get what I want because I refuse to accept anything less."

She licked her dry lips, then swiftly wished she hadn't when his eyes flared with a raw desire that made her heart leap.

"You cannot force me to come down to dinner."

"Actually I could," he mocked. "But if you insist on eating in your bedchamber then I will simply join you."

"Have you taken leave of your senses? You cannot join me."

"Why not?"

"It would cause a scandal."

"A scandal for you, perhaps, but as you so recently pointed out, I am a duke and there is precious little that can tarnish my very old and very respected title." He paused as she shivered, glancing down at her amber silk gown over a silver gauze underskirt. With a frown he moved to collect a matching shawl that she had left at the edge of the bed and carefully wrapped it around her shoulders. "I had forgotten your love for warmth. I shall have a maid light a fire for you while we are at dinner."

She clenched her teeth, refusing to be touched by his seeming concern.

"Do not pretend that you care for my comfort."

"But I do, my dove." His hands lightly circled her neck, his thumb stroking the pulse that pounded at the base of her throat. "I am quite determined to do everything in my power to please you."

"Except leave me in peace," she said huskily.

"Is that what you truly want?" He snared her gaze, his expression brooding. "Peace?"

"Yes," she whispered, even as she knew that was not entirely the truth.

He sensed it as well, his eyes narrowing. "Liar."

"What do you know of me?"

"Not nearly so much as I intend to know. But I can recognize loneliness when it haunts a pair of exquisite blue eyes."

With a burst of alarm Leonida pushed Stefan away, turning from his perceptive gaze.

"Do not."

His hands settled on her shoulders, but he made no effort to turn her around. "Am I wrong?"

"I…miss home."

"Do you truly have a home, Leonida Karkoff?" he whispered.

Her long-buried pain wrenched through her heart, making her feel annoyingly vulnerable.

Stefan had already seduced her body; he could not be allowed to steal her heart.

"What a ridiculous question. I happen to live in one of the finest houses in all of St. Petersburg."

He bent his head to whisper directly in her ear. "A house is not necessarily a home, as I have discovered."

Her eyes fluttered closed as a delicious heat flowed through her body. When Stefan was near she had no fear of being cold.

"You are not happy at Meadowland?"

"I am content…for the most part."

"Contentment and happiness are not the same."

"No, they are not," he said, the hint of wistful yearning tugging at her heart.

Abruptly she turned to face him, her expression wary. Dear lord. What was the matter with her? The Duke of Huntley was the last man who needed or deserved her sympathy.

He was handsome and wealthy and utterly ruthless in getting whatever he desired.

If he was alone, it was by choice, not fate.

"I suppose you will not leave until I agree to join you for dinner?"

Something that might have been disappointment flashed through the blue eyes before his features hardened.

"You are as intelligent as you are beautiful," he taunted.

"And you, sir, are an arrogant bully."

He grasped her chin between his fingers, his gaze focused on her lips.

"You have a quarter of an hour, Leonida. If you do not make an appearance then I will assume you are inviting me to share your dinner in bed."

STEPPING OUT OF LEONIDA'S chambers, Stefan placed his hands flat against the wall and sucked in a deep breath.

He was a fool.

Whether it was because he had allowed his anger at Leonida's attempt to hide from him to impetuously lead him to her bedchamber, or because he hadn't taken advantage of being there, he had yet to decide.

In either case, he was once again hard and aching with no hope of ready relief.

With a muttered curse, he pushed away from the wall and forced himself to continue toward the servants' staircase, where he knew Goodson would be waiting for him.

On cue, the uniformed butler stepped from the shadows, regarding Stefan with a stoic expression.

"Your Grace."

"Well?" Stefan demanded abruptly.

Sensing his employer's tension, Goodson came straight to the point.

"I could not approach as close as I would like since Miss Karkoff's maid was standing guard as if she were one of those savage Cossack soldiers."

"Yes, a most formidable woman," Stefan agreed dryly. He had thought when he entered Leonida's rooms he might have to physically toss the protective Sophy out of his path. "What did you manage to see?"

Goodson cleared his throat. "Miss Karkoff left her chamber shortly after you could be heard going downstairs and went directly to the Duchess's rooms. She remained in there until the maid rushed to warn her of your approach."

Stefan clenched his teeth, leashing his wave of disappointed fury.

He had already suspected that Leonida had some purpose in suggesting that she and Brianna come to Meadowland. And he was not vain enough to suppose it was an overwhelming desire to be closer to him.

Now his only purpose was to discover her nefarious plot.

"Did she take anything from the room?"

Goodson shrugged. "There was nothing in her hands."

"Have her room searched while she is at dinner."

"Of course, sir."

The butler was turning away when Stefan halted him. "Goodson."

"Yes, your Grace?"

"Did Benjamin track down the strangers he caught on the grounds?"

"I fear not." The butler's stoic expression hardened with frustration. "The innkeeper claimed that he has not had any foreign guests for months and no one in the village recognized the description of the villains."

"Have him continue to search through the neighborhood, but request that he be discreet. I would prefer no one realize that I am suspicious of their presence."

"Very good."

This time Stefan allowed the butler to disappear toward the back of the house, slowly turning to study the closed door to Leonida's chambers.

For a moment he brooded on charging back down the hall and bluntly confronting the deceitful woman.

Unlike Edmond, he did not enjoy political intrigue or pitting his wits against a cunning foe. He was a forthright gentleman who expected the same from others. Which was, no doubt, why King George and Alexander Pavlovich rarely called upon him when they had need of guile rather than practical assistance.

It was only the knowledge that Leonida could not be bullied or coerced into revealing the truth that kept him standing in the shadows, his hands clenched at his sides.

"What the devil is your scheme, Leonida Karkoff?" he muttered.

St. Petersburg

THE BORDELLO TUCKED BETWEEN a coffeehouse and furniture warehouse was like many others spread throughout St. Petersburg.

The building was a nondescript brick structure that was surrounded by a wrought-iron fence and guarded by a brute of a man who frightened even hardened soldiers. Inside the front parlor the furnishings were a gaudy, overly opulent combination of plush velvet sofas and fur rugs where a gentleman could wait in comfort for his particular whore to become available. Or, if he preferred, he could join the high-stakes gambling that was offered in the back rooms. Upstairs, the private rooms were individually created to indulge in whatever vice might tempt the jaded members of Russian society.

But it was not the dubious taste in furnishings, or the lovely, well-trained whores that plied their trade that attracted the rich and powerful.

It was instead the absolute discretion that Madam Ivanna demanded of her guests and servants.

A gentleman who stepped through the door could be assured that his presence or his…unusual sexual appetites would never be revealed.

Such a promise of privacy was worth the outrageous sums that Ivanna charged.

Heading up the narrow flight of stairs, Nikolas Babevich was already hard with anticipation at the thought of Celeste and her wicked chains and whips. Such sweet pain was expensive, but well worth every ruble.

Not that he possessed an overabundance of rubles, he acknowledged, a bitter anger burning in the pit of his stomach.

Damn the Countess Karkoff.

It was entirely her fault that he was now reduced to borrowing funds from his nagging sister and dodging the bill collectors who refused to offer him credit for so much as a new pair of boots.

Thankfully he had managed to relieve a drunken Prussian of his purse outside the Opera House last eve or he would have been forced to cancel his standing appointment at this brothel. A near unbearable notion.

Pushing open the door at the end of the long, candlelit hallway, Nikolas licked his lips, expecting to discover Celeste standing in the center of the room, whip in hand.

What he discovered instead was a tall, distinguished gentleman with silver hair and a handsome countenance that was barely lined despite his fifty-odd years.

Sir Charles Richards had arrived in St. Petersburg from England only a few months ago, but had swiftly become a favorite of Prince Michael, younger brother of Alexander Pavlovich.

To most in society he was a charming, intelligent foreigner who was renowned for his impeccable manners and simple elegance, tonight displayed by his plain but exquisitely tailored black coat and dove-gray breeches that were at such odds with the Russian love for flamboyance.

Nikolas was one of the few who suspected that behind his affable smile was a merciless soul that was capable of great evil.

"Good evening, Nikolas Babevich," Richards drawled, his elegant fingers holding one of the small whips that was always so appealing in Celeste's hands, but was nothing less than terrifying when held by the Englishman.

Licking his dry lips, Nikolas cast a covert glance about the barren room, barely noting the various tools of torture that were hung on the walls or the wide bed that was covered in black satin and shackles. Ridiculously he had hoped that Celeste or one of the numerous servants might be lurking in a dark corner.

As if their presence would protect him from the malevolence that filled the thick air.

"How..." Nikolas was forced to halt and clear his throat. "How did you get in here?"

The nobleman's lips curled as he flicked a dismissive gaze over Nikolas's short, unfortunately pudgy figure that was attired in a growingly threadbare jacket in moss green and the too-tight tan breeches.

"There are few doors closed to me," he drawled.

Nikolas clenched his hands into fists. Despite his fear, he wouldn't be mocked by a damned foreigner.

"My congratulations. Now, if you do not mind, I came here for a specific entertainment that does not include spectators."

"Your entertainment will have to wait until after our little chat," Sir Charles sneered, twirling the whip in his hand.

"I told you that the Karkoff bitch refuses to give me the money without proof of the letters. What would you have me do?"

"Did you know the Countess sent her daughter to England? Surrey to be precise."

Nikolas frowned. The Countess Karkoff could rot in hell as far as he was concerned.

"Why should I care?"

"For one thing, it proves there is something in those letters worth discovering. The Countess would never send her daughter on such a journey otherwise."

"Wait," Nikolas growled. "I thought you knew what was in those letters."

"Howard Summerville claimed they must hold nefarious secrets since they were not only written in a mysterious code, but the Duke of Huntley had nearly beaten him to death when he caught him with them in his hands. It was worth taking the chance to discover if the boorish imbecile had truly stumbled across the means of acquiring a fortune or was making his usual empty boasts."

Nikolas stiffened in outrage. He had risked his life on a mere hunch?

"You lied to me."

"I told you what you needed to know." Richards dismissed his accusation with a shrug. "Now, however, Miss Karkoff's presence in Surrey endangers our tidy little plot."

"How?"

The unnerving black eyes narrowed in frigid anger. "Because that is where the letters were last seen, you idiot."

"Does she have them?"

"And how would I know?" Richards tossed the whip onto the bed in an impatient motion. "I sent my servants to search the Duke's home weeks ago, but Miss Karkoff's presence complicates matters."

Nikolas tugged at his wilted cravat, not for the first time

wishing he had never allowed Sir Charles Richards to convince him to take part in the dangerous scheme.

Not that you truly had a choice, a voice whispered in the back of his mind.

Gambling had always been his weakness and when he'd lost far more money than he possessed to the Englishman, he had no choice but to listen to his outlandish scheme. And in truth, the thought of gaining a small fortune with such ease had been a temptation he couldn't resist.

Now he could do no more than curse his stupidity.

"We should never have approached the Countess until we had our hands on those letters."

"You were as eager as I was to claim the fortune. Who would have suspected the Emperor's whore would have the nerve to question your threat?" The dark eyes glittered with a cruel light. "Obviously you were not very convincing."

Nikolas shuddered, his skin crawling with an indefinable fear. "I did what was asked. It isn't my fault the Countess—"

"Shut up," Richards interrupted. "I weary of your excuses."

Nikolas swallowed the lump lodged in his throat. "Fine. We gambled and lost. *C'est la vie.*"

Richards took a step forward, his expression grim. "This is not over. I will have my money."

"How? If the daughter manages to discover those letters then they will know that we have never seen them."

"My men have orders to keep a close eye on the female. If she does manage to uncover the letters they will be able to retrieve them from her."

"And if she does not?"

"Then she will return to Russia with the information that the letters are indeed missing."

Nikolas bit back the urge to point out the numerous flaws in the plan. His existence might be miserable at the moment, but he was in no hurry to meet the death that lurked in his companion's eyes.

"So we wait?"

"No, we cannot allow the Countess to suspect this is a bluff," Richards snapped, a dark edge in his voice making Nikolas relieved that he did not know what was going through his companion's mind. He sensed it would give him nightmares for weeks to come. "I desire you to approach the Countess again and warn her that for every week that passes, the cost of your silence increases by five thousand rubles."

Nikolas took a discreet step backward. "And if she refuses?"

"You will continue to pester her. It will keep her fretting rather than devoting her time to considering how to outwit us." The man's lips curled into a sneer. "Women are incapable of behaving in a sensible manner when they are flustered."

Nikolas's humorless laugh echoed eerily through the room. "Have you ever met the Countess?"

"She is a female." Richards easily dismissed the strong-willed Countess, obviously unaware of the power she could wield. Stupid man. "Keep her terrified that she is about to lose her devoted and very wealthy lover and she will do whatever necessary to keep her life of luxury."

"Why must I be the one to approach her?" Nikolas changed tactics. "It seems to me that I am risking my neck while you hide in the shadows."

Before Nikolas could blink, Richards was across the room, his hands circling Nikolas's throat with enough pressure to prove he could easily snap his neck.

"That is what you are being paid to do, is it not?" he demanded in low, deadly tones. "And believe me, being caught by the Russian officials is the least of your concern. Fail me and I will cut out your heart and feed it to the wolves. Do you understand?"

Nikolas's blood froze in his veins. "Yes."

"Good."

With a derisive motion, Richards tossed Nikolas

against the wall and then pulled a handkerchief from his pocket to wipe his hands. As if he feared he might have been contaminated.

Bastard.

Pushing from the wall, Nikolas jerked his jacket back into place. "And what will you be doing while I am confronting the Countess?"

"I am traveling to Paris. It will be far easier to keep in contact with my men in England."

"So you leave me alone to be shot as a traitor?"

"That, *mon ami,* is entirely in your hands. Do what I command and we both shall be very wealthy gentlemen."

CHARLES STEPPED FROM the torture room, assured that Nikolas would do as he had been commanded. The wretched creature might long to condemn Charles to the netherworld, but they both knew he would never possess the courage to openly challenge him.

Which, of course, was the reason he had chosen the fool in the first place.

A pity he had not been so clever in predicting the Countess's stubborn refusal to hand over the money he so desperately needed.

With an effort, Charles battled back the black fury that had plagued him since he was in the nursery. As satisfying as it might be to slice the bitch's throat, it would not solve his problems.

He had to have money if he wanted to keep his nasty little secrets safe.

A shiver shook his body before he regained command of his icy composure. No. He would not be exposed by a filthy peasant. Even if that peasant was the Beggar Czar, Dimitri Tipova, who reportedly ruled the criminal underworld of St. Petersburg.

Slipping into the room across the hall, he regarded the woman he had ordered to wait for him.

Madam Ivanna was a lushly curved woman who had retained much of her early beauty despite the gray that was threaded through her thick black hair and the wrinkles that fanned beside her wide green eyes. Currently she was attired in a low-cut velvet gown that displayed her considerable charms and matched the decor, but only a fool would miss the shrewd glitter in her eyes.

"Ah, Ivanna, so kind of you to allow me a few moments with my associate." Moving forward he raised her fingers to his lips, relishing her shiver of disgust. Ah yes, shrewd indeed. Unlike most women, Ivanna was intelligent enough to sense the darkness beneath his handsome countenance and practiced charm. "How can I ever repay you?"

She hastily tugged her fingers from his grasp. "It is nothing, I assure you."

"You are certain you would not desire a small token of my appreciation?"

"No, it was my pleasure, *monsieur*."

"A pity." He regarded her with a hungry gaze, his blood stirring at the rich scent of her perfume. It had been far too long since he'd allowed himself to indulge in his little pastime. With a shake of his head, he stepped back. "Still, I suppose this is not the time or the place. I need a means to leave the house without being noticed."

Ivanna heaved a shaky breath of relief, as if sensing how close she had been to glimpsing the true Sir Charles Richards.

"Of course." She waved a hand toward the door. "I can take you out the back entrance."

He caught her wrist, his grip punishing. "I said unnoticed."

"Please, *monsieur*, I do not know what you want," she whimpered.

"Think very carefully, Ivanna."

His fingers tightened, threatening to snap her bones and she gave a sob of surrender.

"There is a hidden passageway that connects my kitchens with the coffeehouse next door." She brokenly confessed the secret known only to those of royal blood.

A cold smile curled his lips. "You are quite intelligent for a whore."

CHAPTER SEVEN

HERRICK GERHARDT ROUNDED the corner, careful to remain out of the flicker of the gaslight that lined the streets of St. Petersburg. Although attired in a plain black jacket and breeches with a beaver hat tucked over his silver hair, there were still too many who would recognize his gaunt features and piercing brown eyes. Even this far from the palace.

The price of being Alexander Pavlovich's closest advisor.

As a rule he found the fear he inspired in others a tool he was swift to take advantage of. It was remarkable what his reputation as a ruthless bastard could achieve.

On this night, however, he was more interested in stealth than intimidation.

Halting next to Gregor, a burly Prussian soldier who was his most trusted guard, he nodded his head to the brothel across the street.

"Is our prey in there?" he murmured, speaking in German as various pedestrians strolled down the street. Prying ears could be anywhere.

"He is. His weekly meeting with the lovely Celeste." Gregor leaned his large body against the iron railing behind him, his strong features settled in lines of stoic patience. Like all soldiers, he understood that the great majority of any war was waiting for the next battle. "The man is nothing if not predictable."

Herrick clenched his teeth. He had been trailing Nikolas Babevich for weeks attempting to discover who he was working for. Thus far he had accomplished precisely nothing. His only solace was that Nikolas had not yet revealed the contents of the letters to anyone.

"If he is so predictable then why have we not yet discovered who is manipulating him?" he muttered.

"Are you still convinced he has a partner?"

"Nikolas Babevich is a pathetic coward who might cheat at cards and steal a man's purse, but he does not have the courage or the intelligence to devise a scheme to extort money from Countess Karkoff." Herrick shrugged, his gaze instinctively scanning his surroundings. No detail was too small to capture his attention. "Besides, I have searched through his past and from all I could discover he has never traveled beyond St. Petersburg. Whoever is behind the scheme must have some contact with England."

Gregor nodded. The soldier knew that Nikolas was attempting to blackmail the Countess, but little more.

"I have reported all the people that Babevich has been in contact with."

"I trust you, Gregor, it is just too difficult to keep a constant watch." Herrick stilled, his gaze narrowing as he watched the tall, distinguished gentleman who stepped out of the coffee shop next door to the brothel. "Well, that is unexpected."

"What?"

"Sir Charles Richards."

"An Englishman?"

"Yes, and a particular friend of Prince Michael."

Gregor straightened, easily detecting the edge in Herrick's voice.

"Is something wrong?"

Herrick paused. He had long ago learned to depend on his intuition, and at the moment his senses were on full alert.

"I am simply wondering why a gentleman who is frequently a guest at the palace would choose to frequent a coffee shop that is more suited to the bourgeois."

A frown touched Gregor's heavy brow. "Perhaps he needed refreshment after visiting Madam Ivanna."

"Perhaps."

"You do not seem convinced."

Herrick lowered his voice as a party of gentlemen weaved their way toward the brothel. Drunken idiots. They would be fortunate to make it out of the neighborhood without being knocked over the head and robbed of their purses. Only a fool would travel the lesser streets of St. Petersburg without well-armed servants.

"When the Prince first befriended Richards I made a few discreet inquiries among my connections in England," he admitted, returning his attention to Sir Charles, who had moved down the street to impatiently await his carriage.

"There was something that concerns you?"

Herrick crossed his arms over his chest. "From most accounts he is precisely what he claims to be, a minor baronet who was well liked among society and respected as a reformer in Parliament."

"Why would such a gentleman choose to leave his home and career to live in a foreign country?"

"Precisely my question."

"And?"

Herrick considered what he had discovered, his brooding gaze noting the manner in which the various pedestrians veered a wide path around the English nobleman. Almost as if they could sense a danger in accidentally brushing against him.

Odd.

"There were rumors, most of them carefully suppressed by Richards's powerful friends, but they were enough to encourage him to leave England and seek a new home far enough away he would not be troubled by scandal," he murmured.

"It must have been a considerable scandal to have forced an English nobleman to travel to St. Petersburg."

"Yes." Herrick's gaunt face hardened. He took personal insult to a foreigner who brought a threat to his city. "Over the past ten years a number of whores were discovered floating in the Thames with their throats slit."

Gregor made a sound of shock. "Richards?"

"There was never any proof, but one of the brothel owners was willing to tell anyone who would listen to her that two of the whores had been regulars of Sir Charles and that he had been the last to see them before they died. Unfortunately, the word of a mere madam could not bring a nobleman to justice."

"But it could cause unpleasant gossip," Gregor murmured.

"Exactly."

Gregor's large hands clenched into fists. Before attracting Herrick's notice, Gregor was a simple soldier who had been the son of a butcher. His humble past gave him a compassion for the peasant class that was all too rare.

"Have any whores in St. Petersburg been found with their throats slit?"

It was, of course, the first thing that Herrick had attempted to discover.

"No, but that does not mean they have not been murdered." He grimaced. "Dimitri Tipova keeps an iron grip on his territory and would rather dispose of any untidy messes than risk being brought to the attention of the authorities."

Gregor gave a disgusted grunt, not at all surprised that even a man with Herrick's power could not penetrate the murky politics of St. Petersburg's underworld.

Dimitri Tipova, the Beggar Czar, was a law unto himself.

"A pity."

"Not entirely. Dimitri has a tendency to inflict his own manner of justice against those who threaten his position."

"If that is true then Sir Charles appears remarkably healthy."

Herrick nodded, his expression thoughtful. "So either there have been no deaths or Dimitri has chosen to punish Sir Charles by a means that did not include the usual torture."

"What do you mean?"

"The Englishman appears to possess enough wealth to live in comfort."

"True." It took a moment for Gregor to follow the direction of Herrick's thoughts. "Ah. You believe that Dimitri is demanding money?"

"I would."

Gregor's gaze snapped back to the brothel as the door was pushed open and a satisfied customer tripped down the stairs.

"A nasty situation, but surely a problem for another day?" he demanded once he had assured himself the gentleman was not Nikolas Babevich.

"Unless he is somehow connected with our current problem."

"You think..." Gregor gave a sharp shake of his head. "No, I have been standing here since Babevich went into Madam Ivanna's. Richards did not come in or out while Babevich has been inside. They could not have been meeting."

"Ah, but you were watching the front entrance, not the hidden corridor that leads from the brothel to the coffee shop," Herrick drawled.

"Hidden corridor?"

Herrick smiled. "Even the most powerful gentlemen enjoy the services that Madam Ivanna provides. They simply prefer their visits to be discreet."

Gregor arched a brow. "So how do you know of the corridor?"

"There is very little that escapes my notice."

"A knowledge that has kept me from making any number of foolish mistakes," Gregor said dryly. "Do you truly believe that Sir Charles is here to meet with Babevich?"

"After weeks of following the fool with nothing to show for my efforts but sore feet, I no longer know what I believe." Herrick heaved a frustrated sigh. "Still, there can be no harm in paying a visit to Sir Charles in the next few days. If nothing else it will allow me to judge whether or not he is intelligent and ruthless enough to conceive a scheme to blackmail the Countess." Reaching out, Herrick laid a hand on his companion's shoulder. "Go home, Gregor. I will keep watch on Nikolas Babevich."

Surrey, England

AFTER YET ANOTHER FUTILE search through the library, the back parlor and the billiards room of Meadowland, Leonida retreated to the garden to enjoy the sun that had broken through the morning fog.

Perching on a marble bench in the center of the rose garden, Leonida lifted her face toward the sky and attempted to ease the tension that gripped her body.

A part of her comprehended that she was wasting precious time. For once Stefan had left just after breakfast to meet with his solicitor in the village and Brianna had taken a carriage to oversee the workers at Hillside.

She was alone except for the servants. A perfect opportunity.

Leonida, however, was weary of her self-imposed task.

She hated deceiving Brianna, who had been nothing but kind and warmly welcoming to her. She hated sneaking about the beautiful estate as if she were a common thief.

And most of all, she hated the situation that made the Duke of Huntley her irrevocable enemy.

If only…

She angrily broke off the futile longing.

What was the point? No matter what her fascination with Stefan, her duty and loyalty lay with her mother.

And Russia.

Nothing could alter the untenable situation.

Almost as if her thoughts had conjured the very man who occupied far too much of them, Stefan suddenly appeared before her, attired in a dark cinnamon jacket and gold waistcoat.

Her heart contracted, her gaze helplessly moving over

his dark features. Dear lord, he was so beautiful. The elegant lines of his features. The sensuous curve of his lips. The broad width of his shoulders.

She shivered, her entire body tingling with pleasure.

"I thought I might discover you savoring the sunshine," he murmured, his eyes darkening as they drifted over the hair she had left free to fall over her shoulders and the sprigged muslin gown that was trimmed with peach ribbons. It was one of her few dresses that had been cut to show the soft curve of her bodice and her breath tangled in her throat as his heated gaze lingered on the ribbon tied between her breasts. "All alone?" he rasped.

It took a moment to find her voice. "Brianna has returned to Hillside to oversee the workers who are refurbishing the parlors. She is convinced they will never properly choose the fabrics for the curtains."

That ruthless will he was so careful to keep hidden was briefly exposed as he planted his hands on his hips.

"So she slipped away before I could halt her?"

"She promised she would do no more than sit on a sofa and search through the fabric swaths that were to be delivered this morning."

"I hope she understands that Edmond will have my head on a platter if anything happened to her."

"No one desires this baby more than Brianna," she pointed out in reasonable tones. "She will not do anything to put herself at risk."

"Hmm." His gaze narrowed. "At least tell me she took a carriage with a groom and outriders?"

"I believe so." She regarded him with a curious frown. "Do you suspect there is danger between here and Meadowland?"

"Poachers always pose a danger. I would prefer you not leave the grounds without an escort."

She rose to her feet at his smooth response. He was lying. Whether it was because he wanted to frighten her so she would remain close enough to keep his eye on or because he feared she might cause Brianna some harm was impossible to determine.

Her chin tilted to a stubborn angle. Perhaps she deserved to be treated with such obvious distrust, but she did not have to enjoy it.

"Unlike Brianna, I have nowhere to go."

His expression eased as a slow, wicked smile curved his lips. "Are you becoming bored with the rather tedious routine of an English country estate, my dove?"

"I have told you I prefer a peaceful existence."

"So you have." He took a deliberate step closer, his scent wrapping around her. "While I insist you possess a more adventurous spirit."

The very air seemed to thicken with an awareness that Leonida desperately attempted to ignore.

"Which only proves you know nothing of me."

"I am discovering more with each passing day," he murmured, his fingers drifting along the edge of her bodice, sending tiny shocks through her body. "I now know that you must be kept warm like a delicate orchid and that you have little taste for spirits. I know you prefer comfort to silly fashion, which says a good deal about your common sense, and that you can spend hours lost in a book that catches your fancy. I know that you harbor secrets that you keep hidden from the world and that you fear your passionate nature."

With a jerk, she stepped back, as disturbed by his intimate knowledge of her as by his lingering touch.

"Ridiculous."

His smile widened. "Shall we stroll to the grotto? Perhaps I can prove the truth of my words."

"You are not nearly as irresistible as you believe yourself to be, your Grace."

"Liar." He once again closed the space between them, his hand cupping her cheek and his thumb softly stroking over her bottom lip. "Does it soothe your pride to know I find you equally irresistible? Most inconvenient, I must admit. You are far more of a distraction than I had anticipated."

"It was never my desire to be a…distraction, I assure you," she muttered, a tingle inching down her spine as her lips brushed against his thumb. "Indeed, I would far prefer that you return your attention to your fields and cows."

His brooding gaze swept over her upturned face. "You should never have come to England, Leonida," he growled.

"I had no choice."

A long, fraught silence hummed between them, the mixture of anger and desire a near tangible force.

At last Stefan wrapped an arm around her waist and led her toward a small stone structure on the edge of the garden. "Come."

She tried to pull away from his tight grip. "No, I…"

"Do not fear, Leonida," he interrupted, his voice edged with frustration. "As much as we both might enjoy a nice tumble in the lilies, I do not have the time to devote to a thorough seduction. I have something I wish to show you."

"What is it?"

"Patience."

She snapped her lips shut, knowing it was futile to argue. Stefan was not the only one with perception. She had learned a great deal about this man over the past few days.

He could be charming and witty and devoted to those he considered his responsibility. He was also stubborn and arrogant and so determined to be a duke that would make his father proud that he would crush anything or anyone who threatened his sense of duty.

Including her.

Ignoring the dull ache deep in her heart, Leonida allowed herself to be steered into the tiny stone building that was topped by a glass dome and guarded by a gargoyle who kept watch over the narrow door.

Stefan waved her inside and with a wary frown she

entered the building, potently aware of his hard male body following close behind. Then, coming to a halt, her eyes widened in startled pleasure as she glanced around the single room.

She was not certain what she had expected, but it certainly was not the whimsical flight of fantasy that was spread around her.

With a shake of her head, she moved to run a hand over the marble dragon that rose from the tiled floor, his mouth opened as if to spray his fire and his golden wings spread wide. Along the far wall a miniature pirate ship was built of polished wood with a sail that could be lowered and a cannon pointed toward an arched window that overlooked the nearby lake. In another corner two sculptured horses stood, complete with tattered saddles.

It appeared to be a vision straight out of a childhood dream and Leonida had no trouble imagining a pair of raven haired, blue-eyed toddlers dashing about the room with wooden swords in hand.

The sharp pang of yearning came without warning and Leonida was startled to discover her hand had unwittingly shifted to touch her stomach. As if her maternal instincts had been suddenly stirred to life.

It was a frightening thought, and one she was careful to keep hidden as she turned to meet Stefan's watchful gaze.

"It is charming."

"My mother had this folly built when Edmond and I were quite young. I believe she hoped such a place would distract us from digging for treasure among her prized roses and tumbling into the lake."

Leonida lifted her brows. The Duchess had not only been a devoted mother, but wise, as well.

"Did it succeed?"

Stefan shrugged. "I spent a great deal of time slaying dragons and sailing the high seas, but Edmond was not satisfied unless his life was in some sort of genuine peril."

In spite of herself, Leonida's lips twitched at the edge of rueful amusement in his voice.

"The two of you are very close."

"Yes." His gaze snared hers, a hint of warning in the blue depths. "There is nothing I would not do for him."

Her flare of humor faded. Enemy, indeed. "And yet he spent a number of years in Russia."

"At the insistence of the Emperor."

"You blame Alexander Pavlovich for your brother's absence?"

"Only in part." A shadow fell across his face. "Edmond… blamed himself for my parents' death. His work for the Emperor not only kept him occupied, but it offered him a reasonable excuse not to visit a home filled with painful reminders." He shook his head, as if clearing away the lingering regret. "Thankfully he has put the past behind him and found his peace."

"And what of you, Stefan?" she could not resist prodding.

"What?"

"When will *you* put your past behind you?"

His jaw tightened, proving her blow had landed, but his brooding gaze never wavered.

"We are discussing Edmond. Now that he has Brianna and the baby, I would not so readily allow him to be lured back to Russia again."

She heaved an aggravated sigh. "So far as I know Alexander Pavlovich has no intention of requesting Lord Summerville's presence."

"He has returned to St. Petersburg."

Leonida felt a measure of relief that the Czar was safely back in his palace, but little more. He possessed her loyalty and gratitude for ensuring her a comfortable existence, but he had simply been too distant for her to ever think of him as her father.

"His advisors will be pleased. As will my mother. The

Emperor's enemies become far too bold when his attention is distracted."

"Which enemies?"

Leonida turned to study the dragon, realizing that she had said too much.

"Why did you bring me here?"

"You seem devoted to exploring Meadowlands from attics to cellar. I did not wish you to overlook my childhood haven."

She refused to react to his deliberate jab. The estate was too large and the staff too numerous for her to keep her search completely hidden. She had to trust her pretense of casual curiosity would conceal her true purpose.

"You did say I could explore the estate," she said stiffly.

"So I did. Of course, I did not realize that you would be quite so thorough."

"You have several lovely works of art."

"And you are interested in art?"

"I appreciate beauty."

His hands landed on her shoulders, spinning her back to meet his hooded gaze. She expected his expression to be one of accusation. He was, after all, dangerously suspicious of her interest in Meadowland. Instead she shivered at the barely leashed hunger that tightened his beautiful features.

"As do I," he rasped.

"Stefan..."

She did not know what she intended to say and in the end it did not matter as his head swooped downward and he caught her mouth in a savage kiss.

Leonida's strangled gasp of surprise was caught in her throat, but she made no effort to push him away as his arms wrapped around her and he yanked her against his hard body.

She tried to tell herself it was pointless to struggle. He was, after all, considerably larger and stronger. Unfortunately, she was too honest to deny the fierce joy that hummed through her body, making her lips part in silent encouragement and her arms circle his neck as she arched even closer.

She had ached for this moment since Stefan had joined her in the garden.

Stefan muttered something beneath his breath, his lips moving restlessly over her face. Her fingers sank into the satin curls at the nape of his neck as his impatient caresses sent jolts of excitement through her.

There was no explanation for the explosive reaction to his touch, and at the moment Leonida did not care. All that mattered were the delicious sensations that curled through the pit of her stomach.

Lost in the pleasure of his mouth nuzzling along the curve of her neck, Leonida was unaware of anything beyond Stefan's arms and it came as an unpleasant shock when he was abruptly thrusting her away.

"Damn," he muttered, heading toward the door. "What is it, Maggie?"

Leonida pressed a hand to her thundering heart as she heard the maid respond.

"Mr. Riddle sent word that the workers have arrived to repair the bridge in the south paddock. They were told not to start without you."

"Thank you. I will be along in a moment." There was the sound of retreating footsteps, and grasping the doorframe Stefan lowered his head, dragging in deep breaths. Several moments passed before he at last turned to regard her with a sardonic expression. "It appears that duty calls. I will inform Goodson not to hold dinner for me." His gaze lowered to her lips, still swollen from his kiss. "Try to stay out of mischief, my dove."

CHAPTER EIGHT

LEFT ALONE IN THE CHILDREN'S folly, Leonida moved to the window overlooking the lake.

A part of her understood she should be returning to Meadowland to continue her search while Stefan was occupied with his bridge, but another part was still reeling from the unexpected surge of desire.

She needed a few moments to collect her scattered wits before returning to her task. And besides, she was not at all certain her wobbly legs could carry her.

Watching the swans glide across the water, Leonida's heart stuttered as the soft sound of footsteps broke the silence. Slowly turning, she watched the shadow fall across the open doorway.

"Stefan…"

She bit off her words, an uneasy alarm coiling inside her as a large man with a brutish face and small, dark eyes as hard as agates stepped over the threshold. Instinctively, she pressed against the wall, noting the rough linen shirt and wool trousers.

Was he a servant at Meadowland? Hardly likely. She had encountered most of the staff over the past few days and would surely recognize him.

Nor could he be a local tenant. None would dare to regard a guest of the Duke of Huntley with such vulgar interest.

Hiding a shiver, she desperately calculated the odds of shoving her way past his hulking form and reaching the door.

As if sensing her thoughts, the stranger prowled toward her, a mocking smile on his lips.

"Miss Karkoff," he said, his voice thick with an accent that sent a chill down her spine. Russian. And no henchman of her mother, of that she was absolutely certain. "I have been waiting for an opportunity to speak with you alone."

"Who are you?"

"Let us just say that a mutual acquaintance sent me."

Gathering her composure, Leonida forced herself to flick a dismissive glance over his shabby clothing.

She was effectively trapped. What choice did she have but to try and brazen her way out of danger?

"I doubt we have any mutual friends."

An ugly smile twisted his lips. "You think you are better than me?" he taunted. "You might have money and fancy clothes, but you are a common bastard. Just like me."

"I have only to scream and a dozen servants will come running. Do you wish to face the English gallows?"

"Oh, you will not scream."

"How can you be so certain?"

"Because you will have to confess to your lover the true reason you have come to England."

She struggled to maintain her disdainful expression even as panic curled through her stomach. He had to be connected to Nikolas Babevich. How else would he know her purpose in coming to Surrey?

But why had he followed her to England? And, more importantly, what did he intend to do to her?

"I am here to visit Lord and Lady Summerville," she said, her tone stiff.

"Nothing so pretty. You have come to steal the letters."

"I do not know..."

"I am not a fool," he growled. "You are here to find the Countess's letters. Which will save me the bother."

Accepting her charade was hopeless, Leonida instead concentrated on his unwitting revelation.

"So, they are here." She tilted her chin. "Which means whoever is attempting to blackmail my mother has been lying when he claims to have them in his possession. The Countess will be quite pleased."

"Not for long," he warned, moving with surprising speed for a man of his bulk.

Before Leonida could react, he had a large, extremely sharp dagger pressed to her throat.

"Are you mad?" she breathed, as outraged as she was frightened. The man smelled of rotting teeth and desperation.

"You will find the letters and deliver them to me."

"Or what? You will kill me?"

"After I spend a few days making you regret having disappointed me." He leered down at her stubborn expression. "Or perhaps it would not be regret. A Russian woman needs more than a soft English steer between her legs. She needs a Siberian bull."

Leonida didn't have to pretend her revulsion. "You are vile."

He deliberately pressed the knife deeper. "I will give you until tomorrow night to bring me the letters. I will wait behind the stables for you at ten o'clock."

"But…" She struggled against the surge of panic. "I do not know where they are."

"Then you had better concentrate on searching for them rather than playing with the Duke's cock."

She ignored his vulgarity. Later she could be horrified by the thought that this hideous man had been spying on her and Stefan.

"What if I cannot find them?"

"Then I will slice your maid's throat and take you someplace where we can be alone. After that…" His smile was one of cruel anticipation. "Well, you will disappear into the cursed fog that smothers this country. Such a tragedy."

"If I disappear the Emperor will not rest until he punishes those responsible."

"A risk I am willing to take. Get me those letters."

She swallowed the painful lump in her throat. "I will not betray Russia."

"Oh, I think you will," he sneered. "Loyalty becomes an indulgence when you have a knife to your throat."

"And what would you know of loyalty?" she hissed.

His features twisted with a terrifying hatred. "You think I should owe allegiance to an Emperor whose soldiers raped my mother and left her in the gutter to die? Or perhaps to the whores who took me in and allowed me to be used by the depraved noblemen who liked young boys?"

She might have possessed a measure of sympathy for his horrible life if he did not have a knife pressed to her throat.

"And your employer?" she instead demanded. "Are you loyal to him?"

"So long as he pays."

"I have wealth. I could pay you a large amount."

"A temptation, I must admit. Unfortunately my—" his eyes flashed with something that might be dread "—employer is not a gentleman who would kindly accept being betrayed."

"You could disappear," she desperately urged. In this moment she would give her entire fortune to be rid of this man. "How would he ever find you?"

"He would find me. And when he did he would make me howl for death." The stranger shook his head, his thatch of greasy brown hair swinging around his face. "No, I will not fail him."

"But…"

"Enough," he rasped, turning the knife so the tip was pressed beneath her chin. "Return to the house and find those letters for me."

"Fine," she breathed, accepting that for the moment she had no choice but to give in to his demands. He was clearly as demented as he was violent. Not a particularly reassuring combination. "I will return to the house."

His eyes narrowed. "And Miss Karkoff."

"What?"

"Do not even think of confessing to the Duke," he warned in lethal tones. "Not unless you wish him to be found floating in his lake."

"You would not dare."

His lips twisted. "Few things would give me more pleasure than choking the life from a spineless English nobleman. What is he without his fortune and servants?" He turned to spit on the floor. "A weak, pathetic waste of flesh who deserves to die. Keep that in mind."

Leonida shivered. Stefan murdered by this filthy bastard? His dark, powerful beauty forever extinguished?

No.

It did not matter what she had to do.

She would never allow Stefan to be harmed.

DRIVEN TO DESPERATION, Leonida raced back to the house and tracked down Sophy, who was flirting with a handsome young footman in the kitchens.

Dragging the startled maid up the stairs, she hastily revealed her confrontation in the garden with the Russian henchman and the necessity of completing her task with all possible speed.

Which meant the time for discretion was at an end.

Leading Sophy directly to the Duchess's chambers rather than requesting her to keep guard, Leonida commanded the maid to search for a hidden safe or any papers that might have been stuffed out of sight. She could only trust to her dubious luck that the army of servants was busy in another part of the house.

Astonishingly, her luck did hold.

At least as far as the servants were concerned.

Unfortunately, she was decidedly out of luck when it came to finding the letters.

After four hours' futile searching, Sophy heaved a sigh

and glanced about the Duchess's bedchamber with the same frustration that smoldered deep within Leonida. "I still say you should just let me get my pistol and shoot the odious jackass who threatened you," she muttered.

On her knees beside the rosewood writing table where she had been searching for a secret drawer, Leonida brushed a stray curl off her cheek. "If I knew where to find him, I would shoot him myself."

"What if we can't…"

"We must, Sophy," Leonida interrupted sternly. "Keep looking."

"Where?" Sophy waved her hands in a helpless motion. "We have searched the chambers from end to end."

Leonida grimaced. The maid had a point. It was difficult to imagine they could have overlooked even the most cleverly hidden safe.

"They must be here," she said, as much to reassure herself as the maid. She had no choice but to find the damned letters. With a shake of her head, she regarded her maid with a frown. "Where do you keep your valuables?"

Sophy shrugged, her round face flushed with weariness. "I don't have many, but I do hide my few coins and best stockings beneath my bed."

Leonida sighed. She'd already checked beneath the bed, a dozen times. And beyond discovering a few stray spiderwebs on the expensive carpet…

Suddenly, Leonida stiffened, her eyes wide with a startling thought.

"Oh."

"What?"

"I just recalled an acquaintance of my mother who had recently installed a safe in her floor." Rising to her feet, Leonida hurried to the edge of the carpet and began tugging it upward. "Help me."

Together the two of them managed to roll the carpet toward the center of the room, revealing a worn wooden floor beneath. A majority of the carpet was, of course, pinned down by the various furniture arranged about the room, but they managed to pull it aside far enough to reveal the barely visible outline of a trapdoor that came complete with a flat, brass handle.

"There it is," Sophy breathed.

They both rushed forward and, bending down, Leonida tugged on the handle, only noticing the small keyhole drilled into the wood when the door refused to budge.

"Damn," she muttered. "We need the key."

Sophy muttered beneath her breath. "Well, it ain't in here."

Leonida straightened, her heart lodged in her throat. Over the past days she had searched through every room in Meadowland, including a brief rummage through Stefan's chambers. A search that had created a strange mixture of horror at her intrusion into his privacy and an undeniable fascination with studying his most intimate possessions.

"I suspect I know where it is," she whispered, a sick feeling in the pit of her stomach.

"Where?"

"Come with me." Taking Sophy's hand, she led her from the room and down the long corridor. "I need you to keep watch."

"Of course," Sophy agreed, only to suck in a dismayed gasp as Leonida halted before the door to Stefan's rooms. "Oh lord."

"Remain here and warn me if someone approaches," Leonida commanded.

"This is a very bad notion."

Leonida battled back a hysterical urge to giggle. Her entire journey to England had been nothing more than a very bad notion.

"I agree, Sophy, but I must do this."

Sophy heaved a sigh. "I suppose."

"I will be as quick as possible. Stay here."

Wiping her clammy hands on her skirt, Leonida forced herself to push open the nearby door and step inside.

As on the first occasion she had entered, she was struck by the sheer masculinity of the room. The furniture was made of heavy English oak and furbished in a pale ocher satin with heavy green velvet curtains. On the walls were a stunning collection of Van Dykes and near the towering window was a floor-to-ceiling bookcase that was enclosed in glass to protect the priceless first edition books.

She shivered as the scent of Stefan teased at her nose, reminding her of the feel of his slender fingers stroking over her skin and the taste of his lips against her mouth. With a shake of her head, she thrust aside the distracting thoughts and headed directly for the desk that was nearly hidden beneath stacks of farming manuals and leather-bound ledgers.

She would have years to recall Stefan and the searing sensations he had stirred to life. Now was not the time to be indulging in fantasies.

Without hesitation, she tugged open the top drawer and pulled out the large ring of keys she had noted during her first search of the room. Surely one of them had to fit the lock?

Shutting the drawer, she hurried out of the room and leaned close to Sophy to whisper in her ear.

"Remain here and watch the stairs," she ordered softly.

Not giving her maid the opportunity to protest, Leonida picked up the hem of her skirt and dashed back down the hall. Entering the Duchess's bedchamber, she crossed directly to the trapdoor and with shaking fingers began attempting to fit the various keys into the lock.

Her rasping breath filled the still air, along with the rattle of metal keys as she slid one and then another into the lock. She had gone through near a dozen before she at last heard a distinctive click, and with her heart lodged in her throat, she pulled the trapdoor open.

Licking her dry lips, she peered into the small, square

space, at first unable to see anything beyond the leather-bound diary covered in dust. Leonida reached to carefully set it aside along with a pearl-studded box that held painted miniatures of a variety of handsome young gentlemen. No doubt gifts from long ago beaus who had been relegated to fond memories by the Duchess. Pulling out the box, she sucked in a sharp breath as she caught sight of the bundle of letters tied with a pink ribbon hidden beneath.

Grasping the bundle, she tugged them out of the hidden space and held them to the light streaming from the window. Her heart turned over in her chest as she recognized her mother's flowing script on the top envelope.

Dear lord, she had done it.

Relief raced through her trembling body. Her mother would be saved, and if she were quick enough, so would Stefan.

For a brief moment her relief was overshadowed by a pain that sliced through her heart, then with a shake of her head, she was replacing the box and journal back into the hidden safe and securing the lock.

She had just managed to roll the carpet back into place when the door was pressed silently open and Sophy stuck her head into the room.

"You must hurry. I just heard one of the maids saying that the Duke has returned."

"I am done."

With only a cursory glance to ensure the room appeared untouched, Leonida gripped the keys in one hand and hid the stack of papers in the folds of her skirt with the other. Then she rushed from the room.

She had just slipped into her chamber when the sound of Stefan's voice echoed through the foyer and up the stairs. Her heart gave another twinge of painful regret before she was firmly pulling her door shut and throwing the bolt.

It was done.

Nothing mattered now but plotting her escape.

"Did you find what you were seeking?" Sophy demanded, her voice a nervous whisper.

Moving to her jewelry box, Leonida stuffed the letters among her pearls and amber necklace and used a small key to lock them inside. It would not withstand any serious attempt to open it, but for the moment it would have to do.

"I believe so," she said, turning around to cross back toward her maid.

"Will you give it to that man?"

"Certainly not."

"But…"

Leonida grasped her maid's hands and regarded her with a somber expression.

"While I am at dinner I want you to pack your bags and when you are certain there is no one about I want you to go straight to the stables of Hillside and collect my carriage."

A mulish frown settled on Sophy's brow. "I will not leave you."

"It will only be for a short time. We must devise some story…" Leonida chewed her bottom lip as she sorted through her mind for a suitable lie. "You can tell Lord Summerville's servants that you received word that your mother is ill and I have allowed you to return to Russia to tend to her. That should hopefully keep them from becoming suspicious of your sudden need to leave."

"I don't understand."

"Once the carriage is away from Hillside I want you to have Pyotr drive it to the line of trees just beyond the lake. Make sure it cannot be easily seen from the road."

Sophy's frown remained. "But what of you?"

Leonida summoned a confidence she was far from feeling. Perhaps if she pretended this hasty plan she was concocting as she went along could succeed, she could make herself believe it.

"I must attend dinner and wait for the household to settle for the night," she said with a grimace, regretfully concluding that she dare not simply bolt. "Only when I am certain that no one will notice my absence can I leave. The more time we have before I am missed, the better."

Sophy took an abrupt step backward, her eyes wide with disbelief.

"You intend for us to begin our return to Russia tonight?"

"I have no choice, Sophy. Once I am gone, I am certain my enemies will follow me and the Duke will be safe."

The maid's lips thinned with disapproval. "I am more concerned for your safety. What if that nasty man is keeping a watch on the house?"

Leonida shivered, the mere thought of meeting the wretched brute in the dark was enough to make her stomach clench in dread.

"No doubt he is," she muttered. "That is why I dare not wait until morning. We must trust the dark will keep us hidden."

Sophy shook her head. "I don't like this."

"Neither do I, but I must get the..." She bit back her impulsive words. Damn. If she did not take care she would never fool Stefan, let alone the enemies chasing her. "Package to Mother before it can fall into the hands of traitors." She swallowed heavily as she recalled the feel of the dagger against her throat. "Or worse."

The maid heaved a sigh and headed for the door. "Very well."

"Sophy?"

"Yes?"

"Warn Pyotr that it might be quite late before I manage to escape. I cannot risk being caught."

"What of your bags?"

Leonida shrugged. "I will take what I can and leave the rest. No doubt the Duke will enjoy tossing my possessions into the fire."

AS WAS HIS CUSTOM, STEFAN retreated to his private study after dinner, intending to review the quarterly reports before his meeting with his secretary in the morning. The cluttered, shabby room had always been a place of peace for him. Within these four walls he could sip his brandy without interruption, surrounded by fond reminiscences. The memory of dangling on his father's knee as the old Duke taught him to manage the accounts. Or standing at the window to study the sprawling lands that would one day be his responsibility.

Tonight, however, it was not his childhood recollections, or even the latest farming manuals that had arrived in the post, that plagued his mind.

No, that honor belonged solely to Miss Leonida Karkoff.

And her peculiar behavior during dinner.

It was not just that she had been quiet. Although Leonida could be one of the most charming and witty females he had ever known, she was by nature reticent. Like himself, she preferred to remain in the background rather than calling attention to herself.

Tonight, however, she had barely spoken a dozen words, her expression distracted, as if she carried a heavy weight on her shoulders.

So what the devil was on her mind? And why could he not shake the urge to seek her out and... What? Demand explanations that she would refuse to give? Offer her comfort she did not deserve? Take her to his bed and put an end to his agony?

With a low growl, Stefan slammed his glass onto his desk, indifferent to the brandy that sloshed onto the polished wood as he turned on his heel and left the cramped room. He resented the restlessness that held him captive. And the vague sense that his orderly existence had been disrupted beyond repair.

This was entirely Leonida Karkoff's fault.

The thought was still uppermost in his mind when he

shoved open the door to his bedchamber to discover the woman of his visions closing the drawer of his writing table.

A raw, savage heat raced through him as he drank in the sight of her slender body covered in no more than a linen night rail with her glorious hair flowing down her back. She was half turned away from him, the flickering candlelight making her gown nearly transparent, revealing the beauty beneath.

Christ.

Barely aware that he was moving, Stefan silently closed the door and turned the key in the lock.

When he had come up to his rooms, he had not been certain what he intended to do.

Now, he did not have a doubt in the world.

Prowling forward, Stefan waited until he was beside her before he spoke.

"What a pleasant surprise, my dove," he drawled, thoroughly enjoying her squeak of alarm as she whirled to face him with wide eyes. "I have been longing for days to lure you into my chambers and here you are, waiting for me like an apparition from my dreams."

She pressed against the desk, as if that small measure of space would keep him from devouring her. Foolish woman.

"Forgive my intrusion, I…"

He arched a brow as her voice faltered and her cheeks flushed a charming pink.

"Yes?"

"I desire to write a letter to my mother and I was in need of parchment."

He stepped closer. Close enough to breathe in the sweet scent of jasmine.

"Parchment?"

"Yes."

"Now why, Miss Karkoff, do you suppose I do not believe you?" he murmured, leaning forward to lay his hands on the surface of the writing desk, effectively caging her between his arms.

She licked her lips as she struggled to meet his heated gaze. "I haven't the least notion."

"No doubt because it is a lie." He rubbed his cheek against hers, savoring the warmth of her satin skin. His restlessness eased, to be replaced by a surge of anticipation. "Like so many others that tumble from those sweet lips."

Her hands lifted to press against his chest. "Must you always be so insulting?"

He shifted to nuzzle the tender spot below her ear, using his body to pin her against the desk as he jerked off his cravat and shrugged out of his jacket. His waistcoat followed, along with his linen shirt. If she wanted to touch his chest, then by God he intended to enjoy it.

Covering her hands, he pressed them firmly to his bare skin. "You would prefer compliments?" He nipped the lobe of her ear. "Very well. Shall I tell you that your hair is the precise shade of summer sunshine and your eyes were surely meant for an angel? Or perhaps you prefer to know how I spend my nights dreaming of removing your clothing so I can devote hours to exploring your alabaster skin?"

With a violent shudder, Leonida attempted to arch from his tender caresses. "So, you do not trust me or even particularly like me, but you are willing to bed me?"

He pressed his mouth to the base of her throat, his tongue stroking over her racing pulse.

"I did not say I did not like you." He nibbled his way down the plunging vee of her night rail. "I like this very much."

She groaned, her fingers flexing until her nails dug into his skin. The tiny prick of pain only intensified Stefan's turbulent need.

"Stefan, you must stop."

"Why?"

"Because..."

Her words came to an abrupt halt as his teeth captured a puckered nipple through the thin fabric of her gown.

"Yes?" he murmured as he teased the beaded tip with his tongue.

"You are so damnably smug," she growled, leaning forward to bury her face in the curve of his neck.

Flames licked through his body, hardening his muscles and making his hands tremble as he tugged her fingers down to the waistband of his breeches.

"Not smug, overdressed. Help me." He lost the ability to think as her fingers fumbled with the hooks, brushing the head of his arousal and sending tiny jolts of pleasure down the shaft. He hastily kicked off his slippers as the trousers slid down his legs. "Christ, what have you done to me?"

"Nothing."

"Liar." At last rid of his clothing, Stefan scooped the delicious bundle of soft woman in his arms and carried her toward the nearby bed. Laying her upper half on the mattress, he knelt on the carpet between her dangling legs. For a moment he simply allowed himself to drink in the sight of her lying on his bed, her golden cloud of hair spread like a halo around her flushed face. Then, with reverent care, he began pushing up the hem of her night rail. "No matter how often I warn myself that I am a fool to allow my lust to overcome my common sense, I cannot resist your temptation."

"Stefan…"

"No," he rasped, lowering his head to brush his lips along her inner thigh. "No more talking. I have to have you, my dove, before I go mad."

She made a strangled sound deep in her throat, her hands clutching the blanket beneath her as he slowly explored the petal-soft skin. The scent of jasmine became even more intense as he neared the juncture of her legs, seeping into his blood until he was drowning in desire.

His fingers slipped beneath her knees, tugging them

farther apart as he ran his tongue through her moist cleft. Her soft scream of pleasure echoed through the room, but thankfully not loud enough to bring the servants running. With a smug pride at the knowledge that he was the first and only man to ever have tasted of her sweet innocence, Stefan licked and teased until she was twisting restlessly beneath him, her hands tangling in his hair as she hurtled toward her climax.

"Please…" she gasped, lost in the throes of passion.

With one last stroke of his tongue he tumbled her over the edge of pleasure, swiftly covering her body with his own as she shivered in bliss.

Her legs were still spread wide and he slid between the cradle of her hips. God, it felt as if she were born to hold him in this precise manner. And perhaps she had been. What other explanation could there be for the ruthless need that held him in its grip?

Not that he particularly cared in this moment what bewitchment she had used to ensnare him. All that mattered was easing the blazing inferno that threatened to consume him.

Cupping her face in his hands, Stefan found her mouth with a kiss just short of savage. Her arms circled around him, her fingers stroking up his spine with a tentative caress. Stefan needed no more encouragement. They had both wanted and needed this since the moment their paths had crossed.

Easing his kiss, Stefan allowed his mouth to drift down the curve of her cheek and along the curve of her neck. His hands explored her shoulders, her arms, and at last cupped her breasts so he could tease her nipples with his thumb. She groaned in encouragement, her nails digging into his back.

Stefan muttered a low curse, abruptly realizing he was dangerously close to a climax. Christ, what was the matter with him? The woman could make him feel like an overanxious school lad with no more than a few awkward touches.

Settling more firmly against her eager body, Stefan

poised his erection at her entrance. He gritted his teeth, desperately reminding himself she was a virgin as he pressed slowly into her heat.

She stiffened at the intrusion, her breath coming in ragged shreds. Stefan forced himself to still until she became accustomed to his penetration, his body quivering at the effort. Only when he felt her tension ease did he begin gently rocking against her, his mouth returning to tease at her nipple as he slid a hand between them and rubbed her tiny bud of pleasure.

Murmuring encouragement in her ear, Stefan quickened his pace, the feel of her tight passage gripping his cock sending shock waves of ecstasy radiating through his body.

He was close…so close.

She arched her hips off the bed, rising to meet his thrusts, then she gasped softly beneath him, her passage clenching about him as she found another release.

The tiny ripples were like a spark to the tinder and, arching his back, Stefan allowed the looming bliss to slam through his body.

CHAPTER NINE

STEFAN WAS NOTHING less than furious as he stormed out of the stables at Hillside.

Not his usual mood after a night of satisfying passion.

But then, he had never before taken a woman beneath his own roof. He far preferred to meet his lovers away from Meadowland. And certainly, he had never had a woman who had sighed with pleasure in his arms disappear in a seeming wisp of smoke during the middle of the night.

"Damn." He slammed the door behind him. "When I get my hands on her..."

"I trust that the *her* you are referring to is not my wife," a dark, familiar voice drawled from behind him.

Spinning about, Stefan watched as his twin brother vaulted from the saddle of his snowy white mount and tossed the reins toward a groom who rushed forward to lead the horse away.

"Edmond." He smiled, noting Edmond's dust-stained appearance. Clearly he had ridden hard from London. Not that Stefan looked much better than his twin, he ruefully acknowledged. Although he had bathed and attired himself in black breeches and a jacket the precise shade of amber of Leonida's favorite necklace, he knew his dark hair was tousled from the numerous times he had run his fingers through the curls and his cravat yanked off and stuffed in his pocket. "I did not expect your return so soon."

Edmond wearily rubbed the back of his neck. "I spoke with the Queen's advisors and did my best to persuade them that it was in her best interest to avoid unnecessary scandal, but I do not hold much hope. Even her closest friends are no longer capable of controlling her."

"She is determined to attend the ceremony?"

"Yes."

Stefan shrugged. "You have done your duty."

Edmond gave a short, humorless laugh. "Let us hope the King agrees with you."

"She is his wife, not yours."

"Thank God." Edmond's hard expression softened, a certain indication he was thinking of Brianna. "And speaking of my wife, I am anxious to see her. Did she accompany you to Hillside?"

"No, she managed to slip away yesterday while I was occupied and came to Hillside to meet with the workmen, so I made it quite clear to my staff that she was to spend today resting."

Edmond lifted his brows. "You are a brave man."

"Thankfully you have returned to bear the brunt of her anger," Stefan pointed out, not at all disappointed to leave his childhood friend in the hands of her husband. Not only was she bound to be furious when she realized she was not allowed from the estate, but he had other matters to occupy his thoughts.

"Indeed," Edmond said dryly. "If Brianna is not here, then may I inquire what brings you to Hillside?"

"I thought you were anxious to be reunited with your wife?"

Predictably Edmond folded his arms over his chest and narrowed his gaze. He might be impatient to be reunited with his wife, but he would not leave until he knew precisely why Stefan was there. Edmond was worse than a mother hen when he thought his brother was troubled.

"Now I am truly curious. Does this have anything to do with my lovely, young guest?"

"Your lovely, young guest has done a flit."

"I beg your pardon?"

Stefan clenched his hands at his sides, recalling his initial sense of stunned disbelief when Goodson informed him that Leonida was missing and that her bed had not been slept in.

At first he had assumed that she had risen from his bed in the earlier hours and had taken a walk in the garden or was once again searching Meadowlands for some mysterious object. It was not until he realized her maid had also disappeared that he more closely examined her chambers to discover a number of her gowns and personal items missing.

His disbelief had altered to fury as he had made his way to Hillside, already knowing he would find her carriage and groom missing.

"She disappeared in the middle of the night, taking her carriage and her maid and God knows what else with her," he gritted.

"Did she leave a message?"

"You believe she would leave a note thanking me for my generous hospitality?" Stefan snarled.

Edmond's gaze sharpened. "I see."

"I am pleased that one of us does."

"Tell me, Stefan, would Leonida have any reason to feel the need to slip away in the dark of night?"

Stefan waved an impatient hand. "That is what I am attempting to determine."

"I was referring to you, dear brother," Edmond said softly. "Did you offer her a reason to feel she must flee?"

Stefan stiffened.

He had, of course, considered the unpleasant notion that Leonida had bolted because of their night together. For any woman the loss of her virginity could be a bewildering experience and she might have overreacted. The thought had oddly twisted his stomach with dread.

Thankfully, he had swiftly come to his senses. Leonida might have been an innocent, but she had readily welcomed him into her body. More than once. And by the end of the night she had been quite bold in her caresses.

Whatever her reason for fleeing, it had nothing to do with the explosive passion between them.

"No."

Edmond appeared unconvinced. "Hmm."

"Take care, Edmond," Stefan warned, not prepared to discuss his erotic obsession with Leonida Karkoff.

Edmond's lips thinned, but he was wise enough to realize that Stefan would not be pressed. "She must have some reason for her abrupt departure," he instead accused.

"I can only presume she completed the task she was sent to perform."

"And what task would that be?"

"Stealing some item from Meadowland."

Not surprisingly, Edmond regarded him as if he feared that Stefan had taken leave of his senses. "You think the Countess Karkoff's daughter is a common thief?"

Stefan snorted. "There is nothing common about her."

"Have you discovered anything missing?" Edmond demanded. "The silver? Mother's jewelry? The Van Dykes?"

Stefan shifted impatiently. He had Goodson searching the mansion, but thus far the butler's meticulous gaze could detect nothing absent or mislaid.

That did not, however, ease the suspicion that clawed through him.

"No."

Edmond studied him with a somber expression. "Stefan, you have behaved in a most peculiar manner since Miss Karkoff arrived in Surrey. Are you quite certain that your unwanted fascination with the woman has not convinced you to view her with suspicion?"

Stefan grimly shrugged aside his brother's accusation. He could not deny his perverse fascination with Leonida Karkoff, but it had nothing to do with his distrust. She had brought that on herself.

"I view her with suspicion because she has devoted the past days to searching Meadowland as if she were on a treasure hunt," he retorted. "She was most particularly interested in Mother's chambers."

"You are certain?"

"Absolutely."

Edmond shook his head. "What could she have been searching for?"

"I would presume it has something to do with Mother's connection to Russia, but the few belongings she brought from St. Petersburg are not excessively valuable." Stefan's jaw clenched. "At least, to no one beyond ourselves."

Edmond scowled, as prickly as Stefan when it came to protecting their parents' memories. "And now she has disappeared," he said flatly.

"Yes."

"What do you intend to do?"

Stefan did not hesitate, turning toward the carriage he had left in the stable yard. "Go after her."

Grasping his arm in an iron grip, Edmond whirled him back to meet his concerned expression.

"Stefan, wait."

"What is it?"

"You are the Duke of Huntley. You cannot simply leap on your horse and dash around the countryside."

Stefan arched a brow at his brother's absurd words. "A lecture on responsibility from you, Edmond?"

"I will admit that I have not always been renowned for my predictable nature," Edmond conceded with a wry smile.

"You have been a rake, a gambler, and you have quite often disappeared for weeks on end without allowing anyone, including me, to know where you have gone."

"All true, but I always had the assurance that my brother could be counted upon to rescue me from any difficulty. Just as so many others count upon you."

Stefan impatiently jerked his arm free. "I know my duty."

"Then you know you must remain at Meadowland. If you wish I can contact my associates in Russia ..."

"No," Stefan sharply interrupted.

A part of him realized he was behaving irrationally. He possessed a hundred servants he could send in pursuit of Leonida, not to mention a local militia who would be delighted to oblige the Duke of Huntley. A much greater part, however, refused to even contemplate allowing anyone but himself the pleasure of capturing the current bane of his existence.

He told himself that it was simply fury at her attempt to betray him, but he knew it was far more than that. Leonida…belonged to him. And until he was prepared to let her go, he would do whatever necessary to bring her back to where she belonged.

"Miss Karkoff is my problem and I intend to deal with her personally."

"So you admit it is personal," Edmond growled.

"This is not your concern, Edmond."

"Damn." Swallowing the urge to continue the argument, Edmond heaved an aggravated sigh. "At least promise me that you will take your servants."

"I am capable of organizing my journey."

Edmond tossed his hands up in defeat. "You do know that you have taken complete leave of your senses?"

Stefan smiled wryly. That was the one thing he was absolutely certain of.

"Go tend to your wife," he murmured, heading to his waiting carriage.

Paris

LEONIDA HAD RASHLY PRESUMED that escaping from Meadowland without alerting Stefan to her flight or having her throat slit by the dangerous Russian lurking near the estate would be the most difficult part of her journey.

Stupid, of course.

Her choice to return to St. Petersburg over land rather

than by sea had been the only sensible decision. Not only would anyone searching for her be bound to look toward the north, but she could not bear the thought of being trapped on a boat with nowhere to escape.

Unfortunately, she was obliged to travel in disguise and without being able to draw on her mother's accounts she was forced to depend on what money she had in her purse. It also meant being stuck in Dover while her groom Pyotr haggled to sell their carriage, locate fraudulent passports and purchase tickets for the ferry, while Sophy searched the shops for a handful of black crepe dresses and veiled bonnets that would hide her from prying eyes. There was another delay in Calais as Pyotr found a suitable carriage that could carry them along the muddy roads that led to Paris.

It was little wonder her patience was stretched thin by the time they reached the outskirts of the city and a particularly nasty rut snapped the back wheel off the carriage. And that her nerves shattered completely when Pyotr informed her after the second day of waiting for the carriage to be repaired that it still was not finished.

She, Sophy and Pyotr stood just outside the limestone-coated hotel with wrought-iron railings and carved garlands above the narrow windows. The hotel could claim little more than reasonable rates and a proximity to *Saint-Honore,* but it was all she could currently afford.

Besides, it was the last place anyone would search for Miss Leonida Karkoff.

"The wheelwright claims he should have the repairs done tomorrow," Pyotr growled.

Aggravated beyond bearing, Leonida snapped open her black lace fan. The narrow streets stifled any breeze, allowing the summer heat to gather among the buildings squashed closely together. The unpleasant warmth made even her feel like wilting. *Mon Dieu.* She was barely able to breathe behind the thick veil on her bonnet and the heavy black crepe gown was beginning to scratch against her damp skin.

"But he promised to be finished today."

Pyotr shrugged. A tall, solid man with a thatch of brown hair and matching eyes, he possessed a stoic calm that Leonida depended upon. It was, in fact, the reason she had insisted he travel with her from St. Petersburg.

"It seems he was called from his shop by the Marquis DeSavois who was in the middle of a race from Paris to Boulogne. The wheelwright only returned this morning."

Leonida heaved a disgusted sigh. "I suppose a mere widow cannot compete with a marquis, no matter how idiotic he might be."

"That does appear to be the case."

"Very well." Leonida wrestled back the frustration that coiled through her. What was the purpose in stomping her feet and screaming like a lunatic? Without the funds to purchase a new carriage, she was stuck waiting for the old one to be repaired. "It seems I shall have to tell the hotel manager we will not be departing after all."

Pyotr twisted his cap in his callused hands. "I am sorry."

"This is not your fault, Pyotr. It was nothing more than an unfortunate accident." Leonida reached to pat her groom on the arm. "Go enjoy your luncheon."

Still perturbed by the delay, Leonida watched as the groom disappeared among the clusters of passing pedestrians, headed for the nearby coffee shop.

"Now what will we do?" Sophy demanded at her side.

Snapping shut her fan, Leonida glanced back at the hotel. The mere thought of returning to her cramped chamber made her shudder. She was angry and frightened and so restless she could barely stand still.

"It seems we have no option but to do what every other woman in Paris does," she abruptly decided.

"And what is that?"

Leonida shrugged. "Go shopping."

"Are you daft?" Sophy hissed in shock. Leonida envied

her maid her light chip bonnet and loose linen gown. "What if you're recognized?"

"Do not worry, I shall keep my face covered."

"I still think..."

"Sophy, the hotel servants are beginning to regard us with suspicion. Not even the most reclusive widow remains forever in her rooms," she firmly pointed out. "Besides, I shall go mad if I do not breathe some fresh air."

"Bah." Sophy waved a plump hand. "The air is foul."

That was true enough. There was not only the unmistakable stench of open sewage, but the narrow street was littered with rubbish that did not bear close scrutiny.

She could only hope the finer neighborhoods were less pungent.

Twining her arm through her maid's, she tugged her away from the hotel and down the street.

"Come, all will be well."

Within a thankfully short time they had reached the wider boulevards that led to the *Palais-Royal.*

The cramped buildings became lavish private residences, the fronts a mixture of classical simplicity and those boasting ornate ornamentation with nymphs and playful deities gazing down at passing crowds. The traffic also thickened, the streets choked with elegant carriages and the public coaches called *cabriolets* that carried the fashionable Parisians and foreign guests to the endless entertainment to be found about the city.

There was an almost frantic air of excitement that was occasionally dampened by a King's Guard who kept close watch upon knots of men strolling down the paved walk or seated outside the numerous coffee shops.

Beneath the brittle gaiety simmered a tension that prickled over Leonida's skin. The atmosphere was charged, as if lightning were about to strike.

She shivered as she tugged the reluctant Sophy toward the nearby arcade. She had always thought St. Petersburg tense with undercurrents of sedition. This, however...lord, it felt as if the blood might begin flowing at any moment.

Entering the arcade that was built of a skeletal iron frame, with a towering glass roof that ran the length of the shops, Leonida swallowed a sigh.

It was a relief to be away from the thundering traffic that offered a messy death for anyone foolish enough to become distracted, but the crush of people wandering through the passage offered little reprieve. Of course, having her slippers trod upon or being jostled by everyone from the highest aristocrats to the most common servants was infinitely better than being toppled beneath a galloping horse.

Allowing Sophy to linger at a toy-maker shop, Leonida strolled past the bookshops and milliners before at last halting in front of a jewelry store that offered a bizarre collection of gem-encrusted beetles made into brooches and even necklaces.

Wondering what fool would actually purchase such a hideous trinket, Sophy barely noted the young lad with a shock of red hair and freckled face darting forward and yanking at her purse until the satin ribbons snapped and he could run off with his prize.

Leonida cursed her inattention, helplessly watching the much smaller body slip easily through the crowd. Thankfully she had most of her stash of money in a pocket hidden in the folds of her heavy skirt, and more importantly, her mother's precious letters were safely concealed beneath the lining of her luggage.

Still, the purse held her favorite handkerchief and the coins she had intended to use for a warm croissant to share with Sophy. It was thoroughly annoying to have it stolen by the unruly scamp.

On the point of giving up her belongings as a lost cause, Leonida watched in surprise as a tall gentleman with silver hair and handsome features grasped the lad by the back of his shirt and lifted him off his feet.

He spoke a few words in the boy's ear before firmly removing her silk bag from his grubby fingers, then with a sharp shake, he lowered the boy to his feet and allowed him to scamper away. Only then did he acknowledge Leonida, offering her a smile as he moved to stand directly before her.

"I believe this belongs to you?" he said in French with a heavy English accent, handing her the maltreated purse.

"Yes, thank you."

Regaining her property, Leonida took a discreet step backward. The gentleman was flawlessly attired in a black jacket and breeches with a silver waistcoat and polished boots. He was clearly a well-bred gentleman and judging by the large diamond winking in the folds of his elegantly knotted cravat, a wealthy one as well. Strangely, however, she found herself instinctively desiring to keep him at a distance. There was something about him that made her sense a cold menace just beneath the surfacc.

"I am not usually such easy prey. I fear I was distracted."

He shifted to peer through the window behind her. "Ah. You were admiring the necklaces?"

Leonida shook off the urge to scuttle away, reminding herself that the man had come to her rescue. The least she could do was be polite.

"In truth, I was wondering if anyone actually purchased such hideous objects."

The man flashed another smile that did not reach his dark eyes.

"I am no longer shocked by what the Parisians consider fashionable. More often than not it is a competition as to who can be the more outrageous."

"Yes, well...I should be on my way."

With a startling speed, he reached out to grasp her hand. "Will you not join me for a coffee? I can assure you that the café just down the passage serves the tastiest pastries in the city."

Leonida tugged, attempting to free her fingers from his tight grip.

"Thank you, but no."

"Come, come, my dear, you cannot abandon me without at least giving me your name."

"Madame Marseau," she grudgingly offered the name she was traveling under.

"You are wed?"

"A widow."

"I see." He leaned downward, as if appearing to peer through her heavy veil. Leonida felt a chill inch down her spine. "And Russian if my ears do not deceive me," he murmured.

"I really must..."

"I am Sir Charles Richards, at your service." He bowed over her hand, ruthlessly ignoring her struggles to be free. "Tell me, Madame, do you reside in Paris?"

"No, I am just passing through."

"How charming, a fellow visitor." He wrinkled his nose in a playful gesture. Leonida found herself wondering if he practiced it before a mirror. "Myself, I am from London and still rather unfamiliar with the confusing jumble of streets, but I should be delighted to offer myself as a guide."

"My stay is far too brief for sightseeing." This time she jerked hard enough that he was forced to release her hand or attract the notice of the fellow shoppers. "Good day."

"At least allow me to give you my card." He smoothly blocked her path, pressing a gilt-edged calling card into her hand. "I am staying at the Montmacier on the Rue de Varenne. If you decide to linger in Paris I hope you will send me a note."

"There is no chance of me lingering."

"Still, if you have need of me, for any reason, I want you to know you can depend upon me."

She frowned. Why the devil was he being so persistent? Did he believe a widow without protection was easily seduced? Perhaps he hoped she was lonely and naive enough to fall into the arms of the first man to show her a bit of attention?

"That is not necessary."

"Who is to know?" He shrugged. "A young lady in Paris can never be too careful."

Her lips twisted as she considered the seemingly endless troubles that had plagued her since leaving Russia.

"I suppose that is true," she said dryly, feeling an unmistakable sense of relief as she caught sight of Sophy weaving a determined path in her direction.

"Remember," he said, his voice low and urgent. "You have only to send word and I will do whatever in my power to assist you."

She shook her head. "Are you always so eager to offer your services?"

"Only to beautiful ladies," he smoothly retorted.

Sophy appeared at her side and without giving the maid the opportunity to catch her breath, Leonida was steering her away from the unwelcome gentleman.

Suddenly her cramped chamber at the hotel did not seem nearly so odious.

"Good day, sir."

CHARLES HELD HIMSELF brutally still as his prey walked away. He did not twitch or blink. Instead, he concentrated on drawing in one breath after another, counting his heartbeats, and willing the red haze that fogged his mind to fade.

She had been there. In his grasp. His hands had itched with the need to grasp her slender throat and demand the letters he knew she had hidden, but there had been too many witnesses, too many King's Guards. All he could do was try and lure her to a more private setting, and even that had been thwarted by the bitch.

Damn her.

For two days he had waited in the shadows for his opportunity to strike. Since receiving his servant's message that the Karkoff wench had managed to slip away and was not to be discovered on any of the roads leading north, he had kept watch on the routes leading from Calais to Paris.

Luck, for once, had been with him. About damned time. And he had recognized Leonida's maid when they had halted at an inn not far from the city. He had directed his newly hired henchmen to ensure the carriage was made unusable while he had returned to Paris to make certain that the wheelwright that was sent for by the groom understood that there was a nice reward to be had if he could prolong the repairs as long as possible.

It should have been a simple matter after that to retrieve the letters, but the worthless woman had refused to leave her rooms at the hotel. Just as annoying, the maid he had managed to bribe claimed that there were no letters to be discovered among Madame Marseau's belongings.

Unconsciously, Charles slid his hand into the pocket of his breeches, smoothing his hand along the small dagger. His hunger was becoming unbearable.

He was still standing there when the red-haired urchin who had nabbed Leonida's purse returned, his ugly face split with a wide smile.

"Did I do it right?" he demanded.

"Perfectly." He flipped a coin that the lad deftly caught. "And here is your reward."

"Is there anything else, *monsieur?*"

On the point of sending the boy away, Charles hesitated.

He had been forced to allow Miss Karkoff to temporarily slip from his grasp, but that did not mean he could not sate his burning need.

There were always women in need of his special attention.

"Actually, there is." The cold that encased his soul began to thaw in anticipation. Blood. Sweet blood. "I want you to take me to your mother."

CHAPTER TEN

LATE THE NEXT MORNING, Leonida stood in the back parlor of the hotel, pacing the threadbare carpet with impatient steps. The swish of her black crepe gown was the only sound to break the silence, her fingers anxiously toying with one of the dozen black ribbons that held the gown together from the high neckline to the heavily flounced hem.

Waiting until a subdued Pyotr left the room and shut the door behind him, Leonida turned to regard Sophy with a blazing frustration.

"*Mon Dieu.* I am convinced we have managed to discover the most incompetent wheelwright in all of France."

"A blustering idiot, if you ask me," Sophy muttered. "I should be very surprised if he even knows how to fix the wheel."

"I am beginning to wonder myself. I will give him until tomorrow morning and then I will insist on another to repair the carriage." Leonida rubbed her aching temples. She had not slept well since leaving Meadowland and the ceaseless worry was beginning to take its toll. "Damn."

Moving to her side, Sophy rubbed a comforting hand down her back. "Ah well, no use pining over what can't be changed. We will be home again soon enough. And there can be no one to know we are in Paris."

"No," Leonida forced herself to agree, although she was not nearly so confident as she wished to be.

How could she be when she felt as if she was being constantly watched when she left her room? And she was absolutely convinced that her belongings had been disturbed more than once.

Of course, it could be the unseen watcher was no more than a figment of her troubled imagination. And maids were bound to have moved a few items during their daily cleaning. Still, her desire to leave Paris became more urgent with each passing moment.

"No one could know."

Sophy regarded her with a sympathetic smile. "You should go and have a hot bath. That will make you feel better."

"What of you?"

The maid's smile widened, a twinkle entering her eyes. "Pyotr mentioned he had a tear in his coat. I told him I would come to his room and darn it for him."

Leonida blinked in surprise. "Sophy."

"If we are to be trapped in Paris for days on end then at least I should enjoy a few hours of harmless flirtation."

"Indeed." Leonida's heart twisted with something perilously close to envy. Harmless flirtation. It was something a woman in her position could never comprehend. Most gentlemen regarded her as a prize to be won for political gain, and the one man who had truly seen her as a woman desirable in her own right now must hold her in utter contempt. She determinedly shook off the dark thoughts and summoned a weak smile. "Enjoy yourself."

With a wink, Sophy left the room.

Left on her own, Leonida briefly considered a short stroll, only to have common sense convince her to climb the stairs to her chamber. The delay of repairing her carriage could not last forever. Until then she would be a fool to risk exposure.

Digging the key from her tiny silk bag, she entered the room and shut the door behind her. Perhaps a hot bath would not be such a bad notion. It would at least give her the opportunity to remove the revolting gown.

She had just stepped over the threshold and closed the

door behind her when a hand clamped painfully over her mouth and she was jerked against a hard male body.

Shock held her motionless, shards of fear piercing her heart as an arm wrapped around her waist, keeping her back tightly wedged against the solid muscles. Then a familiar, exotically male scent teased at her nose as the intruder leaned down to whisper in her ear.

"Did you truly believe you could steal from me and simply slip away, my dove?"

Stefan.

She shivered, a combination of disbelief, fury and a painful awareness battling for supremacy.

No, this was not possible. She struggled against his ruthless grasp, refusing to contemplate the last time she had been held in his arms.

Not surprisingly, he did not allow her to escape, although his hand shifted from her mouth to wrap around her throat.

"Let me go."

"Never," he rasped, his warm breath stroking over her cheek and sending a thrill of excitement down her spine. "You escaped me once, it will not happen again."

She closed her eyes as a haunting regret bloomed in the pit of her stomach. There had not been a night when she had not lain awake recalling his every touch, his demanding kisses, his soft words of pleasure. In an odd way, it pleased her that her last memory of Stefan would be his beautiful face softened and sated as he slept at her side.

Now it would all be destroyed by the fury she could feel vibrating through his body.

"How did you find me?"

"One of my tenants happened to catch sight of your carriage on the road to Dover." His voice was low and dangerous. "It did not take a great deal of imagination to realize you must be attempting to flee to Paris."

"That does not explain how you discovered this hotel."

"I learned that a young widow's carriage had broken down just outside of Paris. I checked with the local wheelwrights and happened to catch a glimpse of your groom and followed him here."

Damn that worthless carriage. If not for the stupid wheel breaking off they would be well on their way to St. Petersburg and Stefan would never have caught her.

"Very clever."

"Not particularly." His grip on her neck loosened to allow his fingers to brush at the sensitive skin. "If I had not allowed myself to be bewitched by a pair of angel eyes and a body meant to torment a man, you would never have been allowed to escape in the first place."

She gritted her teeth, willing herself not to respond to his light caress.

"Escape? I am not your prisoner, your Grace."

He nipped her ear. "You will call me Stefan, and you are now very much my prisoner."

"You have no right."

"No?" he challenged in scathing tones. "As Duke, and by tradition the current magistrate, I have every right to hold a disreputable thief as my captive and return you to Surrey."

A mortified heat flooded beneath her cheeks. Lord, how had she ever allowed her mother to convince her to become involved in her crazy scheme?

Nadia Karkoff might be an expert at manipulation and political maneuvering, but Leonida possessed a deep aversion to deceit.

Which perhaps explained why she was such a dismal failure at it.

"How dare you?" she blustered, her words sounding weak even to her own ears. "I am no thief."

"A thief." His hand cupped her chin. "And a liar as well."

Leonida's embarrassment shifted to anger. Whatever her sins, she had only done what was necessary to protect her mother and the Emperor.

Stefan would do exactly the same in her position.

"I swear if you do not release me, I will..."

"What?" he taunted.

Her nerves simply snapped. She was weary, terrified and not at all pleased to be treated as some sort of hunted animal.

Before she could even consider the consequences, she lowered her chin and sank her teeth into the soft skin between his thumb and finger.

Stefan gave a startled grunt, then with a humiliating ease, he had her off her feet and was striding across the room to toss her onto the bed. Before she could catch her breath, he had landed on top of her, his heavy body pressing her into the mattress.

"Hellcat," he muttered, his eyes dark with an emotion that made her shiver in alarm.

"Damn you." She pressed her hands against his chest, acutely aware of the delicious heat already curling through her stomach. "Why will you not leave me in peace?"

"You know why," he muttered, his tone distracted as his brooding gaze studied her flushed features. "Besides, you have something that belongs to me."

Only brute force kept her from glancing toward the luggage she had tucked in a corner.

"And what is that?" she demanded.

A slow, worrisome smile curved his lips. "I have yet to discover, but I assure you I will enjoy the search."

"You accuse the daughter of the Countess Karkoff without knowing what I supposedly stole, not to mention without proof?"

"Yes."

Her hands slipped against the soft fabric of his dove-gray coat, landing on his shoulders. She shuddered at the feel of hard muscles beneath her palms.

Stefan was no soft, overly pampered aristocrat. He was a man who worked hard to maintain his estate and possessed the ruthless strength to prove it.

"You are outrageous," she breathed.

"I am only beginning," he said huskily, his head lowering to stroke his lips over her heated cheek. "You have no notion just how outrageous I intend to be."

"Stefan, no."

"Why did you come to Meadowland?"

"I did not. I traveled to England to visit Lord and Lady Summerville." She gasped as his fingers tugged at the ribbon holding the high neckline in place. "Stop that."

"A ribbon for every lie, my dove," he warned. "Why did you come to Meadowland?"

"I told you, I..."

Another ribbon was untied, the heavy material of the gown falling open to reveal the thin shift that was all she wore beneath. It was too hot to endure the usual layer of underclothing.

"The truth."

She licked her lips, her heart pounding. "My mother requested that I come to England."

"Specifically to Surrey?"

"Yes."

"Why?"

Her gaze lowered to the simply tied cravat, unwilling to meet his relentless stare as she sought a suitable lie. "I believe she hoped I could discover an interest in an English gentleman since I had refused all my Russian suitors."

"Tut, tut," he murmured, undoing the ribbons to her waist. "A maiden with your pedigree and beauty would never squander herself in the country. Not when you could have dazzled your way through London society."

She made a sound of disgust at his ridiculous words. "I am not the sort of woman who dazzles anyone."

"I must disagree." His gaze ran a searing path down the plunging neckline of her shift, lingering on the hardened tips of her breasts that peeked through the lace. "I have never been so dazzled."

She stirred beneath him, a restless need coiling through her body. "You…"

Her words cut off in a startled moan as he captured the nub of her nipple between his lips. The moistened lace molded to her body, his hot breath making her skin prickle in delight.

"Tell me the truth, Leonida," he muttered.

Her fingers tangled in his hair, her body helplessly responding to his skillful touch. "I cannot."

He shifted to tease her other breast. "Why?"

She struggled to think through the fog of pleasure clouding her mind. "Because my mother is in grave danger."

"What danger?"

He did something with his teeth that made her back arch off the bed.

"I have sworn not to tell."

"How very convenient."

"Are you jesting?" she muttered. "It has been anything but convenient."

"Poor Leonida," he mocked, deftly unraveling the remaining ribbons and pushing the heavy gown off her shivering form. "Shall I make it all better?"

"What are you doing?" she stupidly demanded, her limbs melting beneath the slender hands that roamed with a growing urgency over her skin.

"I have decided the truth can wait, but I cannot," he growled, spreading kisses over the curve of her breasts.

Her breath was squeezed from her lungs, her heart skipping a beat. "Oh."

Lifting his head he regarded her with a tormented gaze. "Damn you."

"Me?" Her eyes widened at his harsh tone. "I have done nothing."

"You have plagued me since you first came to Surrey. I cannot concentrate on anything but you. I have neglected my duties, my tenants and even my brother."

"If you will recall, I left Meadowland. You are quite at liberty to concentrate on whatever you please."

"I will not have peace until I have rid myself of this hellish craving." He caught her lips in a fierce, punishing kiss. "I want you out of my thoughts."

"This hardly seems the best means…" she began, only to choke on the words as he grasped the bodice of her shift and ripped it in two. "Why the devil did you do that?"

"I will buy you another." He groaned as he struggled to yank off his cravat, a flush of color staining his cheeks. "Christ, I will buy you an entire wardrobe. Just kiss me."

Against all sense and reason, Leonida did.

LEONIDA HAD NEVER BEEN STRUCK by lightning, but she was fairly certain she now knew how it must feel.

Quivering from the restrained fury of Stefan's love-making, Leonida sucked in a deep breath as the heavy male body rolled to lie beside her on the mattress, shocks of pleasure still jolting through her lower body.

Good lord…

Unlike the gentleness that marked their first night together, Stefan had unleashed the full power of his desire, taking her with a thunderous hunger that left her drowning in sensations.

Sucking in a deep breath, she turned her head, meeting Stefan's brilliant blue gaze.

Just for a moment the entire world skidded to a halt. The cramped room with its shabby furnishings, the chatter of birds that echoed through the open window that overlooked the back garden, the churning concern at having been caught before she could reach St. Petersburg, all faded away.

A sweet, poignant emotion clenched at her heart.

An emotion that sent a chill of dread down her spine.

No. She was not stupid enough to fall in love with this man.

For God's sake, he considered her a thief and a liar.

And then there was his threat to haul her back to England as his prisoner.

Thankfully oblivious to her shocking thoughts, Stefan folded his arms behind his head and regarded her with a faintly smug smile.

"A most delightful interlude, my dove."

"Interlude?" With a sudden surge she was off the bed and, ignoring her tattered shift, she yanked on the hideous gown. She did not know why she was hurt by his words. So far as Stefan was concerned she was just another woman in a no doubt long line that he had skillfully seduced. Then again, perhaps she should be grateful, she told herself severely, fumbling to retie the numerous ribbons. If she were not already desperate to escape from him, she certainly was now. "I have taken complete leave of my senses," she muttered beneath her breath, shoving her feet into the slippers that had fallen from her feet during the...*interlude*. "Sophy was right."

"Right about what?" he demanded.

She deliberately kept her gaze adverted from his naked body sprawled across the rumpled sheets. "I should have brought a pistol."

He chuckled softly. "It would take more than a pistol to keep me out of your bed."

Arrogant bastard. She wrapped her arms around her waist. "Will you please just go away?"

"Neither of us are going anywhere, Leonida. Not until you have told me why you came to Meadowland and precisely what you have stolen from me."

"I have told you I cannot."

She heard a rustle and peeking out of the corner of her eye, she watched as he slid from the bed and tugged on his breeches.

"Ah yes, the dire threat to your mother."

"It is not amusing." Whirling to face him, Leonida sent him a frustrated frown. "And the threat is not only to my mother."

"Are you saying that you are in danger?"

"Me and anyone who..."

His brows lifted. "Who?"

"Could you not just trust me, Stefan?"

"No." With a shake of his head, he moved to stand directly before her, his hands gripping her shoulders. "That is the one thing I cannot do."

"Why?" She resisted the urge to pull from his grasp. "I would never do anything to hurt you or your family. Indeed, I have done everything in my power to protect you. It was your own ridiculous notion to follow me."

His lips thinned, as if angered by her sincere words. "You knew that I would."

"Actually, I presumed a duke would have more important duties than chasing after an unwelcome guest."

"I never allow anything that belongs to me to slip away."

Swallowing her pride, Leonida parted her lips, prepared to plead if necessary. Before she could speak, however, there was a loud, unexpected bang just outside the window.

Mon Dieu. Had someone just fired a pistol?

Caught off guard, Leonida did not readily recognize the danger. Not until Stefan stumbled forward, a trail of blood running from his shoulder down his bare chest.

CHAPTER ELEVEN

WRAPPING HER ARMS AROUND Stefan's waist, Leonida managed to keep him upright as he struggled for his balance.

"You have been shot," she breathed, still stunned by the unexpected attack.

"Yes, I had surmised as much," he said dryly, managing to steady himself as he turned and headed toward the window.

"What are you doing?" she demanded. "You must lie down."

"And allow the bastard to slip away? Not bloody likely."

She pressed a hand to her heaving stomach, her heart pounding with fear. Stefan had been shot. He might have been killed. And it was entirely her fault.

"For God's sake, do you *want* to be shot again?" she hissed, watching as he pressed against the side of the window and glanced out.

"Damn," he muttered. "Whoever it was has made his escape."

Moving forward, Leonida grabbed his arm and steered him toward the bed. Her concern for the wounded Stefan was for the moment far greater than for the escaping attacker.

"Would you please take a seat? You are bleeding everywhere."

He grudgingly allowed her to settle him on the edge of the mattress, although he appeared remarkably indifferent for a man who had just been shot.

"It is nothing more than a crease."

"I must call for a doctor."

With startling speed he reached to grasp her wrist. "No."

"Do not be a fool, Stefan. You must allow your wound to be properly treated. It might become infected."

"And have all of Paris buzzing with the news that the Duke of Huntley was shot in the private hotel suite of the Countess Karkoff's daughter?" he demanded.

"No one in Paris knows who I am. We could say..."

"Leonida, there would be no means to prevent an investigation. The French authorities would insist upon it."

"And you believe there will be no investigation if the Duke of Huntley bleeds to death in a Parisian hotel?"

His lips twisted. "You will not be rid of me so easily. I have received worse injures cutting wood. If you would be good enough to hand me my jacket?"

She bent down to pluck the jacket from where Stefan had tossed it onto the carpet, her heart giving a faint flutter as she felt the unmistakable bulge of his purse in an inner pocket.

If she could just manage to get her hands on his money she would have the means to flee Paris. And more importantly, the means to lure the danger away from Stefan.

"Why?" she demanded, her voice determinedly steady.

Pulling a tiny flask from yet another pocket, he handed it to her. "This should cleanse the wound as well as any sawbones could do. If you would do the honors?" He flashed a wry smile. "I assure you it will hurt like the devil."

"Good." She readily hid her shattered nerves behind a pretense of anger. "You deserve to suffer for putting yourself in danger."

He winced as she splashed the spirit into the thankfully shallow wound.

"No doubt my brother would fully agree with such an uncharitable sentiment." He pointed toward her forgotten shift at the end of the bed. "Now if you could tear off a length of linen, I believe it should work well enough to bind the wound."

She reached for the shift, tearing off a large square. She

folded it and carefully positioned it over the wound before tearing a small strip to wrap under his arm and around his shoulder to hold it in place.

"I notice that none of your precious clothing is to be sacrificed," she muttered.

"I did promise to purchase you an entire wardrobe." He turned his head to brush his lips over her cheek. "Of course, that promise comes with the condition that I be allowed to rip it off you."

She straightened with a sharp jerk, unnerved by her explosive reaction to his touch.

"*Mon Dieu,* you have just been shot and you are thinking about ripping off my clothes?"

"When you are near that is *all* I think about," he said, his expression revealing he was not entirely pleased with his desire for her. "But you are right."

"What are you doing?" she demanded, exasperated as he rose to his feet, then, grasping the post of the bed, studied the window across the room.

"The shooter had to have climbed the tree to have a clear shot into the room."

She shivered, her stomach twisting with sick dread at just how close Stefan had been to being killed.

Oddly, the knowledge that some criminal might have been watching as she and Stefan had made passionate love, or even the realization that the bullet had more than likely been intended for her, were forgotten beneath the tide of horror at the thought of Stefan lying dead on the shabby carpet.

"I suppose," she muttered.

"Which means it was not simply a stray shot." He turned to stab her with an ominous glare. "It was intended to kill one of us."

"Yes."

"So either someone in Paris has recognized you or I have enemies I did not even know I possessed."

She pressed her hands to her stomach. "You should not have followed me."

"Enough of your games, Leonida. You will tell me the truth," he rasped, muttering a curse as there was a loud knock on her door that made both of them jump in alarm. "Ignore it."

"Madame." The sound of the manager's anxious voice floated through the room. "Madame, I heard a shot. Are you injured?"

Leonida licked her dry lips, welcoming the interruption. "If I do not answer he will come in to check on me."

His jaw tightened, his expression strained from the pain he was attempting to ignore.

"Very well. But Leonida."

"What?"

"This is between the two of us," he warned, his voice lethally soft. "Do not involve anyone else."

She pursed her lips, pushing back the hair that Stefan had so recently unpinned and heading across the room.

"Just stay there and for God's sake be quiet," she muttered.

There was another loud pounding, and, yanking open the door, Leonida stepped into the hall and closed it swiftly behind her.

"Enough," she commanded, conjuring her mother's most imperious expression as she regarded the slender, rather fussy little man with gray hair and somber attire. "Why are you pounding on my door?"

The manager's thin face was ashen as he plucked nervously at his starched cravat.

"A shot," he managed to stutter.

"Shot?"

"I heard a pistol being fired."

"Oh yes, I thought something must have wakened me from my nap." She slowly narrowed her gaze. "Do you mean to tell me that there is some madman in this hotel shooting your guests?"

The manager flapped his hands, nervously gazing down the empty corridor to ensure that no other guests had overheard her accusation.

"No, of course not. This is a respectable hotel. There is no trouble here."

"Then why was there someone firing a gun?"

"I..."

Leonida took swift advantage of his obvious abhorrence at having any sort of disturbance threaten the peace of his guests.

"Perhaps it would be best if I packed my bags. I do not approve of being murdered in my bed."

"Madame, I assure you, there is no danger."

"And what of the shot you heard?"

"A mistake." He straightened his narrow shoulders, happily convincing himself that nothing so bourgeois as an attempted murder could have occurred beneath his roof. "Perhaps one of the maids dropped a tea tray."

"Tea..." Leonida stiffened, struck by a sudden, awful notion. Taking the manager's arm, she steered him toward the nearby stairs and away from the door where Stefan was no doubt listening to the conversation. "Yes, of course. This entire incident has quite overset my nerves. I shall have need of a hot cup of tea with plenty of sugar."

"Of course, Madame." Relieved that Leonida was not about to make a disruptive fuss, the manager readily agreed to her modest request. "I will have it sent up at once."

She leaned closer to her companion, lowering her voice until it was a mere whisper.

"And perhaps you could put in a drop or two of laudanum? I possess a weak constitution."

"Certainly."

"Thank you."

Waiting until the small man was hurrying down the stairs, Leonida sucked in a deep breath and returned to her chamber.

A part of her was horrified by the plot forming in her

mind. She was not by nature a devious, cunning woman who enjoyed outwitting others. Still, a larger part of her understood that she had no choice. Not if she wished to keep Stefan out of his grave.

Entering her room, Leonida closed the door, her heart contracting painfully at the sight of Stefan leaning wearily against the post of the bed. With his dark hair mussed and his face unnaturally pale, he appeared unbearably vulnerable.

As if sensing her unwelcome surge of sympathy, Stefan deliberately straightened, a sardonic smile curing his lips. "You are quite the accomplished actress, my dove. Even I was moved by your touching performance of the delicate widow."

She tilted her chin. "You wished to be rid of him, did you not?"

"I did, but it makes a man wonder if you are ever sincere, or if your entire life is a well-rehearsed performance," he mocked.

"Well-rehearsed?" She gave a short, humorless laugh at the ludicrous accusation. "My life has become one disaster after another."

His gaze seared over her tense expression. "Do you include me as one of those disasters?"

"Absolutely," she lied without hesitation.

Some emotion flashed through his magnificent eyes, but it was gone so swiftly that Leonida was unable to say if it were pique or disgust.

"It is fortunate that my pride is not easily bruised" was all he said.

She snorted. "Your pride, Stefan, is impervious."

"And your ability to distract is beyond compare, but no longer." His expression hardened. "You are going to tell me why you came to Surrey, and more importantly why someone just attempted to shoot a hole through me."

She shook her head, stalling for time. "If you would just return to Meadowland you would be perfectly safe."

"Oh, I intend to travel to Meadowland. And you are coming with me."

His absolute certainty sent a chill down her spine. In this moment she did not doubt that he would willingly tie her to the back of his carriage if necessary to return her to Meadowland.

"No, I have to get to St. Petersburg."

"Why?"

"I have told you. My mother needs me."

"A pity, but she shall have to wait. Until I decide I am satisfied—" he deliberately paused, his gaze skimming down her slender form "—fully satisfied, you are staying with me."

She gritted her teeth. The Duke of Huntley was quite possibly the most stubborn, unreasonable gentleman ever born.

"You have no idea what you are risking."

"I believe I have a very good idea," he said dryly, glancing toward his bandaged shoulder.

"No, you do not," she hissed, not bothering to hide the fear that had haunted her since fleeing England.

He stilled, regarding her with a searching gaze. "Then explain it to me," he urged softly.

For an insane moment, Leonida felt an overwhelming impulse to lay her troubles at Stefan's feet. For all his taunting and threats, she knew he was a rare gentleman who could be depended upon without question. With his assistance there would be nothing and no one who could halt her return to St. Petersburg.

Besides, she hated the lying. The secrets, the constant charade. Most of all, she hated the barriers that kept her from the one man who had ever stirred her emotions.

Whether or not she would have given in to the unexpected whim, Leonida would never know. Just as her lips parted there was yet another knock on the door, interrupting the brief madness.

"Damn," Stefan growled. "Now what?"

Leonida swallowed the lump of regret in her throat. "I ordered tea."

"I have had more privacy in the midst of a carnival."

"Madame?" the maid called.

Stefan muttered a savage curse. "Open the damn door."

Turning, Leonida cracked the door just wide enough for the maid to hand through the steaming cup and saucer.

"Will that be all?" the obviously curious servant demanded.

"Yes, thank you." Using her free hand, Leonida firmly shut the door and turned to regard Stefan with a concern she did not have to feign. Heavens, he looked like he was about to topple over. "Sit down and drink this," she said briskly.

"You sound like my nanny," he muttered, but much to her relief he moved to settle on the edge of the mattress.

"You are pale and obviously weak." She pressed the cup into his reluctant hand. "This should help to revive you."

He reached for the flask that she had left on the bed, wincing in pain at the movement.

"I have what I need to revive me."

She swallowed a sigh. Of course he could not simply do as she requested.

"Drink the tea and I promise I will tell you whatever you wish to know."

His eyes narrowed. "Hmm."

"What?"

"I am wise enough to suspect it will not be nearly so simple." He shrugged, pouring a generous measure of the brandy into the tea before taking a large sip. "Still, I am willing to give you one last opportunity."

She pressed her hands together, not surprised to discover her palms were sweating. The laudanum would do him no harm, she desperately assured herself. Indeed, it was precisely what a doctor would prescribe.

The knowledge, unfortunately, did little to relieve her biting sense of guilt.

"Or what?"

He polished off the last of the tea and set the empty cup on the table next to the bed.

"I will drag you back to Meadowland and hold you there until you confess the truth."

"I thought you intended to haul me back to Meadowland regardless."

"Yes."

"You..." She threw up her hands in exasperation.

He snared her gaze, his eyes glittering with a hectic light. The combination of shock and pain was taking a dreadful toll on his waning strength.

"Begin talking or begin packing, the choice is yours."

She ignored his provoking command, moving forward to place her hand on his forehead, deeply relieved to discover it was cool and dry.

"Are you in pain?"

"I was just shot, Leonida."

"Here." Arranging the pillows against the head of the bed, she gently pressed him backward. "Lean back."

He briefly resisted, then with a heavy sigh, he turned so he could rest against the pillows, not even complaining when she lifted his legs onto the mattress and tugged the blanket over him.

Instead he studied her from beneath half-lowered lids. "I would be much more comfortable if you were to join me."

Her heart lurched with excitement as he patted the mattress beside him.

"I thought you wished to talk."

"We could speak much more easily if you were close."

She grimly refused to acknowledge the bittersweet yearning that stirred in her heart. She had already been foolishly weak in succumbing to Stefan's skillful touch and it had nearly killed him. She would not make the same mistake again.

Instead she forced her heavy feet to the corner to pull

out her case and began packing away the few belongings she had strewn about the room.

"We would not speak at all if I were close," she muttered.

"Perhaps you have a point." He paused as she moved to the small armoire. "What are you doing?"

"I might as well pack as we speak. You did say that I was to be taken back to England."

"Now I truly am suspicious," he mocked, his words faintly slurred. "Good God, leave those hideous gowns behind. You will terrify the natives if they see you strolling about swathed in black crepe."

"You are far too fond of tossing about orders, your Grace."

"I am…" His words faded, as if he were struggling to recall what he was about to say. "Fond of many things, Miss Karkoff," he at last managed to mutter.

Finished with her packing, Leonida slowly turned to discover that her companion's eyes had slid shut.

Walking to the edge of the bed, Leonida gazed worriedly at his pale face.

"Stefan?" she whispered.

His eyes remained shut, but a tiny smile briefly touched his lips.

"I thought you were an angel the first time I caught a glimpse of you," he said huskily, his voice thick.

"No." Her heart twisted with painful shame. "I am no angel."

"I wish…"

"What?"

His head twisted restlessly on the pillow. "I am so sleepy."

"Then rest, Stefan," she murmured, brushing her lips over his brow.

"You…" He struggled to speak. "Bloody hell, you gave me something."

"As I said, I am no angel," she whispered sadly.

Waiting until he had fully lost his battle against the encroaching weariness, Leonida placed a last, longing kiss on his lips. Then, tossing aside the last of her scruples, she tugged his leather purse from his jacket. Grasping her hastily packed bag, she slapped a black veiled hat on her head and hurried from the room.

Stefan's servants would soon come searching for their missing Duke, she reassured her nagging conscience as she hurried down the paneled corridor. They would properly see to his wound, and perhaps, if they had the least amount of sense, they would haul him back to Meadowland while he was still unconscious.

Indifferent to the startled glance from a maid who was carrying an armful of clean bedding, Leonida darted past her to climb the narrow staircase that led to the servants' rooms. She had no notion where Pyotr might be lodged, but she was desperate enough to knock on every door until she found him.

Thankfully for the servants attempting to have a few moments' peace from their demanding employers, Leonida's run of ill luck came to a brief halt as Sophy stepped out of a room and headed toward the staircase.

Rushing forward, Sophy took in Leonida's rumpled appearance and the heavy bag held in her hand.

CHAPTER TWELVE

"WHAT ARE YOU DOING up here?" the maid demanded, her expression troubled. "This is no place—"

"Sophy, thank heavens," Leonida interrupted. "Gather Pyotr and then pack only what you need. I will meet you behind the kitchens."

"What has happened?"

"The Duke of Huntley has happened."

Sophy lifted a hand to her mouth. "He is here?"

"In my room."

"How did he find us?"

"I will explain all later," Leonida impatiently promised. "For now I need you to hurry."

Sensing Leonida's trembling urgency, Sophy gave a sharp nod of her head.

"Of course."

"Be sure to go directly through the kitchens. The Duke is certain to have left his servants to keep watch."

"We shall be there as swiftly as possible."

Trusting that Sophy would fulfill her promise, Leonida turned and hurried down to the lower floor. There were a few raised brows from the kitchen staff, but no one attempted to halt her and, with a brief glance to ensure it was empty, she stepped into the cramped back garden.

There was an unmistakable scent of rotting vegetables and lingering tobacco smoke, but Leonida breathed a sigh of relief as she set down the bag and leaned against the building.

If her nerves had not been twisted into painful knots she

might have appreciated the irony of Miss Leonida Karkoff, darling of St. Petersburg society, cowering behind a cheap Paris hotel, attired in a gown barely fit for a scrub maid, and fleeing from an English duke and God knew how many other enemies. As it was, she conjured no more than a panicked fear as she waited.

To try and distract her mind, she opened Stefan's small purse. She did not expect to find a fortune. No gentleman of sense traveled with large amounts of money. Not unless he desired to attract the attention of the numerous highwaymen that plagued all of Europe.

Still, it was a shock to realize that he had less than fifty pounds in his possession. Certainly not enough to purchase a new carriage, even when added to what she possessed.

Good lord, she would never be free of Paris.

After what seemed an eternity, but was probably less than a quarter of an hour, Sophy and Pyotr hurried into the garden.

"Here we are," Sophy unnecessarily announced, her round face flushed. "What are we to do now?"

"We must leave Paris as swiftly as possible," Leonida announced.

Incapable of being rattled, no matter what the circumstance, the groom moved forward to firmly take Leonida's luggage from her stiff fingers.

"I will get the carriage," he assured her calmly. "Even if I have to point a gun at the damned wheelwright's head to get him to finish it."

Struck by a sudden thought, Leonida reached out to grasp Pyotr's arm. "No, wait. We must leave it. The Duke already knows that it is in the hands of the wheelwright. He might have someone watching the place."

"I hope you do not intend for us to walk to St. Petersburg," Sophy demanded.

"Not if we can possibly avoid such a fate." Leonida scoured her brain for enlightenment, dismissing a number of wild schemes until she at last hit upon the least hare-brained notion. "I wonder..."

"What?" Sophy prompted.

"Sir Charles Richards was excessively determined to offer me assistance. Perhaps he could be persuaded to lend me enough money so we can purchase a carriage."

Sophy frowned. "I thought you said the man made your flesh crawl?"

He had, of course. She could not entirely explain her aversion to the perfectly pleasant gentleman. He was a handsome and charming gentleman of means. But there was no denying that her instinct was to avoid him.

"We are hardly in a position to be overly particular in who we ask for favors," she pointed out, suppressing her shudder of reluctance.

Sophy heaved a sigh. "True enough."

"Pyotr, can you direct us to Sir Charles's hotel on Rue de Varenne?" Leonida demanded. "Preferably by a means that will call the least attention to our departure from the hotel."

"Of course. This way."

There was a brief delay as Sophy insisted on neatly pinning Leonida's hair beneath the veiled hat and smoothing the crepe gown, then they were out of the garden and traveling through a maze of narrow alleys.

They walked in silence, Pyotr leading the way. Within moments, Leonida was utterly lost. From the shadows it was impossible to keep track of where they were headed, but trusting in her groom, Leonida followed his quick pace.

"Good lord. This is certainly a...pungent route," she muttered as Pyotr slowed his steps and peered around the edge of the alley.

"Sorry, Miss."

"No, Pyotr, it was my notion to avoid attention," she reassured her groom. There was no one to blame but herself for their current troubles. "We could not have escaped from the hotel without your assistance."

Sophy clicked her tongue. "Don't be making his head any bigger than it is."

Ignoring the teasing, Pyotr pointed a finger. "The hotel is just across the street."

Moving to stand at his side, Leonida regarded the white stone building with wrought-iron trellises and uniformed servants standing at the door.

Her heart sank at the realization this would not be quite so simple as she had imagined. Respectable women, even widows, did not visit gentlemen in their private hotel rooms.

"I did not consider the notion of how I would actually approach the man," she breathed, silently cursing herself for her stupidity. A woman could hardly request to be shown to a gentleman's apartments.

"Do you want me to fetch the man for you?" Pyotr requested.

"Perhaps that would be for the best. I—" Leonida jerked in surprise as a man approached the hotel, his brutish features and mud-brown hair all too familiar. "*Mon Dieu.*"

Pyotr dropped his bags and pulled a pistol from the pocket of his jacket.

"What is it?"

"That man."

"A rough sort," Sophy said, moving to her side. "I wonder what he's doing at this hotel?"

"He is the ruffian who threatened me in England."

Without warning, Sophy was digging into the small leather case she carried.

"Do you want me to shoot him?" she demanded, pulling out a small pistol.

Leonida choked back a small laugh, not doubting for a moment the bloodthirsty maid would happily shoot the man in the back.

"For God's sake, no."

"He's going to get away."

"Sophy, please put that gun away," Leonida pleaded. "I must think."

The maid gave a shake of her head. "We cannot linger here, Miss Leonida. Soon enough the locals are going to decide that our few coins are worth risking the guillotine."

Leonida glanced over her shoulder, shivering as she realized that several pairs of eyes were regarding them from behind filthy windows.

"Shall I fetch Sir Charles?" Pyotr asked softly.

"No." Leonida sucked in a calming breath. "It is too much a coincidence that Sir Charles is staying at the same hotel as the man who attacked me at Meadowland. I knew there was something odd in his manner during our encounter. Clearly he knew who I was all along." Frustrated fear clenched at her heart. "Still, we have to get out of Paris."

"We could buy tickets on a public carriage," Sophy offered. "There must be some that travel to the north."

"That was my thought, as well, but I fear we would be far too easy to track." Leonida once again went through their limited list of alternatives, heaving a sigh as she accepted there really were none left. "I suppose I have no choice. Now that my presence here is known I might as well present myself to the Russian ambassador and request the funds we need..."

"No, it is too dangerous," Sophy broke in with a stubborn frown.

"Sophy is right," Pyotr added. "If I were searching for you, I would keep a close watch on the Embassy. It is the logical place for you to go."

Leonida understood the risk. It was the only reason she had not approached the Embassy the moment they had entered Paris.

"But I do not possess the funds to purchase a carriage and still have enough to provide for our journey."

A hard smile touched Pyotr's lips. "I will take care of the carriage. Meet me at *Jardin des Tuileries* in an hour."

"How on earth..."

"One hour," he repeated, then before Leonida could protest, he had turned to slip back down the alley.

"Best do as he says," Sophy warned, putting away her gun and gathering the baggage the groom had left behind. "Pyotr can be quite forceful when he has his mind set on a thing."

"Clearly," Leonida said dryly. She bent down to grasp her own case, glancing up and down the busy street. Without her groom, she dare not use the alleys. Which unfortunately meant taking the risk of being spotted by the mysterious Sir Charles. "We cannot wait here."

"No."

Gathering her tattered courage, Leonida waited for the large group of schoolgirls being herded by grim-faced nuns to reach the alley. Tugging on Sophy's arm, she darted among the giggling crowd.

"Hurry, Sophy."

"Where are we going?" the maid muttered.

"It seems we will discover when we get there."

Resisting the urge to glance over her shoulder and ensure they were not being followed, Leonida allowed herself to be swept along with the schoolgirls. It was not until they were several streets from the hotel that she urged Sophy away from the group and headed in what she hoped was the direction of the Seine.

There were the inevitable wrong turns, but eventually Leonida managed to stumble across the *Rue de Rivoli* and, swiftly finding her bearings, she led her maid deeper into the large gardens that were famous for their magnificent statues by Coustou and Maillol as well as the beautifully manicured lawns and shrubberies. It would, perhaps, be more sensible to stroll close to the street where she could easily be seen by Pyotr, but the nearby arcades made her wary.

If Sir Charles Richards was indeed in league with her enemies then he might very well be keeping an eye upon the shops in the hope she would return. She could only trust in Pyotr to find them.

Barely able to breathe, Leonida strolled through the gardens that had been created for Louis XIV by his famous gardener, Le Notre. Her arm was aching from holding her heavy bag and there was a sick sensation in the pit of her stomach, but she dare not halt to rest. Perhaps she was being overly cautious, but at the moment it felt as if all of Paris was searching for her.

They reached the edge of the gardens and Leonida wryly regarded the monument that marked the site where Joan of Arc had been wounded. At the moment she fully sympathized with the poor girl. Being hounded and chased by ruthless enemies was a great deal more nerve-wracking than it seemed between the pages of a book.

Momentarily lost in her thoughts, it came as a welcome interruption when Sophy impatiently tugged on her sleeve.

"There is Pyotr," she hissed.

Turning her head, Leonida spotted the servant standing near the street, his craggy face hard with concern until he caught sight of them. With obvious relief, he lifted his hand and motioned for them to join him.

Leonida hurried forward, Sophy at her side.

"Pyotr, did you—"

"This way," the groom interrupted, turning to lead them down the street, halting at a gleaming black carriage with gold trim and red leather upholstery.

It was sleek and expensive and pulled by a pair of matching gray horses that would each cost more than she currently possessed.

"Good heavens. Where did you get this?"

"I noted it behind the wheelwright's shop this morning." Pyotr smiled with a smug satisfaction. "He obviously had decided to repair it before working upon our own."

Leonida's eyes widened. "You returned to the wheelwright?"

"I approached the shop from the back mews and once I had the carriage I drove about the streets until I could be certain I was not followed," her groom assured her.

"I told you we could trust Pyotr," Sophy said with a fond glance at the groom.

"So you did." Without warning, Leonida began to laugh.

Both servants regarded her as if she had taken leave of her senses.

"What is it?" Pyotr demanded.

"I am just imagining that damned wheelwright's expression when the owner of the carriage discovers it is missing."

WHEN STEFAN AT LAST AWOKE, he briefly wished he hadn't.

Christ. His shoulder ached, his mouth was as dry as an African desert, his purse had been stolen, and Leonida was missing.

Again.

Just as aggravating, his servants and seemingly half the hotel staff were clustered about his bed, all of them fluttering their hands and arguing what was to be done with the unconscious Duke.

With a few short words he had the hotel staff dismissed and his own servants on the hunt for Leonida.

Only Boris refused to obey his commands, stoically insisting on cleaning and tending to the wound before allowing Stefan to change into fresh attire.

The hulking Russian had been Edmond's devoted servant for years and when Stefan had set off from Meadowland he had silently joined the three large grooms that Stefan had chosen to accompany him.

Stefan had dismissed any impulse to send the Russian back to his meddling brother. Edmond was without a doubt stubborn enough to lock him in the cellars of Meadowland if Stefan did not give in to Boris's presence.

Finishing the knot in his cravat, Stefan turned as there was a knock on the door. Before he could move, however,

Boris was crossing the room, his hand in his pocket where he had placed his pistol.

With a frustrated curse, Stefan wandered toward the window, gazing down at the narrow garden.

Night had fallen and the elegant streets of Paris were bathed in the glow of the gas lighting. Even to the most jaded eye it was a beautiful sight, but Stefan barely noticed. His thoughts were consumed with the knowledge that Leonida was out there somewhere. And that someone wanted her dead.

He heard the door close, then the clink of china.

"The tray you ordered, your Grace," Boris announced.

It took Stefan a moment to gather his composure. An explosive combination of fury and a sharp fear that Leonida was already in the hands of her enemy clutched at his heart. The violent emotions were not at all satisfied to be trapped in the damnable hotel awaiting his servants to complete their search.

Thankfully he possessed enough common sense to settle at the small table Boris had procured and forced himself to eat the roasted pheasant and potatoes in cream sauce before pouring a cup of coffee in the hopes it would clear his still foggy brain.

Damn Leonida and her laudanum.

Of course, he had to admire her swift intelligence and brazen courage. What other woman would have so neatly outwitted him?

Settling back in his chair, Stefan sipped at the hot coffee and sternly reminded himself that there was nothing admirable in leaving a man shot and drugged in a nasty Paris hotel room.

Or being so stupid as to dash off with only her maid and groom when she was obviously being hunted by dangerous ruffians willing to put a bullet through her heart.

"What of Miss Karkoff?" he at last demanded, glancing up at the large servant hovering beside the table.

"She is not in the hotel."

"You are certain?" he asked, not putting it beyond the clever wench to have hidden herself in the attics until he had hurried off in search of her.

The large servant who looked more a prize fighter met his gaze squarely, his expression assuring Stefan that not the smallest closet had been overlooked.

"Absolutely."

"Damn."

"She will be found."

"Did you check on her carriage?"

"It remains at the wheelwright's." He paused. "But it seems that another carriage mysteriously disappeared. The owner of the shop is currently attempting to explain the disappearance to a furious Count Schuster."

His brows lifted. "Miss Karkoff stole a carriage?"

"I cannot say that for certain."

With a wry shake of his head, Stefan rose to his feet. Leonida was proving to be aggravatingly resourceful.

"It would seem the chase is on yet again."

"May I speak frankly, your Grace?"

Stefan swallowed a sigh of impatience, already knowing what was on the servant's mind.

"Of course, Boris."

"Perhaps you should consider returning to England." His gaze shifted to Stefan's shoulder. "It is obvious that Miss Karkoff has acquired some very dangerous enemies."

"Yes, she does appear to have spoken the truth in that at least."

"Lord Summerville would be very displeased if you were shot dead."

"I would not be excessively pleased myself."

"He would desire that I return you to your home."

"Your sage advice is duly noted, Boris, but Edmond knows me well enough to realize that once I set upon a course I will not be dissuaded." He offered the servant a faint smile. "You will not be blamed for my untimely death."

Boris furrowed his brow. "As you say."

Stefan stilled, sensing the servant's tension. "Is there more?"

"Miss Karkoff is well loved in Russia. She is one of the few close to the Romanovs who urges a less brutal repression of the peasants and is well-known to generously contribute to a number of charities."

"Commendable, but I am not certain I comprehend your warning."

"Once Miss Karkoff enters Russia only a fool would dare to cause her harm," Boris explained, his voice hard. "Not unless he wishes to be attacked by an angry mob."

Stefan sighed. How the devil had he gotten into such a mess? A deceitful, thieving lover who had drugged him and was now determined to escape him. Mysterious enemies lurking in the shadows. Angry mobs...

Hardly the sort of existence the Duke of Huntley was accustomed to.

Not that he was about to be deterred. When he set his mind on a prize, nothing was allowed to thwart his will. Whether it was a rare first edition, a prized bull or a woman who haunted his dreams.

"Then we must find Miss Karkoff before she reaches Russia."

"There is a vast amount of land between here and St. Petersburg."

"The sooner we begin our hunt, the sooner it will end."

The servant offered a grudging bow. "As you wish."

Stefan pulled on his gloves, his brow furrowed as he recalled the desperation in Leonida's eyes as she had given him one last kiss.

"Boris."

"Yes, your Grace?"

"Can you think of any reason Countess Karkoff would have sent her daughter to England?"

Boris thought a long moment. As Edmond's servant

and confidant, the man probably knew more about the workings of the Russian court than most so-called nobles.

"Countess Karkoff has always harbored great ambition for her daughter, but is also known to be excessively protective of her," he said slowly. "There is only one reason I can imagine she would be willing to put her at risk."

"And what is that?"

"Alexander Pavlovich," he grudgingly admitted. "The Countess has devoted her life to protecting his throne. I don't think she would consider any sacrifice too great."

Without warning a blistering anger ran through Stefan's blood.

The selfish bitch. If it were true, the woman had not only sent her innocent daughter to a foreign land to commit who knew what sort of thievery, but she had put Leonida's life in genuine peril.

If not for him, she might very well be lying dead in this Paris hotel.

"She would sacrifice anything to protect Alexander Pavlovich's throne or her own position of power among the court?" he rasped.

Boris acknowledged the truth of his words with a faint dip of his head. "As you say."

"Damn the woman."

MERE STREETS AWAY, Sir Charles Richards was in a mood as foul as that of the Duke of Huntley.

Granted his hotel apartments were far superior and included a bedchamber as well as an elegant *salle* that was furbished with a great deal of damask and gilt, but he took little pleasure in his surroundings.

Only this morning one of his servants had arrived from St. Petersburg to warn that Dimitri Tipova was growing tired of waiting for his money. Either Sir Charles returned to pay the vast sum or the entire world would discover his nasty little secret.

It was the only reason he had been provoked into such an outrageous scheme.

He *had* to get his hands on those letters before that filthy bandit began spreading word of the missing whores, or worse, decided to have an English nobleman's head mounted on his wall.

Of course, it had been nothing less than a disaster.

Now, he was standing in the center of the *salle,* glaring with icy displeasure at the mammoth servant currently perched uncomfortably on the edge of a delicate chair.

"So, what you are telling me is that after having failed to prevent Miss Karkoff from discovering the letters hidden at Meadowland and allowing her to slip away from England, you have now failed in your task to put a bullet through her heart and instead wounded the Duke of Huntley." His soft voice held a lethal edge that made the servant pale in prudent fear. "A gentleman who is not only wealthy and powerful, but a particular favorite of the King of England."

"It was not my fault."

"No, it never is, is it, Yuri?"

Yuri clenched his meaty hands around the scrolled arms of the chair. "You told me she would be alone."

"And so, instead of waiting until she actually was alone, you risked leading every King's Guard in Paris directly to my door?" Charles purred.

"There were no guards called."

Charles narrowed his gaze. The Duke of Huntley had been shot and the authorities had not been notified? Unheard of.

"You are certain?"

"Yes."

"Why the bloody hell would Huntley allow himself to be shot without demanding justice?" Charles paced the floor, contemplating the strange puzzle. He had been so furious when Yuri confessed that he'd failed to shoot the

Karkoff bitch and retrieve the letters that he had not given much thought to the presence of Huntley. Now he realized that the Duke must have followed Miss Karkoff from England. The damnable brat had obviously made a conquest. "He must be protecting the female."

"It would seem so."

"He cannot be with her constantly. Return to the hotel and finish your task when Miss Karkoff is alone. Do not return without those letters."

The servant cleared his throat. "As to that…"

"What is it now, Yuri?"

"Knowing how much you were wanting them letters I waited a bit and then attempted to sneak into the hotel."

"How very enterprising of you."

The servant flushed at Charles's mocking tone. "I overheard the staff talking."

"And why would I be interested in the gossip of servants?"

"Because they were saying that they seen the Russian widow slipping out the kitchens with a bag in her hand. They were thinking she was attempting to avoid paying her bill."

Charles stilled, a red mist beginning to form behind his eyes. "What did you say?"

Yuri licked his dry lips. "She left the hotel."

"Her servants?"

"Gone."

"And you did not consider the notion of telling me this pertinent piece of information until this moment?" Charles softly demanded.

Not entirely stupid, Yuri surged to his feet, perhaps reading his own death etched onto Charles's face.

"She cannot have gone far. I will—"

"No, I think not." Before the lumbering servant could react, Charles had his dagger pulled from his pocket and thrust into the man's heart. "You have failed me for the last time, Yuri."

CHAPTER THIRTEEN

Prussia

STEFAN HAD NEVER CONSIDERED himself particularly conceited.

Certainly his ducal position had ensured that very few ever dared to question his commands. And his temperament, while not turbulent, was resolute.

Still, it was not until he endured endless days of chasing Leonida through France and deep into Prussia that he became aware that he had never before had his will so annoyingly thwarted.

And he damn well did not like it.

The woman should be at Meadowland—warming his bed, gracing his table, cozily tucked in the library as he read to her from his favorite books. Not risking her neck on some foolish scheme for Countess Karkoff.

Halting at a small village just north of Leipzig, Stefan crawled out of his carriage, pacing the stable yard with short, restless steps as he waited for Boris to return from his questioning of the staff at the nearby posting inn.

He had discovered early in their journey that the presence of the Duke of Huntley made most servants either too tongue-tied to speak or encouraged them to make any claim in an effort to please him. And then there was always the fear that King Fredrick would hear rumors of a prominent Englishman traveling through his territory and issue the sort of invitation that Stefan would find difficult to ignore.

It was far less complicated to allow Boris to approach the natives.

Absently studying the ruins of a castle on a nearby bluff, Stefan attempted to ignore the speculative glances from the passing villagers. He could hardly blame them for their curiosity. It was not often such a sleepy town saw an elegant carriage pulled by two matching black stallions or a gentleman so richly attired in a cinnamon jacket with a cream waistcoat and black pantaloons that were tucked into gleaming Hessians.

At last, Stefan heard the heavy sound of Boris's approaching footsteps and, turning, he stabbed the servant with an impatient glance.

"Well?"

"The stable boy admitted that he recognized the carriage I described and that a veiled lady with two servants spent the night at the inn."

"When?"

"The night before last. We are gaining."

Stefan clenched his hands. "Too slowly."

Boris shrugged. "There is more."

"What?"

"According to the stable boy the widow lingered long enough to trade her elegant carriage for a far inferior vehicle." Boris grimaced. "One that is so common that it could easily be lost among a dozen others just like it."

"Clever minx." Stefan's lips twitched. He was as impressed by her relentless courage as he was relieved at the knowledge that she was still a step ahead of her enemies.

It was absurd how much time he devoted to fretting over her welfare. Christ, he had lain awake last eve worrying whether or not she had a fire to keep her warm. The nights this far north were chilly even in summer.

"She does come from a long line of cunning warriors," Boris pointed out, a hint of pride in his voice. "Czar Peter rebuilt a forgotten land to a massive empire by the sheer power of his will, while Catherine seized the throne and civilized the nation."

"And Alexander Pavlovich?" Stefan demanded dryly, at the moment thoroughly out of charity with the current Czar.

Boris shrugged. "He rescued us from a madman."

"He was not alone in battling Napoleon."

"Ah." A strange smile touched the servant's lips. "I had nearly forgotten. Two madmen."

Stefan lifted his brows, belatedly realizing that Boris had been referring to Alexander Pavlovich's father, Emperor Paul.

The previous Czar had propitiously died when Alexander was a mere twenty-four years of age. No one mourned the loss of the brutal Paul, but the whispers that Alexander had assisted in sending the previous Czar to his timely death, and even stepped over his cold body to take the throne, had haunted the Emperor for years.

"It is a dangerous business to be born a Romanov."

"Russia is a harsh land that breeds those capable of surviving. The weak are not tolerated."

Stefan narrowed his gaze. "Is there something you are trying to tell me, Boris?"

"Englishwomen are taught that being modest and well-behaved are admirable traits," he said, a sudden smile curving his lips. "Although there are those females, such as my wife, who do not heed such teachings."

Stefan snorted, well aware that Janet, who was also Brianna's maid, was firmly in charge of Boris. The woman would terrify the most stout-hearted man.

"Implying Englishwomen are placid and boring?"

Boris shrugged. "They prefer to use charm to beguile a gentleman."

"And Russian women?"

"Passionate, volatile and occasionally dangerous. Most importantly they will not hesitate to do whatever necessary to protect those they love."

Stefan abruptly turned away, a queer ache blooming in the center of his heart.

He could not deny that Leonida made every other woman of his acquaintance pale in comparison. It was not that she was flamboyant or tempestuous. Quite the opposite, in fact. She was much like his mother. A stunningly beautiful woman with a calm composure that disguised a generous heart and a fierce loyalty to her family.

"I will find her," he muttered beneath his breath.

"Best sooner than later."

Stefan turned back to meet Boris's steady gaze. "Is there something you haven't told me?"

"I was not the first to approach the stable boy with questions regarding a young widow with a maid and Russian groom."

"Damn." A chill crept down his spine. "Did you discover anything of who was asking the questions?"

"A fancy silver-haired Englishman who possessed several large guards who the stable boy claimed terrorized the village."

Stefan frowned, caught by surprise. "Englishman?"

"He was quite certain of that, although the man never offered his name."

"This affair grows more confusing by the day," Stefan growled. "What Englishman could possibly be interested in Russian politics?"

"Any number, I should say."

Stefan shook his head. What did it matter? Whoever this Englishman might be, he would not be allowed to harm Leonida. Not even if Stefan had to rip his damned heart out of his chest.

"When did he pass through here?"

"Early this morning."

A sharp unease clawed at him. If he were too late…

"We travel too slowly," he snapped. "We will never catch Leonida at this pace."

"We know she is headed to St. Petersburg. It would be much quicker if we were not forced to halt at every village to inquire if Miss Karkoff has passed through."

"No," he swiftly dismissed the suggestion. "Her enemies are too close. We cannot risk losing her trail."

Boris smiled. "You are concerned for a thief and a deceiver?"

Stefan made no effort to disguise his resolve. "She is mine and I will have her."

A beat passed as Boris considered what his master, Lord Summerville, would desire him to do. Then, obviously deciding that nothing short of knocking Stefan unconscious and hauling him back to England would halt him, he heaved a resigned sigh.

"Not at this pace, you won't."

"True." Stefan turned his head to regard the nearby stables.

"What are you scheming?"

"I want you to hire a mount. I prefer dependability to beauty."

"And then?"

"Then I desire you to travel with my servants to St. Petersburg. I shall meet you there."

"No."

Stefan turned back to discover Boris scowling at him with his arms folded across his barrel chest.

"I beg your pardon?" he said silkily.

"Lord Summerville threatened to have me gelded if I allowed you out of my sight," Boris muttered, refusing to back down. "I have already failed you once, it will not happen again."

Stefan's expression eased. "You failed no one, Boris," he reassured the large servant. "I have long outgrown the need for a nanny, despite my brother's lowly opinion of my skills."

"You may send your servants and carriage to St. Petersburg if you wish, but I am remaining with you."

"And you do not believe that Janet will do her own share of gelding if I allow anything to happen to you?"

Boris chuckled. "My wife is certain to blame her thick-skulled husband and will presume that I got precisely what I deserve."

Stefan rolled his eyes. He did not doubt that Boris would dog his ever step until Edmond was convinced he was safe.

"Very well. Find me a horse and I will speak with my servants."

St. Petersburg
Vasilevsky Ostrov

IN MAY 1703, WHEN THE Emperor Peter first arrived on the island, he had briefly flirted with the notion of building his new Russian capital on the site. For all of his brash will-power, however, Peter had been soundly defeated by nature. The violent storms and unpredictable flooding, along with the constant winds from the Gulf of Finland, made it impractical for the grand city he envisioned.

In the end, he had constructed his fortress on Zayachy Ostrov and his official palaces on the mainland, but he had not entirely given up his scheme for the island. Proclaiming it a location for learning, he had built a museum and observatory as well as St. Petersburg's first university on the eastern side.

The western side was less fortunate. Over the years a series of harbors and warehouses began dotting the bleak landscape, bringing with them an unsavory crowd of rough sailors and peasant workers.

Certainly not a place that the Russian aristocracy cared to visit.

Moving through the dark, narrow warren of streets, Herrick Gerhardt and his faithful guard, Gregor, could feel the threat of suspicious gazes watching their progress toward the abandoned warehouse near the quay.

"If you desired to have your throat slit I can think of several enemies who would be delighted to do the honors in far more elegant surroundings," Gregor muttered.

Herrick smiled, halting in front of the narrow door at the warehouse. The younger man had, quite wisely, been opposed to meeting Dimitri Tipova in the very heart of his criminal empire. After all, more than one foolish official who had sought to put an end to the Beggar Czar had disappeared among the dingy shadows.

Unfortunately, Herrick was in no position to dictate the terms. He was the one to have requested a meeting and since Tipova was hardly likely to risk walking into a trap, Herrick had no choice but to play the game by the criminal's rules.

"I presume you refer to the Summer Palace?" Herrick gently teased his companion.

"The Summer Palace, the Winter Palace, the Senate Square, Kazan Cathedral, the Admiralty, Petropavlovskaya Fortress…"

"Good lord," Herrick interrupted with a chuckle. "Do I have so many enemies?"

"Do not pretend that it is not a source of pride for you."

Herrick shrugged. "If people did not hate me I would not be properly doing my job."

"If others were doing their job properly there would be no need for you to put yourself at risk," Gregor muttered.

"A charming fantasy, Gregor, but no more than that," Herrick softly reprimanded his companion. Whatever his thoughts regarding Alexander Pavlovich, his loyalty was unwavering. He expected the same from those on his staff. "There will always be those who are driven by their lust for power. They will not be satisfied until the crown rests upon their own unworthy heads."

"And you are determined to keep that crown upon Alexander Pavlovich?"

"Better the devil you know."

Gregor offered a stiff dip of his head, unable to deny the truth of Herrick's words.

Alexander Pavlovich might be of a vacillating nature that infuriated his ministers and foreign leaders alike. And there could be no denying he had become distracted and disillusioned over the years. But his love for his people was genuine and his duty to Russia unwavering.

"As you say."

Lifting his hand to knock on the thick door, Herrick was startled as it was suddenly yanked open to reveal a thickset man with a hard face and unmistakable military bearing. At the moment he was wearing a rough smock and breeches, although Herrick would bet his last ruble that was not his usual attire.

A Cossack. Or at least he had been at one time.

"You are Gerhardt?" the man snapped, his gaze taking in Herrick's plain but expensive attire.

"I am."

The man shifted his attention to Gregor. "You were told to come alone."

"This is my guard. He can be trusted."

"You can come with me." The man pointed a finger at Gregor. "He stays here."

Gregor stiffened. "No."

"Be at ease, old friend," Herrick soothed his companion, his gaze never leaving the dangerous stranger. "If Dimitri Tipova desired me dead I do not doubt I would already be lying in a filthy gutter."

The man snorted. "The master prefers to dispose of his enemies with a great deal more decorum. Only bungling fools leave the bodies to be found."

"Vastly reassuring," Herrick commented dryly. "Remain here, Gregor."

The younger man flashed him a sour frown. "You play with fire."

"It will not be the first occasion."

Opening the door wider, the stranger waved a hand. "This way."

Despite the small pistol tucked in a hidden pocket of his black coat and a dagger tucked in his boot, Herrick could not deny a faint unease as he crossed the plank floor. With nothing but moonlight slanting through the broken windows to provide illumination the vast room was shrouded in a darkness that could hide any number of nasty surprises.

Without a word, the man led Herrick to a door that was guarded by two slender men who regarded Herrick with the experienced eye of hardened thieves. They stood aside, but Herrick was thankful he had possessed the foresight to leave his purse and valuables at home.

The door led to a narrow staircase that in turn led to the upper floors of the warehouse and after being scrutinized by two more armed guards, Herrick was led into Dimitri Tipova's private lair.

Herrick was not entirely certain what he expected to find.

Perhaps a huddle of desperate criminals hovering around a fire in some hovel. Or a hidden cellar with rats.

He most definitely had not expected a company of well-trained sentries who possessed the bearing of seasoned soldiers or a shabby warehouse that had been transformed into an exquisite apartment that included a formal parlor, a small dining room, and a library with a collection of books that would be the envy of most Russian nobles.

Thoroughly astonished, Herrick paid no heed as his guide retreated from the room and closed the door behind him. Instead he moved to study the unmistakable Rembrandt hung over a carved marble fireplace.

"Good...God," he breathed.

"I shall take that as a compliment, Mr. Gerhardt," a low voice drawled. "I am quite certain that you are a gentleman who is rarely taken by surprise."

Turning, Herrick studied the man who stepped from a door hidden behind the polished wood paneling.

He was a slender, remarkably handsome gentleman with long raven-black hair that was untouched by gray and pulled into a queue at his nape with a velvet ribbon. His face was thin with aristocratic features and heavy-lidded golden eyes that shimmered with a restless intelligence in the light from the crystal chandeliers.

Attired in a blue velvet jacket with a waistcoat stitched with silver threads and black breeches, he could easily have mixed among the highest of society. In truth, Herrick would swear he had seen nearly identical features on a powerful nobleman just last eve at the Summer Palace.

Perhaps the resemblance should not be unexpected. Many gentlemen littered the streets of St. Petersburg with offspring born on the wrong side of the blanket.

Still, Herrick could not help but accept that his preconceived notions of Dimitri Tipova and how this evening would unfold could not have been more wrong.

The gentleman moved with languid grace to stand beside a mahogany and gilt wood settee covered in Imperial brocaded silk, a faint smile hovering about his finely molded lips.

Accepting that he had been nicely outwitted, Herrick offered a bow of respect.

"Dimitri Tipova, I presume?" he murmured.

"At your service."

Straightening, Herrick discovered himself under inspection from that unnerving golden gaze.

"Thank you for agreeing to meet with me."

"Please, be seated." Waiting for Herrick to settle on a carved mahogany chair with gilded serpents on the back, Tipova toyed with a large diamond stickpin tucked in the folds of his cravat. "I fear my besetting sin has always been my curiosity. My mother swore it would be my downfall."

"And your father?"

The man did not so much as blink at Herrick's smooth thrust. "My father quite wisely suggested that I be drowned at birth."

"But he was willing to pay for your education?" Herrick countered. No Russian serf, no matter how intelligent, was capable of speaking such fluent French without a tutor.

"Willing, no." A sardonic glint entered the golden eyes. "My mother, however, was a formidable lady who harbored great ambition for her son."

"She must be quite proud."

"She is dead."

"Ah." Impossible to know if he grieved beneath that smooth charm. Herrick sensed that few people were ever allowed to see the true Dimitri Tipova. "My sympathies."

"Brandy?" Moving an ebony sideboard, Tipova waved a slender hand. "Or do you prefer tea?"

"Brandy."

Pouring two glasses of the amber spirit, Tipova moved to press one into Herrick's hand before taking his own seat on the nearby settee. Lifting his glass, he flashed Herrick a mocking smile.

"A votre santé!"

Herrick lifted his glass. "To your health."

They sipped the perfectly aged brandy, then, setting aside his glass, Tipova stretched out his legs and crossed them at the ankles.

"Now perhaps you will be good enough to tell me what brings you to my modest corner of the empire?"

"It is my belief that we possess a common enemy."

"Actually, I should say we possess any number of common enemies."

Herrick narrowed his gaze, instantly intrigued by the notion of just how valuable an agent among the underworld could prove to be.

"Indeed?"

Tipova waved a slender hand, clearly satisfied by having planted his seed in Herrick's mind.

"A conversation for another day."

"Very well," Herrick graciously conceded, already determined this would not be his last visit with the astonishing criminal.

"Does this common enemy have a name?"

"Sir Charles Richards."

For the first time, Tipova appeared disconcerted. Then, tilting back his head, he laughed with rich enjoyment.

"I knew you would not disappoint me, Gerhardt."

"You know him?"

Pulling a thin cheroot from his pocket, Tipova lit it from a candle set on the jade inlaid table.

"First I desire you to tell me what interest you have in the Englishman.

"Can I have your assurance of discretion?"

A dark brow arched. "Would you trust me if I gave you my word?"

Herrick did not hesitate. His true talent had always lain in reading a person's character.

"Yes."

The golden eyes flared with an indefinable emotion. "Then you have it."

Herrick came straight to the point. "It is possible that Sir Charles is currently blackmailing a prominent member of the Russian court."

"I see."

"You do not appear particularly surprised."

"I will admit that I am occasionally a wicked man, *mon ami.* I am ruthless, fond of luxury and beautiful women, and not overly concerned with the morals that plague others." He paused, his jaw tightening. "But I am not evil. There is nothing you could tell me regarding Sir Charles that would come as a surprise."

"Evil." Herrick felt an answering revulsion toward Sir

Charles. If the rumors were true the Englishman deserved to be skinned and left for the rats to gnaw on. "Yes, a perfect description."

The brief display of anger was swiftly hidden behind Tipova's engaging smile.

"Besides, I suspected he must be doing something of the sort."

"And why would you suspect such a thing?"

"Because, my dear Gerhardt, I am blackmailing *him*."

Herrick did not bother to act surprised. It was precisely what he had assumed and why he had sought out this meeting in the first place.

"Would you be willing to share the details of what you hold over the man?"

"Only if you are willing to be equally forthcoming."

A flare of insight prevented Herrick from uttering the threat that hovered on his lips. Dimitri Tipova devoted his life to flouting the rules and daring the authorities to try and toss him into prison.

No. He would never be intimidated.

"You know that is not possible," Herrick retorted.

"Then it would appear we are at a tragic impasse."

Herrick drummed his fingers on the arm of his chair, easily shifting tactics.

"Are you are aware that Sir Charles has left St. Petersburg?"

"I had surmised as much."

"Do you happen to know where he has gone?"

"I have a fair notion."

"Will you share the information with me?"

"That depends."

"On what?"

With a smooth motion Tipova was on his feet, moving to toss his cheroot into the fire. When he turned back, Herrick was offered a glimpse of the brutal ambitions that drove this unique man.

"Sir Charles offered me a grave insult. The kind of insult that demands retribution." His lips twisted. "Since you have become involved I must conclude that I have no hope of acquiring the money I requested."

"None whatsoever."

"Then I must have some means to have my justice."

"What do you want?"

A chilling smile curved his lips. "Sir Charles."

"You wish to teach him a lesson?"

"No, Sir Charles is incapable of learning. His impulses cannot be resisted even if he wished to do so, which I assure you he does not." He met and held Herrick's gaze. "The lesson is for any other gentleman foolish enough to flout my rules."

Herrick rose to his feet. "Do you truly believe I will hand over an English nobleman to his certain death?"

"You understand duty, Gerhardt. You have devoted your life to protecting the interests of the Romanovs." Tipova's voice held an edge of cynicism. "An admirable goal perhaps, but who is to protect those poor souls who do not fall beneath the shelter of your fine officials?"

"You?"

The handsome villain shrugged. "Mock if you will, but I do not allow my children to be harmed by anyone."

In a peculiar way, Herrick found himself greatly admiring Tipova. Indeed, it was a great pity the man could not claim his noble blood. He possessed a great deal more courage and intelligence than the majority of the aristocrats who littered the Russian court.

Strolling toward a satinwood desk that held a varied collection of enamel snuff boxes, Herrick absently considered the outrageous request.

On the one hand, he was naturally reluctant to hand over an English blue blood to a self-proclaimed criminal. The relationship between Alexander Pavlovich and George IV was strained at best. Who knew if the fat British monarch would decide to make an unpleasant fuss?

On the other hand, Herrick was swiftly reaching a point of unpleasant desperation.

For the past few weeks Nadia had been besieged by the nasty Nikolas Babevich demanding that she either pay or have her letters exposed to the world. Herrick had attempted to reassure the nervous Countess that there was nothing to fear. Clearly Babevich did not possess the letters or he would have offered proof. Nadia, however, refused to be comforted and since her distress was becoming obvious to the Emperor, Herrick had been forced to follow even the most remote clues to the true master behind the threat.

Which meant he had to get his hands on Sir Charles Richards.

Slowly turning, he offered his host a small dip of his head. "Very well."

The golden eyes blazed with triumph. "You will give me Sir Charles?"

"Yes."

"Your word?"

Herrick smiled. "Will you trust my word?"

"Oddly enough, I will. Most peculiar."

"My thought exactly."

They shared a glance of mutual understanding, then clasping his hands behind his back, Tipova strolled to the center of the delicate Persian carpet.

"Sir Charles was in Paris."

"Paris?" Herrick's brows snapped together. "What business does he have in France?"

"It could be he is attempting to avoid my wrath. A foolish mistake." The criminal deliberately paused. "Or perhaps he was drawn there by the rumors that the charming Miss Karkoff is currently staying in England and desires to keep a close, but secretive, eye upon her."

Herrick froze in unpleasant shock. It did not seem

possible that anyone, let alone a lawless rogue, could know his closest held secrets. It was not only a blow to his considerable pride, but it was a potential threat he would not endure.

"You are not entirely impervious to being hauled before a firing squad, Tipova," he said, his cold warning unmistakable.

"I am rarely stupid, *mon ami*. For me, information is like my priceless treasures." Tipova stroked a finger along an ancient Chinese vase on the mantle. "I collect them for my own pleasure, and only when I am certain of a profit that offers no risk to me do I agree to sell them."

"A dangerous hobby."

Tipova gave a sudden, unexpected chuckle. "Come, Gerhardt, I would not be at odds with you. Indeed, I shall offer you a rather pertinent piece of information to prove my goodwill."

Herrick's hard expression did not ease. "What is that?"

"Before his arrival in St. Petersburg Sir Charles enjoyed a prolonged stay in Paris with an old friend."

"Old friend?"

"A Mr. Howard Summerville who was forced to retreat to the Continent last year when his bill collectors became tediously persistent."

Herrick frowned. "A relation to Lord Summerville?"

"A cousin to the Duke of Huntley, although the rumors are that there is a strain in the relationship between the two families."

Herrick smiled with grim satisfaction. At last he had a direct connection from St. Petersburg to Meadowland. "That is it," he breathed. "Is Sir Charles still in Paris?"

"The last I heard he had left rather abruptly and was traveling north."

"Back to St. Petersburg?"

"That would be my guess."

A sharp fear pierced Herrick's heart. "Why would he return now?"

Dimitri met his gaze squarely. "Obviously because he is on the trail of his prey."

Herrick sucked in a sharp breath.

Leonida.

Damn. What had Nadia been thinking to send her innocent daughter on such a journey? The beautiful Countess had always been impetuous. But this went beyond the pale.

Unfortunately, he had not learned of the scheme until Leonida had already arrived in England. Far beyond his ability to protect her.

Damn. He had to return to his office and begin organizing a search for Sir Charles Richards. Now.

The bastard would not be given the chance to harm Leonida.

Herrick offered his companion a small bow. "I thank you, Dimitri Tipova, for your information. I am in your debt."

"Yes, you are." The golden eyes glinted with a mocking humor. "And I always collect."

CHAPTER FOURTEEN

Russia

THE SMALL INN SOME SIXTY MILES from St. Petersburg was a squat building that appeared to be in imminent danger of being consumed by the encroaching woodlands.

Inside there was little to recommend the shabby establishment to passing travelers. The rooms were cramped with stone walls, rough planked floors and open timber ceilings. Even the private parlor that Leonida requested was a barren room with a dining table in the center of the floor and two cushioned chairs near the fireplace that she had asked be lit despite the grumbling complaints of the slovenly innkeeper.

If she had not been aching from head to toe from their endless flight, not to mention starving, Leonida would never have given in to Pyotr's insistence that they halt for the night. Not only did she doubt the cleanliness of her chambers, but the persistent knowledge she was being pursued by dangerous enemies made it nearly impossible to rest.

Huddled near the fire as night fell and a decided chill entered the air, Leonida desperately attempted to ignore her grimy surroundings and the pervasive scent of fried onions.

Soon she would be home, she bolstered her flagging spirits. Once she had reached St. Petersburg and the protection of her family no one would dare lay a hand upon her. Not even the arrogant Duke of Huntley.

Oddly the knowledge did not offer the comfort she

hoped for. In fact, there was something perilously close to regret tugging at her heart.

Mon Dieu. Had she gone completely mad?

With an angry click of her tongue she forced herself to imagine the luxurious comfort of her mother's home and the blissful peace of being able to spend an entire day without fear of being exposed as a fraud.

She would be safe and happy and, in time, any thought of Stefan would fade to nothing.

Luckily, her thoughts were interrupted by a maid entering the parlor. She preferred not to dwell on the fear that Stefan would never be forgotten. That he might haunt her dreams for years to come.

"Your dinner, Madam," the servant murmured, setting the tray on the table.

"Thank you." Leonida moved to take a seat, grimacing at the bowl of greasy fish stew and loaf of crusty bread that looked to be at least a week old. She had hardly anticipated such an establishment to possess a talented chef, but this was even worse than she expected. "Have you seen my maid?"

The middle-aged female, who was surprisingly tidy, with a pair of shrewd brown eyes, considered a moment. "Last I seen, she was headed toward the stables."

Leonida smiled wistfully. Of course, Sophy would desire some time alone with Pyotr. There could be no mistaking the growing fondness between her two servants.

"Very well. That will be all," she said, dismissing the maid, and resigned herself to eating her dubious meal alone.

Leonida was busy choking down her meal when the sound of raised voices outside the door had her rising to her feet and hastily tugging on her veiled bonnet.

It had been early enough when she had arrived that the taproom had been empty of customers, but it sounded as if it had rapidly filled with the sort of drunken louts who were not happy unless they were starting a fight.

She momentarily debated the wisdom of returning to

her upstairs chambers. At least there she could bar the door against the other guests. Unfortunately, she would have to pass directly by the taproom to reach the stairs, and it did not seem particularly desirable to draw attention.

In the end, the decision was taken out of her hands as the door to the parlor was pushed open and a tall, handsome gentleman entered the room.

Her heart slammed against her chest as recognition hit.

Sir Charles Richards.

Horror held her captive as the unwelcome intruder carefully closed the door and tossed aside his hat and gloves. Then, straightening the lace that peeked from beneath the sleeves of his tightly molded black jacket, he at last strolled across the floor to stand directly before her.

"There will be no need to hide your beautiful face, Miss Karkoff." A cruel smile curved his lips as he yanked off her bonnet and tossed it on the floor. "There should be no secrets between friends."

Cold dread twisted her stomach. She had already suspected that this man was involved with her enemies. Now there could be no doubt.

Resisting the cowardly urge to faint, Leonida instead conjured a stiff expression.

"Sir Charles, whatever are you doing here?"

"Following you, of course," he said blandly, his eyes hard. "You have led me a merry dance, but at last we come to the conclusion of our waltz."

"Pray, why would you wish to follow me?"

"Why?" He reached into the pocket of his jacket to remove a dagger, angling it until the firelight danced off the long, lethal blade. "Because you have something that belongs to me."

Any hope of pretense was forgotten as Leonida hastily backed from the intruder.

"Stay away from me or I will scream," she rasped.

"Now that would be a pity." His fingers stroked the

dagger, as if he took a disturbing pleasure in the feel of the scrolled silver handle. "I have regrettably had the staff of this humble inn gathered into the kitchens with the order to shoot anyone foolish enough to interrupt our charming reunion."

Her mouth went dry, the scream dying on her lips. She would not endanger innocent Russians. And what of Sophy and Pyotr? *Please God, allow them to be unharmed.*

"I find nothing charming in this reunion. Nor will my family when they discover you have accosted me."

He sneered at her sharp warning. "Do you think I fear the mighty Alexander Pavlovich?"

"I think you are a madman."

His features tightened, as if infuriated by her accusation. Then, with an obvious effort, he regained command of his icy composure.

"True. And a rather costly madness as it turns out. Thankfully you are my means of extricating myself from a decidedly nasty situation."

She licked her dry lips. "I have only a few rubles with me…"

Her words broke off with a gasp as he reached out to grasp her arm, jerking her forward to press the dagger against her throat.

"The letters, Miss Karkoff. Give them to me." The point threatened to penetrate her vulnerable skin. "Now."

Leonida's heart thundered so loudly she could barely think. She had always thought herself a woman of unquestionable courage. A true Romanov. It was humiliating to realize she desperately wanted to hand over the letters to be rid of this revolting man.

In truth, he terrified her beyond reason.

There was something…evil that shimmered in those frozen black eyes. As if his soul had been stolen and there was nothing within him but a cold, calculating hatred.

Sadly, the fear had not entirely rattled her wits.

Handing over the letters would accomplish nothing.

Only her own cunning and a great deal of luck would save her from tragedy.

"I do not know what you speak of," she said.

"At any other time I might find a certain pleasure in making you speak the truth, my dear." He lifted his free hand to stroke his fingers over her cheek. "Such beautiful, alabaster skin. So deliciously unmarred. Almost you tempt me." His smile twisted as Leonida shuddered in revulsion. "But, no. Today my haste demands a more brutal tactic." The dagger pressed hard enough to draw blood. "The letters."

She struggled to speak. "I do not have them."

"You think me stupid? I know you traveled to Meadowland."

"My mother was dear friends with the Duchess of Huntley. She wished me to become acquainted with the family."

"She wished to get her pretty hands on those letters." His eyes narrowed. "Do not bother to lie."

She paused for a heartbeat, acutely aware of the unnatural silence that filled the inn. She had never felt so unbearably alone.

"Very well," she at last conceded. "My mother did charge me to find the letters, but they were not there."

"That would be a great deal more convincing if you had not slipped away from the fine estate in the middle of the night with the Duke of Huntley fast on your trail," Sir Charles drawled.

"Of course I left in a hurry," she hastily improvised. "There was a strange man who approached me in the gardens and threatened to kill me. I was frightened, so I fled before he could harm me or my servants."

The dark eyes flashed. "Ah, yes. Yuri. Such a disappointment. You will be happy to know he will never again impose himself on a beautiful young woman."

Her breath caught. "He is…"

"Quite right, my dear. He is dead." There was no regret,

just dark satisfaction. "No doubt his body will eventually be found on the banks of the Seine. You need never fear him again."

"I would be considerably more relieved if I did not have a knife to my throat."

"An unfortunate necessity. If only you would cooperate, our encounter could be far more civilized."

"I have told you I did not find the letters. What more do you want from me?"

The dark eyes flared with a cold fury. "Do you truly believe me incapable of slitting your throat?"

She did not bother to hide her fear. "I not only believe you capable, but I am convinced that you intend to do so regardless of whether I have the letters or not."

"Such a clever little puss," he mocked. "Still, I assure you that your inevitable death can be one of swift ease or it can be messy, and I fear, extraordinarily painful. Your choice, Miss Karkoff, but I do suggest you give me the letters."

Nothing had ever been so difficult as meeting his soulless gaze without flinching.

"I cannot give you what I do not possess."

"We shall soon discover."

His hand tightened on the handle of the dagger, a blaze of anticipation in his eyes. Then, like a gift from heaven, there was a sudden rap on the door. Leonida stiffened, terrified for a dreadful moment that the madman would simply ignore the disturbance. There was a hunger in his expression that revealed the true depths of his sickness. He *wanted* to kill her. As if it was a rare treat he intended to savor.

There was another knock, and with a muttered curse, Sir Charles mastered his composure. Removing the dagger from her throat, he turned toward the door, although he remained close enough to warn her she would be dead before she could take more than a step.

"Enter." At his call the door opened to allow a slender

man, with a sinister scar running down his cheek from his eyebrow to the edge of his mouth, to enter. "Ah, Josef. Have you completed your task?"

The rat-faced man gave a dip of his head. "I searched the rooms."

Leonida held herself perfectly still, aware of Sir Charles's unwavering scrutiny. The least display of concern and he would know that the letters were indeed hidden in her chamber.

"Thoroughly?" Sir Charles demanded.

"I tossed the bed, broke apart the furnishing, and took up the floorboards."

"The cases?"

Leonida held her breath until the stranger shrugged. "Not a scrap of paper to be found."

"You checked through her clothing?"

"Of course." The man flicked a covert glance in her direction and Leonida frowned.

Dear God, did the man suspect the letters had been hidden in the lining of her bag? And if he did, why had he not revealed them to his master?

She had no opportunity to ponder the strange thought as Sir Charles turned to regard her with a lethal frustration.

"You begin to try my patience, Miss Karkoff." He lifted the dagger even as the sound of raised voices echoed through the room. Muttering a curse, Sir Charles glanced toward the doorway. "Now what?"

"I will discover." Josef slipped from the room, returning within a few moments with a dark frown. "Someone has alerted the officials. They are headed toward the inn."

Leonida trembled, not entirely relieved at the notion of the approaching officials. She did not believe for a moment that Sir Charles would leave her alive to reveal his identity.

"Where are Miss Karkoff's servants?" Sir Charles unexpectedly inquired.

"I left them bound and gagged in the stables," Josef admitted, only to ruin Leonida's sharp relief with a careless shrug. "Shall I dispose of them?"

"No," Leonida pleaded, unable to check her dismay. "Please."

"Ah." Sir Charles smiled with a smug satisfaction. "So you are devoted to your serfs, are you? Good." He waved a hand toward Josef. "Have the servants loaded into the carriage."

The man blinked. "Sir?"

"It occurs to me, Josef, that I have in my possession something far more valuable than ancient scandals. What do you suppose the Emperor would pay for the return of his most charming daughter?"

"A king's ransom."

"Or a czar's," Sir Charles taunted as Leonida's eyes flashed with fury.

"Damn you," Leonida muttered, never having felt so helpless in her life.

Sir Charles regarded her with distaste. "Tut, tut, Miss Karkoff. I cannot abide women to use foul language."

Josef stepped forward, his expression sour. "I comprehend taking the wench if she is worth a fortune. But why burden ourselves with the servants? It took three of us to put that groom of hers down and that maid near bit the ear off Vladimir."

The madman waved aside his servant's concern, thankfully missing Leonida's smirk of pleasure at the knowledge Pyotr and Sophy had put up a savage fight.

"My dear Josef, just consider a moment. If we were to take Miss Karkoff alone she would be a constant bother. Such a spirited lass would be honor-bound to try to escape. Or attract unwanted attention. But if she realizes that we shall willingly punish her beloved servants for her misdeeds, I sense she will be considerably more compliant."

"You bastard…"

His hand was moving before Leonida could guess his intent, his vicious slap snapping her head backward and sending her tumbling onto the hard floor.

Standing over her, Sir Charles regarded the blood spilling from her split lip with a disdainful sneer.

"I did warn you, my sweet. I will not tolerate such language."

"TAKE CARE, YOUR GRACE," Boris warned, pulling up his horse as he peered through the night at the small, insignificant inn that bustled with activity. "Something is not right."

Stefan agreed with his friend's opinion, but rather than halting to take stock of the peculiar number of people that filled the small courtyard, he instead urged his weary horse to a quicker pace.

For endless days he had trailed one step behind Leonida, the knowledge she was in danger constantly gnawing at him to the point of near insanity.

Now his heart was lodged in his throat as he headed across the cobbled yard and gestured toward the large, uniformed guard who was shouting orders at a group of cowering peasants.

"You there," he called in perfect Russian.

The soldier scowled, his weathered countenance showing an impatience that was swiftly hidden behind a resigned deference as he took notice of Stefan's expensive greatcoat and the natural air of command.

Moving to the side of Stefan's horse, he offered a dip of his head. "Yes, sir?"

"What has occurred?"

The man grimaced, glaring toward the inn. "Now that is a question I would like very much to be answered. At the moment it is nothing more than a muddle. One servant claims that a gang of brigands swept through the inn, destroying property and kidnapping the guests who they deemed worthy of ransom. Another servant is certain that it was Austrian soldiers who hauled off a poor woman for nefarious purposes."

Stefan's hand tightened on the reins, his jaws clenched so tight his teeth threatened to shatter. Christ. Had Leonida been captured? Was she even now in the hands of her enemies?

By God, he would kill them. Every damned one of them.

"Where is the innkeeper?"

"The fat fool." The soldier nodded his head toward the rotund man who was waving his hands in the air and complaining to anyone stupid enough to cross his path. "You will get nothing from him, except a demand to know who will pay for the damages."

"There must be one witness who is credible?"

"The older maid near the stables appears to have more sense than the others."

"Then I will speak with her."

"Forgive me, sir—" the man halted Stefan with a frown "—but can I ask what interest you could have in this inn?"

Stefan briefly considered ignoring the challenge. He was a nobleman and in Russia that put him above the law. Then, thankfully, common sense overcame his impatience. With the appropriate enticement this man might actually prove to be useful.

"If I can trust to your discretion."

"Of course."

Stefan assumed his most arrogant expression, a ready lie tumbling from his lips.

"I was traveling to St. Petersburg with my ward, who is young and impulsive and inclined to fits of pique when she does not have her own way."

The soldier grunted. "Much like any woman."

"Indeed. This morning we had a rather heated argument when I caught her shamelessly flirting with a mere commoner. When my back was turned she took off with her maid and a groom."

"An English girl?"

"Russian. A golden-haired female with light blue eyes." Reaching into the pocket of his coat, Stefan withdrew one of his gilt-edged calling cards. "I would be excessively grateful if you would keep an eye out for her and send word to me if you should stumble across any hint of her."

"Certainly..." The man's eyes widened as he read the name scrolled on the card. "Your Grace."

Stefan once again reached into his pocket, on this occasion pulling out several coins that he smoothly handed to the man.

"My carriage and servants are traveling in the direction of St. Petersburg. They should not be difficult to discover should you have information for me."

The soldier tucked the card and money beneath his jacket and performed a deep bow.

"You have my word that I will do all in my power to discover the missing girl."

With a nod, Stefan urged his horse toward the maid still standing beside the stables. Boris soon joined him, his expression revealing he had been blatantly eavesdropping.

"He did not believe your story of a ward," he unnecessarily pointed out.

"It does not matter. His only interest is receiving a handsome reward for his efforts. It is to be hoped that he will set a few of his men on the search."

"There will be talk."

Stefan waved away the certain knowledge that the locals would soon be buzzing with the speculation that the Duke of Huntley was chasing after a Russian beauty.

"What do I care? Leonida must be found."

"As you say." Boris reached to grasp Stefan's arm. "Perhaps I should speak with the maid alone."

With a vile curse, Stefan wrenched his horse to a halt. Boris was right, of course. Who the devil could have suspected being a duke was such a bother?

"Be quick about it," he growled, watching as Boris dismounted and moved to speak quietly with the maid, struggling against the near overpowering instinct to charge blindly through the dark in search of Leonida. Dammit. Once he had her back at Meadowland, he was never letting her out of his sight. After several minutes Boris remounted and returned to meet Stefan's impatient gaze. "Well?"

"She says that anywhere from six to ten men arrived from the south and surrounded the inn," Boris said, his words concise. "A few remained outside to keep watch, but at least three entered the inn and forced the staff into the kitchens where they were held by a man with a large gun."

"So she saw nothing?"

"No, but after the men abruptly left, she made an inspection of the premise."

"What did she discover?"

"She says that a young widow was taken from a private parlor along with her two servants."

Even prepared, the words hit Stefan like a physical punch to the stomach.

"Damn."

"She also said that the widow's chambers had been torn apart, as if someone was searching for a great treasure."

Grimly, Stefan gathered his composure. The sooner he finished his business here, the sooner he could be searching for Leonida.

"What could she tell you of the men?"

"Rough and uneducated."

"English?"

"Russian, although she swears that she heard the voice of an Englishman."

That damned Englishman.

What the blazes was his interest in Leonida? And more importantly, what did he intend to do with her now?

"How long ago did they leave?"

"Half an hour, perhaps a bit longer."

Stefan shifted in his saddle, prepared to continue the hunt. "Then they cannot have gone far."

"A moment, your Grace," Boris murmured.

"What?" he snapped.

"The maid mentioned that the widow's belongings had been left behind."

Stefan parted his lips to condemn Leonida's hideous black gowns and veiled bonnets to the netherworld, then he abruptly hesitated.

If Leonida was indeed in the hands of her enemies, she would be terrified by the time he managed to rescue her.

She would surely be comforted by her possessions.

"Gather them."

CHAPTER FIFTEEN

St. Petersburg

HERRICK GERHARDT STOOD at his mirror, putting the finishing touches on his cravat. He was plainly attired, with only his various medals of honor pinned to his black coat to relieve his austere appearance.

His small home in the shadows of the Winter Palace was equally barren of the gaudy grandeur that so pleased the Russian soul. The furniture was solid pieces he had purchased from local craftsmen and the paneled walls were bare beyond a handful of military paintings he had collected over the years.

Spending most of his days among the lavish Russian Court, it was a relief to have a place where he could enter a room and stretch out his legs in comfort.

He had just finished with his morning toilette when there was a knock on the door. He turned as it was pushed open to reveal a young footman with a nervous expression.

"Pardon me, sir, but you have a visitor."

Herrick lifted his brow. He rarely invited guests to his private home and never before he had read through the stack of reports that his various contacts provided each morning. He had not reached his position as Alexander Pavlovich's closest advisor by allowing himself to be caught off guard.

"At this hour? Who is it?"

The footman cleared his throat. "I am not entirely certain, sir."

"I beg your pardon?"

"It is a lady."

Herrick's brows snapped together, sensing a trap. It would not be the first time his enemies had sought to put an end to his undeniable power with scandal.

"Lady?"

"With a veil."

Herrick swiftly considered. It would be simple enough to have the intruder sent away. His staff was a collection of trained soldiers who were eager to protect their commander. On the other hand, the woman might have a genuine purpose in seeking him out.

"Where have you put her?"

"In the breakfast room. I hope I did not do wrong?"

"Not at all." Herrick offered a reassuring smile to the young man. "I will be down in a moment. Please ensure we are not interrupted."

"Yes, sir."

Forgetting himself, the servant offered a salute rather than a bow and scurried away. Herrick chuckled as he reached to pluck a loaded pistol from the dresser, sliding it into the holster beneath his jacket as he made his way to the breakfast room at the back of the house.

Entering the brightly lit room with a pretty cherrywood table and chairs that matched the sturdy sideboard, Herrick studied the slender woman standing beside the French doors.

As his footman warned, the woman was heavily veiled and attired in a black French silk gown that was stylish enough to have cost a small fortune.

So, a woman of society.

Interesting.

Sensing his arrival, the stranger abruptly turned, a slender hand clutching a folded piece of parchment.

"At last," she breathed.

Herrick strolled slowly forward. "Forgive me for keeping you waiting, but I must admit I did not expect a strange woman to be served with my breakfast."

"Not so strange," the woman muttered, impatiently sweeping back the veil to reveal a pale, beautiful face that was framed with glossy black hair only a few shades darker than the wide eyes.

"Nadia." Herrick stiffened in shock. "Have you taken leave of your senses?"

"I had to see you at once."

"You should have sent a message. If it is discovered you were here we will both be answering to the Emperor."

She waved a dismissive hand, as always indifferent to the rigid rules that guided most women of society.

"No one will know and I could not wait."

Dismissing the futile urge to shake some sense into the reckless woman, Herrick instead studied the barely controlled panic that smoldered in the dark eyes.

"What has happened?"

"Here."

Without a word, she shoved the sheet of parchment into his hand. A chill of premonition pricked Herrick's heart before he even read the demand for a hundred thousand rubles in return for Leonida Karkoff.

"How did you receive this?" he asked, his voice harsh with dread.

"It was on my dresser when I awoke this morning."

The bastard had dared enter the home of a countess?

"Did you question your staff?"

"Of course I did," she snapped, wrapping her arms around her waist as violent shivers shook her body. "They claim that they heard nothing during the night and that all the doors and windows were locked tightly this morning. Herrick..."

Taking his companion's arm, Herrick gently steered the growingly hysterical woman to the small settee in the corner of the room.

"Sit down, Nadia," he urged, settling himself beside her to hold her hands in a reassuring grip.

"I should never have sent her to England," she muttered.

Although Herrick was in full agreement, he kept his thoughts to himself. The only thing that mattered at the moment was rescuing Leonida.

"You could not have known just how dangerous or desperate your enemies could be."

Easily sensing his disapproval, Nadia grimaced. "Do not attempt to lessen my guilt, dear Herrick. I thought of no one but myself when I sent Leonida on this mad quest. I was horrified at the thought of Alexander discovering my indiscretion and having it used against him. I thought...he might never forgive me." Tears of regret streaked down her pale face. "Now I will never forgive myself."

"This is doing no good, Nadia," he said sternly. He could not allow the volatile woman to fall into despair. "We must concentrate on Leonida."

As hoped, Nadia brushed away her tears and squared her shoulders.

The Countess might be impulsive and self-centered, but she genuinely loved her daughter.

"You are right," she agreed. "I have my maid gathering my jewels and I have called for my solicitor to discover the precise amount of money I can raise. It will not be enough, but perhaps it will satisfy the brutes."

"No, Nadia. You cannot pay this ransom."

Her brows lowered at his unyielding command. "Do not tell me what I can or cannot do. Leonida is my daughter. I will do whatever necessary to save her."

Herrick muttered a low curse, knowing he had no choice but to reveal at least a portion of his sickening fear. "I had hoped to avoid telling you this, but the man who has been blackmailing you is more than just a greedy opportunist."

"What do you mean?"

"He is...deranged."

She gasped, her eyes wide with horror. "A madman?"

"Yes."

"How do you know this?"

Herrick shook his head. Nadia would not be comforted by the realization his information came from a notorious criminal. "Please, my dear, just accept my word."

"Dear God." She swayed, her ashen pallor revealing the effort it took to hold on to her composure. "You think she is already…"

"No." Herrick refused to even entertain the notion. "He is desperate for the money, so he will keep her alive until he is certain you have agreed to his demands. But I very much fear once he has possession of the money he will no longer consider her of use." Herrick's lips curled in contempt. "Besides, he dare not leave her to reveal his identity."

"But you already know his identity, do you not?"

"He is not yet aware of that fact."

With a jerky motion, Nadia was on her feet, pacing back to the window.

"Do you know how to find him?"

"I have several men searching."

She whirled back to stab him with a frown. "That is not good enough."

"You must trust me, Nadia." He crossed to grasp her shoulders in a firm grip. "Can you do that?"

"I trust you, but I cannot stand aside and do nothing."

"It will not be nothing," he soothed, silently considering the best use of the Countess. His most important duty was to ensure she did not do something foolish that might endanger Leonida. "I need you to continue on as you are."

"Continue on with what?"

"We cannot be certain that this man is not keeping a watch upon you and your household." Herrick's jaw tightened. Sir Charles Richards would suffer for his effrontery. "He did, after all, manage to have a note delivered into your bedchamber."

"*Mon Dieu,* do not remind me," Nadia rasped.

Herrick regarded her sternly, needing her to understand the importance of his request.

"We want the villain to believe you are panicked and attempting to gather the money to pay the ransom. The longer you can keep up the charade the better."

"And what will you be doing?" she demanded.

"I am going to seek assistance in the most unlikely of places."

LEONIDA PACED THE CRAMPED attic with a sense of burning frustration.

The past three days had been a lesson in utter misery, beginning with the bone-jarring flight from the inn and ending with her and her servants being shoved into the attic of this derelict cottage. And just as disheartening was the knowledge it had all been for nothing. The letters she had sacrificed everything to acquire were now left miles behind, hidden among her scattered belongings that could be in the hands of anyone by now.

It could always be worse, of course, she grimly reminded herself.

At least she had not been forced to endure the company of Sir Charles since arriving at the cottage, and while there were always one or two guards to be seen prowling the grounds, only Josef had entered the attic to bring them cold bowls of porridge or lead them to the foul outhouse near the stables.

Still, she could almost feel time slipping away from her.

Shortly after their arrival at the cottage yesterday, she had watched from the window as three of the guards had charged down the road toward St. Petersburg, clearly in a hurry to deliver the ransom note to her mother. Once they had arranged the details with the Countess Karkoff…

Shaking off the morbid thought, Leonida turned on her heel to glare at Sophy and Pyotr. The two were huddled on the floor, refusing to sit on the narrow cot that was the only furniture in the dank space. They were adamant that Leonida be given the one attempt at comfort.

It would have been amusing to fret over the proper protocol when they were being held by a raving lunatic if she were not terrified out of her mind.

"Sophy…" she began, only to snap her lips together as Sophy gave a shake of her head.

"No, I will not do it."

"Neither will I," Pyotr added for good measure.

"Must you two be so stubborn? Nothing can be served by your absurd nobility." Realizing the two would not be intimidated, Leonida sucked in a deep breath and softened her tone. "Indeed, if you managed to escape you could ensure that I am rescued. What could make more sense?"

Sophy sniffed at the perfectly reasonable request. "There is no point in arguing. Neither Pyotr nor I will leave you, and that is all there is to be said."

Leonida pointed a hand toward the window that overlooked the side of the house and the surrounding forest. There was another window that overlooked the front of the house and the overgrown courtyard. Beyond the courtyard was a narrow path, but Leonida had yet to observe any travelers passing by.

"Well, we cannot continue to sit here and hope someone might discover us. This is the first time that the guards are out of sight. We might not have such an opportunity again."

"We must wait." Rising to her feet, Sophy futilely brushed at the dust clinging to her skirt. "Your mother is bound to find the money to pay the ransom and then we will be released."

Leonida pressed a hand to her queasy stomach. "I wish I could be so confident."

"But surely…" Sophy began, her words stumbling to a halt as Pyotr straightened beside her and wrapped a protective arm around her shoulder. His somber expression warned her that he agreed with Leonida's suspicions. "Oh."

"Sir Charles would never have allowed us to know his identity if he intended to release us," Leonida said softly. "He would be ruined."

Sophy pressed a hand to her mouth. "Blessed saints."

"Now you comprehend why you must attempt to escape," Leonida pressed.

"I will not leave you."

Considering the notion of bundling her stubborn maid out the window whether she wanted to go or not, Leonida stiffened as Pyotr held up a hand in warning.

"Someone comes."

There was the sound of footsteps on the narrow flight of stairs. Leonida's heart plunged as Sir Charles came into view, attired in a pristine gray coat and a mocking sneer on his lips.

"Ah, I hope I do not intrude?"

Leonida smoothed her expression, not willing to give the man the satisfaction of witnessing her fear.

"Not at all."

"Good. Then perhaps you will join me downstairs for a light luncheon?"

Her heart missed a painful beat. Dear God. Had her mother paid thc ransom? Was this the end?

"I am not hungry."

The frigid eyes narrowed at her small defiance. "It was not a request, Miss Karkoff."

A small movement from Pyotr warned Leonida that her groom was about to do something stupid. Hastily she moved to put herself between the nobleman and her servants.

"Very well." She tilted her chin. "May I have a few minutes to tidy myself?"

"*Vanity, thy name is woman,*" Sir Charles mocked, his gaze flicking dismissively over her bedraggled form. "You have five minutes to make your appearance downstairs before I send Josef to fetch you. Trust me, you would not care for his methods."

There was a tense silence as the nobleman offered a sardonic bow and turned on his heel to leave the attic.

Watching his departure, Leonida's mind churned with desperation. She had to *do* something. Her pride would not allow her to go down without a fight.

"What do you suppose he wants?" Sophy said, her voice shaking with fear.

"I haven't the least notion, but it cannot be good." Leonida abruptly motioned toward the maid. "Help me out of this gown, Sophy."

"What are you doing?" Sophy demanded, reluctantly moving to unbutton the back of Leonida's black crepe gown.

Leonida ignored the sound of Pyotr's choked cough and the shuffle of his feet as he hastily turned his back on them.

"No doubt it is a waste of effort, but I must feel as if I am at least making some attempt."

Leonida shimmied out of the gown and hastily loosened her corset. Her shift followed the rest of the clothes to the dusty floor. Then, much to Sophy's puzzlement, she tugged the corset back into place and pulled on her dress, waiting for the maid to refasten the buttons.

Snatching the shift off the ground, Leonida crossed to the narrow window that overlooked the front of the house. Pyotr had earlier shoved open the sash to allow a fresh breeze into the stuffy attic, and leaning through the opening, Leonida hung the shift on a nail protruding from the window frame.

Standing at her side, Sophy frowned in concern. "What if one of the guards sees it?"

Leonida shrugged. "They are all careful to remain out of sight of the road. Besides, I can always say I washed it and hung it out to dry."

"You think someone will take notice of it?"

"Not with my luck, but it is all I can think of at the moment."

Leonida's gaze shifted to the empty path. Even if a

miracle did happen and someone passed the cottage there was little hope they would be curious enough at the sight of the shift to investigate. Her only hope was that if someone were actually searching for her and her servants they would catch a glimpse of the undergarment and realize the cottage was not empty.

Without warning the image of Stefan's lean, beautiful face rose to mind.

He had claimed he would not allow her to escape him. That he would follow her no matter how far she ran. Was it possible that he could still be searching for her? Could he reach her before Sir Charles had his money and decided to dispose of her?

With an angry shake of her head, Leonida attempted to dismiss the faint surge of hope that filled her heart.

What man in his right mind would chase after a woman who had lied to him, stolen from him, drugged him and nearly caused his death?

The Duke of Huntley was a stubborn creature, but he was in full possession of his faculties. By now he was no doubt safely returned to England, tending to his lands and appreciating his latest collection of books. If he thought of her at all, it would be with relief she was no longer about to disturb his peaceful existence.

Besides, she had run from Stefan precisely because she did not want him put in danger.

She would never doubt Stefan's courage or his ability to defeat his enemies, but he was at heart a gentleman of honor. Sir Charles, on the other hand, was a man who would happily shoot another in the back. The bastard would do whatever necessary to save his worthless neck.

As if sensing Leonida's dark thoughts, Pyotr moved to grasp her hands, his expression hard with determination.

"We will get out of this."

Leonida managed a strained smile. "I very much hope you are right, Pyotr."

Pulling away from the comfort of her groom's touch, Leonida forced her feet to carry her down the stairs and into the main portion of the cottage.

It was not a vast improvement on the attics.

There was a tiny hallway with a door that led to a small parlor and beyond that to two bedchambers. On the other side of the hallway there was an entrance to the kitchen and pantry. Directly before her was a heavy door that opened to the front courtyard.

She ignored the ridiculous urge to make an attempt at escape.

Not only would she be caught within moments, but Sir Charles had already warned what would happen to Sophy and Pyotr if she tried something so stupid.

Schooling her expression, Leonida stepped into the parlor, prepared as Sir Charles rose from the shabby settee and waved a hand toward the table set in the middle of the wooden floor.

He should have appeared ridiculous, so elegantly attired in the musty room with peeling plaster on the wall and thick cobwebs clinging to the open beams of the ceiling, but instead he simply looked dangerous.

"Allow me, Miss Karkoff." He held out one of the chairs at the table, his dark, unwavering gaze savoring her stiff reluctance as she took her seat and he reached to tuck a napkin into her lap. Only when he had provoked a shudder of revulsion from her did he at last straighten and round the table to take his own seat. "I trust you will forgive such peasant fare, but I am currently without my chef."

"I prefer simplicity," she muttered, pretending an interest in the smoked fish that had been wrapped in traditional wheat pancakes, the roasted duck with a mushroom sauce and stewed apples. In truth it was as unappealing as the vodka he poured in her glass.

Her companion's lips twitched, as if sensing her distaste. "Do you? How odd. I find nothing charming in living without the elegances of life. Indeed, I refuse to do without them."

"Which, I presume, is the reason you are holding me hostage."

"In part." His features briefly tightened. "My chosen style of life has lately become excessively expensive."

She picked at the food on her plate, not wanting to even consider his chosen lifestyle.

"I presume that you have sent your demands to my mother?"

"But of course. The quicker we have finished this unpleasant business the better."

"I could not agree more, but how can you be certain she will meet your demands?"

His chuckle sent a chill down her spine. "So little faith in your own mother? Shame on you."

She forced herself to meet his unnerving gaze. "It has nothing to do with faith, and everything to do with my mother's inability to live within her means."

A hint of complacency marred his handsome features. "Do not fret. From all reports the Countess is hastily scrambling to gather her pretty jewels, her silver and even her prized collection of *Savonnerie* tapestries. Such an enterprising woman shall discover the means to rescue her daughter from my evil clutches. And if not..." He shrugged, downing his vodka in one swallow. "Well, there is always your father. There can be no doubt he possesses the means to pay my demands."

She tilted her chin, infuriated by the thought that this man might be given so much as a ruble. The only thing he deserved was a place in front of a firing squad.

"If my father learns of your treachery there will be no place in Russia you can hide from his justice."

"Then it is a fortunate thing that I have grown quite weary of your grim country," he taunted. "With the proper funds I shall be able to travel anywhere in the world."

"I know where I should like to send you," she muttered before she could halt the words.

His eyes flashed with a cold loathing. "So much spirit. A pity I am not a gentleman who admires a woman with courage."

"Do you admire any woman?"

"Touché." Refilling his glass, he lifted it in a mocking salute. "You are quite right. I find most females repulsive creatures who will lie with a smile upon their lips and barter their soul…" He paused, his lips twisting. "Or even their children, for a few baubles."

Leonida hid a shiver, wondering what had happened in this man's childhood to have created such a monster. Or perhaps it was best she didn't know, a small voice whispered in the back of her mind. She was not so innocent that she did not realize that some mothers were unbearably cruel to their children.

"There are no doubt selfish and wicked women, just as there are selfish and cruel gentlemen," she pointed out, giving up all pretense of eating. "That does not mean that most people are not good and decent."

"You cannot believe such drivel," he scoffed, shoving aside his own plate.

Leonida froze as she caught sight of the carving knife that had been hidden beside the platter of duck.

Dear God. If she could get her hands on the weapon…

Realizing she was staring, Leonida hastily jerked her gaze back to meet Sir Charles's snide smile.

"Why should I not?"

"Your own mother traded her lovely body to entrap the most prized catch in all the empire. Do you believe she ever once thought of how her sordid affair would affect her bastard?"

She refused to flinch at the ugly truth in his words. "I am not a bastard."

"Of course not. Your mother seduced yet another poor

idiot to wed her so she could be certain her precious reputation could be salvaged and she could enjoy all the luxuries she never deserved." He deliberately paused. "And then there is the undeniable fact that when she feared her comfort might be threatened she readily threw her own daughter to the wolves."

She abruptly rose to her feet and angrily moved toward the window that was so filthy she could barely see out the warped panes. She told herself that she was simply attempting to lure him from the table so she would have an opportunity to steal the knife, but deep inside she could not entirely dismiss his hateful accusation.

Over the years, she had resigned herself to the knowledge that her mother would always put Alexander Pavlovich and his position of power first. But that did not mean that she did not occasionally long to find someone who would consider her worthy of being the most important person in their heart.

"I will not remain here and listen to my mother being insulted," she said huskily.

As hoped, Sir Charles rose to his feet to stroll to her side, unable to halt his nasty desire to taunt her.

"Ah, did I touch a tender nerve?"

"Did you bring me down here just so you could insult me?"

Leonida instantly regretted her sharp retort as his smile thinned and that horrifying craving smoldered in his eyes.

"I would like to do a great deal more than insult you, my dear." His hand lifted to grasp her chin in a painful grasp. "You have no notion the effort it has taken me to leave you...untouched. And of course, I have been forced to threaten my men with death to keep them from joining you in the attic. You owe me a great debt of gratitude."

She ground her teeth, refusing to plead for mercy. Damn her foolish pride.

"Gratitude? You kidnap me, hold me and my poor servants against our will in a cramped attic..."

With lightning speed his fingers released her chin and wrapped around her throat, squeezing so tight that black flecks danced before her eyes.

Instinctively, she lifted her hands to pound at his chest, desperate for air.

"That is it, my sweet." He leaned down to whisper in her ear. "Fight me. Scream."

"No," she managed to choke out.

He gave her a sharp shake, pulling back to relish the pain twisting her features.

"Scream for me."

On the point of passing out, Leonida barely heard the sound of approaching footsteps. It was not until a voice spoke from directly at her side that she realized they were no longer alone.

"Forgive me, sir."

With a guttural growl of frustration, Sir Charles shoved Leonida away.

"How dare you interrupt me?"

Lifting a hand to her bruised throat, Leonida struggled to breathe as Josef stood before Sir Charles without flinching.

He was either incredibly brave or as insane as his master.

"I thought you should know that Mikhail and Karl have disappeared," the scarred servant said, his voice devoid of emotion.

"Absurd," Sir Charles snapped. "They are no doubt hunting. Or more likely, lying drunk in the stables. Worthless peasants."

"They were supposed to be on guard duty, but when I checked on them I discovered they were not only missing, but they had taken their belongings and two horses."

Sir Charles stiffened, enraged by the suspicion of treachery among his serfs.

"Bloody hell. I will speak with Vladimir." He waved a dismissive hand toward the still gasping Leonida. "Return the bitch to the attics."

Josef dipped his head. "Of course."

With a profound sense of relief, Leonida watched as Sir Charles left the room, absolutely certain that she had just been saved from certain death.

Not that she was foolish enough to believe that it was more than a temporary reprieve. Sir Charles was convinced he would soon have his ransom payment from her mother and he had no need to rein in his perverted desire to watch her die.

Once he had dealt with his renegade guards, he would finish what he had begun.

Indifferent to her impending demise, Josef waved a hand toward the door.

"This way."

She took a step forward, knowing it would be futile to plead with the man to release her and her servants. Although he had always been polite, he had made it obvious he would not hesitate to kill her if it suited his mood. Then, as she was passing the table, she abruptly halted.

"May I take some food to my servants?" she asked, her throat so tender she could barely speak. "They are no doubt starving by now."

Josef shrugged. "If you wish."

"Thank you."

Gathering the platter of duck, Leonida shifted so she stood between Josef and the table, using one hand to grab the bowl of stewed apples even as her other hand reached for the knife. Placing it on the platter, she piled the pancakes on top, covering the weapon.

At last she turned, her heart thundering as she braced herself to meet Josef's narrowed gaze.

Had he seen? Did he know she had the knife?

Braced for the evil-faced servant to strike, Leonida was unprepared for the mysterious smile that curved his lips.

"After you, Miss Karkoff."

CHAPTER SIXTEEN

HALTING AT YET ANOTHER remote village, Stefan waited for Boris to return from the local pub. He cast an indifferent gaze over the wooden shops huddled along the rough path. It looked remarkably like every other village they had passed through over the past three days.

Poor, grim and unwelcoming.

Not even the afternoon sunlight could soften the bleak atmosphere.

Alexander Pavlovich's attempts at reformation had faltered beneath the unyielding refusal of his fellow noblemen and the constant threat of uprisings, leaving his people to suffer the consequences. Stefan knew it was only a matter of time before the smoldering resentment among the common peasants festered into something truly dangerous.

Sipping the brandy from his flask, Stefan was cataloguing his various aches and pains, including his bullet wound that was slowly healing, when the sound of an approaching horse had him turning his head in surprise.

"That was swift," he said as Boris halted beside him.

The servant shrugged, his face as haggard as Stefan felt. The past three days with little sleep and hard riding were beginning to take their toll on the both of them.

"There was no need to linger."

"Why?"

"I had barely stepped into the taproom when I overheard several locals complaining about a band of ruffians who had been poaching on their lands over the past few days."

Stefan tempered the biting relief that raced through him. The ruffians sounded promising, but the Russian countryside was plagued with brigands. There was no certainty these were the men he sought.

"Do they know where the poachers were staying?"

"One farmer mentioned an abandoned cottage north of the village."

"Have they searched the place?"

"No." Boris snorted at Stefan's startled glance. "The land belongs to the local Count. Why would they risk their necks battling a potential gang of cutthroats for an arrogant landowner who hasn't the least concern for them?"

Stefan swallowed his words of protest. It was impossible for him to imagine his own tenants allowing a band of poachers to roam about his land. Of course, he had always considered his tenants members of his family, not meaningless property to be used for his own profit.

"And the Count?"

"Partaking of the delights in the Summer Palace."

"How far are we from St. Petersburg?"

Boris studied the village, his brow furrowed as he calculated the distance.

"A day's hard ride."

Stefan shook his head. "Why would they linger in such an isolated place when they could easily become lost among the crowds of the city?"

"They hold one of the most well-known ladies in all of St. Petersburg. She would be recognized by even the most humble servant."

"Of course." Stefan sighed. He must be more tired than he realized. A female with Leonida's notorious parents, not to mention her stunning beauty, would be easily recognized in St. Petersburg. He impatiently urged his horse to a trot. "Come. I want to see these poachers for myself."

They had traveled a mile or so along the path when Boris slowed his horse and frowned at the thickening woods.

"Perhaps we should avoid the road," he suggested, his voice pitched low. "If these are the men we are seeking they will be on guard."

Stefan briefly considered. There would be a danger in moving through the dense trees. They could stumble across an enemy before they ever realized they were near. And there was the frustrating knowledge that it would take considerably longer to locate the cottage.

Then again, the bastards were certain to keep a watch on the road. The only chance to approach without warning would be to use the trees as cover.

"I suppose you have a point," he muttered, urging his horse off the path.

Boris grinned as he followed. "For a duke you can be right sensible on occasion."

"What would I do without you, Boris?" Stefan demanded wryly.

"Perhaps you could whisper in your brother's ear just how valuable a servant I have proven to be."

They eased cautiously through the undergrowth, Stefan's attention on full alert. There were more things to be feared than ruffians.

Tigers, and even bears, were known to attack unwary travelers.

"Do not fear, I shall make certain that Edmond is compelled to pay you an exorbitant sum for your assistance." He smiled as he thought of his brother's rapid transformation from rake to domesticated husband. "There are few things I love more than reminding my brother that he is now a staid landowner with numerous responsibilities."

"While you are now the one seeking adventure?"

Stefan blinked at the unexpected accusation. "Not by choice, I assure you. I have never possessed Edmond's love for danger."

Boris slid him a sly glance. "I think you are more alike than you realize, your Grace."

"Of course we're alike. We are twins, for God's sake. Most people cannot tell the two of us apart." He briefly recalled tormenting his nurses and tutors over the years. "A fact that was great fun when we were young."

"I meant your refusal to allow anything to stand in your path once you have set your mind upon a particular lady."

Stefan frowned. "I do not allow a thief to steal from me and escape my justice."

"Hmm." Boris appeared skeptical.

Not particularly surprising. The words rang empty even to Stefan. No man, and especially not a duke, chased a woman from England to St. Petersburg because she might have taken something from his estate.

"Do you have a point?"

Boris shrugged. "What will you do with Miss Karkoff if we manage to rescue her?"

"*When* we rescue her," Stefan growled.

"As you say. Do you intend to return her to St. Petersburg?"

Stefan shifted in his saddle, annoyed by the question. What he did with Leonida was no one's concern but his own. She belonged to him.

That was the end of the matter.

"One problem at a time, *mon ami.*"

Ignoring the warning in Stefan's tone, Boris regarded him with a somber expression.

"I feel compelled to remind you that she is not a penniless serf. Her very powerful and very influential family would take grave insult if she were kept from them."

"They sent Leonida to me. They have no one to blame but themselves if I decide not to return her."

"Your Grace..."

"The future will hardly matter if we stumble into a trap," Stefan growled. "Perhaps we should concentrate on the task at hand?"

Boris ground his teeth, but he was wise enough not

to press Stefan. Instead he returned his attention to scanning the nearby trees, leaving Stefan to stew in his frustration.

He was not so lost to reason that he did not understand that Leonida was a respectable maiden with a family who were powerful enough to offer her protection.

That did not mean, however, he was prepared to play the noble gentleman and simply hand her back to their care.

They had unfinished business.

Until he was satisfied, she was staying with him.

They traveled in silence for several moments, then through the trees, Stefan caught sight of a low stable and just beyond a crumbling cottage set in a small clearing.

"There is a cottage ahead," he whispered, vaulting from his saddle. "Tie the horses here. I want to circle around before we approach."

Boris swiftly had the horses secured, pulling a loaded pistol from his coat pocket.

"Remain here. I will make certain there are no guards hidden among the trees."

Stefan sighed as he pulled out his own weapon. "I do wish you would rid yourself of this habit of treating me as if I am a feeble old woman."

"And I wish you would remember you are a duke. It is not your place to be confronting common brutes."

"Surely I should be allowed to determine my place?" Stefan protested, taking the lead as he threaded his way through the dense woods. This was his ridiculous notion. He would be the one to suffer the consequences.

"You are determined to have me gelded," Boris muttered.

"Take heart, Boris, you will no doubt be killed by our ruffians long before you ever suffer such a hideous fate."

"That is my only hope."

Taking a path that would lead them around the clearing, Stefan kept his gaze trained on the cottage, searching for any hint that the place was not as abandoned as it appeared.

His heart was beginning to sink as they reached the front of the property.

Surely there should be some signal of the ruffians? Guards posted to keep watch. Smoke from the chimney…

Abruptly he halted in his tracks, blinking at the sight of the white garment flapping from the attic window.

"What the devil?"

"It looks like a woman's undergarment."

His brief discouragement was forgotten as a surge of hope tingled through his body.

"I need to get closer."

"For God's sake, be careful."

Reaching the very edge of the clearing, Stefan released his breath on a hiss, easily recognizing the pretty blue bows that ran along the hem of the shift.

"My clever Leonida," he breathed. "She is here."

"How can you be so certain?" Boris demanded, then his expression cleared as he noted Stefan's wicked smile. "Oh."

"Precisely." Returning his attention to the cottage, Stefan studied the shabby disuse that shrouded the building. "It is odd."

Boris crept to his side. "What?"

"The maid at the hotel mentioned six to ten ruffians. Surely they cannot all be within such a small cottage?"

"There are stables in the back."

"Where are the guards?" Stefan shook his head, realizing that he would not find the answer to his questions by standing in the trees gawking. "Come."

Boris muttered a curse, following in Stefan's wake as he continued his circuit toward the back stables. Stefan ignored his disgruntled companion. It was enough of an effort to resist the urge to charge into the cottage and shoot every bastard who crossed his path.

They had nearly reached the stables, still with no guards in sight, when Boris urgently tugged on his arm.

"Wait," the servant hissed.

"What is it?"

Boris pointed at the ground. "Blood."

"No." Stefan's knees threatened to buckle, his heart wrenching to a painful halt at the dark red stain that was splattered over the ground. "Dammit, no."

Boris followed the line of blood leading through the trees, his grim expression revealing he echoed Stefan's fear.

Barely aware he was moving, Stefan trailed behind his servant, his hands clenched at his sides. He would not believe the blood belonged to Leonida. *Could* not believe it.

Fate would not be so cruel as to allow him to come so close only to fail.

"Here."

Coming to a halt, Boris bent down and began to brush aside the branches that had been piled among the tangled undergrowth. Stefan struggled to breathe as a rough blanket came into view. It obviously covered two bodies.

Even Boris faltered for a moment before he could reach forward and yank aside the covering. This time Stefan's knees refused to hold as he sank to the ground, a shattering relief searing through him as he took in the strangers lying in the shallow grave.

"God," he breathed on a shaky breath.

"Both men," Boris muttered, his brow furrowed. "And neither one is Miss Karkoff's groom."

With his numbing fear fading, Stefan was able to take stock of the dead men.

Both were large and attired in simple peasant garb. He judged them to be younger than himself, but with weathered features that suggested a life of hard work and hard drinking.

His attention shifted to the gory bullet wounds that marred each of their temples. They had both been shot at close range. Which meant they recognized and trusted their killer. Or the assassin managed to catch them unawares.

"Do you suppose these are locals who were foolish enough to approach the cottage? Or did our kidnappers have a disagreement among themselves?" He murmured his thoughts aloud.

Boris pondered a long moment. "If the kidnappers quarreled, that would explain the lack of guards."

Stefan rose to his feet and headed back to the clearing. "Let us hope there are a few more bodies littered about the property."

With a grunt, Boris fell into step beside him. "You intend to enter the cottage?"

A cold, ruthless smile curved Stefan's lips.

He had just endured sheer hell while he waited to see if it was Leonida lying in that grave. He was done with stealth.

"I not only intend to enter, but I swear I will kill any bastard who stands between me and Leonida."

LEONIDA STUDIED THE BULKY outline of the knife that she had slipped beneath the long sleeve of her gown. It would easily be noticed by anyone who studied her closely, but if she kept her arm pressed to her side, it might go undetected.

"You are going to do something foolish, I just know you are," Sophy muttered, nervously pacing from one end of the cramped attic to the other.

"At the moment I intend to do nothing more than find a means to hide this damnable knife," Leonida muttered.

"Pyotr, would you tell her not to be an idiot?" the maid demanded, glaring at the groom who stood beside the window, polishing off the last of the duck that Leonida had brought from downstairs. "She's going to get herself killed." Sophy frowned as Pyotr kept his attention trained on the side window. "What are you peering at?"

The groom set aside his plate, his profile tense. "There was someone moving near the stables."

Leonida's heart sank. So much for her hope that Sir Charles's servants had grown tired of waiting for their share of the ransom and had taken off.

"No doubt the missing guards are returning from their morning adventures," she muttered.

Pyotr shook his head. "These were no guards."

"How can you be certain?"

The groom turned to meet her puzzled frown with a wry grin. "None of them would know how to tie a cravat."

A combination of hope and dread surged through Leonida. "Dear God."

"Your mother must have sent the officials to rescue you," Sophy said, clapping her hands together.

"Possibly," Leonida grudgingly conceded. She knew her mother well enough to suspect that she had gone directly to Herrick Gerhardt with the ransom demand. Whatever the Countess's devotion to Alexander Pavlovich, she had always known that it was Herrick who could be depended upon when a problem arose. And if anyone could find her in the vast wilderness of Russia, it would be Herrick. Still, she suspected that if the men that Pyotr had spotted were indeed there to rescue them, they had not been sent by Herrick. Her stomach twisted with sharp fear. "How many men did you see?"

"Two."

"We know that Sir Charles and Josef are downstairs and there was mention of another guard." Leonida absently shifted the knife that poked at her forearm as she spoke her thoughts aloud. "So at least three. If these men are here to rescue us they will need our assistance."

Predictably, Sophy tossed her hands in the air. "Oh lord, you are just not going to be happy until you get your throat slit."

Leonida shivered. "It is certain that my throat will be slit if we do not escape from Sir Charles."

"She is right, Sophy." Pyotr unexpectedly stepped into the fray, his expression stubborn. "We must do what we can."

Realizing she was outnumbered, Sophy folded her arms over her chest. "Fine. But I do not have to like it."

Leonida ignored her pouting maid, concentrating on Pyotr. As desperate as she was to escape, she would not allow her servant to take any ridiculous risks.

"What are you plotting, Pyotr?"

"If I can slip out of the window and join those men then the odds would be nicely evened out."

She hesitated before giving a slow nod of her head. "Be careful. We cannot be certain there are not more guards hidden amongst the trees."

Pyotr grinned. "I will not be caught."

"Here." Leonida reached beneath the cuff of her gown, closing her fingers around the hilt of the knife. "You will need a weapon."

The groom wrapped his hand around Leonida's wrist, preventing her from pulling out the knife.

"I have hopes that our rescuers possessed the sense to come armed." He snared her gaze, his eyes hard with warning. He better than anyone comprehended the full implications if the rescue failed. "Keep this close and do not hesitate to strike first."

She slowly nodded, her nerves tangled into knots as Pyotr shrugged out of his jacket and then, with remarkable athletic ability, squeezed through the window and landed lightly on the ground beneath.

Watching his retreating form, Leonida dared not breathe until he disappeared around the edge of the stables. Even then, she waited, refusing to budge until she was absolutely certain that Pyotr had not been noticed by Sir Charles.

Minutes passed before she at last turned and made her way across the plank floor.

"Where are you going?" Sophy hissed.

"I want to be prepared." Tiptoeing down the stairs, Leonida winced as Sophy clattered down behind her, then silently she turned the handle of the door at the bottom. She grimaced as it refused to budge. Perhaps ridiculously, she had hoped Josef might have overlooked turning the key. "Damn. It is still locked. We must wait."

"Good," the maid muttered.

Rolling her eyes at Sophy's cowardice, Leonida pressed her ear to the wooden panel of the door. A long, agonizing eternity seemed to pass, with the only sound to break the silence the pounding of her heart. She was beginning to wonder if something had gone terribly wrong when at long last she heard the sounds of muffled shouts and the sharp thud of running footsteps.

"I hear something," she breathed, pulling the knife from her sleeve and clenching it with a white-knuckled grip.

At her side, Sophy muttered a prayer, obviously not trusting Leonida's ability to keep her safe.

A good bet, as it turned out.

Still leaning forward, Leonida was unprepared when the door was abruptly jerked open and she tumbled directly into the arms of Sir Charles.

With a small shriek she found herself jerked around until her back was pressed to the madman's chest and one arm wrapped around her waist. His other hand held a silver dagger he pressed to her throat.

"How very kind of you to be waiting for me, Miss Karkoff," he drawled.

Terrified, Leonida still possessed the sense to hide her hand that held the knife in the heavy folds of her gown.

"You bastard."

Hauling her toward the small foyer, Sir Charles pressed the dagger deep enough to break her skin.

"It baffles me that no one has yet cut out that shrewish tongue of yours, Miss Karkoff. An oversight I shall soon rectify."

Leonida desperately struggled against his hold, indifferent to the blood she could feel trickling down her neck. If Sir Charles managed to get her out of the cottage she was as good as dead.

No matter how hard Sophy might pray.

They were nearing the entry to the kitchens when a shadow fell across the floor. Leonida's heart contracted with painful relief, only to plunge in regret as the Duke of Huntley stepped into the hallway, blocking Sir Charles's path to the front doorway.

What was wrong with the aggravating man?

She had done everything in her power to drive him away and keep him safe. He was a duke, for God's sake. He should be at Meadowland, not risking his neck battling her enemies.

Indifferent to her angry gaze, Stefan briefly studied the small wound on her neck, his expression so hard she barely recognized him.

There was nothing of the charming aristocrat in his handsome face at the moment.

His beautiful eyes were as cold as the Siberian winter and his elegant features set in a mask of lethal fury. A predator that was coiled and prepared to strike.

Lifting his arm, Stefan coolly pointed a loaded pistol toward Sir Charles's face.

"Release her."

Holding Leonida as a shield, Sir Charles edged his way into the parlor, growling in anger as Stefan followed him, shadowed by Lord Summerville's manservant, Boris, as well as Pyotr.

"I fear that will not be possible, your Grace," he retorted, his tone defiant despite the obvious fact he was cornered.

Stefan curled his lips in an arrogant sneer. "Are we acquainted?"

Leonida felt Sir Charles stiffen and realized that Stefan had struck a vulnerable nerve.

Sir Charles was jealous of Stefan's superior title.

"I could never claim your lofty position among society, but it is impossible to live in London without enduring the nauseating excitement when the Duke of Huntley condescended to make one of his rare appearances among the *ton,*" he rasped, yanking Leonida even closer as Stefan stepped forward. "Stay back."

"Shoot him," Leonida commanded, preferring a bullet to being at the mercy of the lunatic who held her captive.

"Ah, the devoted Duke is too much a nobleman to risk a helpless female," Sir Charles mocked.

Leonida met Stefan's gaze, her expression grimly determined. "He is going to kill me whatever you do. At least I should be given the pleasure of knowing he is going to die along with me."

Astonishingly, Stefan stretched his lips to a cold smile. "She does have a point and I hate to disappoint a lady."

Sir Charles hissed in surprise. "Do not imagine for a moment that I am bluffing."

Stefan narrowed his gaze. "What do you want of Miss Karkoff?"

"I want what every man wants. Money."

"Very well. How much?"

"No, Stefan..." Leonida began, only to yelp in pain as the dagger dug in deeper.

"Shut your mouth, bitch, the men are negotiating." Waiting until he was confident Leonida was properly cowed, Sir Charles returned his attention to the Duke of Huntley. "One hundred thousand rubles."

Stefan's eyes flashed with a deadly anger, but he remained in bleak command of his composure.

"A great deal of money."

"Not for a duke. Besides, her mother seems to believe her worth such a sum." Sir Charles's short burst of laughter revealed his own opinion of Leonida's worth. "Are you willing to pay?"

"I am willing," Stefan said without hesitation.

"How much do you have on you?"

Stefan shrugged. "Only a few pounds. Unhand Miss Karkoff and once I am in St. Petersburg..."

"And once you are in St. Petersburg you will head

directly for the Summer Palace. You must think me a fool," Sir Charles growled in annoyance, shoving Leonida forward, his dagger still pressed to her throat. "Move aside," he warned as Stefan firmly stood in his path. "Move aside or I will slit her throat."

Stefan's jaw knotted, his body rigid with fury. "You are not leaving this cottage."

"Then you will watch your whore die."

Forced to accept that Sir Charles would happily slide the dagger through Leonida's throat, Stefan gave an impatient motion with his hand, sending Boris and Pyotr out of the room. Then, keeping his pistol trained on Sir Charles, he slowly backed into the hall.

"I will not follow if you release Miss Karkoff," he grated, his eyes dark with a raw frustration as Sir Charles maneuvered Leonida across the room and through the entryway.

Sir Charles laughed as he shifted to keep Leonida between himself and the pistol, backing until he could reach behind and thrust open the outer door. A few more steps and Leonida would once again be in completely in this madman's power.

"Miss Karkoff does not leave my side until I have my reward," Sir Charles warned, tugging her onto the stoop.

"Then have your damned reward," Leonida muttered, shaking her hand free of her skirt and plunging the knife backward and into her captor's side before she could give herself time to consider the danger.

With an agonized shriek, Sir Charles stumbled backward, his dagger slicing a shallow cut through her neck. Then, loosening his hold on Leonida, he clutched at the knife protruding from his side.

Well aware that she might only have moments to scramble to safety, Leonida tried to step forward, crying out in alarm when her legs buckled and she fell to her knees.

The grinding fear she had endured for weeks, not to mention the alarming blood loss from her most recent wound, was taking its toll.

"Leonida," Stefan shouted, reaching the doorway only to come to an abrupt halt as his gaze shifted over her shoulder.

Terrified that Sir Charles was about to pounce on her, Leonida turned her head, summoning her fading energy to fend off his attack.

What she discovered instead was Josef standing next to Sir Charles, his arm around his employer's waist to keep him upright and his other arm extended toward Leonida with a pistol in his hand.

"Tend to the woman," the scarred servant commanded Stefan, warily backing toward the carriage that he had brought from the stables and was now waiting a few paces away. "Sir Charles is no longer your concern."

Stunned by the strange end to the violent encounter, Leonida barely noted Stefan as he rushed to kneel at her side, her gaze never wavering as Josef tossed his near unconscious companion into the carriage and then clamored into the driver's seat, giving a shrill whistle that sent the horses into motion.

A part of her was infuriated by the thought of Sir Charles escaping from justice. The bastard deserved to be shot in the middle of the Senate Square. Another part, however, was desperately relieved to see the back of him.

For the moment she was alive, and while she might never have the pleasure of seeing the monster standing before a firing squad, she at least had the satisfaction of knowing his attempt to blackmail her mother would soon be at an end. And if there was any justice in the world, the wound she had delivered would fester into an infection that would put him in his grave.

With that encouraging thought, Leonida slid into unconsciousness.

CHAPTER SEVENTEEN

DARK HAD FALLEN by the time Leonida awoke. And that was not the only change.

During the hours she had been asleep the cottage had been ruthlessly cleaned, Sophy's efforts no doubt, and Leonida had been included in the thorough scrubbing.

It took only a few moments for her to realize that she had been stripped of her dress and corset and someone had gathered her shift from the attic to pull over her recently washed skin. Even her hair was still damp.

She would have been delighted by the sensation of being thoroughly clean, not to mention deliciously warm from the fire roaring in the stone fireplace, if her throat did not throb with a sharp-edged pain beneath the linen bandage that had been placed over the wound. And if Stefan were not pacing the cramped space of the bedchamber like one of the lions caged in the Tower of London.

When she had first opened her eyes, he had been standing rigidly by the window, his elegant profile tense and his hands clenched at his sides. At her slight movement, he had whirled to face her, his stark relief rapidly being replaced with an explosive anger as she had tentatively lifted her hand to touch the bandage at her neck.

"Never has it been my misfortune to be saddled with such a bloody-minded, impulsive, bird-witted…"

"I will point out that you have never been *saddled* with me, your Grace," Leonida broke in, concentrating on the injustice of being blamed for the ghastly situation rather than dwelling on her bone-deep relief that he was near. She did not want to depend on Stefan to feel safe. "Indeed, I have done my very best to be rid of you."

He shoved a hand through his disheveled hair, appearing oddly vulnerable with his eyes shadowed with a lack of sleep and his jaw in need of a shave. Or perhaps it was because he had at some point shed his jacket and waistcoat and was now attired in nothing more than his fine linen shirt and breeches that clung with tenacious persistence to his long, leanly muscled legs.

The elegant duke had been stripped away to reveal the raw, powerful man beneath.

"Now is not the moment to remind me that you left me drugged and penniless in a nasty Parisian hotel," he rasped, thankfully unaware of her inane thoughts.

"You are right," she snapped, pushing herself to a seated position despite the burning pain of her wound. Sir Charles might be gone, but her mother's letters were still missing. And with no clear knowledge of how to retrace her steps to the inn where they had been left, she had no choice but to entrust the search to Herrick Gerhardt. "I have no time to waste on such foolish arguments."

She reached to flip aside the covers, but with a lunging movement, Stefan was perched on the edge of the bed, his fingers clamping around her wrists.

"You attempt to get out of that bed and I swear to God that I will tie you down."

She trembled at his sudden touch. "I do not take orders from you."

"You will if you have any sense left in that thick skull."

"Your Grace..."

"My name is Stefan, as you well know," he growled, his magnificent eyes snapping with suppressed emotion. "And after weeks spent chasing after you, constantly terrified you were in the hands of your enemies or worse, I do not intend to spend another moment worrying whether you are well or not."

Her heart fluttered at his rough confession, but Leonida dared not be distracted.

"If you are so concerned for my welfare, then why do you insist on remaining in this cottage where Sir Charles and his servants might return at any moment?"

His fingers eased their grip, his thumbs absently stroking the sensitive skin of her inner wrist.

"You are in no condition to be moved and we are far safer here than traveling through the dark. Boris and Pyotr will be on guard. No one will be allowed to approach unnoticed."

"I cannot stay here."

"Why?"

Leonida's mouth went dry at his featherlight caresses. "My mother must be terrified. Sir Charles sent a ransom note."

"Sir Charles." His brows drew together. "Richards?"

Leonida stilled. "You acted as if you did not recognize him."

"We have never met, but his name is familiar...." He abruptly shook his head. "Damn, I cannot recall. There was some ugly bit of scandal that drove him from England."

Leonida thinned her lips. So the English now herded their madmen to Russia?

No wonder Alexander Pavlovich had disliked his journey to the country.

"He is a monster. He should have been sent to the Tower and had his head chopped off."

Stefan's lips twitched. "I will pass your complaint along to the King."

She tugged her arms free. His touch was far too distracting.

"This is not amusing. My mother needs to know I am well."

His brief humor fled as he planted his hands on each

side of her hips and leaned close enough for her to feel his breath brushing her face.

"But you are not well, and until I am convinced you are strong enough to travel you will remain in this bed. I will send word to your mother in the morning."

"No." Her gaze unconsciously lingered on his full lips. They were so temptingly close. "I must leave now. You do not understand."

"Then perhaps you should explain it to me."

She turned her head, glaring toward the dark window. How was she supposed to concentrate when her body was tingling with that potent awareness?

"You know I cannot."

"For God's sake, Leonida, this is no longer a game." His hand cupped her chin to tug her face back to meet his narrowed gaze. "You will tell me the truth. And if you even consider the notion of slipping opium into my tea or knocking me over the head or any other nefarious scheme to escape me, be assured that Boris has been commanded to capture you and drag you back to Meadowland."

She was weakening. It was not just the days of terror when she knew with absolute certainty that Sir Charles was going to kill her and her servants. Or the constant running from enemies.

Or even being forced to endure bad food, shabby inns and a jolting journey over roads that were little better than rough tracks.

No, it was simply that she was tired of the lies.

"I do not understand why you are here," she breathed, searching for the strength to keep her secrets hidden.

"And you presume that I do?" he muttered.

"Stefan…"

"Please, Leonida, I am too weary for our delightful fencing matches. If I am to protect you I must understand the danger."

"I promised my mother."

His nose flared, as if he were offended by her words. "If your mother does not comprehend that her daughter's life is worth more than some damned secret then she does not deserve your loyalty. A fact I intend to point out to the Countess should our paths ever cross."

Leonida was shocked to discover her heart warming at his anger. She could not possibly desire the Duke of Huntley to insult her own mother, she fiercely told herself. But then again, it was a rare and oddly wonderful sensation to know he was angered at the thought of her in danger.

"You would not."

"I would. With the greatest pleasure."

"My mother loves me."

"Perhaps, but she has taken poor care of you." His thumb brushed over her lower lip, sending a jolt of pleasure through her. "I will not be so inattentive."

"I do not need anyone to take care of me."

"Then perhaps I will allow you to care for me," he countered, his gaze lowering to the scooped bodice of her shift. "After the past few weeks I could use a good deal of coddling."

"You will have to acquire your coddling elsewhere," she said huskily.

"We shall see." With obvious reluctance he lifted his gaze. "For now I will content myself with discovering why you traveled to England." His expression hardened into stubborn lines. "Leonida. The time has come."

Leonida attempted to remind herself of the numerous reasons she should keep the truth from this man, not the least of which was the knowledge that the Duke of Huntley was already far too entangled in her life. Instead she could summon nothing more than a sigh of resignation.

"Yes." She shifted to place a measure of space between them. Not that it helped. Stefan's presence filled the entire room. "I suppose it has."

He frowned at her movement, grudgingly allowing his

hand to drop from her chin. "You did not come to Meadowland to be introduced to society or discover a husband."

"No."

"Then why?"

Leonida licked her dry lips, not at all certain where to begin.

"As you know, our mothers were very close to one another before your mother became the Duchess of Huntley. After the Duchess traveled to England my mother maintained a steady correspondence with her."

"I believe we have already established that fact," Stefan pointed out dryly.

"Do you wish me to tell you the truth or not?"

He waved a slender hand. "Proceed."

"It was not long after your mother left St. Petersburg that my mother attracted the attention of Alexander Pavlovich," she continued. "Of course she desired to discuss the relationship with her dearest friend."

"The relationship was hardly a secret."

"Perhaps not, but my mother was foolish enough to reveal the more…intimate details of her affair."

His brows lifted as his gaze drifted over her slender form before returning to meet her wary eyes.

"I must be uncommonly dense because the intimacy of the affair is beautifully obvious."

"I mean that she shared the private conversations between her and the Czar Alexander." She paused, choosing her words with care. "Conversations that should never have left the privacy of Alexander Pavlovich's chambers."

It took a long moment, then with a sudden scowl, Stefan surged off the bed to glare down at her.

"I am dense," he said, his voice edged with anger. "You came to Meadowland to steal my mother's correspondence."

Leonida instinctively hid behind a defensive expression. "The letters were written to your mother, but they were from *my* mother. I surely have as much a right to them as you do."

He snorted. "If you truly believed that flimsy excuse then you would never have lied to my brother and his wife, insinuated your way into my home, and then crept away with my property in the middle of the night."

STEFAN WATCHED THE COLOR flood Leonida's cheeks, her thick tangle of lashes lowering to hide the guilt in her eyes.

Good.

She should feel guilty.

And not just because she had taken advantage of his hospitality to pry through his mother's most private possessions.

"I did what I had to do," she muttered.

His eyes narrowed, his hands curled into fists. "So, I at last know why you were searching through my home."

"Yes."

"Where did you find them?"

"In a safe hidden beneath the floorboards in the Duchess's bedchamber."

"Ah." He recalled the small opening cut into the floor, although it had been years since he had opened it. "Did you take anything else?"

Her gaze jerked up to meet his hard gaze, her expression offended at his question.

"Of course not."

"Why the devil did you not ask me for them?" he gritted, unwittingly revealing the true source of his anger.

She bit her bottom lip. "My mother feared that your loyalty to your king might lead you to refuse my request."

He curled his hands into fists. Damn the Countess Karkoff. She had a great deal to answer for.

"And why would the King of England have any interest in letters written over twenty years ago?"

"He has never hidden his dislike for Alexander Pavlovich."

Stefan shrugged. The two powerful leaders were never destined to be friends. George IV was a gregarious soul who delighted in lavish entertainments and happily indulged his every whim, no matter how outrageous. Alexander Pavlovich, on the other hand, was a quiet, austere man who disliked the pomp and ceremony that was thrust on him.

"George is a vain man who is sensitive to any hint of a slight," he said. "Alexander Pavlovich should not have refused the entertainments that were planned in his honor when he visited London."

Her lips thinned, revealing that her sympathy for the disagreement was thoroughly with Alexander Pavlovich.

"Whatever the reason, I do not doubt the King would be pleased with the opportunity to embarrass the Czar."

He would, of course. But that was hardly the point.

"And you thought I would be an accomplice to such a plot?" he rasped.

She winced. "I did not know you."

"My mother was a loyal Russian until the day she died."

"And your loyalty is to England, as it should be," she swiftly countered.

He gritted his teeth, in no mood to be reasonable. She would never have been put into danger if she had just trusted him.

"We will return to this subject later." He stepped toward the bed. "What is in the letters that you feared would prove to be an embarrassment to Alexander Pavlovich?"

"I do not know."

He muttered a low curse. "I thought we were beyond this foolishness?"

Her eyes flashed with frustration. "I am telling you the truth."

"You traveled all the way to England, played the role of thief, and battled a madman without knowing why you were risking your bloody neck?"

She restlessly stirred on the bed, the shift twisting against her body to outline the perfect curves of her breasts. Stefan sucked in a sharp breath, trying to ignore the brutal awareness that had plagued him since Leonida had opened her eyes.

Until that moment he had been unable to think of anything but the sight of the dagger slicing through her neck. Christ. He was not certain his heart would ever fully recover.

Now, however…

Now he was remembering just how delicious she felt in his arms.

"My mother refused to reveal what she had written and, to be honest, I did not press the issue," she confessed. "There are some secrets best left unknown."

He studied her pale features, at last giving a grudging nod of his head. Alexander Pavlovich's journey to the throne had not been without sacrifice.

Or scandal.

"Yes, I suppose there are." He paused, considering the unpleasant consequences of the letters falling into the wrong hands. "I am still confused."

"Why?"

"Those letters have been hidden away for years. Hell, I did not even know they existed. Why was your mother so suddenly determined to have them in their possession?"

He watched the emotions ripple over Leonida's beautiful features as she overcame her reluctance to confess the truth.

"Because she is being blackmailed."

"Good God."

She grimaced at his astonishment. "You cannot be more shocked than I was."

"Don't be so certain," he muttered, pacing toward the window. He was finding it increasingly difficult to concentrate on anything but the sight of Leonida half-naked on the bed. "What do my mother's letters have to do with the blackmail scheme of a Russian Countess?"

"She was approached by a gentleman who claimed he had the letters and that he would hand them over to Alexander Pavlovich's enemies unless she agreed to pay him a great deal of money."

"Sir Charles?"

"No, it was a Russian who first accosted mother, but it is now obvious that Sir Charles was behind the plot."

"The blackmailer claimed to have the letters?"

"Yes, but my mother did not believe him."

He turned with a frown. "Why?"

Leonida shrugged. "For one thing, he would not produce them to her even when she refused to pay. And for another, he made no mention of the fact that they were partially written in a secret code."

Stefan coughed, unable to imagine his elegant, sophisticated mother writing missives in a secret code.

"Secret code?"

"Knowing my mother the code was nothing more clever than spelling a handful of words backwards or using initials instead of full names," Leonida admitted. "Still, the man who was threatening her seemed to know nothing more than the fact she had written to the Duchess of Huntley and that the letters held the private conversations of Alexander Pavlovich."

"Information you suspect came from Sir Charles?"

She held up a slender hand. "Do you have a better notion?"

He restlessly paced back toward the bed. The letters had been hidden in his mother's room since her death. And he would bet his last quid that Sir Charles Richards had never set foot inside Meadowland.

So how had the bastard known of them?

"None of it makes the least sense."

"At least we agree on something."

His lips twisted. He knew of any number of things they could agree upon. Most of them involving her body trembling beneath him.

"Who besides your mother knew of the letters?"

"She claims no one beyond the Duchess."

"Then how could Sir Charles know of them?" he demanded.

"Perhaps your mother shared the letters with someone who was acquainted with him."

He stiffened, knowing his mother too well to believe such nonsense.

"I cannot imagine my mother revealing the intimate confessions of a friend to anyone, and certainly not a person who would be willing to pass that information to a man such as Sir Charles."

Leonida studied his hard expression, obviously sensing his annoyance at the implication his mother could somehow be involved in the blackmail scheme.

"Then perhaps someone ran across the letters in your mother's safe and told him."

"No one knew of that safe..." he began, only to abruptly sit on the edge of the bed as a distant memory seared through his mind. "Christ."

"What?"

"Howard Summerville." He spit out the name as if it was a curse. And in many ways it was. The spineless creature was an insult to the Summerville name. "My worthless louse of a cousin," he grudgingly explained. "I caught him more than once stealing items from Meadowland. The last time I beat him senseless when I found him digging through my mother's private safe."

She slowly nodded, not appearing particularly surprised by his revelation.

"Would he associate with someone like Sir Charles?"

Stefan made a sound of disgust. "Howard would latch on to Beelzebub if he thought he might drop a quid in his pocket."

Her brows drew together as she considered his condemning description of his cousin.

"That would answer the question of how Sir Charles learned of the letters."

"But not why he would wait so long to approach the Countess," he retorted. "Sir Charles left London years ago."

"He mentioned something of his lifestyle demanding a great deal of money, although I refuse to even consider what his lifestyle might entail." Leonida shuddered, her eyes shadowed with a lingering fear. "I assume he has fallen into debt."

He instinctively reached out to cup her cheek with his hand. He never wanted her to feel fear when he was near.

"Or perhaps he only recently ran across my cousin," he speculated, quite prepared to lay the entire blame on Howard Summerville's shoulders. "The last I heard he was hiding from his creditors in Paris."

She pushed back the golden hair that had dried in a tangle of soft curls. Stefan swallowed a groan, wanting nothing more than to shove his fingers through that pale mass of silk. Instead he forced himself to be content with tucking one of the stray curls behind her ear.

"It does not truly matter how Sir Charles discovered the truth of the letters," she said, her voice not entirely steady.

"Not for the moment," he conceded. "Although I find it astonishing that he would risk blackmailing one of the most powerful women in Russia with nothing more than a suspicion that incriminating letters might exist."

"No doubt he assumed my mother would be so frightened that she would give in to his blackmail without proof of them." She lifted an absent shoulder. "When she refused, he sent his men to England in the hopes that they could discover the letters before I could get them."

His hand dropped to grasp her shoulder, his eyes narrowing in annoyance at her unexpected revelation.

"He sent men to Meadowland?" he charged, then before she could answer, he was struck by a sudden realization. "Of course. The poachers that Benjamin spotted. Why the devil did you not tell me?"

"We have been through this before."

She tried to pull away, but Stefan was in no mood to allow her to escape. Instead he leaned forward, nearly touching her nose with his.

"And we will no doubt go through it again," he threatened, his voice softening as the warm scent of her skin teased at his nose. Even when Leonida was driving him batty, he still wanted her. Desperately. "You will learn to trust me."

CHAPTER EIGHTEEN

LEONIDA REMINDED herself to breathe. The room suddenly seemed smaller, more intimate. And her world reduced to Stefan's beautiful face so close to hers.

Her body might ache and her wound burn with a raw pain, but the urge to forget the horror of the past days in this man's arms was near overwhelming. When Stefan was near she felt protected and utterly safe in a manner that was as unexpected as it was unexplainable.

The knowledge should have terrified her, not sent a comforting warmth through her heart.

Resisting the urge to close that slight distance to feel the intoxicating heat of his kiss, Leonida absently lifted her hand to finger the bandage over her wound.

"We were discussing Sir Charles," she said huskily.

His hands gently skimmed down her bare arms, the light touch sending out tiny shock waves of pleasure. "Were we?"

With an effort, she sucked in a deep breath. No. She could not be distracted. Not until her mother was truly out of danger.

"Yes, we were." She conjured the image of her mother, reminding herself of just how distraught the Countess might be. For all her foibles, Leonida was devoted to her mother. She would never allow her to be hurt. "And may I point out that while we are sitting here he is currently escaping?"

His lips twisted with rueful resignation as he leaned back and studied her with an unwavering gaze.

"As you have discovered, I possess a very long reach. I eventually will make him pay for what he has done."

She rolled her eyes at his arrogance. "Despite your certainty in your skills, I must reach St. Petersburg."

"I have promised to have word sent to reassure your mother."

"And what if Sir Charles reaches St. Petersburg first and manages to convince my mother she must pay immediately?" she demanded.

His jaw tightened at her persistence. "Sir Charles was in no condition to approach your mother. In truth, I am not certain he will survive the injury you inflicted. You may have already stolen my vengeance."

Leonida shuddered. She did not regret stabbing Sir Charles. Or even the thought he might die. Her true concern was that he might survive to hurt another woman.

"We cannot be certain," she muttered.

A silence filled the bedchamber. Stefan studied her with a growing skepticism.

"There is another reason you are so eager to travel to St. Petersburg. Why?"

"I need to be home with my family. Surely that is not so strange after all I have endured?"

"Not strange, but certainly suspicious. You are a complicated woman and you rarely have a simple motive. Whatever your desire to be reunited with your family, there is another reason for your sense of haste." His fingers tightened on her arms, his grip not tight enough to hurt, but warning that he was far from pleased by the thought she was not being entirely honest. "What have you kept from me?"

She glared at his unyielding expression, feeling as if her entire life was being consumed by this man.

"I will agree that you had a right to know why I came to Meadowland. It is your home, after all. But my reason for wishing to return to St. Petersburg is no one's concern but my own."

A dangerous emotion smoldered in his eyes at her deliberate challenge. "No, Leonida, you thrust your way into my life, now you must suffer the consequences. I will not allow you to keep anything hidden from me."

Her heart missed a panicked beat. "I went to England to help my mother, not to thrust my way into your life."

His gaze skimmed down to the revealing shift before returning to her wide eyes.

"And end up in my bed."

Her heart missed yet another beat. "That has nothing to do with the situation."

He leaned forward, his lips brushing over her temple in a featherlight caress. "It has everything to do with the situation."

A bittersweet longing clenched her stomach. If only he were not the Duke of Huntley and she not the Countess Karkoff's daughter. If only they were a man and woman who had no duties or the heavy expectations of their families.

She could so easily fall in love with him.

"Stefan, you must let me go," she whispered.

"Never." His voice held a chilling certainty. "You are mine."

"I am beginning to think that you are the one who is mad."

"Very likely." Pulling back, he captured her wary gaze. "Why are you in such a hurry to return to St. Petersburg?"

Leonida heaved an aggravated sigh. Stefan must surely be the most stubborn, unreasonable man ever born.

Why did she even bother to fight him? Her reward for such skirmishes was nothing more than another dent in her pride, and an ache in her head.

"Because when I was so rudely kidnapped I was forced to leave behind my belongings," she snapped.

An odd expression settled on his elegant features. "And they are so important to you?"

"I had the letters hidden beneath the lining of my bag."

He paused, as if she had at least caught him off guard. A small victory.

"Very clever."

"Not clever at all," she corrected, her expression echoing her sharp pang of guilt. "I kept the letters hidden from Sir Charles, but now I have no means of retracing my steps after I was kidnapped, and even if I could, who knows what the servants at the inn did with my belongings? Anyone could have them."

A slow smile curved his lips. "No, not anyone."

Her breath caught as a sudden hope surged through her. "You…"

"I collected them from the inn," he assured her.

Her hope was forgotten by a sudden flare of puzzlement. "How did you know I was there?"

His smile widened. "There is nowhere you can hide from me, Miss Karkoff."

She snorted at his teasing. "You have no idea how tempted I am to prove you wrong."

His hands trailed slowly up her arms. "Should you not be a great deal more appreciative for my foresight in rescuing the letters from falling into the hands of your enemies?"

"Of course I am appreciative, but…"

Without giving her an opportunity to finish, Stefan swooped downward and covered her lips in a sweet, deliciously stirring kiss.

"I prefer a more tangible method of gratitude," he murmured against her lips, his fingers continuing to brush over her shoulders and up the curve of her neck. Then, reaching the bandage covering her wound, he abruptly pulled back, his eyes glittering with a suppressed fury. "If Sir Charles Richards is not already dead I will strangle that bastard with my bare hands."

"I wish someone would," she said, shivering at the unwelcome memory of Sir Charles's perverted pleasure as he pressed the dagger to her throat. "He enjoyed frightening me. No, he enjoyed *hurting* me. I do not think I was the first woman he had tortured."

"He will never hurt you again." His hand moved from her bandage to trace the line of her jaw. "That I swear."

"I am more concerned for those women who have no protection from such a monster," she said, her voice harsh with concern. "Herrick Gerhardt must be warned."

His thumb brushed the corner of her mouth. "A worry for tomorrow."

"I suppose. For tonight I want…" Her thoughts threatened to vanish as he leaned forward to brush her lips with light, teasing kisses. "Halt that."

"Am I hurting you?"

Leonida pressed her hands against his chest. Of course he was hurting her. Oh, not physically. His touch was pure magic. Which was why, of course, she had been incapable of resisting his seduction. But the knowledge that his life was firmly tied to England and the woman he would one day wed caused a disturbing ache in the center of her heart.

And it would only be worse the longer she spent in his company.

"This is no time for your kisses."

With a deep sigh, Stefan brushed one last lingering kiss on her mouth before pulling back with a rueful grimace.

"Unfortunately you are right."

She ignored her pang of disappointment at his ready agreement. She had more important matters to concentrate upon.

"Where is my bag?"

"I presume that Boris left it in the stables with my horse. Do not be foolish." He firmly pressed her back against the pillows as she made a movement to slide off the mattress. "You will remain in bed, I will collect your bag."

With a stern glare that warned of dire repercussions if she did not obey, Stefan crossed the flagstone floor to lay another log on the fire. Only when he was certain the fire was blazing to his satisfaction did he disappear through the door.

Alone, Leonida was left to ponder the realization that her awkward, near lethal journey was at an end.

She had the letters.

Her mother was out of harm's way.

So why did she feel like crying?

THE RUSSIAN NIGHT AIR was predictably chilly despite the season. Thank God.

After being alone with Miss Leonida Karkoff, Stefan needed the cold breeze to dampen his throbbing arousal.

And his equally aroused temper.

The woman possessed an astonishing talent to do both in the same moment.

So why was he so determined to ignore every sense of decency and simple logic to return her to Meadowland?

He shook his head, dismissing the discomforting question as he crossed the clearing in the front of the cottage.

"Boris?"

"I do not suppose you come bearing food?" a voice demanded from above.

Tilting back his head, Stefan watched the servant nimbly climb down from a nearby tree.

"Not yet." He shrugged. "Miss Karkoff's maid has claimed that her rabbit stew cannot be hurried."

"Women." Boris shook his head. "Luckily I saved a few rabbits to roast over a fire. You are welcome to join me."

"A generous invitation. For the moment, however, I am more interested in collecting Miss Karkoff's belongings."

"Ah." Boris's grimace was visible in the full moonlight. "I meant to tell you, but it slipped my mind."

Stefan frowned, sensing he was not going to like whatever Boris had forgotten.

"What?"

"When I settled the horses in the stables I noticed Miss Karkoff's bag was gone."

"Damn." He was right. He didn't like it. "Was there anything else missing?"

"No. I searched among the trees in the hopes it had simply fallen from your saddle, but I could find nothing."

Stefan did not bother to demand if the servant was certain he had searched thoroughly. If Boris said the bag was missing, then Stefan knew it would not be found.

"It was taken," he muttered, his mind already sorting through the various implications.

"I assume so, but who would want it?"

Stefan shook his head before he reached out to clap his companion on the shoulder. That was a question beyond his ability to answer.

"Keep a close guard, Boris. This adventure is not yet done."

Shoving aside the urge to linger in the cool darkness, Stefan slowly returned to the cottage. His thoughts were churning with possibilities that each seemed more improbable than the last.

Perhaps that was why he missed the narrowing of Leonida's eyes as he entered the back chamber and halted beside the bed.

"I thought you were bringing my bag," she said, her voice low and oddly controlled.

"It is gone."

Before he could guess her intention, she was leaping off the bed, her hair flying about her shoulders.

"What?"

"Damn, stay where you are," he gritted, plucking her off her feet to lay her back on the mattress. Then, when it was obvious she intended to fight him, he sat on the edge of the bed and grasped her arms in a tight grip.

"What have you done with the letters?" she hissed, her eyes bright with accusation.

He frowned. Christ, she was beautiful with her face flushed and her glorious hair spread across the pillow. He was wise enough, however, to resist the urge to yank her into his arms.

The vixen was quite capable of drawing blood when she was in this mood.

"I told you..."

"You told me that you had them and then you return to claim that they have mysteriously disappeared." Her suspicious glare seared over his face. "Did you go to order your servant to hide them?"

It took Stefan a long moment to realize that the wench was actually accusing him of stealing the damned letters. His hands tightened on her arms, infuriated by the knowledge she still refused to trust him.

"Have you taken leave of your senses?" he demanded, his voice low and threatening. "If I wanted to keep the letters from you I would never have told you I retrieved them to begin with."

"Perhaps it just now occurred to you what they are worth."

"Are you suggesting, Miss Karkoff, that I am intending to use my mother's letters to extort money from the Countess Karkoff?"

She licked her lips, suddenly appearing uncertain. "I..."

"Ah, but why halt there?" he silkily demanded. "Maybe I shall destroy Alexander Pavlovich and make my own bid for the throne. I do have a remote connection, after all."

She at least possessed the grace to appear embarrassed by her insulting accusations. If only momentarily. Refusing to meet his hard glare, she lowered her head.

"If you do not have them, then where are they?"

"Obviously they have been stolen."

"By who?"

The question had been plaguing him since Boris had revealed the luggage was missing.

"It could have been anyone. A local who strolled past

and thought the bag might have money stashed inside." He shrugged. "Or one of Sir Charles's guards."

Her head abruptly lifted, her eyes wide as she appeared to be struck by a sudden thought.

"Josef," she breathed.

"Who?"

"The man who helped Sir Charles escape."

Stefan had a brief memory of a small, scarred man who had appeared to haul Sir Charles into a waiting carriage. At the time he had been so consumed with the blood spilling from Leonida's wound that he had no interest in the roughly attired peasant, or the madman he was helping to flee.

"He was not in the cottage when we entered," Stefan said, speaking his thoughts aloud. "So it is entirely possible he caught sight of our approach and decided to hide in the woods to avoid capture."

She chewed her bottom lip, her eyes troubled by some inward thought.

"He was the one who searched my rooms at the inn. He told Sir Charles he could not find the letters, but at the time I wondered if he knew more than he was willing to reveal." She shifted restlessly beneath his grip. "Perhaps he deliberately left them behind in the hopes he could return later and retrieve them without Sir Charles realizing his betrayal."

Stefan prepared himself for yet another battle. The fear for her mother was already etched on her tight features. Within moments she would be once again demanding that they return to St. Petersburg.

Regardless of the fact she was in no condition to travel.

Or that he was in no condition to allow her to escape.

"That would make sense," he conceded. "But if he discovered I had been so kind as to deliver the letters into his hands, why would he bother to rescue Sir Charles?"

Her brow furrowed. "I do not know."

"Those letters have caused a considerable amount of

trouble," he snapped, frustrated by Leonida's constant concern for her mother. Did she never think of herself or her own needs? "Why the devil did you not just burn them?"

"My mother wished to keep them."

"Why?"

"She..." There was a brief hesitation. "She is a very sentimental woman."

Stefan's lips thinned at the absurd lie. He did not need to be able to read Leonida's mind to realize that the Countess Karkoff wanted the letters for some nefarious purpose of her own.

No doubt she hoped to use them to protect herself, and her position, from the always unpredictable Romanovs.

"No, she is a very cunning and calculating woman." He held her gaze, his expression grim. "She desired the letters to protect herself and was willing to sacrifice her own daughter to get her greedy hands on them."

"That is not true."

"Why do you defend her?"

"She is my mother."

"Then she should behave as one. And you should have more sense than to fall in with her dangerous schemes."

Her eyes narrowed, never one to be intimidated. Strangely it was one of the qualities he admired most about her.

"Do not attempt to tell me you would not risk your neck for Lord Summerville," she countered. "Or that he would not do the same for you."

He snorted, knowing he could not argue with her logic. Only last year Edmond had pretended to be Stefan to draw the danger away from his brother. That did not mean, however, that he was willing to allow Leonida to continue with her reckless behavior.

Once he had her back at Meadowland she would be protected as she should be.

"Yes, but I would also blacken his eye for being ridiculous enough to put me in danger in the first place."

"If I decide to blacken someone's eye it will not be my mother," she warned.

His annoyance abruptly faded as his gaze swept over her defiant expression.

For all Leonida's ability to stir his anger and exasperate him beyond measure, not to mention the manner she had tossed his peaceful life into utter chaos, she was still the most fascinating woman he had ever encountered.

"You truly are an ungrateful brat," he chided, loosening his grip to stroke the satin skin of her upper arms. "Your mother shoves you into the hands of Sir Charles and you have no word of complaint, while I rescue you from the madman and you desire to blacken my eye."

Her expression remained unyielding, but Stefan did not miss the delicate shiver. She could spit fire all she wanted, but she still responded to his touch. The knowledge was absurdly satisfying.

"I left Meadowland so you would not be put in danger," she said, as if that excused her mad flight into the path of Sir Charles. "If you had remained where you belong then you would not have been put in the position to rescue me from any madman."

He shook his head at her convoluted logic, but he could not halt his slow smile. "You are concerned for my welfare?"

Her lashes fluttered down to hide her expressive eyes. "I would not want you hurt because of Russian conspiracies."

He chuckled, lowering his head to bury his face in the thick golden curls, breathing in her warm, jasmine scent.

"Why can you not just admit that you care?"

"Not wishing someone dead does not mean…" Her words broke off in a groan as his lips discovered the sensitive spot just below her ear. "Oh."

He nipped the lobe of her ear. "Can you at least confess that you desire me?"

"I do not want to," she rasped, even as her head arched back to invite his caress.

"Leonida." He trailed his lips over her cheek, careful to keep his touch light. He was acutely aware of her painful injury. Any further seduction would have to wait until she was fully healed. "My sweet dove. I will not allow you to slip away again."

She reached to clutch at his shoulders, the heat of her hands searing through the thin linen of his shirt.

"I must go home."

Her words hit him like a blow. Did she truly believe that he would allow her to walk away?

He pulled back, a disturbing fear clutching his stomach as she lifted her lashes to reveal an unexpected determination.

"No. My carriage will be waiting in St. Petersburg. Return to Meadowland with me."

She shivered, wrapping her arms around herself. "You know that is not possible."

With an effort, Stefan contained his burst of frustration, instead rising to his feet so he could cross the room and stir the fire. He had devoted his entire adult life to avoiding the complications of women who desired more than he was willing to offer. Perhaps it was the irony of fate that ensured the one woman he refused to allow out of his life was so determined to leave.

The flames flared and crackled, filling the small room with heat. Setting aside the poker, Stefan turned to meet her guarded gaze.

"Anything is possible."

"If it were known I was staying beneath your roof without Lady Summerville to act as guardian my reputation would be in tatters."

"Then you can stay at Hillside," he easily countered. "I know Brianna would be delighted to have your companionship. Especially now that she is confined to the house."

"And your brother would be wishing me to the netherworld."

He leaned against the rough stone wall, knowing quite

well that Edmond would readily open his home if he thought it would please his brother.

"I can ensure Edmond is welcoming."

"No, Stefan." Her voice was low, but unhesitating. "My place is in St. Petersburg."

CHAPTER NINETEEN

LEONIDA PULLED THE BLANKET over her trembling body and settled deeper against the pillows as Stefan paced the floor. She was still annoyingly weak from her injury. Or at least, she told herself it was her injury. What else besides the shock and loss of blood could make her hands tremble and her skin feel cold and clammy?

She was not about to admit that the unpleasant sensations were entirely due to the thought of her bleak future without Stefan.

Reaching the window, Stefan abruptly turned on his heel and paced back toward the bed to glare down at her undoubtedly pale face.

"And what waits for you in St. Petersburg beyond your mother?" he abruptly demanded.

She swallowed her sigh of frustration. Why was he making this so difficult?

Deep in her heart she ached to do whatever necessary to keep Stefan in her life. But her logic understood that she would court nothing but disaster to give in to her desires.

What did he offer beyond thc risk of scandal? Desire, of course. What else? Fleeting affection?

Life had taught her that affection was as undependable as it was costly.

Just look at the mess she was in because of her devotion to her mother.

"I happen to have a very full life with a number of friends and several charities that depend on me," she informed him stiffly. "And of course, with Alexander Pavlovich's return to the Summer Palace there will be a number of society events to attend."

"I thought you disliked parties," he accused.

"They are not my favorite means of devoting an evening, but we all do what we must." She met his gaze squarely. "A duke is not the only one with duties."

"And if your mother or the Emperor decides that it is time for you to wed?"

She blinked, startled by the unexpected question. "They decided it was time for me to wed several years ago. Thankfully, that is a decision no one will make for me."

His beautiful face was hard, unreadable. "And you have decided that you have no need for a husband?"

Leonida paused, uncertain what he wanted from her. He appeared annoyed by the thought her parents would press her into marriage and even more annoyed by the fact she would never be wed against her will.

Impossible man.

"No, I am just certain that I have yet to encounter a gentleman who has convinced me that a life with him would be preferable to sacrificing my independence," she said tartly.

His brooding gaze swept down her slender form covered by the blanket.

"You would consider marriage a sacrifice?"

"Would you not?"

It was his turn to pause, seeming to give the offhand question serious thought.

"It would, of course, depend entirely upon my potential bride."

Leonida flinched at the painful thought of Stefan with his eventual bride. She would be English, of course. One of those sweet-tempered debutantes that had been trained from the cradle to pander to a gentleman's vanity. And beautiful.

A lovely English rose.

"This is a ridiculous conversation," she muttered.

His jaw tightened, but he readily allowed himself to be diverted. "Then let us return our attention to more important matters."

"The only important matter is finding those letters."

"You are not going to distract me, Leonida." He settled on the edge of the bed, a dangerous shimmer in his eyes. "I did not travel across the continent to return to England alone."

Her mouth went dry, starkly aware of the tantalizing awareness prickling over her skin. The urge to curl against the warm strength of his chest and feel the comfort of his arms wrapping around her was near unbearable.

Instead she grimly reminded herself that she was no clinging female who needed a gentleman to tell her what she was or was not going to do.

"Then I fear you are going to be disappointed."

"No." He leaned forward, his hands braced on each side of her waist as he loomed above her. "I am not a man who accepts disappointment."

"The choice is not yours to make. I am returning to St. Petersburg and there is nothing you can do to halt me."

"You should know better than to challenge me," he drawled, a dangerous edge to his voice. "I would prefer you come with me willingly, but I am not opposed to convincing you of the pleasures to be found in our journey to England."

Leonida was absurdly relieved by the spark of anger at his smug assurance that he could bend her to his will. It was much easier to ignore the craving to close the small distance and lose herself in his kisses when her pride was injured.

"Are you threatening to hold me against my will?"

"It would not be against your will for long." He bent to brush his lips along the curve of her ear. "We both know the only reason you are resisting your desire to be with me is fear of scandal."

Leonida hid her shiver of pleasure, her hands lifting to press against his chest.

"You arrogant..."

"Not arrogant, determined."

"Arrogant," she fiercely repeated. "And no better than Sir Charles."

Stefan sucked in a sharp breath, abruptly pulling back to regard her with an insulted expression.

"You would compare me to that bastard?"

She ignored her prick of guilt. She had allowed this man to beguile her too many times. She could not risk being lured back to England and disaster.

"Sir Charles was just as eager to hold me against my will and force me to obey his commands. How are you different?"

"The madman was prepared to blackmail your mother and slice open your throat," he gritted.

"My point is that I am not a bit of property to be claimed by some man. I am perfectly capable of deciding what I desire for my future."

He held himself unnaturally still, his elegant features rigid in the flickering firelight.

"So you are prepared to walk away from me without regret?"

Without regret. She swallowed the near hysterical laugh.

"It is for the best."

"The best for you or me?" he rasped.

"Both."

He leaned so close she could feel the brush of his breath on her face, their gazes locked in a silent battle of wills.

Sensing that he was caught between the urge to kiss her into compliance and the more uncomplicated choice of tossing her over his shoulder and carrying her off, Leonida breathed a small sigh of relief when the door was shoved open and Sophy entered bearing a wooden tray.

"Here we are. Freshly baked bread and rabbit stew."

With a muttered curse, Stefan rose to his feet, regarding Leonida with a glare that made her stomach clench with unease.

"I will stand guard so Pyotr can eat his dinner," he said, his eyes narrowing. "This conversation is not finished."

He brushed past the startled maid, slamming the door behind his retreating form.

With an unfathomable smile, Sophy continued her path to the bed, waiting for Leonida to scoot to a sitting position before laying the tray across her legs.

"Dare I ask what conversation I interrupted?"

Leonida tore apart the warm bread with more force than absolutely necessary.

"The Duke of Huntley is insufferable."

"And what man is not?" Sophy asked. "They always believe they know what is best and find it impossible to accept a woman might be capable of thinking for herself."

"Exactly," Leonida muttered, suddenly realizing just how hungry she was as she swallowed a large spoonful of the savory stew.

"And even more insufferable when they are obviously in the wrong, and yet refuse to admit as much."

"I do not believe they ever accept the notion they might be wrong."

With a chuckle, Sophy busied herself with straightening the blanket covering Leonida and arranging the pillows.

"Then again, they do know how to keep a woman warm at night."

Leonida snorted, refusing to acknowledge the flutter in the pit of her stomach at the thought of Stefan keeping her warm.

"So does a blanket."

Sophy straightened with an arch smile. "And they do come in handy when a woman is being kidnapped by a madman."

Leonida concentrated on her dinner, a heat crawling beneath her cheeks.

"Not when they intend to kidnap you in return."

"The Duke intends to kidnap you?"

"He has threatened to take me back to Meadowland whether I am willing to go or not."

"Has he?" There was a short pause before the maid gave a sudden laugh. "Well, well."

Leonida jerked her head up, her brows drawn together in a frown of disbelief. "I do not know why you look pleased. Stefan should obviously be locked in Bedlam."

"A gentleman is rarely capable of thinking clearly when he has fallen in love with a woman," Sophy said, her tone smug.

"Love?" Leonida's voracious appetite abruptly disappeared. With a sharp movement she set aside the tray, her heart oddly heavy. "That is absurd."

"Is it?"

"Yes. The Duke of Huntley might desire me as a temporary mistress, but lust has nothing to do with love."

"A gentleman does not risk his life for lust."

"He does if his pride is injured." She shook her head. "Believe me, Sophy, the Duke wants nothing more from me than a brief affair."

"And what is it that you want?"

Leonida leaned back against the pillows, not allowing her thoughts to dwell on the perilous question.

"Peace."

IT WAS A WEARY HERRICK GERHARDT who rode past the precisely constructed buildings of the military settlement despite the bright morning sunlight.

He had not rested since yesterday when he had received a cryptic note along with a roughly drawn map from Dimitri Tipova suggesting where he might search for Miss Karkoff. He had barely paused to change clothing before gathering Gregor and his horse and charging from St. Petersburg.

As he neared the location, however, the instinctive

wariness that had kept him unscathed, despite the vicious Russian politics, had urged a measure of caution.

Only a fool would completely trust Tipova and he did not intend to tumble into a trap.

Not that his discreet inquiries along the way had provided him with much more than vague rumors of a disruption at a local inn and a strange Englishman who was searching for his missing ward.

He had hoped that the commander of the local settlement might be capable of providing more reliable information.

Shifting in the saddle that had grown more uncomfortable by the hour, Herrick urged his horse to a brisk pace, his gaze absently skimming over the encampment.

His military soul approved of the tidy rows of connected structures that housed the soldiers and their families. As well as the rigidly divided fields the soldiers planted to provide their food.

His heart, however, flinched at the grim atmosphere that lay like a sullen cloud over the entire settlement.

Where were the children who should be at play? Or the women gossiping and whispering as they tended their laundry? Or even the men laughing together as they shared a bottle of vodka?

Ah, Alexander Pavlovich, why are you so blind to the seething resentment?

With a shake of his head, Herrick passed the soldiers standing guard at the edge of the settlement and joined Gregor, who'd waited patiently at the side of the main road.

Bringing his horse to a halt, Herrick watched his companion easily vault back into his saddle, wryly considering the advantages of youth. At the moment his entire body ached and his tired eyes felt as if they had been rubbed raw with sand.

What had happened to the time he could endure a day of battle and then ride the entire night to engage in the next campaign?

"Did they have any information?" Gregor demanded, his bulky body attired in a plain black coat and breeches that matched Herrick's modest style.

Herrick hoped to avoid any unnecessary attention among the peasants.

"They confirmed the rumors of an inn being attacked by a group of ruffians and a woman being taken against her will," Herrick said, keeping his searing fear caged beneath his stoic composure.

He could not think clearly if he allowed his emotions to cloud his judgment.

"Do they know where they took her?"

"The Commander claimed that he has been keeping watch on the road and that all carriages have been halted to ensure that the villains did not pass."

"So they must still be at the cottage."

"Yes."

Gregor studied him intently, sensing Herrick's hesitation. "You do not seem convinced."

Herrick smiled wryly. There were disadvantages to hiring a soldier with intelligence rather than one content to mindlessly follow orders.

"The Commander also mentioned that one carriage passed late last night at a dangerous pace and nearly ran down the guard when he attempted to halt the driver." His fingers tightened on the reins, his horse shifting with unease beneath him. The thought that he could be so close to rescuing Leonida only to have Sir Charles slip past him was enough to make him howl with frustration. "He said the guard was certain there was only one male passenger, but it is impossible to know for certain."

"That is troubling." Gregor glanced toward the nearby soldiers, his brow furrowed. "What do you wish to do?"

"For the moment we have no choice but to continue on to the cottage and pray that Miss Karkoff was not in that carriage."

Gregor's lips twisted as he returned his attention to Herrick.

"I suggest we continue on rather quickly. I do not like the stares we are receiving."

Herrick grimaced as he urged his horse into a slow trot, glancing over his shoulder at the gray buildings and silent fields.

"It is a pity," he muttered. "The settlements were a sound notion in the beginning. How better to increase the size of the military while allowing the men to be with their family and provide their own food?" He shook his head. "But under Akartcheyeff's rule it has created more problems than it has solved."

Gregor gave a philosophical shrug of his shoulders. "Soldiers do not make dependable farmers. Not when they are forced to practice their drills for hours each day or to drop their plows when the Commander calls them to duty."

"No, and the brutal treatment by most of the commanders has not improved the situation." Herrick felt the age-old regret tug at his heart. "Akartcheyeff will never learn that it is respect, not fear, that inspires true loyalty."

Gregor's face hardened. He had endured three years of Akartcheyeff's cruel temper.

"He was trained under Emperor Paul. Perhaps it is not so strange he would prefer a regimental authority to what he would consider coddling."

"Treating a man with dignity is not coddling," Herrick grated.

Gregor shot him a wry glance. "I am not the one you must convince."

Herrick slowed his pace as the fields lining the road were replaced with a mixture of hawthorn and birch trees with the occasional cedar. The trees dangerously obscured his view.

"I have done what I can and I dare not press too hard," he admitted. "My fear is that the Czar's habit of charging from one extreme to another will convince him to replace the General with a man such as Prince Alexander Golitsyn."

Gregor gave an abrupt laugh. Golitsyn's unwelcomed influence on Alexander Pavlovich was creating as many problems as Akartcheyeff. Herrick considered himself a religious man, but the zealous extremes that were beginning to creep through the palace were yet another concern.

"You do not wish to witness the settlements becoming monastic barracks?" Gregor asked, already knowing Herrick's opinion.

"No more than I wish the men to spend their days standing before the altar and merely praying for their crops to grow."

Gregor chuckled. "Careful, Gerhardt, you shall be accused of being a heretic."

"Mystical nonsense. It has done as much damage as Metternich," he muttered, the bitter words tumbling from his lips before he could halt them. Breathing in a cleansing breath, he shook his head. "Forgive me. I am tired or I would not allow my tongue to be so free."

"You need never apologize to me or fear that your words will be repeated," Gregor said, his voice low with sincerity. "Unlike many, you do know how to inspire loyalty."

Herrick managed a weary smile. "A loyalty I depend upon, my friend. And the reason I requested you join me on this delicate mission."

Gregor cast a glance toward the thickening trees. "Ah yes, our mission. Do we have a plan if Miss Karkoff is at the cottage?"

"We kill Sir Charles and return her to her mother."

"You believe it will be so simple?"

"Thus far nothing has been simple, but I cling to futile hope," Herrick drawled, reaching into his pocket to pull out his loaded pistol. "Take care, the cottage should be near."

"Nearer than you imagine, Herrick Gerhardt," a voice drawled from the edge of the trees.

Herrick brought his horse to a calm halt while his companion cursed and fumbled for his pistol. Reaching out, Herrick laid a restraining hand on the young soldier's arm. He recognized that voice.

"No, Gregor," he commanded, turning his head to watch the burly servant step from the shadows. "Boris. I am not certain if I am more shocked at the realization that you have not yet been shot by a prudish Englishman or that you have appeared in this precise location. May I assume that Lord Summerville is near?"

"Lord Summerville remains in England. I traveled to Russia with the Duke of Huntley."

Herrick didn't bother to hide his shock. It had been several years since Huntley had journeyed so far from England. Which begged the question of why he would choose to do so now.

"And what would bring the Duke here?" he demanded.

"No doubt it was the same reason that brought you here."

Herrick's tension coiled as he realized what the man was implying.

"Is Miss Karkoff..."

"In the cottage with her maid, Sophy," Boris was swift to assure him.

Painful relief surged through Herrick as he tossed his reins toward Gregor and slipped from the saddle. He was not too late. Thank God.

"And Sir Charles?"

Boris grimaced, his hands planted on his hips. "The last we saw of him, he was in a carriage headed toward St. Petersburg with his servant."

Herrick crossed toward the edge of the road, noticing a narrow trail leading through the trees. No doubt the cottage lay beyond.

"You allowed him to escape?" he barked.

Boris smiled. As Edmond's personal servant he had

rarely displayed more than a grudging deference toward anyone beyond Summmerville.

"Not entirely unscathed. Miss Karkoff managed to lodge a knife in his gut. There is a decent chance that he is currently suffering a painful death."

Herrick clenched his hand on the pistol, infuriated by the thought of the sweet child being forced to protect herself.

"Leonida stabbed him?"

Boris lifted his brows. "I do not know why you should pretend to be shocked. The woman is a hellion who would terrify any man with a bit of sense."

"Has she been harmed?"

"She was wounded."

"Damn." Herrick stepped toward the path, anxious to return her to the safety of St. Petersburg. "I must see her."

With a movement that was surprisingly swift for such a large man, Boris was blocking the path, his expression unreadable.

"She is already healing. There is no reason to fret."

Herrick stilled, belatedly recalling he still had no notion why the Duke and Boris were in Russia. He did not like mysteries.

"Boris, are you attempting to block my path to the cottage?"

"Miss Karkoff is still sleeping. There is no reason to awaken her."

"Allow me to warn you that I am tired and in no mood for games. You will take me to Miss Karkoff," he commanded, his voice low and lethal. "Now."

There was a rustle in the undergrowth before a tall form attired in a dark green jacket and fawn breeches stepped onto the path.

Herrick's eyes narrowed as he realized that Stefan had recently bathed and shaved the face that was so remarkably similar to Edmond's.

So, the men had not recently arrived at the cottage.

The knowledge sent a chill down his spine. Did the Duke know why Leonida had been sent to England? And more importantly, if had discovered the truth, what did he intend to do with the information?

Although Edmond had spent years as an advisor to Alexander Pavlovich, his older brother's loyalty had always remained with England.

As if sensing Herrick's suspicion, Huntley allowed a slow, taunting smile to curve his lips.

"Do not blame Boris," he drawled. "He is merely following my orders."

CHAPTER TWENTY

STEFAN FOLDED HIS ARMS over his chest, attempting to disguise his annoyance with Herrick Gerhardt's untimely arrival.

A deep part of him understood that he could not actually drag Leonida back to England. She was not some village maid without family or connections. But he had known that with enough time he could persuade her that their affair was not yet at an end.

He had never been as notorious a rake as his younger brother, but he knew when a woman enjoyed his touch. Christ, he had only to be near her for the air to heat with frustrated passion.

With the proper inducement, he could prove to her that it was futile to deny the need that bound them together. They were both trapped until desire had run its natural course.

The arrival of Herrick, however, had stolen any opportunity to slip Leonida away. The stern, ruthless man would have Stefan locked in the Czar's dungeons if he suspected Stefan intended to lure Leonida back to Meadowland. And his bed.

"I must admit this is a rather odd place to find the Duke of Huntley," Herrick said, his expression guarded.

"You have my full agreement."

"Would your presence have anything to do with Miss Karkoff?"

Stefan deliberately glanced toward the two servants who eyed each other warily.

"Perhaps we should have this conversation in private?"

"If you wish." Together they moved down the path, Herrick's pistol glinting in the dappled sunlight. A silent threat that Stefan did not miss. Damn him to hell. "Tell me, is Leonida badly injured?"

Stefan halted, turning to stab Herrick with an irritated frown. Herrick's concern came far too late. He should never have allowed Leonida to be put in danger.

"No, but she has endured a brutal ordeal and it will take longer for her emotions to heal than her wounds."

Herrick's face drained of color. "Did Sir Charles..."

"I do not believe so," Stefan rasped, knowing that the older man feared Leonida had been violated. The fear had haunted him, as well. "But he most certainly enjoyed terrorizing her and her servants. It is a fortunate thing she possesses such courage. A lesser woman would be utterly shattered."

Herrick recovered his composure, smoothing his expression to an unreadable mask.

"Leonida's courage could never be questioned."

"No, only her good sense." Stefan deliberately paused. "And the intelligence of her advisors."

Herrick's jaw tightened as the thrust slid home. "May I inquire what your interest is in the Countess's daughter?"

"She was a guest in my home," Stefan smoothly retorted. "Or at least she was a guest until she stole my mother's letters and slipped away in the midst of the night."

Herrick arched his brow, disguising any reaction to the realization that Stefan was aware of Leonida's reason for being in England.

"And you followed her?"

"You are fortunate I did. Sir Charles had every intention of killing her. If not for me you would be searching for a corpse."

"Boris mentioned it was Leonida who stabbed Sir Charles," Herrick countered, scraping against Stefan's pride.

He would never forget the sight of Leonida trapped

against Sir Charles, the dagger pressed to her throat as the crimson blood dripped down her pale skin.

The vision would be seared into his mind forever.

"We have already determined her courage, but she had no means to fend off an entire gang of ruffians," he said coldly. "It was sheer luck I managed to get here before Sir Charles slit her throat."

Herrick flinched as Stefan struck back. "What do you want, Stefan? A medal? No doubt Alexander Pavlovich would be pleased to pin the Order of St. Vladimir on your chest."

"I want to comprehend how the Countess could sacrifice her innocent daughter to save herself from scandal."

The older man's expression was dangerously hard and Stefan did not doubt that if he were anyone but the Duke of Huntley the old soldier would have him clapped in chains and disappearing into a damp cell.

"I appreciate your concern for Leonida," he said, his tone revealing that he was anything but appreciative of Stefan's interference. "But you will not be allowed to meddle in Russian affairs."

"Russian affairs?" Stefan's temper flared. "Damn you, Leonida was very nearly killed."

"I realize the gravity of the situation and I assure you that Leonida will be well protected once she has been returned to her family."

"That has yet to be decided."

"Your Grace..."

Belatedly realizing now was not the time for this particular argument, Stefan overrode the older man's outraged words.

"I think you should know that the letters Leonida stole from my home are now missing."

Herrick's lips thinned, his obvious desire to make certain that Stefan understood he had no claim to Leonida thrust aside by the more pressing concern of the lost letters.

"Do you have any notion of who might have taken them?"

"Leonida suspects that the servant who assisted Sir Charles to escape might have taken them for his own purpose."

"Damn," Herrick muttered, clearly distracted. "They must be found."

"Without the assistance of Leonida."

Herrick snapped his attention back to Stefan, his eyes hard with warning.

"You speak for her?"

"Someone needs to."

"Forgive me, your Grace, but I fear you overstep your bounds."

"I was not the one to risk her lovely neck by sending her to a foreign land to play thief while a madman haunted her every step."

The old soldier stepped forward, his jaw tight. He was not a man accustomed to having his warnings ignored. A pity for him that Stefan was not so easily cowed.

"Miss Karkoff is no longer your concern," Herrick growled.

"This entire situation remains very much my concern." Stefan allowed a superior smile to curve his lips. "If you will recall, the letters that have caused such trouble belonged to my mother."

"You are in Russia now, not England."

"Is that a threat, Gerhardt?"

The man returned Stefan's smile, too wily to be lured into open confrontation. There was a reason he had been Alexander Pavlovich's longest serving advisor.

"I am merely pointing out that you are a visitor and it will be the Czar's decision how long your stay might be."

Stefan shrugged aside the warning. His lofty position might not make him utterly immune to the Emperor's anger, but it did offer him a protection few others could claim.

Alexander Pavlovich would not be anxious to further

strain the relationships between Russia and England, no matter what his opinion of King George.

"You believe that Alexander Pavlovich will force me from the country?"

Herrick refused to back down. "If need be."

"Take care," Stefan said softly. "If I am forced to leave I assure you that Leonida will accompany me."

The very air prickled with menace as both men battled to dominate the other.

"That is a very foolish boast, your Grace. Perhaps you do not comprehend just how attached Alexander Pavlovich is to Leonida. You do not want to incur his wrath."

"If he was so attached, he would never have allowed her to be put in danger."

"He did not..." Herrick snapped his lips shut as he realized just what he had admitted.

"He does not know of the letters, does he?" Stefan mocked, knowing it was the one true weapon he held over this man. "Or the fact that the Countess was being blackmailed."

Herrick's jaw clenched, his expression hard as he sought to regain the ground he had lost. "You are an intelligent gentleman with a brilliant future in England. Why would you entangle yourself in the Countess's private matters?"

"I became entangled the moment Leonida arrived in Surrey."

The danger in the air thickened. "The Romanovs owe a debt of gratitude to your family, so I will offer you a word of warning. Leonida is a precious jewel of the Empire. Should anyone, no matter what his title or position, dare to harm or insult her, you can be certain that justice will be done."

Stefan scowled. Herrick Gerhardt had always been fiercely devoted to Alexander Pavlovich, and it was only to be expected his loyalty would extend to Leonida, but Stefan found himself bristling at the man's possessive manner.

Leonida was not the property of Russia.

She was *his.*

"Thus far the person who has caused her the greatest harm is her own mother," he snapped.

Herrick leaned forward until they were nearly nose to nose. "Return to England, your Grace, before you…"

"Herrick?" A soft female voice had them both spinning toward the path leading from the cottage. Stefan's heart gave its familiar jerk at the sight of Leonida, her slender form swathed in her ugly black gown and her face heart-rendingly pale. With her throat still bandaged and her eyes shadowed from lack of sleep, she had never appeared so fragile, or so in need of his strength. Stefan instinctively stepped forward only to freeze when she gave a choked cry and without warning flew down the path to throw herself in Herrick's waiting arms. "Oh, thank heavens."

THE HOME OF VANYA PETROVA was an elegant St. Petersburg townhouse built near the Fontanka Embankment. Like its owner, the mansion was a mysterious combination of lavish beauty and hidden secrets.

Vanya had for years been a ruthless supporter of Alexander Pavlovich, using her wealth and power to bolster the young Czar's original claim to the throne and then keeping an eye upon the treacherous nobles and various secret societies that had proven to be a constant threat over the years.

It had, indeed, been Vanya who had first approached Edmond to assist her in her covert efforts and happily lured the young, impetuous nobleman into one dangerous situation after another. A fact Stefan had depended upon when he had arrived unannounced on her doorstep.

Stefan had met Vanya on occasion over the past years, but he was counting on her heavy obligation toward his brother to secure her assistance during his visit to St. Petersburg.

Thus far his hasty plan had been successful.

A satisfied smile touched his lips as he glanced about the guest chambers he had been given. The lilac wall panels and satinwood furnishings held a hint of a European influence, but Vanya's love for Russia was obvious in the lush velvet curtains, the delicate ornaments that sparkled with expensive jewels and the polished wood floor that was too beautiful to cover with a carpet.

A decidedly welcome change from the nasty inns that he had been forced to endure for weeks.

Another welcome change was the tailor that Vanya had insisted be brought to her home to provide a suitable wardrobe for the Duke of Huntley. Although his carriage had arrived in St. Petersburg, he had not packed the elegant evening clothes that would be necessary to move among the Romanov Court.

Now, three days after his arrival, he was attired in a precisely cut mulberry jacket stitched with gold and a champagne waistcoat. His black pantaloons were a soft knit that clung to the hard muscles of his legs, and his shoes sparkled with diamond buckles.

Choosing an Oriental knot for his cravat and brushing his raven curls to frame his lean face, he appeared every inch the powerful Duke of Huntley prepared to be entertained by the Emperor of Russia in his Summer Palace.

A fortunate thing, since the gilt-edged invitation had arrived just after breakfast.

He unconsciously grimaced as he absently stroked the enamel snuff box in his hand. His first inclination had been to ignore the royal summons. His only purpose in St. Petersburg was to be near Leonida until she came to her senses and returned to Meadowland. In the meantime, he had no interest in socializing among the always treacherous Russian Court.

Unfortunately, his visits to the Countess Karkoff's home had been a pointless waste of time. The butler had turned him away at the door, claiming the Countess was ill and that Miss Karkoff was tending to her care. Since he had not yet reached the point of being willing to break down the door and carry Leonida off, he had no choice but to hope she would eventually make her appearance at the palace.

Besides, not even a lofty English duke could ignore an invitation from the Czar without attracting unwanted attention.

His resigned thoughts were interrupted by a sharp knock and Stefan turned to watch as the door was thrust open and Vanya Petrova sailed into the parlor.

A tall, curvaceous woman, Vanya was still beautiful with her silver hair and handsome features. This evening she was attired in a green crepe gown that perfectly matched the stunning emeralds hung about her neck with sable trim along the hem.

Closing the door behind her, Vanya's blue gaze made a critical survey of Stefan before a smile curved her lips.

"A vast improvement," she said, her English only faintly accented.

Stefan slid his enamel snuff box in a pocket beneath his jacket and straightened his cuffs.

"I knew I could trust you to create a miracle. Your exquisite sense of fashion is exceeded only by your beauty."

Vanya clicked her tongue although a pleased blush stained her cheeks.

"And I thought it was Edmond who inherited your father's gilded tongue."

"False rumors that I suspect came from my brother."

"Ah." She sent him a significant glance. "Speaking of rumors."

He grimaced. "Please, Vanya, I have not yet had my first brandy."

"Allow me."

With a regal grace, Vanya moved to the brass inlaid table to pour a measure of brandy into a glass. Returning to Stefan, she pressed it into his hand and watched as he tossed it down in one swallow.

"I do not suppose this can wait until I return from the palace?" Stefan muttered, placing the empty glass on the nearby mantle.

"It could, of course," she said succinctly.

"Very well, you cunning minx." He conceded defeat with a sigh. He would be a fool to walk into the poisonous atmosphere of the palace without all the information he could gather. "Tell me of these rumors."

"The first is that Leonida was sent to England to discover whether an English suitor would appeal more to her than those Russian hopefuls that she has already rejected."

A peculiar resentment flared through his heart. "Have there been many?"

Vanya lifted a silver brow. "Many?"

"Many rejected suitors?"

"More than a dozen that I know of, and no doubt many more who I do not," she admitted, her tone casual but her gaze piercing.

He clenched his jaw. Now was not the moment to dwell on the thought of Leonida being swarmed by anxious suitors. He had promised Boris he would at least attempt to remain civilized.

"Let us return to the rumors."

Vanya's full lips twitched. "Well, there are those who are speculating that Leonida found you no more pleasing than any other man and returned to Russia only to have you follow her in the hopes of changing her mind."

No more pleasing? The woman had melted in his arms like warm butter.

"And what are the others speculating?"

"That you were the one to dislike the match and Alexander Pavlovich commanded your presence to bring you up to snuff."

"So either I am a lovesick swain, or a marionette on the Czar's strings? Lovely."

Vanya toyed with a square-cut emerald that dangled from her ear. "What did you expect?"

"Can I not simply desire to visit my mother's homeland without ulterior motives?"

Vanya's laughter echoed through the large parlor. "My darling Stefan, you are in St. Petersburg. Nothing is done without ulterior motives."

He could not argue with her logic. The royal sport in Russia was gossipmongering. How many noble families had been destroyed by stray whispers?

"So which rumor do you believe?" he abruptly demanded of his companion.

She studied him for a long, unsettling moment. "I believe that you are more confused than any of us as to your reasons for being here."

The undeniable accuracy of her words wrenched a startled laugh from Stefan.

"Edmond always claimed that you were as crafty as a fox."

"And a dependable friend." Her expression softened as she moved to place a hand on Stefan's arm. "Stefan, you must take care."

He met the pale blue gaze, keeping his own expression guarded. He had told Vanya nothing more than the fact he had traveled to St. Petersburg to complete unfinished business between him and Leonida, but the woman was far too clever to be easily deceived.

She already suspected more than he desired.

"Am I in danger?"

Her fingers on his arm tightened. "My loyalty toward Alexander Pavlovich will never waver, but the Czar grows more unpredictable with every passing year. If he believes your arrival in St. Petersburg is connected with Miss Karkoff, he will demand to know your intentions."

Stefan was not impressed. What father allowed his

daughter to be sent to England without ensuring she was properly cared for?

"I did not realize he took such an interest in the young lady."

Vanya's lips thinned as she was forced to acknowledge Stefan's rebuke.

"It is admittedly haphazard and at his convenience, but your arrival is certain to recall it to mind."

Stefan covered her fingers that lay on his arm, regretting his sharp words. Vanya had been nothing but kind since his ill-mannered intrusion into her home.

"I appreciate your concern, but I cannot ignore an invitation to the Summer Palace."

"No, but you can avoid incurring the Czar's wrath."

Stefan smiled wryly. "I seem to hear that with monotonous frequency."

"No doubt because it is excellent advice."

"I promise to do my best," he soothed, attempting to lighten the mood. "So, before I walk into the hornet's nest, do you have any other words of warning for me?"

With a shrug she stepped back, obviously accepting that she had done all she could to keep Stefan from disaster.

"There are the inevitable squabbles among the minor nobles and the Austrian ambassador is currently out of favor, so if he sends you an invitation it would be best to refuse." She paused, an expression of distaste rippling over her striking features. "You will also discover the Court littered with peculiar gentlemen and ladies who claim to be mystics. It is important that you disguise your opinion of their absurdities."

"You forget I have spent time in English society. Ignoring absurdities is as obligatory as a properly tied cravat."

Vanya's smile returned. "I suppose I should also warn you that you will not be particularly welcomed by those gentlemen who had hoped to claim Leonida as a bride. At least not if they believe you to be a rival. There are many who are convinced that marriage to her will further their position in society."

Stefan's brows snapped together. Leonida wed to further the ambitions of some worthless buffoon? Never.

She deserved a man who could appreciate her rare combination of sweet innocence and fiery courage. A man who would lavish her with his undivided attention and make certain she understood just how extraordinary she was.

A man like himself.

"If that is true then it is little wonder she has refused to wed," he said, caught off guard when Vanya tilted back her head to laugh with rich humor. "What is so amusing?"

"Miss Karkoff is unwed because she has not yet discovered a man worthy of her heart. Such an intelligent and spirited woman would be foolish to settle for anything less."

Stefan's scowl remained. Somehow he had the sense that he was included in those men whom Leonida found unworthy.

"And precisely what makes a man worthy?"

"That is for her to decide." Vanya pursed her lips. "I do hope for her sake, she will consider carefully before committing to any man. A woman in her position has the luxury of remaining independent for as long as she desires."

Even knowing the woman was attempting to provoke him, Stefan couldn't halt the stab of annoyance.

"It is little wonder you are considered a danger to young ladies of society," he said tartly.

"Because I believe that women are capable of making their own decisions? The world is changing, Stefan. Women are no longer the property of men."

"A pity," he muttered.

"Hmm."

"What?"

"You sound remarkably like your brother before he at last accepted he would have to put aside his pride and earn the trust of the woman he loved. No doubt you intend to be just as stubborn."

Stefan froze, refusing to consider why the accusation had made his heart clench in alarm. Edmond's stormy courtship of Brianna had nothing in common with his desire for Leonida.

Nothing at all.

"Good God, I am suddenly relieved that I am forced to endure dinner at the palace," he retorted. "An evening in the Emperor's company is fraught with far less risk than sharing a brandy with you, my dear. At least with Alexander Pavlovich I stand a fair chance of coming out unscathed."

She shook a warning finger in his face. "A wise man does not praise himself going into battle, he praises himself coming out."

CHAPTER TWENTY-ONE

PETERHOF, THE SUMMER PALACE of the Emperor of Russia, was a tribute to Emperor Peter's fascination with the seas and the sheer force of his will.

Stretching along the Gulf of Finland, the grand palace separated the upper and lower parks that had been designed by the French architect Leblond, a student of Le Notre who had created the Versailles gardens. Leblond (along with his fellow architects) secured his own fame with his exquisite Grand Cascade that began at the front of the palace and directed the channel of water through sixty-four fountains and past hundreds of gilt bronze statues that glorified the sea gods and goddesses. At the bottom of the Cascade was the mighty Samson Fountain that Peter had constructed to proclaim his victory over Sweden.

The palace itself had been built with large windows and terraces to admire the view, and beneath Peter's daughters' rule it had been expanded by Rastrelli. The talented architect added a floor to the central Baroque building and connected two sweeping wings with golden domed pavilions at each end.

It truly was a masterpiece, Leonida had to acknowledge as she stepped from the carriage and paused to admire the brilliant yellow structure trimmed with white that glowed like a jewel beneath the flames of a thousand torches.

A pity that her nerves were so tightly knotted that, for once, her invitation to the palace was more a punishment than a treat to be savored.

Allowing herself to be swept along with her large party of elegantly attired companions, her heart thudded with a painful dread.

Damn Stefan.

When Herrick had arrived at the cottage to return her to St. Petersburg she had been certain that she had seen the last of the Duke of Huntley. She was once again surrounded by the protection of her family and any hope he could have harbored at continuing their affair was at an end. What could possibly keep him in Russia?

The aggravating man, however, refused to accept the inevitable.

He had shown up at her house demanding to see her, and while she had managed to have him turned away, she had discovered this morning that he still possessed the means to force a confrontation.

Why else would he have accepted an invitation to dinner with Alexander Pavlovich?

The devious duke had to know that she would be terrified at the thought he would expose her mother's foolishness to the Czar and confess her true reasons for traveling to England. What better means of forcing her from her home?

Clenching her teeth, Leonida climbed the wooden steps of the Gala Staircase. About her the milling guests whispered in awe at the dazzling display of gilded garland and flowers that decorated the white walls along with golden mythological statues tucked into shallow alcoves. Even the wrought-iron railing was decorated with traces of gilt.

Leonida paused on the wide landing, pretending to study the two female statues representing spring and summer that towered on pedestals connecting the railing. It was more than a simple appreciation for their flowing robes and graceful features. She needed to escape her chaperones without the tedious necessity of inventing some excuse.

Once certain she had escaped notice among the crowd, Leonida continued up the stairs, determinedly heading toward a side door once she reached the formal hallway rather than continuing on to the reception rooms. From there she hoped to be able to scan the guests from the shadows. She had to find Stefan before he could meet with Alexander Pavlovich.

She had just reached the door when a hand reached to grasp her arm, keeping her from her escape.

"Leonida?"

She swallowed a sigh of resignation as she turned to greet the older man attired in a plain black jacket and white waistcoat.

This was one gentleman she could not dismiss with a frown.

"Herrick."

Waiting for her to perform a graceful curtsy, Herrick regarded her with a suspicious gaze.

"I did not realize that you would be attending tonight. Alexander Pavlovich mentioned that the Countess was still recovering from her illness."

Leonida smoothed her hand down the gold satin ball gown that was embroidered with rubies along the low-cut bodice and tiny puff sleeves that barely caught the edge of her shoulders. Her pale curls were loosely piled on top of her head and a wide ruby ribbon encrusted with diamonds encircled her throat, disguising the cut that was rapidly healing.

She had told herself that she had chosen this particular gown because the Czar would expect her to appear at her best. It had nothing to do with the infuriating Duke of Huntley.

"Princess Rostovsky was kind enough to request I join her party," she retorted.

If she hoped that would be enough to send Herrick on his way, Leonida was doomed to disappointment.

"I trust the Countess will soon be fully restored to health?"

She smiled with rueful amusement. When she had first returned home her mother had been nearly hysterical with relief, barely allowing Leonida out of her sight. Then Nadia had learned that the letters were once again missing. She had taken to her bed, refusing to believe that her world was not coming to a ghastly end.

"We both know she will not be fully recovered until the letters are returned and the danger of scandal is at an end," Leonida said, her voice pitched low.

"It is not in Nadia's nature to hide from trouble."

"She is still blaming herself for my unexpected adventures and has convinced herself that she is destined to be properly punished by having her sins exposed to Alexander Pavlovich."

Herrick shook his head, a hint of impatience rippling over his gaunt face. "She has always possessed a love for the melodramatic. I will speak with her."

"You are always welcome, Herrick, but I am not certain that even your powers of persuasion will persuade Mother to leave her bed."

"I will simply point out that her continued absence from the palace is stirring the Czar's suspicion that she is avoiding his company." A glint of humor softened his dark eyes. "If that fails I shall say that the Court is beginning to whisper that Alexander Pavlovich has at last wearied of her and has banned her from his presence."

Leonida chuckled, easily imagining her mother's horror at the mere thought. She would be scrambling from her bed before her maid could pull back the covers.

"You are a devious man, Herrick Gerhardt."

"I should be, I have had years of practice." He reached out, cupping her chin to study her pale face. "Now, my dear, why do you not tell me what you are doing here?"

Leonida cursed the luck that had crossed her path with this all too shrewd man. He knew her far too well.

"I was invited. Is there a reason I should have declined?"

"You know that the Duke of Huntley will be attending?"

"Will he?"

Herrick narrowed his piercing gaze, not fooled for a moment by her innocent tone.

"Leonida, if you even consider the notion of putting yourself in danger again I will have you put in shackles and hauled to Siberia."

She pulled away from his grip with an aggravated sigh. There were moments when she wearied of being treated as a witless child rather than a grown woman.

At least Stefan…

No. She would not allow herself to think of him as her tender lover. She was furious with him.

"And how could I possibly be in danger surrounded by the Czar's personal guard?" she demanded. "Not to mention that Pyotr refuses to allow me out of the house without him at my side. He even rode beside the Princess's carriage tonight, as if I were going to be attacked in the middle of St. Petersburg."

"There are many varieties of danger," Herrick observed in a hard voice. "I do not trust the Duke."

Leonida blinked, rather startled by the older man's reaction to Stefan. He had always been devoted to Edmond. Surely the brothers were not so different?

"You believe he is a threat?"

"I believe that he is a man fascinated by a woman and that he is not thinking as clearly as he should." The older man shifted, as if discomfited by the conversation. "He could easily tarnish you with scandal."

Equally ill at ease, Leonida glanced toward the passing guests. How could Herrick possibly suspect Stefan's desire to have her in his bed?

Surely the Duke had not been so tasteless as to reveal their brief affair?

"I have agreed to trust you to retrieve those horrid letters," she said stiffly. "You must trust me to manage the Duke of Huntley."

Herrick's expression tightened. "And how do you intend to manage Huntley?"

Since she hadn't the least notion, Leonida could have happily kissed the uniformed servant who halted directly beside Herrick and performed a deep bow.

"Pardon me, sir, but the Emperor has requested your presence."

Herrick waved an impatient hand, sending the footman scurrying away.

"Leonida."

"Go to the Czar, Herrick," she urged, managing a confident smile. "I will be fine."

"If he harms you…"

"Go."

ACCUSTOMED TO THE TEDIOUS formality that surrounded a royal evening of entertainment, Stefan attempted to remain philosophical as his carriage crawled behind the long line of carriages leading toward the steps of the palace. He had waited days to see Leonida, he reminded himself as he fidgeted with impatience. A few more minutes would hardly matter.

Unfortunately, he could not entirely forget Vanya's blithe reference to Leonida's determined suitors. The thought that she was even now smiling as some man kissed her fingers or led her onto one of the shadowed terraces was enough to twist his stomach into a painful knot.

By the time his carriage reached the sweeping front steps, Stefan was climbing out before the footman could assist him. Brushing past the small clusters of guests, he rapidly made his way up the steps and entered the vestibule where he handed his hat and gloves to the servant waiting beneath the large portrait of Emperor Peter.

Belatedly aware of the curious glances trained in his direction, Stefan forced himself to take a breath and make his way to the upper floor at a dignified pace, occasionally nodding in the direction of vague acquaintances.

The Emperor was already curious about the Duke of Huntley's presence in St. Petersburg. He would not call more attention to himself by dashing through the palace like an imbecile.

Reaching the top of the limewood steps of the Gala Staircase, he paused to study the various guests. Most were gathered together in an effort to see and be seen, although a few were admiring the large portraits that lined the walls.

His hands clenched as he realized that Leonida was not among the crowd. Then, from the corner of his eye, he caught a glimpse of curls the shade of morning sunlight.

An excitement he had no intention of examining fluttered through the pit of his stomach as Stefan thrust his way past a lady attired in a hideous puce gown and her whey-faced daughter. He was not about to allow his prey to escape.

Not again.

Keeping his gaze trained on the golden curls, Stefan pushed his way to the edge of the gathering, a predatory smile curving his mouth as he caught sight of Leonida's delicately carved profile.

So his instinct had been right. She was here. His body tightened with a scorching need as he moved forward. He had spent too many nights lying awake, aching to feel her in his arms. He was damned well not spending another night with nothing more than empty frustration.

Almost as if able to read his thoughts, Leonida glanced at him over her shoulder and then deliberately slipped into a side chamber.

With long strides he was following in her wake to enter the small living room with Chinese silk on the walls and an embroidered divan that echoed the Oriental theme near the fireplace. Assuring himself they were alone, he firmly closed the door. A pity there was no lock.

For a moment, he leaned against the wooden panels of the door, simply appreciating the sight of Leonida as she stood in the center of the room.

Christ. She shimmered like a golden angel in the candlelight.

An alarming warmth filled his heart, spilling through his body. With a low growl he pushed from the door and stalked toward her. It had been too long since he had felt her pressed to his body.

Her eyes widened at his relentless approach, as if sensing his barely leashed hunger. And then he had his arms wrapped around her and the disquiet that plagued him for days slowly eased. She fit against him with astonishing perfection.

"Leonida," he muttered, his lips restlessly stroking over the satin skin of her face, her warm jasmine scent clouding his mind with pleasure.

For a precious moment Stefan could feel Leonida melt against him, a soft moan of pleasure wrenched from her throat. He shifted to claim her lips in a kiss of blatant need, allowing the distant clamor of elegant guests to fade until it was just him and Leonida alone in the world.

Then the sound of a string quartet soared to life in the reception hall, breaking the spell. Leonida stiffened, raising her hands to press against his chest and turning her head to escape the demands of his kiss.

"Stefan, no," she said huskily. "I must speak with you."

Denied her lips, Stefan nibbled a path down the tender curve of her neck, careful to avoid the ribbon that hid her wound.

"Later," he murmured against the rapid pulse beating at the base of her throat.

"You must halt."

"Why?"

"Do you want to be discovered?"

Stefan smiled. In this moment he was indifferent to

who might come across them. Or what the consequences might be.

He needed her. Now.

"What I want is you." He pulled back, his gaze sweeping greedily over her beautiful face. "Come with me, Leonida. There must be privacy to be found in this vast monstrosity."

She jutted her chin, but Stefan did not miss the blush staining her cheek.

"The palace is not a vast monstrosity," she inanely argued. "Most visitors claim it is even more beautiful than Versailles."

Stefan snorted. "Yet another monstrosity, but at the moment I have little interest in discussing architecture."

"Neither do I."

Heat blazed through his body. "Then let us find someplace where we can be assured we will not be interrupted."

She trembled as he pressed her against his hard arousal, but with a sudden motion she was pushing her way out of his arms.

"No, this is not why I came here tonight."

Stefan gritted his teeth. His overwhelming impulse was to sweep her off her feet and lay her on the nearby divan. Whatever Leonida's protests, he sensed her yearning. He did not doubt he could overcome her ridiculous barriers and seduce her.

Instead he planted his hands on his hips and fought back his male instincts.

Ridiculously, he did not want to compel her capitulation. He wanted her to admit she desired him with a force that equaled his own.

Pride? Or something more dangerous?

Impossible to know.

"I do not care why you came, only that you are here," he growled. "I knew you could not hide forever."

"I have not been hiding."

He deliberately lowered his gaze to the mouth still swollen from his kisses.

"How could such beautiful lips utter such dreadful lies?"

She brushed her hands over the shimmering folds of her gold gown. A certain indication she was not as composed as she wished him to believe.

"Not wishing to receive you in my home is not hiding. My mother has been ill."

"Predictable." Stefan shook his head in frustration. "You were nearly killed because of her selfish refusal to admit the truth and she is the one to seek sympathy."

She stiffened at his harsh words, her expression settling into mulish lines that he recognized all too easily. She would protect her mother to the gates of hell. No matter how unworthy the Countess might be.

It was a loyalty he grudgingly admired even as he wanted to shake some sense into her.

"You know nothing of my mother and it most certainly is not your place to judge her," she snapped.

"And what is my place, Leonida?" he countered. "I am allowed in your bed, but not allowed to protect you from those who take advantage of your overly generous heart?"

Heat flooded her cheeks. "You have no place. What happened between us is over."

With a hiss of anger, Stefan prowled forward, backing her against the wall.

"It is far from over," he warned, planting a hand on either side of her head to glare down at her stubborn expression. "I am not a fool. I feel you tremble when I touch you. I taste your pleasure when our lips meet. You still desire me."

Her eyes darkened with an awareness she could not hide. "No. I cannot."

"Cannot?" His voice thickened, his gaze mesmerized as her tongue peeked out to wet her lips. "You already have."

"A mistake I do not intend to repeat."

"Dammit, this is not a mistake." He leaned down,

brushing her lips with a lingering kiss. "This is a miracle. Why do you deny your need?"

"Because I will not be your mistress," she said, her voice low, as if the words were wrenched from her. "Not ever."

He flinched. "Leonida…"

"No." She turned her head, refusing to meet his frustrated glare. "I came here to speak with you. Nothing else."

Stefan abruptly stepped back. Damn the woman. Why did she have to complicate what should be a simple affair?

She had come to his bed willingly enough. Hell, she had been nothing less than eager.

Now she behaved as if his only purpose was to ruin her life.

"And why, after three days of ignoring me, would you have a sudden urge to speak?" he snarled.

"Because I need to know what you intend to say to Alexander Pavlovich."

"What…"

He bit off his words, his hands clenching as he realized the implication of her words. It was not mere chance that she was at the palace. Or because of some furtive desire to cross his path.

She was here because she feared that he might reveal the ugly truth of her trip to England to her father.

Why the devil had he not considered such a possibility?

His sharp, humorless laugh echoed through the room. "Of course. I have always considered myself to be quite an intelligent gentleman, but when it comes to you, my dove, I seem to be no more than a half-wit."

She frowned warily, as if trying to judge his reaction to her accusation.

"You have not answered my question."

Stefan turned to pace toward a lacquered table that held a priceless collection of Chinese vases, his mind churning. Whatever his annoyance at the realization Leonida was eager to believe the worse of him, he was not above using her assumption to his advantage.

"How did you know I was invited to dine with the Emperor tonight?" he demanded.

Leonida paused, clearly reluctant to reveal her source of information.

"Our cook has three daughters," she at last admitted. "The youngest is a chambermaid to Vanya Petrova."

"And she thought it necessary to share my plans?"

"There are few secrets in St. Petersburg."

"I will keep that in mind."

She made a sound of impatience. "Why are you here, Stefan?"

Slowly he turned, meeting her fretful gaze. "Not even I can ignore a summons from Alexander Pavlovich."

"And when he demands to know why you have traveled to Russia?"

His gaze drifted down her slender body, lingering on the ribbon tied about her neck to disguise her injury. His own bullet wound was nearly healed, but the memory of how near he had come to losing this woman would be forever seared into his mind.

How the hell did she expect him to simply walk away?

"That depends entirely upon you, Leonida."

"What do you mean?"

He crossed his arms over his chest. "I possess no particular inducement to deceive the Czar Alexander. Indeed, it would be the height of foolishness to risk such a powerful man's displeasure."

Her expression hardened. "You did not mind risking his displeasure when you threatened to kidnap me."

"Ah, but the reward would have been worth the cost," he drawled. "Now I have no reason to lie."

"It is not lying to avoid revealing my purpose in coming to England."

"A fine distinction."

She stepped from the wall, her curls shimmering like liquid gold in the candlelight and her eyes the pale blue of the finest sapphires.

Stefan swallowed a groan as his body clenched with an impatient surge of lust.

"There is no reason for him to suspect that my visit was more than a desire to become acquainted with England," she said, seemingly impervious to the torture she was inflicting on him.

"You are not so innocent as to think the Emperor will not demand to know what occurred during your time at Meadowland and why I chose to follow you back to St. Petersburg."

"Which only proves that you should never have come here."

"Why should I not?" Stefan shrugged. "I have nothing to hide."

"This is absurd." She glared at his mocking expression. "If you reveal the truth you will only cause Alexander Pavlovich further distress."

"He has endured both scandal and disappointment before."

"And he still carries the wounds," she retorted. "Why burden him with more?"

He stepped toward her rigid body, unable to deny a smug satisfaction at the fluttering pulse visible at the base of her throat.

He did not believe for a moment that it was fear making her heart race.

"So you only desire to protect the Czar Alexander?"

"Of course."

"And your mother?"

She shifted restlessly, easily sensing his derision toward the Countess Karkoff.

"Yes."

"And what of me?"

She faltered, a hint of uncertainty flaring through her eyes.

"I do not understand."

"Thus far the only reason you have given me to hold my tongue is for the benefit of the Czar Alexander and your mother," he said smoothly. "Why should I hazard Alexander Pavlovich's anger should he discover that I hid the truth from him?"

She waved a hand in a dismissive motion. "There is no danger of him discovering the truth."

"Then you have the letters?"

"No, but..."

"But?" he prompted as her words faded.

"Herrick Gerhardt is confident that he will be capable of tracking them down."

He took another step forward, drawn to her with an irresistible compulsion. He was well and properly bewitched, he acknowledged, brushing a finger down the length of her stubborn jaw.

"And in the meantime they might be used to once again blackmail the Countess, or worse, sold to those willing to make your mother's confessions a source of public humiliation for the Emperor," he insisted. "If that were to occur, Alexander Pavlovich is bound to hold me at least partially responsible for not warning him of the potential threat."

She shivered, making no effort to pull away from his lingering touch. "You intend to tell him?"

"Unless you can convince me it is in my interest not to."

Frustration rippled over her beautiful features. "Do you have no concern for Russia at all?"

"Why should I?"

"It was the homeland of your mother. You did say that she remained loyal to the crown."

Stefan narrowed his gaze, reminded of the numerous risks that Edmond had taken in the name of Alexander Pavlovich.

"My family has done its duty to the Russian Empire," he said, his voice edged with warning. "You are going to have to find some means beyond guilt to keep my lips closed."

"And what would those means be?"

A wicked smile curved his mouth. "I think they should be fairly obvious."

"Why you…"

Her hand lifted to slap his face, but with a smooth motion Stefan captured her wrist and brought her fingers to his lips.

"Careful, Leonida."

She glared at him with impotent anger. "If you think for a moment you can threaten me into sharing your bed then you must have lost your wits, along with any claim to chivalry."

"Gentlemen with chivalry are inevitably a tedious bore," he murmured against her palm.

"It is not surprising *you* would think so."

He chuckled, indifferent to her insult. "Has it occurred to you that such a paragon of virtue would never be capable of understanding how a proper young maiden could manipulate her way into a man's home and then seduce him so she could escape with his property?"

He heard her breath catch. "I did not seduce you."

"What a poor memory you possess, my dove." He shifted her hand to kiss the sensitive skin of her inner wrist. "Perhaps you need to be reminded of your power over a hapless gentleman."

She groaned softly before wrenching her arm away and rubbing it against her skirt. As if she could wipe away the feel of his touch. And her violent reaction.

"You are merely attempting to distract me."

He lifted his brows, allowing her to escape. They both knew she was vulnerable to his touch. "I thought we were negotiating."

"I do not negotiate with my body," she hissed.

"A pity," he countered, not entirely teasing. "But you were the one to assume that I intended to demand your presence in my bed in exchange for my silence."

"You…" She muttered something beneath her breath,

no doubt damning him to the netherworld. "What do you want, Stefan?"

"Nothing more nefarious than your companionship."

"My companionship?"

His smile faded as he reached to grasp her chin. He wanted to ensure there would be no confusion.

She would not be allowed to avoid him.

"You will no longer turn me away when I call upon you at your home," he said, his tone uncompromising. "And if I issue you an invitation I will expect you to accept without complaint."

"You want me at your mercy?"

"A charming notion, but at the moment I will be satisfied with the knowledge you will not be able to scurry back to your home and slam the door in my face. Do we have a deal?"

Her eyes flashed with fury. "Damn you."

"I shall assume that means yes."

CHAPTER TWENTY-TWO

HERRICK ALLOWED THE UNIFORMED servant to lead him through the maze of rooms, swallowing a sigh as he halted before the chamber that had once been Emperor Peter's private study.

He had briefly hoped that Alexander Pavlovich had requested his presence to fend off some bothersome diplomat who was plaguing him with demands. It was not an uncommon occurrence.

But if they were meeting in this room, then it meant that what he had to say was private rather than state business.

And he could already guess just what was upon the Czar's mind.

Briefly considering the pleasant notion of continuing on to the side door that led to the gardens, Herrick squared his shoulders and stepped into the study. There was no purpose in putting off the inevitable.

Closing the door behind him, Herrick allowed his gaze to roam over the shadowed chamber. It was one of his favorite rooms in the entire palace. Unlike most of the public rooms, there was no gilt or jewels or glittering chandeliers. Instead there was a somber beauty in the carved oak paneling and exquisite parquet floor. The furnishings were equally simple with a heavy writing desk and shelves that contained a collection of leather-bound books. In a place of honor was Emperor Peter's large globe set in a wooden stand that spoke of his expertise in navigation.

The only splash of color was the three large portraits

hung on the paneling. The largest, of course, was of Peter in shining armor and the second of Czarina Catherine on horseback. The third was of Alexander Pavlovich attired in his military regalia.

His gaze at last landed on the Czar, who was standing beneath his own portrait, a wistful smile on his still handsome countenance.

A tall, imposing figure attired in an elegant blue coat that precisely matched his shrewd eyes and black pantaloons, Alexander Pavlovich's golden curls had begun to recede, but he retained the charm that had been his most potent asset over the years.

"Herrick."

"Sire." Herrick performed a bow. "You wished to speak with me?"

"Yes." The Emperor waved a hand toward the desk. "Brandy?"

"No, I thank you."

The Emperor turned to regard his portrait as Herrick crossed to stand at his side.

"You have served me faithfully a number of years, *mon ami.*"

Herrick chuckled as he studied the portrait. It had been painted shortly after the victory over Napoleon Bonaparte. A time that had been filled with glory and national pride.

"Indeed. It is almost impossible to recall the young, idealistic men we used to be."

"Too idealistic," the Emperor said on a sigh. "Had I known the burdens of wearing such a heavy crown, I would have allowed the Corsican Monster to keep Moscow."

Herrick grunted in disgust. Napoleon might have been a military genius, but his overweening pride and belief his grand army was indestructible had made his defeat as certain as Russia's glorious victory.

"The fool could not even hold on to Paris in the end,"

he retorted. "And surely you would not condemn us to the rule of the fat Bourbon King?"

The Czar's gaze instinctively shifted to the imposing portrait of Catherine.

"No, Grandmother would have cursed me from her grave. She was determined to have me upon the throne."

"A wise choice."

"Was it?"

"I never had a doubt."

Alexander Pavlovich turned to regard Herrick with shadowed eyes. "We should all be so fortunate to share your confidence. I am plagued with constant doubt."

Herrick was careful to keep his expression unreadable. The Emperor's fits of melancholy were becoming increasingly worrisome. Unfortunately he could battle against traitors and secret societies and even assassins, but he had no weapon to keep Alexander Pavlovich safe from his own fears.

"Is there something particular upon your mind?" he asked gently.

With an effort the Emperor shrugged off his dark mood, the blue eyes sharpening with the force of his shrewd mind.

"Yes, Herrick, there is."

"How may I serve you?"

Moving to the desk, Alexander Pavlovich poured a glass of brandy. "You may inform me what game the Countess Karkoff is playing."

"Game?"

"Nadia has many talents, but the ability to deceive me is not among them. I have known she was troubled since my return to St. Petersburg. I did not press her because I assumed she would be comforted by Leonida's return, but matters have only become worse." Alexander Pavlovich leaned against the desk as he sipped the brandy. "Now she refuses to even leave her bed."

Herrick shrugged, silently cursing Nadia for forcing him into the discomfiting encounter.

"You did say she sent word she was ill."

"If she was truly ill then she would not have declined the offer of my personal physician, nor would she have pleaded that I not visit until she is fully recovered. Nadia adores having others fuss over her."

"True enough."

"My first thought, I will admit, was a suspicion that Nadia had taken a lover."

Herrick's brows rose in genuine astonishment. "Nadia has been ever faithful, Sire."

Seemingly reassured, Alexander Pavlovich studied Herrick with a steady gaze.

"Something is preying upon her. I want to know what it is."

"Then should you not be having this conversation with the Countess?"

"Not if I wish to discover the truth."

Herrick's lips twitched. The Countess had never been famed for her honesty if a lie would suit her better.

"You wish me to question her?"

"Herrick, you are not foolish enough to pretend that you are not fully in Nadia's confidence," the Emperor warned softly. "She has always depended upon you when she is in trouble. And, of course, there is nothing that occurs in St. Petersburg that does not reach your ears."

Herrick grimaced, knowing he was cornered. The Emperor was not stupid, despite his habit of ignoring troubles he preferred to leave in the hands of others. When he demanded answers, he expected to get them.

"Do you trust me, Alexander?" he asked.

"With my life," the Czar admitted without hesitation.

"Then I think it best that you accept that it is in your interest not to know the precise details of Nadia's difficulties."

The Emperor drained the last of his brandy and set aside the glass.

"Is she in danger?"

Herrick considered a long moment. "I do not believe so."

"And what of Leonida?" the Czar pressed. "Is she involved?"

"Unfortunately."

"That was why she traveled to England."

"Yes."

Alexander Pavlovich pushed from the desk, his emotions carefully concealed as he absently crossed toward the large globe.

"I find it beyond my ability to imagine what such a journey could accomplish."

"Nothing more than a number of sleepless nights, I assure you," Herrick said dryly.

The Emperor frowned. "It does not surprise me that Nadia would send her daughter on a reckless adventure, nor that Leonida would find it impossible to refuse her mother's plea for assistance, but I am rather disappointed in you, *mon ami*."

"I had no notion of the scheme until Leonida disappeared from St. Petersburg. I was…" Herrick chose his words with care. Alexander Pavlovich, after all, was devoted to Nadia despite her reckless nature. No doubt it was in part her impulsive, vivacious character that was so different from his own gravity that attracted him. "Not pleased. Thankfully she has been safely returned home."

"Yes, she has returned." The Emperor turned his head to snare Herrick's gaze. "But not alone."

"I presume you are referring to the Duke of Huntley?"

"Rather odd he would choose to visit St. Petersburg the precise moment that Leonida returns from England."

"Not odd," Herrick muttered. "Dangerous."

"Should I be concerned?" Alexander Pavlovich demanded with a lift of his brows.

Herrick bit back the words that would have the Duke of Huntley hauled off by Imperial Guards. His personal annoyance at the man's relentless pursuit of Leonida was hardly worth a war with England.

"There is no doubt that the man is obsessed with Leonida, but I do not believe he would intentionally harm her," he grudgingly conceded. "Still, he does not appear to be thinking clearly at the moment."

"And what of Leonida? Is she equally fascinated?"

"Unfortunately."

"Why unfortunately? It would be a fine match."

Herrick's brows lowered at the Emperor's unexpected approval. "Assuming the Duke is prepared to offer marriage, she would be expected to leave St. Petersburg and live in England. The Countess would be devastated."

Alexander Pavlovich shrugged, his expression pensive. "Perhaps it is time for Leonida to seek her own happiness rather than constantly attempting to please others."

"You would not object to her wedding an Englishman?"

The Emperor sighed. "Both Nadia and I have been far too selfish. I only wish Leonida to be given a man who will love her as she deserves."

Herrick swallowed his words of protest, abruptly realizing that his possessive affection for Leonida was clouding his judgment.

He was so accustomed to having her depend upon him as she would a father that the thought of her turning to another man left a large hole in his heart. It was little wonder he had wanted to lodge a bullet in the Duke's arse.

Rather ironic that it was her true father that had to point out just how wicked it would be to keep her from finding happiness with a man who could offer her the love and devotion she so desperately craved.

"St. Petersburg will be empty without her," he said mournfully.

A small, perceptive smile curved the Emperor's lips. "You know, Herrick, perhaps you should consider choosing a wife and producing children of you own. You would be a doting father."

Herrick shuddered, heading for the brandy.

"God forbid."

THE JOURNEY BACK TO St. Petersburg had proven to be an agonizing test of endurance for Sir Charles.

Fleeing from the cottage, he had barely managed to stanch the blood pouring from his knife wound before falling unconscious. He had awakened in a squalid barn, so consumed with fever and pain that he was incapable of doing more than shivering on the dirt floor and cursing his weakness. Even worse, he had been plagued with nightmares of his childhood, at times crying in fear as he heard his mother's voice whispering in his ear.

He had no clear notion of how much time had passed before his fever at last broke and Josef had once again loaded him into the carriage and continued the excruciating journey. He remained weak, but as the hours passed he turned his thoughts from his pain and instead concentrated on his plans for revenge.

By the time they reached St. Petersburg he had imagined killing Leonida Karkoff a hundred different times, a hundred different ways.

Each more satisfying than the last.

The burning fury gave him a measure of strength as they at last came to a halt. At least enough to haul himself out of the carriage and peer around his surroundings with a jaundiced gaze.

Clutching the door, he studied the shabby warehouse that appeared grim beneath the bright sunlight and the distant quay that had been battered by the sea.

This was a part of St. Petersburg that a gentleman of his breeding did not willingly visit.

For good reason.

"Where the devil have you brought me?" he rasped, glaring at Josef as the servant tied off the reins of the horse and joined him. "I told you to take me to my house."

The scarred face twisted as Josef smiled with mocking amusement.

"I presumed that the fever had addled your wits. Unless

you truly desire me to deliver you into the hands of the Countess's guards?" The servant shrugged. "They are no doubt waiting for you there."

"Do not get above yourself," Sir Charles snapped.

"Do you want me to keep you from the dungeons or not?"

Sir Charles cursed the wound that left him dependent on his servant. The feeling of vulnerability did nothing to improve his foul mood.

"I prefer the dungeons to falling into the hands of Dimitri Tipova," he muttered.

Although his dealings with the leader of the underworld had been through the criminal's various underlings, he had heard rumors that Tipova hid among the dredges of society.

"And do you not think Tipova has his men keeping watch on your house?" Josef demanded. "I doubt a man who is feared throughout St. Petersburg is stupid."

He was right, damn him. Anyone searching for him was bound to keep guard on his home. Still, he had to find some means of retrieving the contents from the hidden drawer in his desk. Not only did it contain his forged passport that would be his only means of leaving Russia and what few funds he had left, but it held the various mementos he had collected from his victims over the years. Those were irreplaceable.

"I cannot leave Russia without my possessions."

Wrapping an arm around Charles's waist, Josef began leading him toward the warehouse, the crash of waves against the distant wharf the only sound to break the silence.

"It will take you at least a week to heal enough to travel. By then we will find a means to retrieve what you need," Josef assured him.

Charles stumbled on the uneven paving, the movement sending a jolt of searing pain through his side.

"This is that bitch's fault," he gritted. "I intend to see her in hell."

"All in good time."

"I want you to keep a close eye upon her. She will not be allowed to escape me again."

Josef angled his way to a side door, ignoring the trash piled beside the stone building.

"She believes herself to be protected now that she has been returned to her home. She will be there waiting when you are prepared to punish her."

The image of Leonida Karkoff pleading for mercy as he sliced his dagger through her throat sent a rush of anticipation through his body.

"A punishment I intend to savor."

"We will both be savoring a firing squad if we are caught by the guards." Josef reached out to tug open the heavy wooden door. "That's always assuming we are not captured by Tipova's men first."

Stepping into the large empty room that was shrouded in dusty shadows, Charles grimaced in disgust.

"What is this place, beyond a haven for rats?"

Josef urged him into the center of the rotting floor, his expression unreadable.

"I frequently stay here when I have need of disappearing from the streets."

"It is filthy."

"It is not so bad as that."

"Have you taken leave of your senses?" Charles sneered. "I am not a nasty peasant who is content to wallow in the muck."

"I am, of course, devastated you are displeased with my home, Sir Charles, but as they say, beggars cannot be choosers," a low voice drawled.

Stiffening in alarm, Charles glared as a slender man, with raven hair pulled into a tail at his neck and startling golden eyes in a narrow face, appeared from the shadows.

A mere serf, he told himself, although there was no mistaking the expensive cut of his claret coat and the aristocratic lines of his features. Even his boots were glossy enough to please the most meticulous nobleman.

No doubt he stole the clothes in the hopes of fooling the natives.

He was not so easily deceived.

Still, he could not deny the chill of unease that trickled down his spine.

"Who the hell are you?" he growled.

The stranger strolled forward, a mocking smile on his lips. "I have had many names and many guises over the years."

"I am in no humor for games."

"Now that is a pity since the game has just begun. One I have been looking forward to for a very long time."

Charles struggled against the instinctive urge to back away from the approaching man. By God, he did not cower before peasants.

"Do you impress the local serfs with your pretense of a true gentleman?" he scoffed.

"The local serfs are wise enough to hate true gentlemen." Coming to a halt, the man crossed his arms over his chest. "I impress them with my willingness to kill anyone who dares stir my temper."

"If you are hoping to frighten me then you are wide of the mark."

"Now who is pretending, Sir Charles?"

Charles gritted his teeth. If he were not injured the mocking idiot would already be dead.

"I have no need for pretense."

The man took another step forward, standing close enough to peer down his long nose at Charles.

"You bluff and bully as if you are a man of courage when at heart you are nothing more than a pathetic coward who preys on the weak."

Charles jerked at the accusation. No. This man could not know the truth. It was impossible.

"Enough of this foolishness. Either you leave or my servant will put a bullet in your heart," Charles rasped, a savage sense of triumph easing his discomfort as Josef readily pulled a loaded pistol from his pocket.

Gallingly, the stranger merely laughed, unperturbed by the gun pointed directly at his heart.

"So you would hide behind a nasty serf?" the man tossed Charles's words back in his face. "Is that what is considered bravery among true gentlemen?"

"Josef, be rid of this fool," Charles barked.

Without warning, the man tilted back his head to laugh with rich enjoyment. "Yes, Josef. Be rid of the fool."

"At last," Josef muttered, whirling on his heel to directly point the pistol at Charles.

Charles stumbled back, too shocked to fully comprehend what was occurring.

"What the blazes is the matter with you?" he demanded of his servant.

The stranger's laugh once again echoed through the empty warehouse.

"You did not believe I would allow you to escape from St. Petersburg without keeping an eye upon you? We have unfinished business."

Realization hit with a vicious blow. This was a trap. And he had fallen into it like a bumbling buffoon.

Cold dread coiled through his stomach, his knees so weak he could barely stand.

"Tipova," he breathed.

The master criminal offered a mocking bow. "At your service."

"You bastard."

"That I am. And quite proud of the fact."

"I suppose you believe you are excessively clever?"

"At least moderately clever." Dimitri cast a glance toward his treacherous servant. "What do you think, Josef?"

"No more than moderately."

"Brutally honest as always." The golden eyes shimmered with a smug amusement. "I do hope that he proved to be rather more respectful during his service to you, Sir Charles."

Charles licked his dry lips. His fury at having been so easily duped was swiftly giving way to sheer terror. Dimitri Tipova had not gone to such trouble to bring him to this warehouse merely to taunt him.

He had to find some means of escaping from this mess.

"Why have you brought me here?" he asked, his voice coming out in an embarrassing croak.

Tipova narrowed his gaze. "Do not be tedious. You know quite well why you are here."

"I will have your money…"

His words were cut brutally short as Tipova smashed his fist into Charles's mouth.

Tumbling backward, Charles groaned in agony. His lip was split and it felt as if someone had thrust a hot poker through his side. His vision momentarily clouded, making his heart clench with panic. Slowly his eyes cleared and he belatedly wished that he had passed out.

Gazing upward he found Tipova hovering over him with a feral hatred etched on his face.

This was more than a man angered by the loss of his money or the inconvenience of replacing his dead whores.

His revulsion toward Charles was a tangible force in the air that held no mercy, no compassion.

"Your attempts to blackmail Countess Karkoff have accomplished nothing more than your humiliation," he said, his lips curling with scorn. "Now you have nothing to offer me beyond your slow and painful death."

Cowering on the floor, Charles desperately clutched at his only hope of avoiding his horrifying fate.

"You will be shot for this," he hissed. "I am a nobleman. You cannot harm me without answering to the Emperor."

Tipova crouched down beside him, his golden eyes glowing with a terrifying anticipation.

"Actually I have been assured by those in authority that I am quite at liberty to do whatever I please with you. It was not at all wise to kidnap the Emperor's daughter."

"You lie."

The words had barely tumbled from his lips when Tipova deliberately pressed a knee hard against his knife wound, making Charles convulse in anguish.

"Did Miss Karkoff do this to you?" Tipova murmured, digging his knee deeper. "Obviously a spirited wench. I really must meet her."

"I will slice open that whore's throat," he gasped.

"Ah. It bothers you to be bested by a mere woman," the bastard taunted. "You like them at your mercy, do you not? It makes you feel less a worthless coward when you abuse a frightened, helpless creature."

"Go to hell."

Tipova reached into Charles's pocket to remove his favorite dagger.

"Eventually, but not before I have sent you ahead to prepare the path," he murmured, stroking the razor-sharp blade down Charles's cheek.

Charles's heels burrowed into the rotting planks of the floor as he futilely tried to scoot away from the dagger. The fear he had created in his victims was not nearly so pleasant when he was the one beneath the blade.

"Please," he whimpered, tears rolling down his cheeks. "I will find the money for you. I swear."

"Too late."

Charles screamed as the dagger sliced through his face.

CHAPTER TWENTY-THREE

ALTHOUGH IT HAD BEEN LATE when Leonida returned from the Czar's dinner, she was up with the sun, attiring herself in a peach silk carriage gown with ivory lace around the hem and a triple strand of pearls around her neck to hide the nearly healed wound. Her hair she left loose to tumble about her shoulders, too restless to remain still long enough for Sophy to style it in a more elegant knot.

The sense of restlessness continued to plague her as she finished her breakfast and retreated to a small parlor that overlooked the sunken rose garden.

It was a charming room with pale yellow silk on the walls and French furnishings that were painted gold and covered in a cream satin. The tables were topped with agate and held a collection of delicate cameos. The ceiling had been painted with a scene of cupids dancing among the clouds.

It was not the beauty of the room, however, that drew Leonida. Instead it was the morning sunlight that streamed through the high arched windows that made it her favorite.

Curling on a low sofa, she attempted to lose herself in a book, refusing to ponder her brief encounter with Stefan the night before or the message he pressed into her hand just before leaving the palace.

If she had learned nothing else over the past weeks, it was that she was wasting her time to attempt to make sense of the Duke of Huntley.

Several hours passed before the sound of approaching footsteps had Leonida setting aside her book, her heart leaping with what she told herself was annoyance, although it felt remarkably like anticipation.

She was smoothing her hands down her skirt when Pyotr entered the room. Since her return to St. Petersburg he had hovered about her as if he were a mother hen.

"Huntley is back. Shall I send him on his way?"

Leonida rose to her feet. "No, Pyotr, please have Sergi show him in."

"You are certain?"

She forced a smile. She had never been less certain of anything. Just being in Stefan's company was enough to toss her into a maelstrom of confusion. Her mind warned her to treat the man with a cold indifference. Surely her apathy would eventually convince him to halt his foolish pursuit? But only a few moments in his company and she was a seething mass of emotion. Like a schoolgirl in her first throes of calf-love.

"Of course." She managed to get the words past her stiff lips.

"Then I will fetch Sophy."

"That will not be necessary."

"You can't be with the man without a companion," Pyotr growled.

"We will not be staying. The Duke has requested that I join him for a drive."

The groom's expression hardened with suspicion. "And you agreed?"

"Obviously."

"Why?"

"That is between Lord Huntley and myself."

Pyotr was clearly displeased with her sudden decision to meet with the man she had deliberately avoided for days.

"Then I will join you."

Her expression softened, her heart warming at his unwavering concern.

"Thank you, Pyotr, but there is no need."

"Have you forgotten there is a madman still loose who has every reason to want you dead?"

Leonida shivered. She had been haunted by nightmares since returning to St. Petersburg. At least she had until last night.

For some reason her dreams had once again been filled with a raven-haired, blue-eyed gentleman who set her blood on fire.

"I am not likely to forget."

"Then you need to be protected."

"A task that is now in my hands," a dark voice murmured from behind Pyotr.

"Stefan," Leonida breathed, her heart slamming against her chest as the tall, lean gentleman brushed past the groom and crossed the room to raise her fingers to his lips.

"Lovely as always, my dove."

For a moment Leonida's mind refused to function. Good lord, he was so beautiful. The elegantly chiseled features. The thick raven curls. The blue eyes that could shimmer with humor or darken with tenderness.

Her hands itched to reach up and sink her fingers in his hair and tug his head down so she could kiss those sensuous lips. She ached with a frustrated desire that became worse with every passing day.

With an effort, she gathered her thoughts and, turning toward the doorway, she nodded to the silver-haired butler who hovered behind Pyotr.

"Thank you, Sergi, that will be all."

The elderly servant cast an outraged glare toward Stefan before performing a stiff bow. Clearly the Duke had forced his way into the house, offending the poor butler who was unaccustomed to such a determined gentleman.

"Very well."

The man shuffled away and Leonida returned her attention to Stefan, who was smiling with an unrepentant satisfaction.

"There was no need to bully my servants," she chastised.

"I am weary of waiting on your doorstep."

"I agreed to join you," she muttered. "I do not go back on my word."

"Then blame my lack of manners on my eagerness to be at your side."

"You can be at her side in the shelter of her home," Pyotr said from across the room. "There is no need to drag her about St. Petersburg."

Stefan's lips twitched, but his gaze never strayed from Leonida's face.

"Since Vanya Petrova was kind enough to lend me use of her carriage there will be no need to actually drag Miss Karkoff."

Pyotr snorted, unimpressed with Stefan's quip. "It is still dangerous."

With a rueful sigh, Stefan turned his head to meet the groom's sour gaze.

"Do not fear, Pyotr, I have brought a groom and two outriders to stand guard. Miss Karkoff will be well-protected."

"I do not like it."

"Perhaps not, but I am certain that Miss Karkoff is weary of being trapped in this house," he pointed out gently. "She is no longer a prisoner and she deserves to feel the sunlight on her face."

Leonida's heart threatened to melt. No one but Stefan had ever bothered to notice her craving for the delicious warmth of a sunny day or the need for a room heated by a fire. Perhaps it would seem like nothing to most women, but to her it was…astonishing.

"I will be fine, Pyotr. Remain here and keep a watch upon Mother."

The groom muttered something beneath his breath, but with no authority to keep Leonida confined to the house he gave a grudging nod of his head. "If you insist."

Ignoring the man's warning glare, Stefan took Leonida's

arm and escorted her through the house, pausing at the front door while she pulled on a chip bonnet with peach ribbons. Then, allowing Sergi to open the door, he led her down the stairs to the open black carriage with white leather seats.

Leonida vaguely recognized the servant holding the reins of the matched pair of grays, as well as the two side riders who were attired in the Duke's uniforms. She had occasionally caught sight of them during her stay at Meadowland.

She was surprised, however, that Boris was not among the guards. She had sensed that he was aggressively determined to remain at Stefan's side until they returned to England.

Once they were settled, the carriage jerked into motion, the sharp sound of hoofs striking against the cobbled streets echoing through the quiet neighborhood.

Leonida remained silent as they headed away from the house, savoring the delicious sunlight that poured over her with welcoming warmth. Stefan had been right. She had been lingering in the house too long.

Not that she intended to admit as much to the man seated far too close to her side.

He was already arrogantly certain she found him irresistible.

"Where are we going?" she at last demanded as they clattered over a narrow bridge leading away from the city.

"I thought you would enjoy a drive through the countryside," Stefan retorted, shifting so he could face her. "Does that please you?"

"Do you truly care if I am pleased or not?" she asked tartly.

He ignored her question, instead reaching out to lightly touch the shadows beneath her eyes.

"You look tired. Are you not sleeping well?"

"Well enough."

"What is troubling you, Leonida? Are you plagued by nightmares?"

She swallowed a sigh. The man was annoyingly perceptive. A fine talent when it came to his staff and tenants, but she preferred to keep some thoughts to herself.

"At times."

"Has Gerhardt discovered any trace of Sir Charles?"

She grimaced. "Not that he has mentioned, but he rarely shares all that he knows."

His hand cupped her cheek, the warmth of his palm rivaling the heat of the sun. She swallowed, barely keeping herself from rubbing against that soft touch like a contented cat.

"I could keep you safe at Meadowland. At least until the bastard has been captured."

She regarded him with an exasperation that was not entirely feigned. "You are truly the most stubborn man I have ever encountered."

His thumb brushed her bottom lip with an unnerving intimacy. Thank goodness they had reached the edge of the city and were away from prying eyes.

"I would not need to be so stubborn if you would just be reasonable."

"And by reasonable you mean giving in to your every command?"

"It would be a beginning."

She rolled her eyes. "It is little wonder you have not yet wed. I feel pity for your poor wife."

An indefinable emotion flickered through his magnificent eyes. "Do you?"

"Yes," she said, pretending her heart did not clench with a vicious stab of pain.

"There is no need. When I care for a woman I willingly devote myself to her happiness." He leaned forward to whisper directly in her ear. "She will be utterly and fully content."

She shivered at the rush of exquisite awareness that tingled through her body. "Arrogant as well as stubborn."

His lips brushed along the curve of her ear, his breath a caress against her neck. "You would vanquish a lesser man," he assured her. "Unless, of course, you prefer a lapdog?"

She hastily scooted from his disturbing touch. Another moment and she would be a helpless puddle of need.

"I prefer a gentleman who can respect my ability to make my own decisions and not run roughshod over my opinions," she snapped.

He draped an arm along the back of the seat, his brooding gaze moving restlessly over her upturned face.

"I have no intention of running roughshod over your opinions, only your fanciful belief I intend to hurt you."

"Demanding that I be your mistress would hurt me," she said, her voice pitched low so it would not carry to the servants.

He narrowed his gaze in frustration. "My only demand has been that you allow me the opportunity to enjoy your companionship. Any decision to share more than conversation will be made by you."

RECOGNIZING THE STUBBORN expression that had settled on Leonida's face, Stefan allowed a silence to descend on the carriage.

Damn it all. He was not stupid. He had seen her eyes light with pleasure when he had walked into her parlor. He could feel her response to his touch.

So why did she continue to push him away?

The woman was enough to make a sane man consider becoming a monk.

Turning his head, he studied the passing scenery. It was that or hauling Leonida on his lap and kissing her senseless.

Not that he was able to ignore her presence at his side. Even as his eyes narrowed in resignation at the sight of the dispirited serfs who tended the fields, his entire body pulsed with awareness.

Her jasmine scent teased at his nose and the heat from her body seeped through his clothing. He would have better luck ignoring another shot to his back.

At last the carriage slowed, turning on a tree-lined drive. Ahead was a large stone building with a columned terrace and statues of Greek gods keeping watch from the roof.

It was the parkland, however, that appealed to Stefan. Beyond the formal garden and reflecting pool, the unpretentious beauty of nature had been left untouched.

Whatever his opinion of Russian politics, he possessed a deep admiration for the raw, untouched splendor that was all too rare in England. It pleased him in the same manner as Leonida pleased him.

Both were willful, untamed and filled with surprises.

His groom pulled the horses to a halt before the wide terrace and climbing from the carriage, Stefan turned to hold out a hand to the frowning Leonida.

"Why are we here?" she demanded, grudgingly allowing him to help her step onto the graveled drive.

He threaded her arm through his own, keeping a firm grip. She was quite capable of bolting when she discovered the surprise he had in store for her.

"You have become too thin," he said, guiding her up the stairs. "I have hopes of tempting your appetite."

She stiffened in alarm. "My appetite will hardly be improved by being thrust amongst strangers."

He smiled. "Trust me."

She clicked her tongue. "I grow weary of those words."

Before he could respond the door was pulled open to reveal a short, gray-haired housekeeper with a round face and welcoming expression.

She dipped a small curtsy. "Your Grace. Miss Karkoff. Welcome. If you will follow me?"

Turning, she headed across the paneled foyer to the curved stairs. Leonida shot Stefan a frustrated glare, but, too well behaved to cause a scene, she followed in the servant's wake. Reaching the upper floor, the woman halted at the nearest door and stood aside as Stefan and Leonida entered the room.

It was a small, cozy chamber with paneling on the bottom of the walls and the upper halves painted with pastoral scenes. There was a green striped sofa set beneath a window overlooking a distant lake and matching chairs near a porcelain stove. In the center of the room was a cherrywood table laden with a number of covered dishes.

"I believe that you will find that I have provided all that you requested," the housekeeper murmured.

"It is perfect. Thank you." Reaching beneath his jacket Stefan pulled out a large coin and pressed it into the servant's hand. "That will be all."

"Very good."

With a knowing smile the woman turned to disappear down the hallway and Stefan closed the door, silently turning the key that had been left conveniently in the lock.

Unaware that they were soon to be completely alone in the house, Leonida had drifted toward the table, her brow wrinkled in puzzlement.

"Who owns this place?"

He pulled out a chair, waiting for her to have a seat before gently removing her bonnet and rounding the table to settle on his own chair.

"Vanya Petrova, although she chooses to keep her connection to this particular home private."

"Why?"

He chose his words with care. Vanya rarely revealed her efforts to protect Alexander Pavlovich.

"There are occasions when she prefers to meet with her associates in secret," he said, filling her plate with poached salmon with a delicate mushroom sauce, roasted pheasant and potatoes in mint.

Taking her plate, Leonida glanced toward the closed door. "So we are alone?"

He filled his own plate then poured them each a glass of the wine.

"My servants will remain on guard outside. There is no danger."

"That depends upon your notion of danger."

He slowly smiled. "Come, Leonida, I have requested your favorite dishes." He did not allow himself to consider the fact he had kept such a close watch on Leonida that he knew precisely what she preferred. "What is the harm in a simple luncheon?"

Placing a linen napkin in her lap, Leonida picked up her fork. "I am bound to regret this."

"I promise to ensure you have nothing to regret."

A flush touched her cheeks at the intimate edge in his voice and ducking her head, she concentrated on her meal. Stefan did not press his advantage, instead taking pleasure in watching her eat the delicately prepared meal.

She had grown far too thin from her grueling journey back to Russia, and worse, it was obvious she was not sleeping well. It goaded his most primitive urge to protect her.

Only when her plate was empty did Leonida lift her head, her composure once again intact. "Did you speak with the Emperor?"

He sipped at his wine. "Only briefly."

"I suppose he demanded to know your reason for visiting Russia?"

Stefan shrugged. In truth, he had been pleasantly surprised by his encounter with Alexander Pavlovich. The Emperor had naturally been curious by his unexpected arrival, but he had not probed as Stefan had expected. Instead, he had accepted Stefan's blithe explanation with remarkable ease.

Of course, there had been a speculative gleam in the older man's steady gaze. As if he knew more than Stefan would be comfortable admitting.

"He did," Stefan admitted.

"And?"

"I assured him that after your departure from England I became concerned at the notion of traveling such a vast distance with only servants to bear you company. I desired to make sure you arrived safely."

Her brows lifted. "He believed you?"

"Who can say for certain? Alexander Pavlovich is notoriously capable of keeping his thoughts to himself. At least I have not yet been tossed into the dungeons."

"An oversight that would no doubt be corrected if he discovered you have brought me to this remote house without a proper chaperone," she dryly retorted.

With a smile Stefan shifted his chair until he was seated close to her side.

"As you have repeatedly informed me, there are some things best kept from the Emperor."

"When it is convenient for you," she reproached.

"Convenient for the both of us," he murmured, reaching for a strawberry and pressing it to her lips. "Allow me."

She sank her teeth into the berry, her breath quickening. "I am capable of feeding myself."

"Obviously, but this is far more enjoyable," he rasped.

"What if I bite your fingers?"

His body tightened, his gaze captured by the drop of juice that clung to her bottom lip.

"You can bite me anywhere you desire."

"Do not tempt me."

With a chuckle he lowered his head to lick the juice from her lips. "That is precisely what I am attempting to do," he whispered.

"Stefan."

"You taste of strawberries." He stole a kiss. And then another. "I love strawberries."

Her hands lifted to his chest, but she did not press him away. "You have not finished your meal."

"What I hunger for cannot be found on my plate." He

traced her lips with his tongue, then kissed a path to the curve of her neck, halting at the edge of the pearls. "Christ, I have missed you, Leonida. The feel of your skin, the scent of your hair, the soft moans you whisper in my ear."

She shuddered, her head tilting back in silent encouragement. "We should not be here."

Stefan continued downward, exploring the line of her shoulder with slow, lingering kisses.

"Do you want me to return you to your home?"

"I…"

"Leonida?"

There was a long, agonizing pause. Continuing his soft caresses, Stefan swallowed his urge to demand she put them both out of their misery. He had waited this long for her willing capitulation; he would not ruin it with a few ill-chosen words.

Preparing himself to endure yet more frustration, Stefan nearly shouted in relief when Leonida heaved a soft sigh and her arms curled around his neck.

"No."

"Thank God," Stefan growled.

Rising from the chair, he scooped Leonida in his arms and carried her to the nearby sofa, tenderly laying her on the cushions before straightening and tugging off his clothes.

Acutely aware of Leonida's heated gaze watching his jerky movements, Stefan was fully aroused as he knelt beside the sofa. Who the devil knew that stripping for a woman could be so erotic?

Grasping a handful of golden curls, he leaned forward to claim her lips in a greedy kiss, his free hand slipping beneath her to tug at the ribbons of her gown.

She tasted of strawberries and sweet temptation. A heady combination that spread through his body, drowning the world to leave only Leonida and his aching need. Roughly pulling her gown off her slender body, he impatiently struggled with her corset and thin shift.

Once rid of the bulk of her attire, Stefan dragged his mouth from her lips, spreading kisses down her throat before pausing to savor the tightly budded nipples. He smiled as she moaned in pleasure, her back arching as he continued his path over the flat plane of her stomach.

She was so tiny, so delicate. Like a fragile jasmine blossom.

Stroking his fingers down the backs of her legs, he tugged off her slippers and followed them with her silk stockings.

Slowly pulling back, Stefan studied her bare form lying against the sofa, her golden curls shimmering in the slanting sunlight.

She was stunningly beautiful, of course. But that did not explain why his heart squeezed with an alarming sense of fulfillment. As if something vital had been missing from his life until this moment.

Dislodging the dangerous thought from his mind, Stefan shifted to kiss the tips of her dainty toes, ignoring her breathless giggles. He intended to taste every delicious curve, every elegant line.

His decision made, he explored the slender length of her leg as she squirmed beneath him. At last reaching her upper thigh, Stefan tugged one leg off the sofa to spread her wide for his caresses. He moaned as he realized she was already damp with anticipation, her musky scent making his erection jerk in response.

He had dreamed of this precise moment for far too many nights. Now his body threatened revolt before he could fully savor the delectable encounter.

With a tortured moan, he shifted to run his tongue through her moist heat, delighted by her choked shriek of pleasure. This was how he wanted her. Warm and wet and boneless with need.

Stefan continued to tease her tiny bud, reveling in her soft pants and broken pleas for release. Only when he was certain she was on the crest of her climax did he poise himself above her, gazing down at her smoldering gaze with a sense of awe.

His woman.

His and his alone.

"Leonida," he groaned, not certain what he was demanding.

Not until she lifted her arms and plunged her fingers into his hair, dragging his face down for a searing kiss.

"Please, Stefan."

He did not make her ask again. Cupping her face in his hands, he positioned himself at her entrance, then with one hard thrust, he penetrated her to the hilt.

She bowed beneath him, moaning in satisfaction as he stroked with an increasing urgency. His intention to be gentle was swiftly forgotten as her legs wrapped around his waist, her hips moving in time to his fevered pace.

"God, Leonida, you feel so good," he panted, his heart thundering and his body clenched with his building climax. "So damn good."

"Stefan…" Her words broke off with a cry of release, her eyes squeezing shut as she shuddered in bliss.

Stefan growled as he felt her tiny convulsions rippling over his erection. The exquisite sensation tossed him over the edge, and giving one last thrust his orgasm slammed into him. Time seemed to halt as he allowed his seed to pump into her womb with stunning pleasure.

Christ.

CHAPTER TWENTY-FOUR

LATER THAT EVENING, Stefan was in his private chambers in Vanya Petrova's house, leaning against the window as he watched the sun set over the city.

It was a striking view, he had to admit. The golden domes glowed with dazzling beauty beneath the lingering rays and the carved angels appeared prepared to take off in flight.

A far different sight from the grime and soot of London.

Of course, a part of his pleasure with the current scene might simply be his overall sense of goodwill.

Although he had returned to Vanya's two hours ago to bathe and change into a dove-gray coat and silver waistcoat with gray pantaloons, he was still basking in a glow of contentment.

Toying with the diamond stickpin in his crisply starched cravat, Stefan fondly recalled the afternoon in the arms of Leonida.

He had just reached the memory of their third bout of lovemaking when the door opened and Boris stepped into the room. Turning, he watched as the servant closed the door behind his large form, crossing the polished floor with a suspicious expression.

"You are appearing particularly pleased with yourself," Boris accused. "I presume your luncheon went well?"

"It was…magnificent," he murmured, frowning as Boris abruptly laughed. "You find something amusing?"

"I am always pleased to witness that daft expression on a man's face. It proves I am not alone in my suffering."

"Daft?"

"Like a man who has been hit upside the head with a shovel." Boris reached out to pat Stefan's shoulder with a smug smile. "It happens to all of us eventually."

Stefan's frown deepened, his warm glow threatened by a sudden chill. He had devoted an immense amount of effort to pretending his obsession with Miss Leonida Karkoff was something that would swiftly pass.

He did not appreciate Boris attempting to ruin his excellent fantasy.

"Nothing has happened beyond a pleasant interlude with a beautiful woman," he retorted sharply.

"Ignoring the truth will not make it go away." Boris grimaced. "To be honest it only makes matters worse in the end."

"Enough." Stefan shook his head, perfectly capable of ignoring any truth he desired. "Did you manage to get into Sir Charles's home or not?"

The servant smirked, but he was wise enough to allow Stefan to turn the conversation.

"Surely you did not doubt me?"

"Since I had not yet received word you had been arrested, I was reasonably confident in your success. Did you catch sight of the bastard?"

"No, he has not been to the house for several weeks." Boris smiled wryly. "But I did catch sight of at least a half dozen men keeping watch on the house."

Not surprising. Stefan had expected the Countess to have guards looking for Sir Charles. And of course, Herrick Gerhardt would have his own men searching. It was a damned wonder that half of St. Petersburg was not milling outside the bastard's house.

Which made it all the more astonishing that Boris had managed to slip into and out of the house without being halted.

"It is no wonder he has avoided the place," he muttered.

Boris shrugged. "He could be dead."

"I would never be so fortunate. Did you discover anything that might reveal where he is hiding?"

"There were a handful of invitations, but no private correspondence. Either he destroys his letters or he has no one who cares enough to write."

"Damn." Stefan considered their few options. "What of his accounts? Does he frequent a brothel or coffeehouse?"

"There were bills from a number of establishments, mostly his tailors and the local grocer. He is deeply in debt."

It was disappointing, to say the least. How the hell did he find Sir Charles when he didn't know where to start the search?

He paced the room, something tickling at the back of his mind. What was it? Something Leonida had said. Something…

With an abrupt motion he turned back to Boris. "Leonida mentioned an accomplice," he said.

"Do you have a name?"

"Not yet." He grimaced. It would be a simple matter to demand the name from Leonida, but he had no desire to force her to recall anything connected to Sir Charles. Besides, she was bound to make a fuss if she realized he was searching for the murderous nobleman. He would have to find a different means of acquiring the information. "Did you find nothing of worth?"

There was a short pause before Boris reached beneath his jacket and pulled out three leather bags held closed with drawstrings. He tossed them on the top of a jade-inlaid table.

"These were hidden in a locked drawer of his desk."

Stefan crossed to tug open the first bag, pulling out the official English passport.

"Forged papers. He will need these to travel out of Russia without being halted by Gerhardt's men." He reached for the second bag and dumped out a handful of coins. "A few rubles." He reached for the last and largest bag, pulling open the drawstrings and shaking out a strange combination of buttons and ribbons and two cheap brooches. He frowned in confusion at the obviously feminine objects. Why would a man keep such trinkets protected in a locked drawer? They must have some meaning for him. Leaning forward, Stefan realized there was something staining the ribbons. The candlelight flickered and suddenly he was stepping backward, a sick disgust rolling through his stomach. Blood. "Holy hell."

Boris shuddered. "Exactly."

"He is truly mad."

"Yes."

Overcoming his revulsion, Stefan gathered the sordid mementos, along with the passport, and tossed them into the burning fire. He shivered, imagining Sir Charles among the flames. The sooner the man was sent to hell the better.

"Leonida will never be safe so long as he is out there."

"Do you want me to keep a watch on the house?"

"It would seem that it is already closely guarded." He restlessly moved to collect his hat and gloves from the dresser. "I will learn the name of his associate. Perhaps he can be persuaded to reveal where the bastard is hiding."

"Then I wait." Boris watched as Stefan tugged on his gloves. "Another dinner at the palace?"

Stefan smiled, his lingering horror thankfully replaced with a stab of anticipation. Leonida had promised she would be in attendance. Even though it had only been a few hours, he was anxious to be at her side.

"What can I do?" he teased, opening the door. "The Emperor is obviously charmed by my company."

"Or he has laced your food with hemlock."

Stefan laughed. "Thank you, Boris."

"Always pleased to be of service."

Heading out of Vanya's townhouse, Stefan discovered his carriage awaiting him and within less than an hour he had navigated the thick traffic and reached the reception rooms of the palace.

He paused just inside the doorway, his gaze sweeping over the glittering crowd. At first glance there was no sight of Leonida.

Was she late? Or had something happened?

His heart squeezed with unease and he was debating the wisdom of going in search when the crowd shifted and he was distracted by the sight of golden curls.

Leonida.

His anxiety eased, but as his hungry gaze skimmed over her white lace gown worn over a silver underskirt and diamonds shimmering about her neck, he realized that he had been unable to see her earlier because she was surrounded by a horde of elegant gentlemen, each of them vying to gain her attention.

Even as he watched one of them leaned forward to whisper in Leonida's ear, his fingers stroking down her bare arm.

A biting anger exploded through him, his hands clenched at his sides. Damn the preening buffoons. They would soon discover the danger in pestering his woman.

Oblivious to everything but the sight of Leonida, Stefan charged forward, nearly bowling down the gaunt, silver-haired gentleman who deliberately stepped in his path.

"Your Grace," Herrick Gerhardt said, his voice hard.

For a crazed moment, Stefan continued forward, determined to knock the old soldier out of his way. Another man was touching Leonida. He would rip off his damn arm and shove it down his throat.

Then, catching sight of the dark eyes that held a ruthless warning, he grimly forced himself to halt. Gerhardt was quite capable of having him tossed from the palace with a nod toward one of the numerous guards.

Dammit. He was a duke. He was not accustomed to having others meddling in his affairs.

"Gerhardt," he growled.

The older man impaled him with a cold glare. "You will find the Emperor in the Throne Room."

"A rather obvious location," Stefan dryly retorted. "I will make my bow in a moment."

"I regret having to disagree, but you will make it now."

Aware of several gazes trained in their direction, Stefan deliberately adjusted the cuffs of his jacket, disguising the fierce emotions clamoring through him behind a mask of cool composure.

"You seem to forget, Gerhardt, that I am not a loyal Russian servant. I do not take orders from you."

"I am not speaking for the Emperor, but as a gentleman who truly cares for Leonida and her happiness."

A possessive fury clenched his heart.

"An even more dangerous proposition," he said, his voice low, lethal.

"Do not be an idiot, Huntley, she is like a daughter to me," Herrick snapped.

Stefan was far from reassured. Whatever the older man's feelings for Leonida, his one purpose was to halt Stefan's pursuit.

Something Stefan would not tolerate.

"And you believe you can keep me away from her?"

"If it was at all possible, I most certainly would," Herrick admitted in icy tones. "Unfortunately, all I can do is attempt to prevent you from causing scandal."

Stefan's brows snapped together at the ludicrous accusation. Was the man utterly blind? "The only scandal is you allowing Leonida to be besieged by a pack of worthless fribbles. It will be a miracle if she is not trampled."

"Those fribbles have been besieging Leonida since she was first introduced to society. There is no danger of gossip unless some fool charges across the room and begins snapping and snarling like a hound protecting his favorite bone."

A tiny voice in the back of Stefan's mind whispered that

Gerhardt was speaking only the truth. And that if he were capable of rational thought, he would accept that he was overreacting.

He gritted his teeth, doing his best to ignore that unwelcomed voice. "Have you considered the notion that Leonida might appreciate being rescued from the bothersome pests?"

"No." Herrick's expression was as hard and unyielding as granite. "And neither would you if you were concerned for Leonida rather than your own selfish jealousy."

He jerked at the sharp attack. "What are you implying?"

"Leonida has little in common with her mother."

"I am well aware, not to mention excessively grateful, of that fact," he snapped.

"The Countess has always been a vivacious woman who enjoys flouting the dictates of society and prefers to attract attention," Herrick continued, ignoring Stefan's interruption. "Leonida is quite the opposite. The speculation that has followed her from the day she was born has been a never-ending burden. She will not thank you for creating a scene."

Stefan's gaze turned back to Leonida as he forced himself to take stock of her brittle smile and the stiff set of her shoulders. Unlike so many women, she truly disliked the swarm of gentlemen clamoring for her attention. She did not coyly flirt while deftly keeping the men at bay. She did not giggle and blush at their comments. She did not pout when they glanced away.

In truth, she looked like she would be quite happy if she could disappear behind one the towering Russian vases.

Hardly a woman who would preen to have her jealous lover storming to her side and tossing the worthless peacocks through the nearest window.

Of course, understanding that he would only embarrass Leonida did not ease his burning need to stake his public claim upon her.

"You cannot expect me to ignore her for the entire evening."

"I expect you to behave as a gentleman."

Stefan wrenched his gaze from Leonida, silently acknowledging the irony of Herrick's words. From his earliest memories he had always tried to do what was right, what he believed to be his duty, while Edmond rebelled. No one acquainted with him would believe he needed to be reminded he was a gentleman.

Or that in this moment he did not give a damn about his family's prestigious name so long as Leonida remained out of his grasp.

Wrenching his gaze from the woman who could torment him even from afar, Stefan gathered his unruly thoughts and forced his attention back to his companion.

If he were forced to obey the ridiculous rules of society, then he would not allow the entire night to be a complete waste.

"And what is my reward?"

"You might avoid a public execution."

Stefan folded his arms over his chest. "Come, Gerhardt, you have asked a favor of me, I surely deserve one in return."

"What do you want?"

"It is a trifling matter, really."

"That I very much doubt."

"I want to know the name of Sir Charles's accomplice."

Herrick stiffened, his expression suspicious. "Why?"

"Humor me."

"This is a Russian matter…"

"The name," Stefan grated.

The two men regarded one another, their gazes locked in silent combat. Then, as if realizing that Stefan would not compromise, Herrick muttered a low curse.

"Nikolas Babevich," he gritted. "Do not interfere, Huntley."

Stefan smiled. "I really must make my bow to the Emperor."

Before Herrick could reach out to halt him, Stefan was smoothly moving away, winding his way through the crowd until he could locate a uniformed footman to carry a message back to Boris at Vanya Petrova's house.

THE BALLROOM WAS CONSIDERED a masterpiece of the palace. The walls, painted a soft ivory, were broken by a double row of arched windows draped in crimson velvet that glowed beneath the brilliant crystal chandeliers. The floor was patterned parquet and the ceiling painted with a vision of Persephone leaving the underworld.

The Emperor was seated on a dais at one end of the long room while at the other end a string quartet played upon another dais. In between a hundred couples twirled in a dazzling waltz.

All quite lovely, but Leonida felt nothing but relief as she slipped through an antechamber and made her way onto a back terrace. The night air was chill, but the relief of being away from the choking crowd overcame her discomfort.

Strolling to the stone railing, she absently gazed over the vast orchard, breathing deeply as she sought to ease the tension that had gripped her the entire evening.

She had never particularly enjoyed such events at the palace. She far preferred the few occasions the Emperor had invited her to a private meal and the rare enjoyment of his undivided attention. Tonight, however, had been even more trying than usual.

Not only had she been plagued by the usual idiots who assumed she could offer them a claim to Alexander Pavlovich and the power of his throne, but there had been no means of ignoring the Duke of Huntley.

Oh, he had been well mannered enough. Remarkably well mannered.

When he had first entered the ballroom she had

expected him to defy propriety and cross directly to her side, indifferent to his duty to the Emperor or the rabid tattle mongers that would have taken sordid delight in his obvious interest in Leonida.

But, after a short conversation with Herrick, the Duke had properly headed for the Throne Room, and while Leonida had been constantly on edge, he had thankfully kept his distance throughout dinner and later when Alexander Pavlovich had led his guests to the ballroom.

She might have assumed he had lost interest in her after their long afternoon of lovemaking if it had not been for his heated gaze that had followed her every movement.

There had been a smoldering hunger in those magnificent blue eyes that warned his desire for her was as strong as ever. And shockingly, her body had readily responded to his lingering stare.

Even as she had politely chatted with her dinner partners and accepted a waltz with an elderly admirer, her heart had pounded in her chest and her stomach had fluttered with excitement. She felt gloriously alive. Just as she had when he had held her in his arms and kissed her with a thrilling desperation.

The realization terrified her.

She was uncertain how much time had passed when the sound of approaching footsteps could be heard over the soothing fountains. There was no need to turn about to know who approached. She could be blind and deaf and still sense when Stefan was near.

Busy preparing herself for the encounter, Leonida did not turn when she felt him halt directly behind her. A mistake. She had no warning when he grasped her shoulders and with one yank whirled her around so he could haul her against the hard muscles of his chest.

"Christ, I thought I would never have a moment alone with you," he muttered, his head bending down to claim her lips in a savage kiss.

Leonida instinctively gripped his shoulders, her knees going weak at the jolt of painful pleasure that surged through her. He tasted of fine cognac and male need. A heady combination that she was helpless to resist.

Closing her eyes, she allowed herself to become momentarily lost in the sheer pleasure of his kiss. There was little use in pretending she did not enjoy his lovemaking. Not when he could feel her shivers of pleasure.

He groaned low in his throat, his fingers running a restless path down her spine. Still, it was not until she felt the tug of a ribbon that held her gown together that she was jerked out of the sensual spell he was weaving.

"Stefan, you must behave yourself," she chided, firmly tugging out of his arms.

"What do you think I have been doing this entire bloody night?" he rasped, the torchlight revealing the slash of color along his cheekbones and the pained frustration that smoldered in his eyes.

A frustration that resonated deep within her.

She unwittingly backed up until she was pressed against the stone balustrade.

"I will admit that I have been pleasantly shocked to discover you can behave as a proper gentleman," she said, attempting to lighten the thick atmosphere.

His lips twisted. "Not willingly."

"Did Herrick threaten you?"

"He reminded me that my last desire is to ever hurt you." His gaze seared over her face, his hand reaching out to trace the plunging line of her lacy décolleté. "Of course, there is no need to reveal my first desire."

She batted away his hand, her skin tingling from his light touch.

"Stefan, anyone could wander into the garden."

"Will you come for a drive with me tomorrow?" His jaw knotted as she hesitated. "Leonida?"

Swallowing the painful lump that threatened to choke

her, Leonida turned to stare blindly at the shadowed orchard. The mere fact she so dreadfully desired to share another stolen afternoon in his company warned her that she was playing with fire.

Every passing day ensured that much more disappointment when he left.

"I have agreed to accept your invitations," she muttered, making her reluctance clear.

With a harsh sigh, Stefan moved to lean against the railing, his profile hard with annoyance.

"Will there ever come a day when you do not feel the need to keep me at a distance?"

"No."

"Why?"

It was a question she would never answer. If he truly understood the power he held over her…

No. The mere thought was unbearable.

"How long do you intend to remain in St. Petersburg?"

He paused, as if caught off guard by her abrupt question. "My plans are not entirely fixed."

"You have been away from your estate for a number of weeks. Are you not concerned that you might be needed?"

"Edmond is capable of overseeing Meadowland."

His voice was smooth, but Leonida did not miss his slender fingers tapping a restless beat on the stone railing. He was far more concerned about his absence than he was willing to admit. Perhaps even to himself.

"He has his own estate and Brianna to consider," she pointed out softly. "He cannot be expected to shoulder your duties forever."

He turned his head to stab her with a sullen glare. "Are you attempting to be rid of me?"

"I do not need to make an effort," she said, her expression grimly stoic. "We both know you will soon have to return to your responsibilities."

"It will not be forever."

"You belong in England."

His hands clenched the railing, his knuckles white. "And where do you belong, Leonida?" he rasped.

She flinched as he deliberately struck at her deepest yearning.

Had she been fresh from the schoolroom and her head filled with dreams, she might have held on to the hope that Stefan could offer her the love and sense of security she longed for.

Thank God she was old enough to understand that fairy tales were best left behind in the nursery.

"I suppose I am still searching."

For some reason her answer appeared to annoy him. His brows drew together and his lips thinned.

"You can as easily search in England as in Russia."

"And when you weary of me?"

"Who is to say I will weary of you?"

She shook her head. "How long do your affairs usually last? A few weeks? A few months?"

"I have never had an affair with a woman such as you." He tenderly tucked a stray curl behind her ear. "Never."

With an effort she ignored his fingers as they trailed down the line of her jaw. She would not allow him to distract her. He might wish to disregard the inevitable end of his desire for her, but she could not afford to be so indifferent.

"Even if you do decide to continue our relationship, what do you expect of me once you are wed?" she charged, her heart clenching with a ruthless pain. "Do you intend to keep me in one of your cottages so you can visit when you are not occupied with your wife and estate?"

He sucked in a sharp breath, pushing away from the railing so he could prowl across the terrace with short, jerky steps. Obviously, he had not considered the complications of having her in England.

Turning back toward her, Stefan shoved his fingers

through his hair. "I have no intention of wedding in the near future."

His tone indicated he considered his answer an end to the matter. Leonida, however, had no intention of allowing him to dismiss the futility of their connection.

"Why not? It is your duty to produce an heir, is it not?"

"Edmond has thankfully shouldered that particular responsibility."

"Perhaps."

"Perhaps?" His gaze narrowed. "I assure you, there is no perhaps about Brianna carrying a child."

"You are not the sort who allows another to *shoulder* his responsibilities." Her tone dared him to defy the truth of her accusation. "Besides, you will never be satisfied to live alone in that vast house. It demands a family."

Stefan returned to his pacing, his expression tight. "Meadowland has stood for centuries, it will no doubt survive a few more years without a duchess."

Leonida leaned against the railing, a sick sensation in the pit of her stomach. But why? She had already accepted that Stefan would wed. And that his bride would be a perfect English debutante. It was ridiculous to feel such a bleak sense of sorrow.

"Why have you not wed?" she said, unable to stop the question that continued to plague her.

He halted near a torch, the firelight making his skin glow with a rich sheen.

"You informed me that no woman of sense would have me."

She rolled her eyes. As if he were not magnificently aware that he was the most sought-after gentleman in all of England.

"Women tend to lose all sense when offered the opportunity to become a wealthy duchess. I do not doubt you have had willing women tossing themselves at your noble feet since you left the nursery."

"You would only accuse me of arrogance if I agree."

"Then why do you not have your duchess?"

Stefan turned his head, regarding the orchard as if the answer could be found among the fruit-laden trees.

Leonida discovered herself fidgeting as the silence stretched, suddenly wishing she had not pressed. She sensed she was not going to like the answer.

"I have yet to encounter a woman who could replace my mother in the hearts of my people," he at last admitted, his voice so low she barely caught the words.

"Or in your heart," she whispered, straightening from the railing as ridiculous tears filled her eyes.

She had been right. She did not like the answer.

How would Stefan ever be capable of caring for another when he was haunted by the ghosts of those he had lost?

He stepped forward, his brow furrowed. "We were discussing our future, not some mythical wife."

"There is no future to discuss, Stefan." She tilted her chin. "It is impossible."

His gaze raked over her slender body, deliberately reminding her of the hours he had devoted to pleasuring her. "Obviously it is not," he gritted. "Why will you not accept that this passion that burns between us is far from sated?"

"Because I need more."

"More of what?"

"More than you can offer."

Anger flared in his eyes at her sharp words and he reached out to grasp her arm. Leonida, however, swiftly stepped to the side, avoiding his hand.

Then, with her chin held high, she marched across the terrace and back into the brightly lit palace.

She had no power to ease the demons that plagued him.

Until Stefan could accept his loss and learn to trust his emotions to another, he would be forever alone.

CHAPTER TWENTY-FIVE

STEFAN WATCHED LEONIDA disappear from the terrace, his hands clenched at his side.

He could easily have halted her retreat. Just a few swift steps and he could have her tossed over his shoulder and headed into the privacy of the orchard. He had no doubt once he had her alone he could prove she was just as eager for his touch as she had been earlier in the day.

Instead he remained frozen in place, his anger a tangible force that swirled through his body.

At least, he told himself it was anger. Otherwise he would have to admit that the searing emotion was… anguish.

Because I need more than you can offer.

His jaw clenched as her low, cutting words continued to echo through his mind.

What the devil was wrong with the woman?

There was no man who could offer a woman more than he could.

He possessed an enviable position among society, excessive wealth he was delighted to squander on his lovers, a rather handsome countenance and a steady temperament.

Most certainly his previous mistresses had never complained. Hell, they had used every feminine trick available to keep his interest.

Obviously Leonida envisioned some paragon of male perfection that no gentleman could hope to achieve.

Damn the aggravating wench.

Standing alone in the dark, Stefan sucked in deep breaths as he attempted to calm his churning emotions. Leonida alone could create such havoc. Usually without even trying.

So why did he not simply leave?

Stefan shook his head. The question had plagued him since leaving Meadowland, and he was still no closer to an answer. Perhaps he never would be.

"Huntley."

Lost in his dark thoughts, Stefan jerked in surprise as the voice sounded from below the railing.

With a frown he moved to the edge of the terrace, peering over to discover Boris standing in the shadows.

"What are you doing here?"

Stepping back, Boris allowed the torchlight to fall across his face, revealing his grim expression.

"I think there is something you need to see for yourself."

"Now?"

"Yes."

Stefan hesitated. He knew that Boris would never have traveled to the palace unless he had discovered something he considered urgent, but then again, the thought of leaving at this precise moment was far from appealing.

Even now Leonida would have returned to the ballroom, her devoted suitors swarming around her.

What if her unreasonable annoyance toward him led her into some sort of foolish behavior? Women were always unpredictable. An angry woman…well, there was simply no telling what she might take it into her mind to do.

"Does this have anything to do with Sir Charles?" he demanded.

"Only in part." Boris waved a hand toward the far side of the orchard. "I have a carriage waiting behind the stables."

"You are certain this cannot wait until tomorrow?"

"Quite certain," the servant retorted, his voice bleak.

Stefan cast one last glance toward the palace before

heaving a sigh. Perhaps it was just as well he could not return to the ballroom. In his current mood he was bound to do something he would later regret.

"Very well."

Without bothering to return for his hat and gloves, Stefan angled across the terrace to the broad steps that led to the orchards.

In silence Boris joined him, leading him along a dark path to the elegant stables that were as elaborately constructed as the palace. As they neared, however, Boris circled away from the splashes of torchlight that filled the cobblestone yard and the milling grooms that were playing cards or throwing dice as they waited for their employers to return home for the evening. Only when they were once again cloaked in darkness did he approach the back of the sprawling stone buildings.

Wondering if Boris's secretive behavior was simply a symptom of his long years of playing spy for his brother, or if something more nefarious was troubling him, Stefan wisely held his tongue as he climbed next to Boris onto the high bench of the carriage. With a crack of the whip, Boris sent the restless bays into motion, traveling down a narrow path that led to a side entrance to the grounds.

Once they were through the gate and headed toward the outer fringe of St. Petersburg, Stefan turned toward his companion, determined to have his answers.

"Can you tell me where we are headed, or is it to remain a mystery?"

"No mystery. I received your note and decided to discover what I could of Nikolas Babevich."

Stefan arched his brows. "Without me?"

Boris shrugged. "I presumed you would be more pleasantly occupied."

"As did I," Stefan curtly admitted.

"Ah." Boris shot him a knowing glance. "Troubles with Miss Karkoff?"

"Miss Karkoff is nothing but trouble."

"You didn't seem to think so earlier this evening," the servant reminded him. "Course, a woman can steal a smile from a man's face just as quick as she can put it on."

Stefan snorted, turning his head to regard the brightly lit homes that they rushed past. Most of the houses were still built of stone and boasted gardens with marble fountains, but they were noticeably smaller than those closer to the palace and the facades without the ornate decorations.

"Truer words were never spoken," he muttered.

"Tomorrow no doubt your smile will be back," Boris said, slowing the carriage as they rattled over one of the numerous bridges that connected the sprawling city.

"Unless I come to my senses and return to England before I lose what wits I have left."

"So you keep saying, but here we are. Have you asked yourself why?"

Stefan gritted his teeth. He should have learned not to discuss women with his companion. Boris was ridiculously happy in his marriage to Janet. What did he know of a female who tormented a man one moment with her willing kisses and the next treated him as if he were her long-sworn enemy?

"Are we headed to Babevich's?"

Boris turned onto a narrow street. "Yes, it is not far."

"Have you spoken with him?"

"No."

Stefan heaved a sigh of impatience. "Boris, if this is some sort of jest it is not amusing."

"This is no jest." Boris's features twisted with a sudden revulsion. "Trust me."

Unease crept down Stefan's spine as his companion slowed the bays and halted before a narrow house that had a crowd of guests spilling from the front terrace and a number of carriages blocking the street.

Boris was a stoic man who was rarely ruffled. If he had

discovered something that could rattle his composure it had to be extraordinarily disturbing.

"It appears that he is entertaining," he muttered, searching the house for some sign of trouble. "Is Sir Charles among the guests?"

Boris leaped from the carriage and tied off the reins next to a long line of vehicles.

"Babevich's house is around the corner," he corrected as Stefan joined him. "It is best we walk through the mews. I would prefer no one notice the carriage."

Stefan did not protest as Boris led him through a dark alley despite the stench of rotting garbage and the nearby outhouse. In truth, he was far more concerned with what lay ahead than rubbish that threatened the gloss of his boots.

Whatever had spooked Boris was bound to be unpleasant, to say the least.

Tugging open a back gate, Boris held his finger to his lips, as if Stefan needed to be reminded to keep his mouth shut as they blatantly trespassed into a stranger's garden. Perhaps not surprising. It was Edmond who had devoted himself to such dangerous games while Stefan was quite content to be a law-abiding citizen.

Of course, since meeting Leonida he seemed to make a habit of flouting all conventions.

How ironic would it be for him to be the brother who ended up in Alexander Pavlovich's dungeon?

With a shake of his head at his ludicrous imaginings, Stefan managed to avoid breaking his knees on the low marble benches that dotted the garden, although his pants did not fare as well as he snagged them more than once on the overgrown roses. Clearly Babevich had not bothered to hire a gardener in a number of months.

Nor had he bothered with repairs to his house. Even in the moonlight, Stefan could detect several tiles missing from the roof and a gutter hanging at an odd angle. No doubt during the daylight the slow decay was even more apparent

Which of course would explain why he was desperate enough to throw his lot in with Sir Charles. Only an idiot or a man on the edge of ruin would attempt to blackmail the Countess Karkoff.

Boris ignored the back door leading to the servants' quarters and instead rounded the side of the house. Stefan's steps slowed as the darkness was broken by a square of light that shimmered through the French windows.

Damn. He had expected the house to be empty. Intruding on a man in his own home was a dangerous business.

Seemingly unaware of Stefan's unease, Boris climbed the flight of stairs that led to the narrow balcony in front of the French doors, his hand reaching into his coat to pull out a pistol. With no weapon, Stefan felt disturbingly vulnerable. A sensation that only worsened as Boris stepped directly before the light that spread across the balcony.

Was the man demented?

Far more cautiously, Stefan halted at the edge of the French doors and, craning his neck, peered inside. He had already been shot once during the course of his adventure. He wasn't anxious to step in front of another bullet.

At first glance he could detect nothing out of the ordinary. The parlor was narrow with shabby furnishings arranged around a cheap carpet thrown over the worn floor. The walls had once been a green satin although they had faded to a muddy yellow and the light of the chandelier gleamed dully off the collection of dubious paintings.

Babevich not only needed a housekeeper, but a lesson in fine art.

Wondering why Boris would be gazing so intently at a seemingly empty room, Stefan shifted farther onto the balcony to study the far end of the room.

It was then that Stefan at last noticed the body sprawled on the carpet next to the stone fireplace.

His breath lodged in his lungs as his gaze slid over the stranger's pale face surrounded by tangled brown hair and down the motionless body covered in rumpled evening clothes that were stained red by the blood leaking from the wound in the center of his chest.

His fear of flying bullets was forgotten as he reached for the handle of the French door, cursing as it refused to open.

"Go for assistance, Boris," he gritted.

The servant laid a restraining hand on his arm. "It is too late, Huntley. The man is dead."

It took a moment for Stefan to accept the truth. But as the man continued to lie frozen in a pool of his own blood, his sightless eyes staring at the ceiling, he heaved a resigned sigh.

"Is it Babevich?" he rasped.

"Yes."

Stefan didn't have to ask how Boris could be so certain. The dutiful servant would already have searched the house.

"Did you find anything..."

His words ended in a shocked hiss as his gaze strayed away from Babevich's wounded chest and he belatedly noticed that there was nothing but a bloody stump sticking from the cuff of his jacket. Hellfire. Some sick bastard had chopped off Babevich's hand.

Stefan swayed, his stomach heaving. No wonder Boris had been so grim.

"Christ."

"Exactly." Boris tightened his hand on Stefan's shoulder. "We need to leave before the officials arrive."

Stefan sucked in a deep breath. Could he just leave the man lying there like a bit of rubbish? It seemed...indecent.

But then again, what could he do? The man was dead and Stefan's presence at the house would only involve him in a nasty scandal. After all, the authorities were bound to demand to know why he was lurking around the house. What could he say? The man had been blackmailing Countess Karkoff?

"Yes," he at last muttered.

Wrenching his gaze from the macabre scene, Stefan followed in Boris's path as they retraced their steps to the waiting carriage.

Distantly he was aware of the laughing chatter that drifted from the surrounding homes and the bark of a dog roaming the streets, but remained too consumed by the memory of Babevich's bloody end to take notice.

It was not until they had retrieved the carriage and were swaying down the dark street that he managed to shake off his lingering sense of shock.

"I have never..." He shuddered, his mouth dry. "Sir Charles is no better than an animal."

Boris kept the restless horses at a slow but steady pace, weaving his way through the thickening traffic.

"I fully agree, but I do not believe he was responsible for Babevich's death."

Stefan grunted in surprise. He had never considered the possibility that anyone else could have attacked Babevich.

"Who else would be so anxious to keep him quiet?" he demanded. "And do not imply the Countess Karkoff or Alexander Pavlovich. They would never be so indiscreet."

"No, it was Tipova."

"Tipova?"

"Dimitri Tipova. The Beggar Czar." Boris flashed a hard smile. "Although you would have your tongue cut out if you called him that to his face."

"A criminal?"

"He is far more dangerous than a mere criminal. There is nothing that occurs among the streets of St. Petersburg that he does not control. Alexander Pavlovich might be the Emperor of the nobles, but Tipova is the ruler of the peasants."

Stefan was not particularly shocked. Even in London a nobleman understood that once he left the comforting confines of Mayfair he was at the mercy of the local thugs.

"What makes you suspect the Beggar Czar?"

Boris hesitated, almost as if he regretted sharing his

thoughts. Stefan frowned. Did the servant have something to hide?

At last, Boris tugged the horses to a halt before a small park and turned on the seat to meet Stefan's curious gaze.

"Babevich's hand was chopped off."

Stefan shuddered. "Yes, I had noticed, although I am doing my best to put it from my mind."

"That is Tipova's means of allowing others to know that he was responsible for the killing."

"Good God, he desires people to know he is a savage?"

"Of course. Such a man does not rule by laws or charity to others. His only weapon is fear and he wields it without mercy."

Stefan found himself intrigued by his companion's matter-of-fact acceptance of Tipova's brutal habits. Not many men could stomach the business of chopping off limbs.

"How do you even know of this man?"

Boris shrugged. "I have not always been employed by your brother."

Realization took a moment to hit. "You were a criminal?"

"Nothing more shocking than pinching a few wallets, but I most certainly would have gone down that path if not for a young man who caught me in a bumbling effort to steal a gentleman's walking stick," Boris admitted.

"Tipova?"

"The same."

"What did he do?"

"He hauled me to a public execution and told me I would be next if he ever caught me on the streets again." The moonlight revealed his wry grimace. "Then he hauled me back to my mother who near beat me to death."

Stefan sudden comprehended Boris's refusal to condemn Tipova as a ruthless bastard. For whatever reason the man had shown enough compassion for a young boy to keep him from becoming yet another of the thieves that choked the poorer quarters of the city.

Of course, there were those who would consider his employment with Lord Summerville not much better than being a common criminal. God only knew how many laws his brother had encouraged him to break.

"How old were you?"

"Ten."

"What of Tipova?"

"Barely shaving."

Stefan lifted his brows. "And he was already cutting off hands?"

"A precocious youth with ambition."

"A bit more than precocious," Stefan muttered. "I thought nothing could be more dangerous than Russian politics."

"A wise man avoids those who lust for power, whether rich or poor."

Two drunken noblemen stumbled through the park, abruptly reminding Stefan that the hour was growing late.

"I am willing to accept that Tipova is responsible for Babevich's murder, but what is their connection?"

"Most likely he owed Tipova money. Or was foolish enough to offer Tipova some sort of insult."

Stefan glared into the dark. Each time he thought he was a step closer to capturing Sir Charles he discovered his hopes thwarted.

"Damn. You found nothing in the house that might reveal where Sir Charles is hidden?"

"No."

"So, a dead end." His chuckle lacked any hint of humor. "Quite literally."

Boris shook the reins, sending the horses into motion.

"Sir Charles is not a gentleman capable of discretion. If he is in St. Petersburg then he will soon reveal his presence."

"Until then, Leonida remains in danger."

AFTER ABANDONING STEFAN on the terrace, Leonida desired nothing more than to collect Sophy and return home.

She did not enjoy such gatherings under the best of circumstances. Now it seemed like little more than torture.

Thankfully, she possessed far too much pride to give in to the cowardly impulse and, pasting a brilliant smile on her lips, she returned to the crush of guests, determined that no one, especially not Stefan, would suspect her heart was breaking.

Why should she offer him the satisfaction of knowing he had wounded her? He considered her nothing more than a temporary mistress he would soon toss aside.

She kept the thought uppermost in her mind as she danced with one eager gentleman after another. But as the evening wore on and Stefan remained conspicuously absent, her anger began to shift to confusion.

Why would he exit the palace without taking his leave?

Was he too angry to even speak with her? Or had he at last accepted that she would never be content with what he was willing to offer and decided to wash his hands of her?

The very thought sent a crippling pain through her heart.

Mon Dieu. What had she done?

Slipping to the edge of the crowd, Leonida began making her way to the far doors. She had endured enough. She could not continue with her charade any longer.

"Leonida."

Intent on her escape, it took a moment for Leonida to realize that the crowd had abruptly parted to reveal the Emperor.

Her startled gaze skimmed over Alexander Pavlovich's elegant uniform and the Cross of St. George that glittered with magnificent glory before returning to meet his angelic smile.

"Sire," she murmured, sinking into a deep curtsy.

Waiting for her to straighten, the Emperor held out his arm. "Will you join me?"

"Of course." Acutely aware of the avid gazes that watched their slow progress across the room, Leonida cast a covert glance at her father's profile. It was not often that her father sought her out in such a public setting. "It is a lovely gathering," she at last murmured.

Alexander Pavlovich regarded his guests with a jaundiced smile. "Vultures. They smile and fawn, while plotting to steal my crown. There is not one of them I trust." He turned back to meet her startled gaze. "Except for you, *ma petite.*"

"I am always your loyal servant."

"You have such a good heart." He patted the hand she had rested on his arm. "I wonder if Huntley is worthy of it?"

Leonida stumbled, then caught herself. Why should she be surprised? Alexander Pavlovich might appear oblivious to the world about him, but there was very little that he missed.

And while Stefan had not caused a blatant scene, he had not been exactly subtle in his unwavering attention.

"It does not matter if he is or not," she admitted, her voice carefully devoid of emotion. "He has no interest in my heart."

"Do you desire me to rid St. Petersburg of his presence?"

It was what she should desire. Instead her heart plummeted to the pit of her stomach.

"There is no need. Soon enough he will feel compelled to return to England."

Alexander Pavlovich heaved a wistful sigh. "I have forgotten what it is to be so young and naive."

Leonida's lips twisted as she recalled the past weeks. What would the Emperor say if she revealed the adventures she had endured since leaving St. Petersburg?

"I am not so naive as others assume."

With a smooth motion, the Emperor led her into a small alcove, turning her to study her face with a curious expression.

"I have seen how the Duke watches you. He is bewitched."

"A passing infatuation."

"And what of you?"

A ridiculous blush stained her cheeks. "Me?"

"Do you love him?" the Emperor asked gently.

"I..." The lie faded on her lips. The steady blue gaze demanded the truth. "Yes." She heaved a deep sigh. "I am such a fool."

"There is nothing foolish in loving another. Only in the decisions you make for that love."

Leonida frowned. It was unlike the Emperor to speak to her with such intimacy. So why now?

Had Herrick revealed more than he should have?

"Do you intend to warn me against the Duke?"

Rather than answer the question, he tugged her deeper into the alcove, motioning toward the ivory-and-gold-striped settee.

"Have a seat. We can be private here."

Leonida perched on the edge of the cushion, holding herself stiff as the Czar joined her on the settee. They were mere paces from the ballroom, but the clamor had receded to a near bearable din.

"I sense I am to receive a lecture."

"No lecture, only the natural concerns of a father." He smiled faintly as she jerked in surprise at his claim of parentage. It was a thing acknowledged, but never spoken out loud. "I have no desire to see you unhappy."

Bemused, she considered her words with care. Alexander Pavlovich might be speaking to her as a father, but he was still the Emperor of all Russia. If he concluded that the Duke of Huntley had hurt or insulted her, he might very well feel compelled to seek justice.

That was the last thing she desired.

"Do not fear." She managed a faint smile. "I am not the sort of female to sit around pining for what she cannot have."

He reached to take her hand. "I am more concerned that you will allow your emotions to urge you into an affair you will only regret."

"Sire..."

"Please allow me to finish, *ma petite*," he interrupted her mortified stammering. "I have no intention of prying into your privacy, but I desire you to carefully consider your future."

"My future?"

"You might have inherited your mother's beauty and her undoubted charm, but you have little in common with her."

"Very little," she said dryly.

"Understandable, of course," he said, his expression pensive. "Nadia's childhood was filled with such bleak loneliness that she was bound to crave the excitement and affection denied her."

Leonida grimaced. How often over the years had she rued her mother's insatiable need to shock society? Even at times hiding in the shadows when Nadia was behaving at her most outrageous.

Only now did she realize that Nadia's brittle *joie de vivre* was her means of denying her grim past.

"She never spoke of her childhood until..." Leonida caught herself before revealing her mother's latest troubles. "Lately. It does explain her love for attention."

Alexander Pavlovich's expression softened. "Ah yes, she does keep society from becoming miserably dull. It is her disdain for convention that has forever fascinated me, and the reason our relations have continued throughout the years."

"Mother is quite devoted to you."

"Yes, I believe she has been content with what I could offer her," he said, a glimmer of regret in his eyes. They both knew that while Nadia could claim a portion of his heart, Alexander Pavlovich had never been a faithful lover. "You, however, have quite different needs than Nadia. You would never be satisfied with a man who could provide nothing more than a fine home and an enviable position in society."

She lowered her gaze to study his strong fingers covering her hand, her heart suddenly heavy. He was right, of course. There might be a part of her that was willing to sacrifice whatever necessary to keep Stefan in her life, but something inside her would wither and die.

"No."

He gently squeezed her fingers. "There is a gentleman waiting for you who will love you with his entire heart. Do not settle for less."

"Thank you," she said softly.

A shadow fell across the entrance and they turned to watch a uniformed servant enter the alcove and perform a deep bow.

"Ah." With a weary sigh, the Emperor lifted her fingers to his lips. "Duty once again rears its ugly head. Take care of yourself, *ma petite*."

Leonida rose to her feet, straightening her shoulders.

Yes.

If she did not care for herself, then who would?

CHAPTER TWENTY-SIX

STEFAN WOKE LATE after a restless night. In truth, it was a wonder he had managed to sleep at all. Stumbling across dead bodies was not precisely the best means of ensuring sweet dreams.

And it had not helped that when he had at last returned to the palace it was to discover Leonida had already left.

Dammit. How much longer must they play this frustrating game?

If she were beneath his roof then she could no longer hide from him. Which was the precise reason he needed to find the means of convincing her to return to England.

The sooner the better.

A hot bath helped to ease the knots of frustration, but he was still plagued by a strange sense of foreboding as he attired himself in a copper jacket and ivory waistcoat that he matched with brown breeches and glossy Hessians. In the intricate folds of his cravat he placed an emerald stickpin that was his only ornament beyond his heavy signet ring.

Leaving his chambers, Stefan made his way through the large house to discover Vanya in her private breakfast room decorated with green damask silk wall panels and pretty Chinese vases.

The older woman was seated at a small table, appearing remarkably pretty in a morning gown of Berlin silk with drop pearl earrings.

"Good morning, Stefan." She waved a hand toward the

sideboard that held a set of silver trays. "Will you join me for breakfast?"

"I would be delighted."

His stomach growled as he moved to fill his plate with freshly baked ham and coddled eggs before joining his hostess at the table.

Sipping her tea, Vanya studied him over the rim of her cup. "You look pale. Did you not sleep well?"

Stefan grimaced. "It was a…difficult evening."

"I trust you were not foolish enough to quarrel with Alexander Pavlovich?"

"I have thus far avoided that particular fate, although I cannot say the same for some others."

Her lips quirked as she watched him polish off his ham. "I presume you speak of Leonida?"

"I shall never understand women."

"You are not intended to." Vanya batted her lashes. "It would remove our irresistible cloak of mystery."

Stefan poured a cup of the coffee, not at all amused. "Then how is a man to know what the devil a female wants?"

"It is not a matter of a man knowing what a woman wants, but whether he is prepared to offer what she *needs.*"

He frowned, attempting to ignore the tiny whisper of disquiet that pricked his heart. What Leonida needed was him. Nothing else.

"You speak in riddles."

"Or you simply choose not to understand."

He pushed aside his plate, his hunger suddenly vanished. Why did women always have to complicate matters? Leonida enjoyed his home, she desired him, and when she forgot to treat him as the enemy, she took pleasure in his company. It was only because of her mother that she was so reluctant to become his mistress.

"It is too early for me to follow your confusing logic, Vanya."

"You are truly as difficult as your brother." Vanya shook

her head. "Just consider what Edmond's life would have been like had he been foolish enough to allow Brianna to slip away."

His gaze lowered to study his fingers, which tightly gripped the coffee cup. Losing Brianna would quite likely have destroyed his brother. But Edmond had been in a position to tumble madly into love. Stefan would never have such a luxury.

"I am not Edmond. Besides, you are hardly in a position to throw stones." He lifted his head to glower at his companion. He did not spend a great deal of time in Russia, but he was well aware that Vanya had enjoyed a long-term affair with Mr. Richard Monroe. "How long have you refused to make an honest gentleman of Monroe?"

"Too long," Vanya promptly admitted, a soft smile curving her lips. "Which is why we are to be married next summer."

"You are to be wed?"

She chuckled at Stefan's blatant shock. "I had planned the wedding for Christmas, but I wish for Brianna to attend so I postponed the ceremony until she and the babe can travel."

Stefan abruptly rose to his feet. The strange ache in his heart was not envy. It was…disbelief.

Why would Vanya wed after years of enjoying the perfect affair?

"This entire city has gone mad."

Vanya shrugged, unperturbed by his sharp tone. "Perhaps."

Stefan paced toward the window, absently noting the earlier rain had eased to a mere drizzle. Leonida would be pleased. She disliked the rain. For him, however, the gray clouds seemed to suit his mood.

He did not like the feeling that he was chasing after Leonida, constantly remaining one step behind.

What if she slipped away?

No. He would never allow it to happen. He would have her no matter what the cost.

The sound of the door opening at last had him spinning about to regard the young footman who entered the room with a small silver tray in his hand.

Vanya rose to her feet. "Yes, Anton?"

"A message has arrived for Lord Huntley."

A tingle of excitement raced down his spine as he crossed the parquet floor. It had to be from Leonida. Who else would write to him in St. Petersburg?

Had she at last come to her senses?

"Thank you," he murmured, plucking the folded parchment from the tray.

The servant backed from the room, leaving Stefan standing in the middle of the floor, his excitement fading as he recognized the writing scrawled across the paper.

"Is it from Leonida?" Vanya asked.

"No." He broke the wax seal. "It is from Edmond."

Vanya offered a small curtsy. "Then I will leave you to enjoy your letter in private."

"Do not bother. Edmond can barely be forced to sit long enough to sharpen a quill. I will be shocked if he managed to scribble more than a few words." Unfolding the parchment, Stefan discovered that his brother had actually managed a half page. Of course, deciphering the illegible writing took a considerable effort. Several moments passed before he abruptly crumpled the letter and tossed it aside. "Damn."

Vanya hurried to his side, her face pale with concern. "Is it Brianna?"

"No, it is my steward," he swiftly assured the older woman. "He was clearing the north field and a tree fell on him."

Her concern remained although it was obvious she was relieved to know that Brianna was safe.

"Was he hurt?"

"Both legs were broken, but Edmond claims the doctor has assured him that Riddle will make a full recovery."

"Thank God."

"Yes, he was very fortunate." Stefan was deeply relieved that the injuries had not been worse. Riddle had been his steward since the death of his father and his dedication to Stefan had ensured that Meadowland had thrived beneath his care. He would be impossible to replace, both as his steward and one of his dearest friends. "Still, he will be laid up for several weeks, if not months."

"Can I be of assistance?" Vanya broke into his thoughts.

"I fear not." He squared his shoulders. "I must return to Meadowland."

"Of course. Do you wish a carriage?"

Stefan shook his head. "No, I must travel by ship, it will be far quicker. I will send Boris to the docks to check the schedules."

"How soon do you intend to leave?"

Duty demanded that he leave immediately. Without Riddle there was no one to oversee the tenants or take charge of the inevitable problems that plagued such a large estate. Edmond could not be expected to devote every day to Meadowland when he had his own estate and family to care for.

His jaws clenched. Duty be damned.

He would return to Meadowland. But not until he had Leonida on the ship with him.

"As soon as I have completed my unfinished business."

Barely aware he was moving, he had nearly reached the door when Vanya's voice brought him to a halt.

"Stefan."

He glanced impatiently over his shoulder. "Yes?"

"Leonida is not a village maid. You cannot compel her to leave her family."

He smiled with grim determination. "You underestimate my powers of persuasion."

"She does not want your persuasion."

"She wants me. And she is damned well going to admit it."

AFTER A MORNING OF RELENTLESS rain, the sun at last broke through the gray clouds and spilled its warmth over St. Petersburg.

It was a welcome change for Leonida as she pulled aside the curtain in the carriage and allowed the sunshine to pour through the small window. The mornings she spent at the local orphanage were always difficult. She did what she could to ease the suffering of the children, but it was never enough. Her only consolation was the continued hope that she could convince her father to provide the schooling the children so desperately needed.

The carriage rolled to a halt before her mother's house and the door was pulled open by the ever-present Pyotr. She had stepped onto the still damp pavement when a movement in the rose garden at the side of the house caught her eye.

"Mon Dieu," she breathed, her gaze skimming over Stefan as he paced from one end of the garden to the other, his body tense with overt impatience.

"Do you wish to drive on?" Pyotr whispered in her ear. "He is bound to go away eventually."

"That is what I tell myself, but he keeps returning."

"Like a bad rash."

A grudging smile touched her lips. "Exactly."

"There is no need for you to meet with him. It would not trouble me to send the Duke on his merry way."

Leonida briefly wished it could be so simple.

It was cowardly, but the thought of avoiding the inevitable confrontation with Stefan was tempting. Especially when she was not nearly as certain as she should be that she could remain firm in her decision to bring an end to their ridiculous affair.

She had devoted hours last night to pacing her room while she lectured herself on all the reasons she was a fool to continue her relationship with Stefan.

They were numerous. And sensible.

And necessary.

The only problem was that it was all well and good to decide that she could no longer risk being in Stefan's company when she was alone and quite another to stand firm when he was near.

How often had she made the decision to put him out of her life only to allow herself to be cajoled and bullied and seduced into continuing their affair?

Aware of Pyotr's worried gaze, Leonida tilted her chin and straightened the skirts of the sprigged muslin gown trimmed with white gauze that she had matched with an emerald-green sash.

"I appreciate your offer, Pyotr, but I am capable of dealing with his Grace," she forced herself to say.

"Are you certain?"

No. Absolutely not.

She pasted a smile on her face. "Of course."

Pyotr heaved a resigned sigh. "I will not be far."

With a pat on his arm to reveal her appreciation for his concern, Leonida moved to the small gate and entered the rose garden.

Her heart gave its familiar leap as Stefan caught sight of her and prowled forward, his elegant features set in an expression of dark impatience.

"At last," he growled as they both halted near the marble fountain, his hands clenched at his sides as if resisting the impulse to reach out and grab her. "Where have you been?"

Leonida met his glare with a cool composure. At least on the surface. Inside, her blood was racing and her stomach clenched with a bittersweet awareness.

He was just so annoyingly beautiful.

"Not that it is any of your concern, but I have been to the orphanage to ensure the boots I purchased were delivered to the children," she snapped, stirring the coals of her anger in an effort to ignore the tingles of excitement that refused to be dismissed. "It is shocking how merchants will attempt to cheat the children if I am not there to keep them honest."

His lips tightened. "I suppose it is no use in pointing out the danger of visiting such a place?"

"None whatsoever."

"Why am I not surprised?"

Her eyes narrowed as she belatedly noted the shadows beneath his magnificent eyes and the tension etched onto his elegant features. "Something is troubling you. What is it?"

He stiffened, as if caught off guard by her perception. Then his lips twisted with a reluctant amusement. "You know me so well."

"Are you going to tell me what has happened?"

Stefan's brooding gaze swept over her face, lingering a heart-stopping moment on her lips before returning to her wary eyes.

"Edmond sent word that my steward was injured in an accident."

Leonida pressed a hand to her lips. Although she had only been at Meadowland for a short time, she had come to know and respect Stefan's devoted servants. Especially the steward who always had a kind word when she crossed his path.

"Mr. Riddle?"

"Yes."

"Is he badly hurt?"

"He has broken both legs."

"Oh, no. The poor man." Her concern deepened at Stefan's grim expression. "Will he walk again?"

"According to Edmond he should make a full recovery."

"Thank goodness."

He nodded, his thoughts seemingly distracted. Leonida wrapped her arms around her waist, beginning to sense his presence in the garden was not just to reveal his steward's accident.

"I must return to Meadowland."

Even knowing this moment was bound to come, Leonida was shocked by the crippling pain his words caused.

To never see his beautiful face again. Never to hear his low, seductive voice whispering in her ear. Never to feel his warm, hungry kiss demanding a response.

She abruptly turned to stare blindly at the water spouting from the marble nymph in the middle of the fountain.

"I…see."

His hands gripped her shoulders, the heat of his body burning through the back of her muslin gown.

"Leonida, I have no choice."

"When do you leave?"

"As soon as possible."

She curled her hands into fists, her nails biting into her palms until they drew blood. She would not to cry. Not yet. What did she have left but her pride?

"Of course." She kept her voice low, carefully controlled. "I hope you will give Lord and Lady Summerville my regards."

"That is all you have to say?"

"I wish you a safe journey."

His fingers tightened on her shoulders, and with a sharp jerk, he turned her around to meet his scorching gaze.

"Dammit, Leonida."

"What do you want?" She wildly shook her head. "Tears? For me to beg you to remain?"

"You know what I want."

She squeezed her eyes shut, unable to meet the brilliant demand of his gaze.

"No, Stefan."

"Leonida, I have no time for these games," he rasped, pulling her hard against his chest. "I intend to be on the first ship to England. And you will be with me."

"This is no game." She struggled as he wrapped his arms tightly around her. A futile effort. "I have told you over and over that I will not be your mistress. Why will you not accept my decision?"

He lowered his head to whisper directly into her ear. "Perhaps because you *are* my mistress."

"No."

"Shall I take you to your bedchamber and prove otherwise?"

She steeled herself not to shiver, but the potent pleasure was undeniable. He was leaving and her body ached to know him one last time.

"Stefan…"

He buried his face in the curve of her neck. "You make me crazed."

"Then you should be pleased to leave me behind."

"Never."

It was the absolute certainty in his voice that had her struggling out of his grasp. The man was insufferable.

"You cannot force me to accompany you."

Their gazes tangled in a battle of wills.

"Is that a challenge?" he gritted out.

"It is the truth." She tilted her chin, refusing to be intimidated. "As you well know."

"What I know is that you need me, whether you are willing to admit the truth or not."

She ignored the painful ache in the center of her heart. "Surely you don't mean to imply that I cannot survive without you? I assure you that I have done quite well on my own."

"Have you?" he taunted.

"Yes."

His eyes darkened with a loneliness that was echoed deep within her.

"No, my dove, you have hidden from your life, pretending to be a part of the world while always keeping yourself separate."

She sharply turned away, hiding her expression from his penetrating gaze.

"That is absurd."

"I have watched you," he relentlessly persisted. "I have seen how you smile and mouth the proper words, but remain careful to hold others at a distance."

She flinched. How did he always know where she was the most vulnerable?

"Just because I do not care for society does not mean I do not have a full and happy life."

"Happy?"

"I am..." The lie would not pass her stiff lips. "Content."

"You are alone."

"I have my family."

"Family?" he mocked. "They are no doubt the reason you push everyone away."

She spun back to stab him with an angry glare. "What is that supposed to mean?"

He cupped her chin in his hand, his expression hard, despite his surprisingly gentle touch.

"You have been disappointed on too many occasions. You fear that if you allow another into your heart they will only use you for their own selfish advantage."

Her humorless laugh filled the garden. "A fear well founded with most gentlemen."

A faint color touched his cheeks as her thrust hit its target. "I only want to take care of you."

"No, you desire to use my body until you weary of it."

His gaze slid downward with a tangible force, lingering on the gentle swell of her breasts before at last returning to her heated face.

"You forget, in return I am offering you full and complete use of my body. You may take advantage of me whenever and wherever you want." His voice thickened. "Surely that is a fair trade?"

Heat curled through the pit of her stomach, threatening to undermine her determination. She took an instinctive step backward. "Not for me."

Her words snapped his fragile control, his eyes blazing with frustration. "Christ, what will it take to make you admit you desire this affair as much as I do?"

"More than you can offer."

"So you keep saying. How the hell can you know if you will not even tell me what it is?"

She wrapped her arms around her waist. What would he say if she told him that she wanted nothing less than his heart?

A pain lanced through her. She knew the answer without even asking.

It was the one thing he would never offer her.

"You claimed that I live in loneliness, but you are no different," she charged, eager to divert his attention. "When was the last time you enjoyed London society or filled Meadowland with guests?"

"I have duties..."

"Oh yes, your precious duties." She did her own share of mocking. "You hide behind them so you do not have to search your soul and realize how empty it is."

CHAPTER TWENTY-SEVEN

WITH AN EFFORT, STEFAN reined in his temper.

Damn. Why did he allow this woman to stir his anger with such ease? It was not as if he possessed a volatile nature. Quite the opposite. But the moment he was in Leonida's company he was suddenly at the mercy of emotions he did not even know he possessed.

No wonder he too often lost the upper hand in dealing with the aggravating female.

Moodily, Stefan studied Leonida's beautiful alabaster face. Her expression was set in stubborn lines, but he did not miss the hint of tears that shimmered in her eyes. She was clearly troubled at the thought of his departure. So why the hell did she continue to fight him?

"Do you intend to drive me away by stirring my anger?" he abruptly demanded. "Is that your last defense when another comes too close?"

She wrapped her arms around her waist in a protective gesture.

"But you are not close."

He laughed at the ludicrous words. "I would say that we have been as close as two people can possibly be."

"Physical intimacy can occur between complete strangers. It is meaningless."

"If you truly believed that then you would have had a dozen lovers." His gut twisted with savage fury at the mere thought of Leonida in the arms of another. He would quite likely kill the bastard. "Instead you have given yourself only to me."

"While you have had any number of lovers, no doubt," she snapped.

He smiled, fiercely pleased by the edge of jealousy in her voice. "I will have no other while we are together."

"Do not restrain yourself on my behalf." She sniffed, pretending an indifference he did not believe for a moment. "You are at liberty to take as many lovers as you want."

"I need only one. Return with me to Meadowland and I will prove just how insatiable that need is."

He stepped forward to pull her back into his arms, but with a swift movement she was darting out of his reach. Did the blasted woman expect him to chase her around the garden?

"Enough, Stefan." Her unsteady voice was harsh. "I will not be traveling to England and that is the end of the matter."

The end? He shook his head. The woman might be stubborn, but not even she could deny the ruthless need that bound them together.

"You truly will allow me to leave without a hint of regret?"

Her eyes darkened. "It is for the best."

"Liar."

"Stefan, please…just go."

For a crazed moment his frustrated anger threatened to overcome his rational mind. She wanted him. That much he knew beyond a doubt. And if she were too stubborn to admit it, then by God, he would toss her into his carriage and haul her to the ship by force if necessary.

It was the memory of Vanya's words that halted him in his tracks.

It is not a matter of a man knowing what a woman wants, but whether he is prepared to offer what she needs….

His jaw tightened. Of course. How could he have been blind for so long?

Leonida Karkoff might be a fascinating combination of

sweet innocence and fierce courage, but at heart she was a woman like any other.

Abruptly he turned on his heel to pace toward the nearby fountain.

"You intend to force my hand, do you not?" he rasped.

"Now what are you implying?"

"As usual I have been embarrassingly dim-witted when it comes to you." He turned to meet her puzzled gaze. "Odd, considering that women have been angling to become my bride since I inherited my title."

For all her undoubted intelligence, it took Leonida a long moment to at last comprehend his meaning.

"*Mon Dieu,*" she breathed, pretending shock at his accusation. "You think…you honestly believe I…"

"That in return for continuing our delicious affair you expect me to make you the next Duchess of Huntley," he smoothly completed.

Without warning she had launched herself forward, beating her fists against his chest with a shocking anger.

"You bastard."

Startled, Stefan grasped her wrists and glared down at her flushed face.

What the devil was wrong with the woman now?

Was he not making the ultimate sacrifice? How dare she act as if he had just insulted her?

"If I were a bastard then we would not be in this particular situation," he growled. "No one could expect Miss Leonida Karkoff to wed a commoner."

"Your arrogance is beyond belief," she hissed.

"There is no arrogance in knowing the worth of my position."

"Perhaps the women in England are blinded by your grand Dukedom, your Grace, but I have spent my entire life surrounded by royalty." Her eyes glittered like sapphires in the sunlight. "If I desired a title I could have wed two counts, three barons, a French *duc,* and half dozen princes."

His jaw clenched. "All of them no doubt as poor as paupers, not to mention old enough to be your father."

"Ah." A tight, angry smile curved her lips. "So you are not only a duke, but you are wealthy and handsome, as well. How could I possibly resist?"

"I do not expect you to."

Her eyes darkened with an emotion that was perilously close to pain as she jerked her arms out of his grasp.

"Are you..." She was forced to halt and clear her throat. "Truly asking me to marry you?"

Was he?

Ridiculously, his mouth was dry and his heart thundered in his chest.

For years he had refused to consider the thought of installing a duchess at Meadowland. Oh, he had briefly flirted with the notion of taking Brianna as his bride. She had, after all, been a part of life for years and she loved the estate as much as he did. More importantly, he had known his parents would surely have approved of such a choice.

Now, however, he could not pretend that his need for Leonida had anything to do with Meadowland. Or the future of the Huntley family.

It was pure, selfish desire.

"I have told you that I will not return to England without you," he said, his voice rough. "If I must wed you, then so be it."

An unnerving silence filled the garden as Stefan waited for Leonida to respond. He did not expect her to swoon. Or even to cry out in joy. She possessed too much pride for such overemotional displays.

But he assumed that there would be a measure of satisfaction in her expression. She had what she wanted, after all.

Instead her expression hardened, a glint of grim resolution chasing away the lingering hurt in her eyes.

"'Then so be it'?" She threw his words back in his face. "What a romantic proposal. I am quite swept off my feet."

Stefan stiffened in outrage. "If you expect me to get on my knee then you are sadly mistaken. I have no need to beg for my bride."

Her chin tilted. "I cannot imagine how Edmond managed to win Brianna if he possesses your lack of finer feelings."

"He kidnapped her," Stefan gritted.

"*Mon Dieu.* Are all Englishmen such barbarians?"

He clenched his hands at his side. It was that or shaking some sense into her thick skull.

"When it comes to overly stubborn females."

She instinctively backed away, as if sensing his violent mood. Wise woman. At the moment the scorching anger that raced through him made a mockery of his usual calm composure.

"I can only hope you are jesting," she muttered.

"You have demanded I give you more," he grated. "If it is not to become my wife then what the bloody hell do you want?"

"The fact you even have to ask proves you are incapable of giving me what I need."

He shoved his fingers through his hair. The woman was destined to put him in an early grave.

Or more likely Bedlam.

"I have offered you everything I possess."

"Yes, I suppose you have." Her voice was low, resigned. "Goodbye, Stefan."

In shocked disbelief, Stefan watched as she walked toward the house with a stiff dignity.

Christ. She was leaving.

Standing motionless for several long moments, Stefan ignored the crushing urge to follow in her wake. He had offered her his name and his pride on a platter, only to have it tossed back into his face.

He was done dancing to Miss Leonida Karkoff's tune.

Spinning on his heel, Stefan stormed from the garden, collecting his carriage from the mews behind the house.

If the wretched woman thought she could manipulate him with her ridiculous games then she was in for a rude awakening. His days of chasing after her like a hound in heat were done.

Despite the heavy traffic, Stefan returned to Vanya's house with admirable speed. Of course, he had left behind several furious Russian pedestrians who had hurled curses when he had near run them down and a number of grooms who had been forced to swerve their vehicles out of his path or risk a collision.

Once at the townhouse, he tossed the reins to the waiting footman and charged up the steps. During the brief journey he had nurtured the smoldering sense of betrayal at Leonida's rejection. He wanted to be in a blazing fury.

His anger was certainly preferable to acknowledging his aching sense of loss.

Ignoring the butler who pulled open the door at his approach, Stefan crossed the foyer, intending to head directly to his rooms. The sooner he was out of Russia the better.

Of course, it could not be so simple.

He had just reached the sweeping staircase when Vanya appeared from a side parlor.

"Stefan." She came to an abrupt halt as she caught sight of his tousled appearance. "I assume from your expression that your business with Leonida did not go well?"

"The woman is…" He snapped his lips shut. Surely he had made enough of a fool of himself for one day? "It no longer matters. Has Boris returned?"

"Yes. He said he would wait for you in your chambers."

He stepped toward the stairs. "Thank you."

"Stefan."

It was the thick concern in the older woman's voice that halted his retreat. Turning, he regarded her with an impatient frown.

"I am in rather a hurry, Vanya."

"Tell me what happened between you and Leonida."

"I asked her to accompany me back to England and she declined."

She flinched at his raw tone. "Did you tell her of your feelings?"

His humorless laugh echoed sharply through the foyer. "I asked her to be my bloody wife."

Absurdly, the older woman shook her head in resignation. "But did you speak to her of love?"

A jolt of alarm shot through his heart. He was not about to discuss his confused jumble of emotions toward Leonida. He had ignored them for weeks. He intended to keep ignoring them.

"I appreciate your hospitality, Vanya, but I must see to my packing. With any luck I shall soon be on a ship to England." His lips twisted. "And sanity."

"Stefan…"

Vanya's plea fell on deaf ears as Stefan grimly climbed the stairs and made his way to his chambers. He would not waste another moment on Leonida Karkoff.

She was a mistake he intended to scrub from his memories.

Shoving open the door, Stefan entered his private parlor. Boris was seated on a settee near the window, sipping from a silver flask as he stepped over the threshold, but with a grimace the servant rose to his feet and tossed the flask in Stefan's direction.

"You look in need of refreshment, Huntley."

Without hesitation, Stefan took a deep drink from the flask. The vodka seared down his throat, landing in his stomach with a fiery explosion.

"Good God," he rasped, tossing the flask back to his companion. A few more sips and Boris would have to carry him onto the ship. "Do you have the schedule?"

Boris nodded. "There is a ship that leaves in two hours."

"Can we get passage?"

The servant grimaced. "For the proper price."

It was what Stefan had expected. What sea captain

didn't feather his own nest by accepting bribes? As a rule, Stefan deplored such behavior. It was always the poorest passengers that suffered. Today, however, he would have bought the whole damned ship and tossed everyone aside if it meant being rid of this demented country.

"The cost does not matter."

Boris pocketed the flask and folded his arms over his barrel chest.

"So I suppose the only question is how many tickets will I need to purchase?"

Stefan clenched his jaw at the deliberately provocative question.

"I will make a bargain with you, Boris."

"I am listening."

"I will buy you as many barrels of vodka as you desire for the journey so long as I never have to hear the name Leonida Karkoff again."

Boris slowly smiled. "Never heard of the woman."

WAITING FOR STEFAN'S CARRIAGE to charge out of the mews at a breakneck speed, Leonida returned to the garden.

She would be damned if she would allow any of the servants to see her crying over the Duke of Huntley.

Besides, she could not bear the thought of being closed in. Not in this moment. She needed to feel the summer breeze and the sun on her skin. How else would she melt the frozen pain that held her captive?

Choosing a marble bench near the back of the garden, Leonida allowed the tears to fall freely. The wrenching sadness would pass, she told herself. It might take a few days. Or weeks.

Or months.

But in the end she had made the right choice.

Mon Dieu. There was nothing she wanted more than to be Stefan's wife. It had nothing to do with becoming the

Duchess of Huntley. Or claiming a prestigious position in English society. It was simply the desire of a woman who loved a man beyond all bearing.

But Alexander Pavlovich had been right.

Even if Stefan were willing to give her his name for the sake of his passion, how long would it be before she began yearning for an affection he could not feel? Or worse, how long before Stefan came to regret having a wife he could not love?

It would destroy her.

And eventually it would destroy Stefan, as well.

She lost track of time as her tears slowly came to a halt and she wallowed in her misery. Soon she would gather her composure and return to the house. Life, after all, had not come to an end just because Stefan was leaving Russia.

Her mother was still in danger and until they could find some means of discovering who had the letters, the Countess would never feel safe. And, of course, there was still Sir Charles. Until he was caught, the streets of St. Petersburg would never be safe.

She was on the point of returning to the house when the sound of the back gate being pushed open had her on her feet.

"Pyotr?" she called, instinctively moving to investigate who had entered the garden. "What are you..." She came to an abrupt halt, her heart squeezing with terror as she easily recognized the slender man with a jagged scar running down his cheek. How could she ever forget him? He had helped Sir Charles hold her captive. "No."

Opening her lips, Leonida prepared to scream. At least one of her servants was bound to be close enough to hear. Before she could make a sound, however, the small man clapped a hand over her mouth and lifted the gun he held in his other hand.

"Forgive me, Miss Karkoff, but I cannot allow you to draw attention to my presence." A chilling smile touched his lips. "I will remove my hand, but know I will not hesitate to shoot if you attempt to attract notice."

Trembling with fear, Leonida waited for the servant to pull his hand away. Although he had managed to shave and change into a clean pair of trousers and linen smock since the last occasion she had seen him, Josef still managed to appear menacing. And she did not doubt for a moment he would pull the trigger.

"What are you doing here?" she asked huskily.

"My employer desires your company." He jerked his head toward the small carriage just beyond the mews. She had been so lost in her thoughts that she had not even heard it approach. "If you will accompany me peacefully I assure you that no harm will come to you."

"Never." Her words throbbed with sincerity. "I would rather you shoot me now than to be in the hands of Sir Charles again."

Surprisingly, his thin face twisted with disgust. "Sir Charles. Bah. I would never work for such a depraved coward."

"Do you take me for an idiot? I have not forgotten one ghastly moment in your company."

"Nothing more than a charade." The man shrugged. "My true employer was anxious to keep track of Sir Charles. It would not do to have him disappear before he was brought to justice."

Charade? Justice? Leonida shook her head, anger and confusion beginning to overcome her fear. This had to be some sort of trick.

"And it did not trouble you that he kidnapped an innocent woman and nearly slit her throat?"

"I did my best to keep you alive." He caught and held her gaze. "Even you must admit that."

Her lips thinned. She was not about to admit any such thing. Not when he was pointing a gun at her heart.

"All I know is that you were traveling with Sir Charles

and rescued him before he could be put in a grave where he belongs."

"You were allowed to have your bit of flesh, but his life was owed to another."

Leonida jerked in shock. "He is dead?"

Josef shook his head, as if he had said more than he intended.

"Your questions will all be answered if you will simply get into the carriage."

She shivered. "I do not trust you."

"Very wise, but on this occasion I have been commanded to treat you with exquisite care. Always presuming you cooperate."

"What do you want of me?"

Noticing her instinctive glance toward the house, Josef reached out to grasp her arm and began hauling her toward the open gate.

"I admire your attempt to distract me long enough to be discovered by one of your servants, but I really must insist that you get into the carriage."

With the gun pressed to her side, Leonida had no choice but to give in to his demands. Even if she could scream for help before the rat could shoot her, she would never put her servants at risk.

They reached the carriage and Leonida had only a glimpse of the large groom, who sat on the driver's seat, before being shoved into the dark interior. Unfortunately, the glimpse was enough to reveal that the man possessed the hard, detached expression of a seasoned soldier. She would find no mercy from him.

Huddling on the surprisingly clean leather seat, Leonida kept her wary gaze trained on Josef as he sat opposite her, the gun held in his hand but no longer pointed in her direction. Not that she was deceived. One wrong move and he would shoot.

They traveled in silence, the only sound the sharp click

of horseshoes against the paved road. Leonida was too terrified at the lingering dread she was about to be delivered to Sir Charles to chatter, and Josef was obviously not the sort to believe in social niceties.

It was at last the realization they were traveling over one of the bridges to the outer islands that shook her out of the strange stupor.

"Do you intend to tell me where we are going?"

"No."

Her hands clenched, her anger flaring. Was she being taken to a remote spot so no one could hear her scream? Or was it simply more convenient to drop her body in the sea after her throat had been slit?

Neither possibility eased her looming panic.

"It does not really matter." She forced the words past her stiff lips. "As soon as it is known that I am missing the entire Russian Army will be scouring the city for me. You and your mysterious employer will learn what happens to those who anger the Czar."

Unexpectedly, Josef smiled. "You do have spirit for a fancy wench."

She grimaced. "More like stupidity."

"No, I have seen your courage." Even through the shadows she could detect the hint of admiration in his eyes. "Not many females would have survived Sir Charles."

More unnerved than pleased by his words, Leonida cleared the lump from her throat.

"Your flattery will not save you from being executed."

"You will be returned home long before Alexander Pavlovich can gather his forces."

"We shall see," she muttered, far from reassured.

Again a tense silence filled the swaying carriage. Leonida gritted her teeth. It was taking all her effort not to give in to the panic that thundered through her.

She would not lower her pride with futile hysterics.

After what seemed to be an eternity the carriage at last

pulled to a smooth halt and Josef shoved open the door to crawl out. Leonida grudgingly followed, her gaze swiftly taking in the three-storied warehouse built of gray stone that was situated along a shabby quay.

At first glance the place appeared abandoned with overgrown weeds and trash piled along the side, but Leonida was not deceived. Even from a distance she could see several large forms outlined behind the numerous windows.

Guards keeping watch.

"What is this place?" she demanded, resisting the urge to struggle as Josef grasped her arm and firmly led her to a side door.

"Follow me."

As if she had a choice in the matter.

Grimly concentrating on not stumbling over her hem, Leonida nearly missed the sounds that began to fill the air. Startled, she turned to regard Josef's hard profile.

"Are those children?"

He met her gaze with a faint smile. "Did you think only nobles could produce brats?"

She frowned. The sounds came from behind the warehouse, as if the children were playing in the sunshine.

"Why are they not at the orphanage?"

"We take care of our own when we can."

We? Nothing could make her believe that Sir Charles had the least interest in caring for children. The man was a coldhearted monster. So who did Josef mean? Was this some sort of secret lair for criminals?

"By training them to be thieves?" she hazarded.

Oddly the man appeared offended by her comment. "By giving them a roof over their head, food in their bellies and the chance to learn how to read. Which is more than your orphanage can offer."

She did not bother to hide her disbelief. "You are teaching them to read?"

"And to do their sums."

"Even the girls?" she demanded, easily able to determine the high-pitched laughter that could never belong to a boy.

"Of course." Reaching the door, Josef pulled it open and waved a hand toward the dark interior. "After you."

Desperate to distract her mind from the potential monster waiting in the shadowed depths, Leonida concentrated on Josef as she stepped over the threshold.

"Who is responsible for the children?"

"For lack of an appropriate chaperone, I have taken charge of the urchins," a voice replied from the shadows of the large, cavernous room.

She came to a halt, her hand pressed to her racing heart. "And you would be?"

The man stepped into the light from a nearby window, appearing absurdly out of place in the grimy setting.

Good…heavens. He was quite honestly one of the most handsome gentlemen she had ever encountered.

Tall and slender, he had dark hair that was pulled into a tail at his neck, the better to reveal his elegant, bronze-kissed face. His eyes were a startling gold that shimmered in contrast to the black velvet jacket, and his lips curved into a smile of pure temptation. In the shaft of sunlight a diamond flashed from the folds of his crisply tied cravat.

He should have been standing in the formal confines of the Summer Palace, not in an abandoned warehouse.

As if sensing her astonishment, the man moved forward to take her hand, lifting it to his lips.

"Dimitri Tipova," he murmured, allowing his mouth to linger far longer than manners dictated. "It is my great pleasure to meet you at last, Miss Karkoff."

This was the infamous Beggar Czar?

Too confused by the unexpected encounter to be as frightened as she should be, Leonida frowned.

"You look familiar. Have we met before?"

Amusement smoldered in his golden eyes. "I do not

move in your elevated circle, although you have no doubt crossed paths with my father."

A blush touched her cheeks. "Oh."

"Not all bastards are so welcomed as you, *ma belle.*" He glanced toward the back windows of the warehouse. "Which is why I opened my little school."

Tugging her hand from his warm grasp, Leonida studied the handsome criminal with a wary puzzlement.

"Why have you brought me here?"

His gaze trailed a warm path down her body. "In part I desired to meet you."

"Why?"

He chuckled at her blunt suspicion. "You are somewhat a saint among the serfs."

"Saint?"

"Your kindness to those in need does not go unnoticed."

She nervously glanced over her shoulder, discovering Josef standing patiently beside the door. Had she fallen asleep in the garden? Certainly this all seemed like more a nightmare than reality.

"And that is why you had me kidnapped?"

"An unnecessary evil, for which I hope you will forgive me. Unfortunately, there is a rather large bounty on my head. It did not seem wise to call upon you at your home." The dark gaze took another sweep over her slender body. "Of course, had I known your beauty was even more stunning than rumored I might have considered it a worthy risk."

"Sir…"

"Dimitri," he smoothly interrupted. "I am no gentleman."

"What do you want of me?"

"We shall discuss that in a moment, *ma belle.*" His slender hand lifted to tuck a stray curl behind her ear. Oddly, Leonida was not frightened by the intimate gesture. Or even offended. Instead, she could not deny a growing curiosity about this complex man. "First I have information that I believe will be of interest to you."

The edge in his voice sent a sudden chill down her spine. "Does the information have anything to do with Sir Charles?"

"Intelligent as well as beautiful, a most charming combination." Taking her hand, Dimitri Tipova placed it on his arm and turned to lead her toward a door on the far side of the room. "Come, I have tea waiting. We shall discuss the sad end of Sir Charles over freshly baked gingerbread."

CHAPTER TWENTY-EIGHT

REGRETTABLY FAMILIAR with the perils of traveling by sea, Stefan remained settled in Vanya's carriage, far away from the crowd of waiting passengers and the unpleasant stench that permeated every dock around the world.

There were few things worse than the smell of rotting fish and unwashed bodies.

Outside the tiny window of the carriage he could view the large ship that would soon carry him to England. Thank God. For the first time since his mad flight he realized just how much he missed his rambling old house and the well-tended fields. He had been a fool to ever leave.

Once he was back at Meadowland and surrounded by the familiar companionship of his family and tenants, Leonida would soon become nothing more than a stale memory.

He grimly held on to that thought, as if it could keep at bay the howling emptiness that swept through his soul.

Watching the crew scramble about the deck of the ship, Stefan breathed a sigh of relief as Boris tugged open the carriage door. He wanted to be away from this place.

Away from the temptation of Miss Leonida Karkoff.

"They are preparing to board."

Climbing out of the carriage, Stefan grimaced as the pungent scents assaulted his nose.

"You have seen to the luggage?"

"It is safely stowed, along with your servants."

Placing his beaver hat on his head, Stefan angrily tugged at the cuffs of his moss-green jacket.

"I was a fool to come to Russia."

"Not a fool." Boris clapped a comforting hand on his shoulder. "You would have regretted letting her go without a fight."

"And yet I still lost her."

Boris frowned at Stefan's harsh tone. "Perhaps in time she will come to her senses and realize she can't survive without you."

The memory of Leonida's obstinate expression as she had walked away from him seared through his mind.

"Perhaps," he muttered, knowing even as the word left his mouth it was never to be.

The knowledge was a festering wound in the center of his heart.

Stepping back, Boris waved a hand toward the dock that was now nearly empty.

"We must go."

"Of course." Commanding his reluctant feet to carry him forward, Stefan was abruptly spinning back toward his carriage as he heard the sound of horse hooves thundering in his direction. His breath squeezed from his lungs as he easily recognized the rider. "What the devil?"

Boris grudgingly moved to stand at his side. "What is it?"

"Pyotr."

Boris grabbed his arm. "Huntley, we have no time to waste." He muttered a curse as Stefan wrenched his arm free and headed directly for the Russian groom who was dismounting from his winded horse. "Huntley."

Ignoring his companion's attempt to halt him, Stefan stalked to stand directly before Pyotr.

"What are you doing here?"

"Is Leonida with you?" the servant demanded, not bothering to disguise his alarm.

Stefan frowned. Why the devil would the man think Leonida was with him? Unless…

She was missing.

A stark, savage fear gripped Stefan's heart.

"No."

"I had hoped…" The man shook his head, already turning back toward his horse. "No matter. *Bon voyage*, Huntley."

Stefan grabbed the back of the groom's jacket, yanking him around to meet his scorching gaze.

"Dammit, Pyotr, tell me what has happened to Leonida."

"I don't know," the man reluctantly admitted. "She was in the garden, obviously upset after your visit. I checked on her several times, but when I returned to bring her a tea tray she was gone."

Stefan's heart refused to beat. He knew Leonida too well to believe she would wander off without telling Pyotr of her destination. Not when she was well aware that her faithful servant would panic the moment he discovered her missing.

Christ. Sir Charles obviously had survived his wounds. And now he had Leonida.

"Why the hell did you ever leave her alone?" he rasped.

Pyotr attempted to disguise his sense of guilt behind a fierce scowl.

"It was obvious she desired her privacy. Besides, I was close enough to hear if she cried out."

"And you truly imagine a madman would allow her the opportunity to scream for help?"

Pyotr leaned forward, stabbing Stefan with an accusing glare. "It was not me who left her crying alone in the garden."

His hands clenched at his sides as an agonizing remorse pierced him. He did not need Pyotr to point out the obvious.

He should never have left her. Not when he knew there was a possibility that Sir Charles might still be alive and in a mood for revenge.

Bloody hell. He should not have left her regardless of Sir Charles.

It had been his wounded pride that made him storm from the garden. He had offered Leonida all he possessed and she had flatly rejected him. Or at least, that was what he had told himself.

So you intend to force my hand...

Stefan winced as he recalled his mocking words. Christ. It was no wonder she had attempted to slap his face.

Edmond would laugh to know how he had bungled his first proposal. Especially since Stefan rarely allowed his brother to forget his clumsy pursuit of Brianna.

Looking back he realized that he'd felt as if he were being manipulated into a declaration against his will. Only now could he accept that he had simply been...terrified. The answer to his proposal had mattered far too much, so he had treated it as if it did not matter at all.

And had received precisely what he deserved.

Vanya had tried to tell him. To warn him.

Leonida was not a woman who would ever trade her body to grasp position or power. And she most certainly would never be content with a man who could offer no more than a transitory passion.

For God's sake, she had told him.

I am not my mother...

Without warning Boris was at his side, jerking Stefan out of his bleak thoughts.

"Huntley, we must board," he said, glaring over his shoulder at the large ship. "The captain is bleating he will leave without you. As if I did not pay the fat pirate three times what the tickets were worth."

"Leonida is missing," he said, the very lack of emotion in his voice revealing the depths of his fear.

"Damn." Boris paused, then cleared his throat. "I thought the woman was no longer our problem?"

"He is right, your Grace," Pyotr added. "Get on your ship. I will find my mistress."

"You should not have lost her to begin with," he snapped.

Boris regarded him with a frown, no doubt wondering if he had surrendered to madness. "Huntley?"

"Christ." Stefan sucked in a calming breath. He had to think clearly. Leonida's very life might depend upon him. "Return to England, Boris. Tell Edmond I will return as swiftly as possible."

Boris threw his hands in the air. "I knew that woman would manage to keep you here."

Pyotr narrowed his gaze. "Are you implying that this is some ploy to—"

"I don't imply, Pyotr," Boris interrupted, using his considerable bulk to loom over the smaller groom. "If I thought Miss Karkoff was attempting some nasty trick I would say so."

"Enough," Stefan snapped, his control hanging on by a fragile thread. He glared at the belligerent Russian. "Do you know anything beyond the fact Leonida has disappeared?"

Pyotr shrugged. "One of the maids claimed she saw a black carriage pull away from the mews and a..."

Stefan stepped forward as the man's words trailed away. "What?"

"She said there was a small man with a face like a rat."

"That hardly describes Sir Charles."

"No, but it describes his devoted servant."

Realization hit Stefan like a blow. "Josef."

"Yes."

Turning, Stefan slammed his fist into a nearby brick wall, indifferent to the shock of pain that raced up his arm. His thoughts were consumed with the horror of Leonida being in the clutches of the lethal madman.

Boris grabbed his arm, as if afraid that Stefan might do himself more damage.

"We will find her, Huntley."

"How?" Stefan whirled back, a violent fear shuddering through his body. "We do not even know where to begin the search. Sir Charles could have taken her anywhere."

"I will return and question the neighbors," Pyotr abruptly decided. "Perhaps one of them noticed something that will be of assistance."

Stefan gave an absent nod. Knowing the curiosity of most neighbors, it was worth the attempt.

"Very well."

Leaping back into his saddle, Pyotr glanced down at Stefan.

"What do you intend to do?"

Stefan grimaced. Did he truly have a choice? He was not about to race around blindly, simply hoping to stumble across Leonida. No. He needed assistance, and there was only one man in the position to help.

"I am going to find Gerhardt."

The groom allowed a whisper of hope to ease his grim expression. "You believe he knows where Sir Charles is hidden?"

"If he does not, he at least has the ability to gather enough soldiers to search the city. House by house, if necessary."

PERCHED ON THE EDGE of the settee, Leonida sipped her tea from a cup made of Wedgewood china and allowed her gaze to roam over the elegant parlor.

She could sense Dimitri Tipova regarding her with an unwavering interest, but she was still attempting to reconcile the sophisticated decor that currently surrounded her with the shabby exterior of the warehouse. Who could ever suspect that such a place would hide priceless Rembrandts and a collection of jade figurines that would make her mother swoon with pleasure? And the books…even from a distance she could tell they were well-worn with use rather than simply put on display.

Dimitri Tipova was proving to be an astonishingly complex man.

And a dangerous one, a voice whispered in the back of her mind. She would be a fool to allow his smooth charm to lull her into a sense of complacency. She sensed he could be as ruthless and cold-blooded as Sir Charles in his own way.

"More tea?"

Setting aside the cup, Leonida warily returned her attention to the gentleman negligently sprawled on a chair directly opposite her.

"Thank you, no." She ran her damp hands down her skirt. There was no means to hide her fear. "Please, will you tell me why you have brought me here?"

"Of course, *ma belle,*" he murmured, glancing toward the door leading to the private chambers. "That will be all, Josef."

The scarred servant lifted a brow. "You are certain? She is a tiny thing, but she is cunning."

Dimitri chuckled, seemingly content to have his commands questioned. A rare quality for most leaders.

Indeed, the only other gentleman she had encountered who treated his servants with such respect was Stefan.

Leonida crushed the thought of the Duke the moment it flared painfully through her mind. She dare not be distracted. Not now.

On this occasion, she could depend upon no one but herself to survive this encounter. Stefan would not be riding to the rescue.

"I have hopes that we shall soon come to an understanding," Dimitri drawled, interrupting her futile thoughts. "Keep a close guard on the road. I prefer not to be surrounded by the Emperor's Guard without warning."

"Very well." Josef performed a sweeping bow. "Miss Karkoff."

Waiting until the servant had left the room and pulled the door closed behind him, Dimitri pointed a slender finger toward a small box wrapped with a bow on the inlaid ebony table in front of her.

"I have a gift for you."

She licked her dry lips. "What is it?"

"Open it and see."

With stiff reluctance she collected the box and tugged off the silver ribbon. Pulling off the lid, she prepared herself for what lay inside.

Surprise stabbed through her as she caught sight of the flawless diamond that glittered against the black velvet cloth lining the box.

"A stickpin?" she muttered in confusion, then without warning she realized that she had seen the diamond before. "*Mon Dieu.* This belongs to Sir Charles."

"Yes. He has no further need of it."

Leonida jerked up her head to meet the cruel satisfaction that glittered in the depths of his black eyes.

"He is dead?"

"Quite dead."

A shudder of sheer relief shook her body. "Thank God."

Dimitri dipped his head. "I thought you would be pleased."

"I am," she swiftly agreed, holding out the box as if it contained the plague. "But I want no reminders of the monster."

The handsome criminal leaned forward and gently closed her fingers around the box.

"Then sell it and donate the money to the orphanage. It seems a fitting end to Sir Charles."

Beneath the force of his dark gaze, she swallowed her instinctive revulsion. He was right. Sir Charles's taint was gone from the world and the large diamond was worth a great deal of money. She could purchase a number of supplies for the children.

"Yes. Thank you."

Dimitri settled back in his chair. "I assure you, it was my greatest pleasure."

She paused, studying the lean, dangerous face with a curiosity she could no longer keep at bay.

"Why?"

"Sir Charles was a rabid animal who needed to be put down."

She frowned, not surprised at the description. She

already suspected as much. But how would this man even know of Sir Charles?

"He harmed someone you cared for?"

"I care for all those who are not considered worthy of being protected by Alexander Pavlovich and his guards." A hint of steel edged his voice. "Sir Charles tortured and murdered women for his own perverted pleasure. It could not be tolerated."

Leonida was wise enough not to protest the man's disrespect toward his Emperor. It was not, after all, as if she could argue her father's lack of concern toward the tragedy of the serfs.

Instead, she concentrated on the knowledge that Sir Charles was well and truly dead.

"Did he suffer?"

A feral smile curved his lips. "Very much."

"Good."

As if surprised by her fierce response, Dimitri tilted back his head to laugh with rich enjoyment.

"You possess the soul of a warrior and the heart of a saint." The dark eyes studied her with an unnerving intensity. "A pity I cannot keep you."

With a sharp motion, Leonida rose to her feet. She was not entirely certain he was teasing.

"If that is all..."

"But it is not." His voice held a thread of warning. "Please, return to your seat."

Her heart thundered, but she forced herself to reclaim her place on the settee. It was not as if she could escape.

Not until Dimitri Tipova was prepared to let her go.

If he did intend to let her go.

"What else could we have to discuss?"

"According to my sources, Sir Charles was not alone in his attempt to blackmail your mother."

Her burst of fear was forgotten as her eyes widened in shock. "How did you..."

"There is very little that occurs in St. Petersburg that does not reach my ears." He overrode her disbelieving words, his expression unreadable. "And Nikolas Babevich has never been discreet."

She shivered. Was there any secret this man had not ferreted out? It was uncanny.

"My mother will never pay him the money he has demanded," she said, her tone defensive.

"Never fear, Miss Karkoff. Babevich has happily joined Sir Charles in the netherworld," he drawled. "Well, perhaps not happily. As I recall there was a great deal of screaming involved."

A trickle of sweat inched down her spine. Just how much blood was on this man's hands?

"What did he do?"

"He was foolish enough to owe my gambling establishments a great deal of money."

"I…see."

His smile mocked her barely concealed unease at his callous manner.

"Do not mourn his passing, *ma belle.* He was a liar and a thief who was plotting to murder his own sister to gain her inheritance."

Her spine stiffened. She was not troubled by the thought that Nikolas Babevich was dead. After all, he had done his best to terrify her mother into giving him an enormous fortune. And any gentleman who would throw his lot in with a man such as Sir Charles was bound to possess his own share of evil.

No, she was far more unnerved by the knowledge that her current companion could shrug aside murder so lightly.

It was hardly reassuring for a woman he had just kidnapped.

"I am surprised you did not wish for him to succeed in acquiring his inheritance if he owed you money," she muttered.

"My pesky conscience occasionally overcomes my

business sense," he admitted, smoothly rising to his feet to cross toward the marble fireplace. "Such as now."

"Now?"

Opening an enameled box on the mantle, Dimitri plucked out a stack of letters tied with a frayed ribbon. He turned, smiling at her suddenly wide eyes.

"I believe these belong to your mother."

Leonida slowly rose to her feet, her heart refusing to beat.

The letters. So, Josef *had* stolen them from her bag. How else could Dimitri have gotten his hands on them?

Now the question was, what did he intend to do with them?

She forced herself to meet his dark, steady gaze. "What do you demand for their return?"

His brows arched with an inbred arrogance. "I do not barter like a common merchant, Miss Karkoff. I offer you the letters with my compliments."

Leonida would be the first to concede that she was innocent in the ways of criminals, but she was not stupid.

"You would not have brought me here if you did not want something."

His soft chuckle brushed over her as he moved with the grace of a stalking panther to stand directly before her.

"Ah, such a clever little minx. I will admit that when I do someone a good deed, I expect the favor to be returned."

"And what favor would you demand?"

He shrugged. "Who is to say?"

"I have little influence with Alexander Pavlovich."

"Do not worry. It will be nothing that will be beyond your powers to provide."

Leonida was not nearly so confident. Thus far, Dimitri had played the role of charming host, but she had not forgotten he had readily admitted to killing two men.

Did she truly wish to be in debt to such a man?

Even if it did mean getting her hands on the damnable letters?

"I…"

Her lips snapped shut as the door to the private chambers was thrust open to reveal Josef.

"There are men approaching," the servant announced.

Dimitri was swiftly on alert, but his expression was more amused than terrified.

Clearly he assumed he was more than capable of dealing with whatever was approaching.

And Leonida suspected his confidence was hard-earned.

"Guards?" Dimitri demanded.

"A handful. Along with Gerhardt." Josef's gaze slid to Leonida, a taunting expression on his narrow face. "And the Duke of Huntley."

"Stefan?" Leonida made a sound of staggered disbelief. The servant must be mistaken. Stefan was on a ship bound for England. And even if he were not, he had made it painfully clear that he had washed his hands of her.

Why would he put himself at risk to attempt to rescue her?

"Ah. It would seem your escorts have arrived. Be sure and give them my warm regards," Dimitri said, shoving the letters into her hand before motioning his servant forward. "Josef, please accompany Miss Karkoff downstairs."

Before Leonida could protest, the servant had moved to grasp her arm and began hauling her toward the door.

"Come with me, Miss Karkoff."

Unable to battle against Josef's determined grip, Leonida glanced desperately over her shoulder. Dimitri stood in the middle of the expensive carpet, his arms folded over his chest.

"The favor?" she demanded.

A wicked smile curved his lips. "I will send word if the day arrives when I need your assistance."

"That is not particularly reassuring."

His dark chuckle followed her as Josef tugged her out the door and down the steps.

"Au revoir, ma belle."

CHAPTER TWENTY-NINE

THE FIGHT BEGAN THE MOMENT that Stefan appeared on Herrick Gerhardt's doorstep and continued even after the older man had gathered his horse, along with several grim-faced soldiers, to lead them from the city to the northern island.

It was only to be expected, of course.

Both men were born leaders and harbored a fierce male sense of possession toward Leonida. With their tempers rubbed raw with fear at her disappearance, the sparks were bound to fly. Only their overwhelming need to find Leonida kept them from coming to blows.

They rode ahead of Boris and the other guards who had wisely fallen back to avoid the crossfire, both keeping a close watch on the crumbling warehouses that dotted the rough landscape.

"I have warned you, your Grace, that I will not allow you to meddle in Russian affairs," Herrick gritted out, angling his horse toward the path leading directly toward the quay.

Stefan's fingers clutched the loaded pistol in his hand. "And I have warned you that I will not allow Leonida to be used as a pawn in your murky games. You should have told me of Dimitri Tipova's involvement."

The dark eyes snapped in his direction. "Just as you should have told me of Nikolas Babevich's murder," he countered. Stefan had only grudgingly admitted he had stumbled across the dead body when it was obvious Herrick was considering wasting their time by searching for Sir Charles and Leonida at Babevich's house. Of course, when he described the gruesome method of the man's death, it had in turn forced the older man to confess Tipova's interest in Sir Charles, and the possibility that the Beggar Czar might at least have some knowledge of Leonida's disappearance. "Besides, why should I speak to you of Leonida at all? Are you not preparing to leave St. Petersburg? Leonida is no longer your concern."

A blaze of emotion seared through his body at the older man's taunt. For once he made no effort to ignore or dismiss the unnerving sensations. He was done pretending.

To himself and to others.

"Leonida will be my concern until the day I die." His low, husky voice throbbed with sincerity. "No doubt she will continue to plague me even after I am in my grave."

Herrick's gaunt face remained set in bleak lines, but the dark eyes flickered with a ready comprehension of Stefan's vow. Whether he approved or not was impossible to know.

"And your return to England?"

Stefan shrugged. "It will be delayed until I have wed my future Duchess."

"If she will have you."

A dark, ruthless pain slashed through Stefan's heart, but he refused to give in to despair. He would not believe that he had ruined all hope. It was…unbearable.

"Until I met Leonida I considered myself excessively clever, now all I can claim is an ability to learn from my mistakes," he said. "She will have me, even if I must devote the rest of my days to earning her heart."

Herrick's brows lifted. "Heart?"

"Yes."

"Perhaps you are not quite so dim-witted as I first supposed," the older man muttered.

Stefan ignored the insult, his gaze narrowing as he realized they had passed by most of the buildings until there was only one unkempt structure huddled near the quay.

"Is that the warehouse?"

"It is."

"Then why are we dawdling?"

"Huntley, wait." Herrick reached out to grasp Stefan's arm. "It could be a trap."

"I do not care."

Yanking away from Herrick's grip, Stefan dug his heels into his horse to send him bolting down the street to the warehouse. He had not lied. If Dimitri Tipova knew anything of Leonida's disappearance then he would risk any trap to discover the truth. What meaning did his life have without the woman he loved?

Passing through the broken gates, Stefan was charging across the paved yard when the door to the warehouse was shoved open and a small, golden-haired woman stepped into the fading light.

"Leonida."

Not waiting for his horse to come to a halt, Stefan leaped from the saddle, running toward Leonida the moment his feet hit the ground. He absently noted that the door to the warehouse had been closed behind Leonida and that Herrick and his guards had spread out to ensure that no one could approach without warning. A wise precaution that he was delighted to leave in Herrick's capable hands. His only concern was the beautiful woman who walked toward him with an uncertain expression.

"Stefan?"

At last reaching her side, Stefan ran desperate hands over her body, frantic to assure himself that she was not injured.

"Are you hurt?"

"I am fine."

Gripping her shoulders, his anxious gaze seared over her upturned face. "You are certain?"

"Quite certain."

The vicious tightness clenching his chest eased as he at last accepted she was safe.

"What happened?" he rasped. "How did you get here?"

"Josef appeared in the garden and forced me into his carriage." She grimaced, but it was more a gesture of aggravation rather than lingering fear. "I do wish people would stop doing that."

His fingers instinctively tightened on her shoulders, his gaze turning toward the warehouse.

"I will kill the bastard."

Her hands lifted to press against his chest, genuine fear flashing through her beautiful eyes.

"No, Stefan. It is too dangerous."

His brows snapped together. Did she not comprehend his primitive need to punish any man foolish enough to threaten her?

"He cannot be allowed to escape," he snarled.

"I would bet my entire fortune he has long since disappeared. Besides, I have assured you he did me no harm."

"He kidnapped you."

"Only to bring me here so I could meet with Dimitri Tipova," she said, as if that excused the bastard. "I will admit that I was frightened, but he did nothing to hurt me."

His brows snapped together. "Why would Dimitri Tipova wish to meet with you?"

"He wanted me to know that Sir Charles is dead."

Stefan sucked in a sharp breath. During the long, harrowing afternoon, he had been ravaged with thoughts of Leonida being in the hands of Sir Charles.

Now a sharp, biting relief raced through him.

He could not bear the thought of Leonida enduring more anguish.

"Tipova killed him?"

"Yes." She shuddered, her arms instinctively wrapping around her body in a protective motion. "I was not the only woman he hurt. He had to be stopped."

"That doesn't explain why he kidnapped you."

"He wanted to give me these."

She lifted her hand, and for the first time Stefan noted that she clutched a small box along with a stack of letters tied with a ribbon. It did not take a great deal of intelligence to speculate what they were.

"My mother's letters." He captured her guarded gaze. "Tipova had them?"

"Yes."

"How?"

She wrinkled her nose. "Josef stole them as we suspected, but he never truly worked for Sir Charles. He was a spy for Dimitri Tipova."

Stefan possessed little interest in Josef or his loyalties. He was far more concerned with Tipova and why the leader of the underworld had felt compelled to kidnap Leonida to return a handful of letters.

Such a man did not do things out of the kindness of his heart.

"And what did he demand for them?"

"I am not entirely certain."

"Leonida…"

"Stefan." Before he could guess her intention, Leonida had lifted a hand and placed it across his mouth, effectively silencing him. "I want to know what you are doing here."

It was not the fingers that halted his demands to know precisely what Dimitri Tipova had required of her. Instead it was the uncertainty that shimmered in her eyes.

He never desired for this woman to doubt him again.

Gently he grasped her wrist, tugging her fingers from his lips to press them against his cheek. "I think it should be obvious I was searching for you."

"You are supposed to be on a ship to England."

"So I was." He shook his head. Christ. He had come so close to destroying his future. "Thank God, Pyotr came to warn me of your disappearance. I might have been well out to sea by the time I came to my senses. Boris might never have forgiven me if I forced him to swim miles back to St. Petersburg."

Her expression remained guarded, as if she feared he was playing some cruel trick. The sight made him flinch with regret.

"Did you take a blow to the head?" she demanded.

"The blow, my dove, was to my heart." He lightly kissed her fingers before placing them in the center of his chest. "A blow that I no doubt richly deserve, but one I hope you will heal."

"Stefan?"

Indifferent to the numerous gazes watching them with avid curiosity, Stefan abruptly wrapped his arms around her slender waist and buried his face in the curve of her neck. He needed to feel her warmth melting away the icy fear that had gripped him for the past hours.

She was safe.

Now he had to convince her to take yet another risk.

"Bloody hell, I have been such a fool."

She trembled, but thank God, she made no effort to pull away.

"I have no intention of arguing," she muttered.

"No, I do not suppose you do." He breathed deeply, savoring the sweet jasmine that filled his senses. How had he ever thought he could survive without this woman? "I have known since the moment you crossed my path that I wanted you. Hardly surprising. You are astonishingly beautiful. But I could not understand why you fascinated me more than any other woman I have ever known."

The box and letters fell to the ground as she raised her hands to rest them tentatively against his chest.

"Because you thought me a liar and a thief."

He pulled back, willing her to see the sincerity that was etched on his face.

"True, but even when I suspected that you were in my home under false pretenses, I could not halt my obsessive need to make you mine." His smiled ruefully. "I should have known in that moment you were a danger to more than my sanity."

"So you decided to take me as your mistress?"

He grimaced at his blind arrogance. Not that he hadn't paid a painful price for his conceit. This woman had led him on a merry chase from England to Paris to St. Petersburg.

"That was the only means to have what I desired without confessing the truth," he said.

She frowned. "The truth of what?"

"That I was terrified."

She blinked, clearly taken aback by his blunt honesty. "Of me?"

"Of acknowledging the feelings that you stirred deep inside me," he admitted without hesitation. The time for dissembling was long past.

A lingering hurt darkened her eyes. "Because I am not the Duchess you envisioned for yourself?"

He swallowed his disbelieving laugh. This beautiful, clever, frustratingly courageous woman was even more wondrous than he had ever hoped to have as his Duchess. Instead he concentrated on soothing her painful doubts.

"Because loving you forced me to consider my future rather than clinging to my past."

"Love?" she whispered.

The last rays of sunshine stroked over her face, shimmering in the brilliant gold of her hair. His arms tightened around her as his blood stirred and his muscles hardened with awareness.

She was so damned beautiful.

"It was ironic, really," he said, his voice thickening. "I devoted years to fretting over Edmond's guilt at my parents' death while blindly ignoring my own ghosts. It was not until you entered Meadowland and filled it with your golden light that I realized how dark it had become."

Her expression softened. "You mourned your parents."

Stefan shook his head. He was not so forgiving of his years of willful deceit.

"I hid behind my duties so I would not have to accept their loss. They would have been vastly disappointed in me."

Her hand lifted to gently touch his face. "I refuse to believe they could ever be disappointed in you."

"But it is true," he insisted, leaning into her touch. He craved it with a wrenching force. "As you said, Meadowland is not just a house. It is a home meant to be filled with a family." He deliberately paused. "*Our* family."

He felt her stiffen beneath his hands, a wary hope darkening her eyes. "Are you proposing, your Grace?"

"I am offering you my name, my worldly possessions and my heart, Miss Karkoff." He lowered his head to murmur against her lips. "I promise to always keep you warm no matter how cold the weather. I promise you will always have books and quiet evenings, and I promise that you will always be first in my life. I love you. For now and all eternity."

With a low cry, Leonida threw her arms around his neck and pressed her face to his chest, just over his pounding heart.

"And I love you."

Happiness exploded through him at the simple words. "So will you be my Duchess?"

The brief happiness was replaced by a jolt of panic as she pulled back to regard him with an unreadable expression. "There is something you have forgotten to offer me."

"Leonida?"

"When we were in the garden you…"

"No, my dove," he groaned, pressing his lips to her mouth in a quick, silencing kiss. "Please do not remind me. I cannot bear to recall how I behaved. I was an ass."

He lifted his head to discover her regarding him with a startlingly mischievous expression.

"You were, but you did offer me the full and complete use of your body." Her hands shifted to run her fingers through his tousled hair. "Is that no longer to be included in your proposal?"

"Christ." He breathed out a shaky sigh of relief, resting his forehead against hers. "Tease me like that again and I will toss you over my shoulder and take you to the nearest priest."

Her wicked chuckle tightened his muscles with an equally wicked pleasure. "You did not answer my question."

Shifting to ensure his body protected her from the gazes of the gathered men, Stefan gripped her hips and pressed her hard against his rising erection.

"Do you need further proof?" he asked huskily.

Heat flooded her cheeks, assuring Stefan that he was not the only one suffering from a frustrated hunger.

Good.

It was not at all fair that he should be alone in his need. Besides, he could always hope her desire for him would urge her into a swift wedding.

A very swift wedding.

"Perhaps when we have a bit more privacy," she said.

He groaned at her soft promise. "Does this mean you agree to be my wife?"

Like the sun breaking through the clouds, a slow smile lit her face.

"Did I ever have a choice?"

His laughter filled the air. "Never."

EPILOGUE

THE WEDDING OF THE Duke of Huntley and Miss Leonida Karkoff was a quiet, simple affair attended only by the Countess, the Emperor and Herrick Gerhardt.

There would be another wedding once they reached Surrey, of course, to satisfy the demands of the Church of England, but none who attended the ceremony could doubt that even the most lavish affair could surpass the solemn beauty of Stefan and Leonida exchanging their vows.

Had two people ever gazed at one another with such love?

At last the wedding party made their way to the ship waiting to carry the couple to England. After tearful good byes the Emperor returned to the Summer Palace, while the Countess entered her carriage and disappeared from the dock.

Climbing onto his waiting horse, Herrick headed toward his home, only to come to an abrupt halt mere blocks from the dock. Damn. He had hoped he could dismiss the worry that had been needling him throughout the morning. Instead, it was only becoming more persistent.

Although Nadia had appeared genuinely delighted as she watched her daughter become the Duchess of Huntley, there had been a sadness in her dark eyes that haunted him.

He would not be capable of settling down until he discovered what was troubling the Countess.

Wryly acknowledging he was worse than a meddlesome old woman, Herrick altered his route, at last halting his horse before Nadia's lovely home. Then, climbing the steps, he allowed the butler to show him to a back parlor.

Stepping over the threshold, he found Nadia standing next to a fire that blazed in the marble fireplace, appearing far younger than her years in a pale blue gown over a silver satin slip with a row of silver roses that trailed over her shoulders and down the low-cut back. It was little wonder that the Emperor had found her an irresistible temptation.

She glanced up at his entrance, a hint of curiosity in her dark eyes.

"Herrick. Please join me."

With a smile he moved to stand next to her, leaning against the mantle as he folded his arms over his chest.

"A charming ceremony."

"It was, indeed."

He narrowed his gaze. "And, of course, Leonida made a beautiful bride."

A wistful smile touched her lips. "Any bride is beautiful when she loves her husband as Leonida loves Stefan."

Unease whispered through Herrick. What was plaguing the woman?

She surely could not be disappointed in the marriage? Although the Duke of Huntley was more English than Russian, he possessed a lofty position and enough wealth to make any mother swoon in delight.

"Thankfully Stefan appears equally devoted."

"More than devoted. He is besotted."

Herrick's expression softened, suddenly realizing that it was not disappointment that he could sense.

"Regrets, Nadia?" he demanded softly.

"Not for myself." She absently toyed with a lacquer box set on the mantle, her eyes distant with remembered guilt. "I made the choices that made me happy, but I do regret that I did not understand that my daughter could never be satisfied with a society marriage."

Herrick grimaced. They had all been selfish when it came

to the sweet, all too biddable child, each using her to fill some emptiness in their lives yet giving her very little in return.

"No, Leonida has always needed love," he admitted.

Nadia sighed. "I failed her."

"Nonsense," he stoutly denied. The Emperor's dangerously brooding mood had lightened the moment of Nadia's brilliant return to society. Herrick would not allow her to retreat back to her rooms in a need to wallow in her guilt. "Leonida has grown into a beautiful, intelligent and confident young woman who would make any mother proud. What more could you desire?"

Seeming to come to a decision, Nadia squared her shoulders and flipped open the lid to the lacquer box.

"I desire to know she will always be safe."

Herrick's eyes widened as she pulled out the bundle of letters that had been the source of endless troubles over the past months. He had only a brief glimpse of them when he had escorted Leonida from Dimitri Tipova's warehouse, but he easily recognized the frayed ribbon.

"Nadia?"

She laughed with mocking amusement at his surge of concern, then with a casual motion, she tossed the entire stack into the fire.

"Do not fret, Herrick. I have learned my lesson."

Herrick stepped from the fire as it rapidly consumed the aged parchment, his brow furrowed. The last thing he had expected was for Nadia to destroy the letters. Not after Leonida had nearly lost her life to retrieve them.

"I thought you considered the letters a means to protect your future?" he accused.

Nadia shook her head, her expression somber. "I willingly placed my fate in the hands of Alexander Pavlovich. I shall stand at his side no matter what the future might hold."

Herrick hid his astonishment as he crossed to pour two glasses of brandy. For all of Nadia's charm, she had always been a selfish woman at heart.

Was it truly possible she had learned to put others before herself?

With a shrug, he returned to his companion and pressed a glass into her hand. All that mattered was Nadia's continued loyalty to the Emperor.

"Leonida never did reveal what Dimitri Tipova demanded for the return of those letters," he murmured. The Beggar Czar had occupied a great deal of his thoughts over the past days.

Herrick was not a man who allowed such a valuable asset to slip through his fingers.

"If he is as cunning as you have claimed, he will not dare trouble Leonida," Nadia easily dismissed the threat. Like too many nobles she had no understanding of the power a man without a title could wield. "Not unless he wishes to incur the wrath of the Duke of Huntley."

Herrick could not argue with her logic. Dimitri Tipova was not a stupid man.

"True enough. Stefan would kill him without a thought." He abruptly chuckled, pondering the criminal's reaction to Herrick's determination to have him in his service. "Besides, Tipova will soon have other matters to occupy his mind."

Nadia narrowed her gaze. "I sense you are plotting to lure the poor man into one of your nefarious schemes."

"Not today." Lifting his glass, Herrick offered a toast. "To Leonida."

Nadia touched her glass to his. "Leonida."

ONCE SETTLED IN THEIR elegant cabin, Leonida wandered to the deck of the ship, watching as St. Petersburg became a distant speck on the horizon.

A small smile curved her lips as she recalled the last occasion she had traveled away from St. Petersburg.

Who could ever have suspected the adventure that was awaiting her? Or the joy that she would discover?

Pondering the strange twists of fate, Leonida ignored

the brisk breeze that tugged on her green velvet pelisse edged with sable, and the crew who bustled past her. It was not until a pair of warm, muscular arms wrapped about her waist and hauled her against a broad chest that she was enticed from her private thoughts.

"You have a rather wistful expression on your face, my dove," Stefan murmured, his lips brushing the curve of her ear. "Are you sad to leave your home?"

Leonida shivered, her body melting with a familiar heat. Over the past days it had been impossible to find a moment alone with Stefan. Now she was anxiously anticipating her wedding night.

"I will miss St. Petersburg, but my home is with you," she assured him softly.

With gentle care he turned her in his arms, studying her with a searching gaze.

"*Our* home."

"Yes." A sense of utter contentment warmed her heart. "And besides, we have promised to return for Vanya's wedding."

Lowering his head, Stefan stroked his lips teasingly over her mouth. "Did we?"

Her arms lifted of their own accord, wrapping around his neck as a thrilling anticipation clenched her stomach.

"You are not going to distract me," she warned.

His lips shifted to spread a line of tormenting kisses down the curve of her throat.

"No?"

"No."

He chuckled as she ruined her threat with a shaky moan of pleasure.

"Liar."

Pulling back, she regarded him with a stern expression. "You are very certain of yourself."

The lean, beautiful features softened with an expression that tugged directly at her heart.

"The only thing I am certain of is my love for you."

Framing his face in her hands, Leonida raised herself on the tips of her toes to press her lips to his mouth.

"And mine for you, my magnificent Duke. We are now bound together for all eternity."

"Thank God." Without warning, Stefan was sweeping her off her feet and heading directly toward the stairs leading to the private cabins. "I am too old to be pursuing my wife across the continent."

She chuckled. "But you did it so very well."

He gazed down at her with eyes already smoldering with passion.

"Ah, but I intend to do even better at keeping you."